EMORY'S GIFT

W. BRUCE CAMERON

WHEELER PUBLISHING
A part of Gale, Cengage Learning

GALE
CENGAGE Learning·

Detroit • New York • San Francisco • New Haven, Conn • Waterville, Maine • London

Copyright © 2011 by W. Bruce Cameron.
Wheeler Publishing, a part of Gale, Cengage Learning.

Wheeler Publishing Large Print Hardcover.
The text of this Large Print edition is unabridged.
Other aspects of the book may vary from the original edition.
Set in 16 pt. Plantin.

LIBRARY OF CONGRESS CATALOGING-IN-PUBLICATION DATA

Cameron, W. Bruce.
   Emory's gift / by W. Bruce Cameron. — Large print ed.
    p. cm.
   ISBN-13: 978-1-4104-4147-8 (hardcover)
   ISBN-10: 1-4104-4147-4 (hardcover)
   1. Large type books. [1. Human–animal relationships—Fiction. 2. Grief—Fiction. 3. Grizzly bear—Fiction. 4. Bears—Fiction. 5. Junior high schools—Fiction. 6. Schools—Fiction. 7. Family life—Idaho—Fiction. 8. Idaho—History—20th century—Fiction. 9. Large type books.] I. Title.
PZ7.C1442Emo 2011b,/c7>
[Fic]—dc23   2011024802

Published in 2011 by arrangement with Tom Doherty Associates, LLC.

Printed in the United States of America
1 2 3 4 5 6 7 15 14 13 12 11

To my parents, Bill and Monsie Cameron,
who never lost faith and often
had to put their money where
their mouths were to prove it.
Because of you, I'm me.

PROLOGUE

I thought I saw Emory today.

He'd be pretty old for a grizzly bear: I last saw him when I was in the eighth grade, slightly more than twenty-five years ago. Male grizzlies can certainly live into their late twenties, but it's not typical, and had I not been so excited I would have realized that the huge male I spotted clambering out of the river was simply too spry to be who I thought he was.

Though I am a bear biologist by education and training, I've spent most of the past year examining dirt, of all things. Specifically, the dirt on the banks of rivers where bears congregate.

Ursus arctos horribilis, the great grizzly, is normally reclusive and shy, but he abandons his antisocial ways to stand virtually shoulder-to-shoulder with other bears during a salmon run. Bear etiquette demands they keep their fishing grounds pristine, so when it comes time to relieve themselves they wander up on shore — hence my interest in dirt.

My name is Charlie Hall, and I'm an expert in the proverbial question "Does a bear poop in the woods?" Yes, yes, he does; and his droppings, rich with nitrogen from salmon and seeds from all the berries he consumes of a summer, create a fecund stew along the riverbanks, leading to incredible biodiversity and trees fully 20 percent taller than their less richly endowed cousins growing farther inland. The bears hunt for grubs, turning the soil like farmers. Grizzlies, I tell anyone who will listen, are nature's gardeners.

The question, you see, is not what a bear does in the woods but, rather, what good does a grizzly bear do when he gets there? To those of us engaged in a desperate attempt to save the species from extinction, the answer to this question is crucial.

My back had been complaining for about an hour when I screwed the top on the last container of soil, dumped my heavy tool belt to the ground, and stretched with a groan. It was at that moment, my hands reaching up to the sky as if in supplication, when I caught sight of a massive bear, eight hundred pounds and more than four feet tall at the shoulder. He was a male, a bear I'd never seen before, rearing up on the bank of the Clearwater River in Montana, standing in low grass. His fur was silver tipped, "grizzled," and his head was broad. His nose was high — probably sniffing *me,* because the forty yards separating us was nothing to a creature whose sense of smell was nearly as sharp as a hound dog's. The bear was on my side of the river, his face mostly turned away from me, but there was something in his profile, something in the way he stood . . .

"Emory!" I shocked myself by yelling. I clumsily stood, pushing the brush away from my face. "Emory!"

If I were to write a book on how to behave around an animal so powerful he can kill an elk with one blow, rule one would have to be: *Don't ever yell at a grizzly.* Rule two would be: *Don't ever startle a grizzly.* And rule three: well, if you were stupid enough to chase a grizzly bear, as I was doing, a book probably wouldn't be of much use to you. But certainly rule three would be: *Don't ever, ever run after one.*

I've read that the chances of a person dying from a bear attack are about the same as a person dying from a lightning strike. I've always thought, though, that if you

9

actually are hit by lightning, your odds of dying from it go up dramatically. The same might be said about the mighty grizzly, an amazing, top-of-the-food-chain predator with astoundingly sharp claws, flesh-tearing teeth, and powerful jaws. Your best chance of surviving a grizzly attack is to not have one.

When the bear I thought might be Emory turned toward me, I saw two things immediately. First, it wasn't Emory: the black stare from those eyes was entirely different from the warm intelligence I remembered in Emory's gaze. Second, this bear was spooked, as stressed as bears get.

And I, of course, was the source of his stress.

I heard his teeth clank together like a metal gate banging shut, three quick successive bites at the air that told me this bear felt his life threatened by my approach. *His* life threatened. Saliva flew — when grizzly bears are about to attack, they drool, adding a menacing sheen to their long, sharp fangs. And, just before they charge, they pound the ground with their feet.

I had a canister of bear repellent attached to my belt. My belt was maybe fifteen or twenty yards behind me, lying where I'd tossed it. I spread my arms wide, letting the bear know I was just human, nothing to be afraid of.

"I'm sorry," I said in a quaking voice.

The bear slammed his front paws down on the dirt.

I took a slow, careful step backward. A grizzly bear can run thirty-five miles an hour and can turn more adroitly than a fleeing squirrel. He was twenty-five yards from me. If I sprinted for the bear spray, I might make it halfway.

"It's okay," I said reassuringly, trying to calm both of us.

The bear showed me his teeth, snapping them together, saliva flying.

"Please." I took another step backward.

The bear pounded his paws on the dirt. I inhaled carefully.

He charged.

Eight hundred pounds of angry tooth and claw came at me with his head low and his murderous gaze intent. *Run,* my inner voice screamed. It was a straightforward attack, swift and silent. *Run!* But I stood, holding my ground.

"Hey," I said tremulously, and then he was there, right *there,* so close I felt the blast of heat from his breath as he chuffed at me and veered away. He ran another ten feet laterally and then stopped, staring at me.

11

They call it a bluff charge. Among bear experts, there's a joke: it's only called a bluff charge by the people who live through one. For everyone else, it's just a charge. A bear feels threatened and he wants you to leave, so he storms at you, makes it clear that this is the one warning you're going to receive.

I was backing up, still talking, trying to keep the heartbeat out of my voice. "Okay, easy bear, good bear, it's okay. It's okay." I didn't look him in the eye; that's an aggressive act.

My fingers were trembling when I got to where I had left my belt. I unhooked the bear spray. When I looked up again, the bear had disappeared into the brush.

Needless to say, I didn't pursue him.

It took more than five minutes for the wash of adrenaline to dwindle, for my heart to finally stop beating at my ribs, for my fingers to regain enough strength to put my belt back on. I started gathering up my soil samples. That was it for me; I was done for the day. I felt nauseated and weak, sweat trickling from my forehead.

If he had been Emory, I allowed myself to wonder finally, would he have reacted any differently? Did I think he would recognize me, be glad to see me?

I sighed, a bit disgusted with myself. Was

12

I a bear biologist because I was interested in the species or because I was on a foolish lifelong quest to catch just one more glimpse of the bear who had so completely changed my life?

CHAPTER ONE

"What do I do if I'm in the woods and I run into a cougar?" I asked, starting off with one of his favorites.

"Cougar," Dad responded, nodding.

My stomach tensed. It was my favorite game, not because I really thought I'd encounter a cougar or a wolverine or any of the other animals I'd ever mentioned but because of the way it engaged my father. When we first moved from suburban Kansas City to our home both high and deep in the Selkirk Mountains of Idaho, my father lectured me all the time about how the woods were full of predators, but the gravity of his instructions had been drained away after five years without incident, so that now we just ran through the list and he repeated his warnings in what had gone from conversation to ritual. He set his fork down on his plate, gathering his thoughts. I leaned forward eagerly, as if I'd never come up with "cougar" before.

My father wasn't a big man. When he stood with other men he seemed to be on the shorter side of average, and his hands were small, though they worked well enough with wood to keep food on our table. Over the past two years he'd lost a few pounds and it didn't look good on him; his neck seemed too small for his collar and his reddish brown hair was often unkempt.

"Nobody has seen a cougar in a long time, Charlie."

"They're out there, though," I insisted. There were notices posted at the state campsite that warned hikers of mountain lions, aka cougars, aka pumas, aka panthers.

"They are out there," my dad agreed. "But a cougar probably isn't going to be after you," he said. "Most times you see a cougar, it will be running away."

"But if it's not," I insisted, my eyes pleading with him to stay in the game.

"But if it's not." He nodded.

I relaxed.

"Well, let's see, how much do you weigh, now? Twenty pounds? Twenty-two?"

My father was teasing me. I made a fierce muscle, my biceps quivering in alarm as I forced it to make what meager appearance it could muster. I had blond hair like my mother and the same brown eyes as my dad. As I proudly regarded the small lump of sinew I called my biceps, I could see the nearly invisible blond hairs sticking up out of my tan skin.

"Eighty-five," I announced.

Dad grinned. "You don't weigh eighty-five pounds, Charlie." Then the grin died, his eyes drifting toward the head of the table. There was a time when the woman who once sat there weighed a mere eighty-five pounds, when her weight was obsessively monitored and announced and analyzed, all for no ultimate good whatsoever. There was no doubt that this was what he was thinking as he looked at Mom's empty chair.

"Cougar," I reminded him.

He turned back to look at me. I still had his attention. "Well, a young cougar, one that isn't good at hunting, he might think a bite-sized boy like you could make a tasty meal. When they first get kicked out of the den they're hungry and wandering around, trying to find a territory they can call their own. Especially the males, they need a huge area. They don't want to run into a person — humans used to shoot them on sight and sort of selected out the bold ones, so the only mountain lions left are descended from the timid ones. But they could be danger-

17

ous if they're hungry enough, or if they feel threatened."

"So if it's hungry . . . ," I prompted.

"Okay, so if it's hungry, the first thing is, don't run. If you're running, a cougar's just a big cat. Ever see a cat jump on a string? It's instinctive."

"So stand still."

"Right. Stand up big and tall. If you've got a stick nearby, hold it up over your head, but don't throw it or point it. What you want is for that cougar to see you as a meal that's going to cost him, put up a real fight."

Dad said this last with less enthusiasm, tiring of the game already.

"Grizzly bear." *Please, Dad. Please keep playing.*

"Oh." Dad waved his hand. "You're not going to see a grizzly around here, Charlie. Last one seen in this part of Idaho, had to be thirty years or more ago. They're practically extinct in the lower forty-eight."

"But still. If I saw one."

My plaintive insistence carried a lot of despair that my father could have picked up on if he'd been paying attention. I was losing him. No matter what I did, I couldn't seem to hold his attention for more than a few minutes at a time, anymore. I could've danced around directly in front of him, waving my hands, crying out, "Dad, look at me! Here I am," and he'd somehow lose sight of me.

His gaze drifted back to the empty chair at the other end of the table.

"Dad?" *Why don't you love me? How can I get you to love me?*

"Dad!"

His glance seemed a bit surprised, as if he couldn't quite remember who I was.

"Grizzly bear? If I did see one."

He sighed. "Charlie."

"Grizzly," I insisted.

He looked within himself, consulting his inner encyclopedia. "Thing about a grizzly is it probably isn't looking to eat you. If it is, you'll know because it'll act like it doesn't care you're there. It won't look at you, it'll pretend it's foraging, but every time you see it, it's gotten closer. That kind of bear you treat just like a cougar; you talk loudly at it, you back away, you get yourself a weapon, and if it attacks, you fight. Go for its eyes. Let it know that as far as unplanned meals go, you're not worth the bother."

A wiser child would have quit the game right there, but I kept pressing: "What if I just run across one, by accident? One with cubs?"

"Mother grizzly is just like a black bear.

19

She's defensive; she just wants to protect her cubs. You back off; you try to get as much distance as you can from those cubs without running. If she attacks you, you curl up, protect your head and neck with your arms, and play dead. Lie there until she's long gone."

"What if it's a male? Dad? What if it's a male grizzly? What then?" A certain shrill desperation crept into my voice.

Dad didn't hear me. He was looking at the end of the table, seeing his wife, maybe, or maybe just seeing the hole she'd left in his life when she died. I knew he'd be unresponsive now, a shell of himself, and that he wouldn't see me, either, not even when I got up from the table to do the dishes. It was as if I didn't exist.

When this happened, it felt like there were not one but three ghosts living in the house.

He said only two more words to me that night. I was in bed, lights out, lying there as silent as the house had been since dinner. My window was open a crack, cool mountain air flowing deliciously across my body. I heard my father ease out of the chair in the living room, snapping off the light next to where he had been reading. He came down the hall and stopped in the dark rectangle of shadow that was my open door:

I felt him standing there, looking at me sprawled in a blanket of moonlight. "Tomato cages," he said.

And then he was gone.

"I hate you, Dad," I murmured into my pillow, the sound too quiet for even my own ears. I didn't hate him, of course. He was my whole world.

Sometimes I allowed myself the horrible contemplation that maybe my father hated *me.* Maybe he knew what I had done. The thought made my heart pound; it could wake me up at night with the sensation of drowning in cold water.

I didn't have a name for it, this thing. It was my awful secret, my awful, horrible secret. If my dad knew, if he had even a strong suspicion, it would explain how a father might come to hate his own son. Wouldn't it? How would he ever forgive me, when I couldn't even forgive myself? I was a bad person, though the only other human being who knew what I'd done had died a year ago last April.

That night I heard Dad sobbing in his bedroom, a choking noise that filled me with dread and fear. He never cried in front of me, not once, but this was far from the first time I'd heard him down the hall, facing his pain alone.

I was hurting, too. Why didn't he come out of his bedroom and ask about me, his only child? We never talked about what was the most significant event of our lives. We came back from the funeral as if the only reason we were together was that we had shared a ride, and each went our separate way into our grief as soon as the last well-meaning neighbor departed from our home.

It was as if Dad had an awful secret of his own, but everyone knew what it was. Mom was dead. That was the secret.

It happened to me, too, Dad.

It was August of 1974, and I'd just turned thirteen. I was small for my age, several pounds shy of the eighty-five I'd boasted of at dinner. Our home in northern Idaho bordered state land for miles and miles in every direction and when we'd moved there a few years prior I thought it was paradise. Mom had loved it.

We used to have real family conversations when she was alive, not just animal games but discussions about my future, the war in Vietnam, what they were building at Dad's shop. Now my dad would let a whole day go by without initiating a dialogue — I knew, because I'd tested it once, but it made me so heartsick that I broke the silence the next morning, babbling ceaselessly just to beat back the loneliness. That night's final exchange had been typical.

"Tomato cages."

The wire tomato cages were sitting out in the square patch of lumpy earth that used to be Mom's garden, looking like skeletal soldiers filled with a twisted circulatory system of brown, dead plant stalks from the year before.

One Mother's Day long ago I'd presented Mom with flags I'd made for the tops of the cages. They were just strips of white cloth the art teacher provided, but I'd laboriously painted "Tomato" on them, seeing them in my mind as pennants snapping in the wind out in the garden, serving notice that the tomato cages were for tomatoes and not corn or potatoes or zucchini. In reality they hung limp from their wire frames, the letters illegible in the folds.

Mom said she loved them. She never pointed out that tomato cages are supposed to be narrow at the bottom and wide at the top — I'd crafted flags for *upside-down* tomato cages. From that year forward she placed the tomato cages so that they looked like miniature oil wells out in the garden and at the end of each growing season would carefully roll up the flags and then duct-tape the roll so that the flags wouldn't be affected when the tomato cages were stacked in the pole barn.

Mom had had a good October day two years before, tending to her garden, preparing it for the winter and for a spring planting the doctors correctly predicted she wouldn't see. I helped her do some raking and told her she didn't have to tape the flags on the tomato cages. By that time I knew how stupid I'd been and was embarrassed that the neighbors might see our upside-down cages and think I was just a kid.

"We should just throw those out," I said.

"Nonsense, Charlie. I love my flags," Mom said. I was growing up, in my eyes, but she sometimes still treated me as a child.

She tenderly taped each flag in a thick roll atop the cages, then straightened, putting a hand to her face. "Whew. Let's put these away tomorrow; I need to go lie down."

The way I remembered it, she never really got out of bed after that, not in a way that didn't make me feel as if she were invisibly tethered to it. By April of the following year, my dad and I were standing numbly in a spring snowstorm, listening to Pastor Klausen talk about what a wonderful woman Laura Hall was, while the wet built up on the casket in a way that made me want to towel it off to save the gloss from being ruined. My dad held my hand and his fingers were like ice.

Most of the people wore black. I resented the ones who gave me pitying glances and I resented the ones who lacked the courage to look at me and I resented the ones who reacted to the wet weather with distressed expressions. I knew it wasn't fair, but there was nothing fair about any of it.

I didn't cry until we got back home, where Mom's presence was still everywhere, palpable, defying the unreal fact of her death. And then, when I cried, it was as much out of guilt for what I had done as anything else.

So that's why I hated my father for bringing up the tomato cages. Why now? Why did he even care?

Touching them was the last normal thing my mother had ever done. As long as they still stood sentry out there in the garden, it was as if they were waiting for a woman who was coming back any time now.

The next morning, instead of obeying my father's instructions to yank the tomato cages, I deliberately chose to embrace a glorious disobedience. I'd long before discovered the small tin in my father's bedroom drawer that contained the key to the gun cabinet. I loved to pull the guns out and sight down on small prey in the backyard and "pow!" they'd be blown to imaginary bits. The .30-06, a huge, heavy rifle, had a small telescope on top, two thin hairs intersecting on pretend wolves and bears across the valley. The slugs rolled around in my hand with a thrilling weight and snicked into place when I loaded each weapon.

Dad told me when we first moved to Idaho that when I was big enough he'd teach me how to handle guns. But he was never going to teach me; he hadn't even opened the cabinet in two years.

I spread a kitchen towel on the table and lined up my tools. I glanced at the sweep hand on the clock and saw that it was just ten seconds away from 11:50 A.M. I decided to see if I could disassemble a weapon in two minutes, the way recruits did in boot camp movies. The second hand passed over the 12 and I began confidently dismantling my dad's .30-06 rifle.

I went further this time than ever before, basically taking the gun completely apart. I examined each piece of metal, a few of them very small, as I freed them from the main assembly, placing them on the towel like a surgeon lining up scalpels before an operation.

Just before noon I realized I'd failed to track when my two minutes were up, but it didn't matter because I'd just heard something that made me freeze, my eyes wide open, disbelieving.

We seldom got much traffic up in these hills beyond town. Anyone turning off the paved road, County Highway 206, was either lost or on his way to one of only six houses clustered up here on Hidden Creek Road. A long climb, full of switchbacks, would take you to our place, and a little farther on you'd crest the hill and then make your way back down to join Highway 206 again, the downward half of the loop just as steep as the upward half.

I knew that climb well. The school bus always went to the opposite end of Hidden Creek Road first, so that our house was the last stop. This was fine for the morning because it meant I had a few more minutes to sleep in, but in the afternoon I was too impatient to make the full loop and would get out with a handful of other students who lived just off Highway 206. Then I'd run home, my breath getting ragged as I chugged up the steep switchbacks on Hidden Creek Road. And I mean *run,* because my mom was sick and I wanted to see her and make sure she was okay.

I never told her the reason I raced up Hidden Creek Road as if being pursued by

27

outlaws was that I was running home to her, but I'd like to think she knew. She was always glad to see me. Walking in the front door to her welcoming smile was often the high point of the day.

Whenever a vehicle turned off the pavement and headed up our way, we could hear it in the valley. I'd long ago learned which sound meant the mail truck was coming; which clanking, grinding noise meant that the neighbor lady Mrs. Beck was driving her husband's stick shift; and which throaty roar meant that my father's Jeep had turned the corner.

It was this last sound that came to me clearly through the open kitchen window now. What was he doing home? Did work let out early?

And what really mattered: I had just a few minutes before my father came into the house and saw me sitting there with his forbidden rifle broken apart on the table. I jumped up and my motion jerked the kitchen towel and the gun parts fell to the floor in a shower of metal.

CHAPTER
TWO

The sound of the front door opening co-incided perfectly with the firm click of the gun cabinet door as I shut it. I whirled and faced my father, who stood on the threshold and stared at me. Behind me I could feel the .30-06 rifle vibrating in its slot. I'd reas-sembled it with an alacrity that would put a smile on the face of any drill sergeant, but I was still standing right in front of the cabinet with no excuse for why I was there, guilt painted all over my face. I eyed my father with fear. I read in his expression that he knew what I'd been doing, and my heart sank with it.

"Charlie?" he said, his tone puzzled.

I drew in a breath. My fists clenched the gun cabinet key in my hand, its tiny teeth digging into my palm.

"Charlie? You're not ready?"

I blinked at this, unsure.

"Get a move on. It's Saturday; did you

forget what day it was?"

Truthfully, I had. It was summer vacation, and I had lost all sense of the calendar. Saturdays my father took me to the YMCA for junior-lifesaver training. I was supposed to be wearing my bathing suit.

"Oh!" I could have laughed with relief. I ran down the hall, stealthily replaced his key, then tiptoed back to my bedroom and slipped into my trunks and grabbed a towel. He was already back out in the driveway when I emerged from my bedroom and skipped past the gun cabinet, giving the rifles a parting glance.

Dad started the Jeep as I slid in. He backed out of the driveway and we bumped along in silence.

The air was so clear it seemed to shine as the Jeep rattled down the curvy, rutted road. I looked out at the perfect day and tried to think of something to say to my father.

The county road snaked along next to the river, Dad's thickly treaded tires buzzing on the pavement. When we first moved to Selkirk River five years ago, I noticed the quick transition from utter wilderness to town, a sudden clutch of buildings jumping up from the riverbank as if in surprise. It was like, I told my mom, a house here and a house there got together and said, *Well hey, we might as well have a town while we're at it!*

Selkirk River put everything it had into about five square blocks and then seemed to lose ambition. Downriver the homes and occasional stores continued a ways, and the shop where my dad's employer turned out customized furniture parts was another couple of miles in that direction, but after that there was nothing to the south until you got to the city of Sandpoint. Up north there were only mountains and Canada, both seeming to stretch forever.

My dad wheeled into the parking lot of the YMCA, turned off the Jeep, and then twisted in his seat to look at me. I felt a rising, unspecified guilt and cast about for something to attach it to. Could he know about the rifle?

"I need to talk to you, Charlie."

"Yessir." I swallowed.

"It's about where I was this morning. Do you remember me telling you I had business to take care of?"

He'd never told me that. I could recall with absolute clarity everything my father had said to me the past month, the past two months, maybe even stretching all the way back to Mom's funeral, because he spoke so seldom now. I wondered if this meant he was talking to me in his head, like I often

31

did with him, and that he was confused over what was real and what he had imagined.

"I don't remember that."

He thought about it. "I guess I meant to. Charlie, I've decided to go into business with Rod; you know Rod Shelburton, has that ranch where we all rode horses a couple times? Him."

Dad was watching me intently. I tried to understand what sort of reaction was expected of me. "Okay," I finally said.

"The thing is, I'm investing some money with him. What's left from your mom's life insurance after we paid off the medical bills. You understand? So it's like it's not just my money. It's our money, Charlie, yours and mine both. So in a way, I'm investing for the both of us." With that, he stuck out his hand like we were closing a business transaction.

I guess I'd known there was some money after my mother died, but I never thought of myself as having any claim to it. I gripped Dad's hand and shook it, baffled.

"Okay then. You have a good time in Lifesaving."

I was dismissed. Still a bit unclear, I swung out of the Jeep and headed toward the building. I heard the Jeep start up behind me but didn't turn around to wave,

because I hated when I did that and my dad wasn't looking at me to wave back. My hand would just hang there in the air, waving at nothing, noticed by no one.

I was one of only two eighth graders in Junior Lifesaving. The rest were seventh graders and one sixth grader. Seventh graders were in the lowest grade in junior high school and considered to be among the most worthless life-forms on the planet. They were referred to as "sevies." I didn't talk to them or acknowledge them because they were so far beneath me.

I had been a seventh grader myself until just a few weeks ago.

Back in my bedroom I had a photograph taken of me when I was in Little League in Prairie Village, Kansas. I'm standing there with the rest of my teammates, and here's why the picture was on my wall: I was a big kid. Not the biggest on the team but easily one of the three or four largest. My coach called me Slugger.

What happened then was we moved to Idaho and the clean air and water apparently stunted my growth. I just stopped growing, stopped gaining weight. As I stood shivering and wet by the indoor pool at the YMCA, I was acutely aware that I was shorter than any of the despised sevies and

barely had any height on the sixth grader. Every one of my ribs was clearly on display, and my scrawny legs stood storklike out of baggy swim trunks, as if someone had put shorts on a tomato cage.

Our instructor's name was Kay. I thought of her then as an exotic older woman, but looking back on it I suppose she was no more than eighteen or nineteen years old.

I had decided to take junior-lifesaving classes because I harbored a fantasy about saving Joy Ebert, a blond, blue-eyed girl in my grade, from the river rapids. She'd be drowning and I'd plunge in and pull her to safety and she would love me and marry me. I had been in love with Joy since fourth grade and had even talked to her a few times.

Then I went to the first junior-lifesaving class and Joy was forgotten: I was totally in love with Kay. Kay had a thin figure she kept wrapped in a taut one-piece bathing suit — both of us had some blossoming to do, I figured, so maybe she wouldn't care about our age difference so much. In a part of the country where the faces were as plain and uniformly bland as uncooked biscuits in a pan, Kay was deliciously exotic, some kind of Asian blood adding spice to her look. Now it was Kay, with her short

hair and almond-shaped eyes, whom I pictured rescuing from the river waters; she would be pleased one of her students had learned so well and she would love me and marry me.

I was sort of big on the idea of marriage, which was somewhat of an unusual attitude for an eighth-grade boy, but I liked the permanence it implied. You married a girl and she was yours forever; there was even a law about it.

"Now these are your manuals," Kay said to us, holding up a pamphlet with the Red Cross on it. "Who wants to pass them out?"

As one all seven of us surged forward, and Kay backed up, laughing a little. "No, I mean one person to hand them out. Here," she said, turning to Danny Alderton. "Pass these out."

The rest of us tried to hide our jealousy.

Danny Alderton was a neighborhood friend, though at that moment I didn't have much use for him, because Kay had picked him over me. He lived up the road from us, next door to the Becks. His skin turned a little pink, his freckles burning, as he accepted the pamphlets and handed one each to his classmates. "Here," he muttered as he thrust one at me.

"Be sure to study the chapter on mouth-

35

to-mouth resuscitation," Kay lectured us. "Once you have someone out of the water, you need to make sure their lungs are clear, and you need to give them mouth-to-mouth until they can breathe on their own. In two weeks, we'll have a class on it. Okay? You don't need to wear your swimsuits that day. We'll be practicing the whole session. Yes, Matthew."

The sixth grader had his hand up. I never asked Kay questions lest she thought I was unworldly. That's why God invented sixth graders.

"What do you mean, 'practicing'?" Matthew asked. His teeth were chattering from the cold and it gave his question a trembling-with-fear quality.

Kay didn't understand the question. "What do you mean what do I mean?"

Matthew struggled to put it into words. He gestured to us, his classmates. "Practice?" he asked tremulously. "On who?" As in, *do mouth-to-mouth with each other?*

The thought hadn't occurred to me, but now that Matthew had brought it up I figured if his assumption was correct I'd probably skip that lesson.

"Oh," Kay said, getting it. She shrugged. "On me."

She turned away to pick up some life rings

and thus missed the shock that passed over our faces. I was so flabbergasted I forgot my boycott of the seventh graders and exchanged stunned expressions with them.

I realize times have changed, but it was a more simple era then, and I had never before kissed a girl. The previous year a torrid wave of making out had rampaged through the school like a fever, but it had passed me by as if I had been inoculated. The idea that my first lip-to-lip experience would be with a womanly woman like Kay drenched me with excitement and dread.

We spent the afternoon pulling each other out of the water. Half the time I simulated drowning and half the time I simulated saving, but all of the time I was in a full-out swoon, going through the motions. In two weeks I would be mouth-on-mouth with a *woman.* I had an *appointment.*

Dad picked me up and asked me how my lesson went and I said, "Fine." He asked me if I wanted burgers for dinner and I said, "Fine." He suggested I go fishing in the creek while he went back to work with Mr. Shelburton; I said, "Fine." I was in a fog.

What pulled me out of my daydreamy state was what I saw as I headed out the back door with rod and creel. My father had been busy while I'd been dragging fake drowning seventh graders out of the water at the YMCA.

Mom's tomato cages were gone.

Our paved driveway descended steeply from Hidden Creek Road and swooped into the two-car garage, which was set into the ground floor of our house. If you ignored the curve and went straight, a dirt driveway branched off and ended ten yards away at a pole barn. It looked more like a big garage than anything, with a two-car-wide garage door in front and a person-sized door on the side.

The top of the side door was glass, so I didn't have to go inside to confirm that the tomato cages were stacked in a neat pyramid over on the far wall; I just peered in the window. I stared at them for a long time.

What was I going to do, put them back? Then it would be by my hand, not my mom's, that the cages stood sentry in the garden.

I didn't understand why my father didn't see any value in leaving Mom's things alone. I hated it when my dad's older sister came to town after the funeral and cleared our home of Mom's clothing and shoes; I despised the way he acted as if her toothbrush in the bathroom meant nothing to him and tossed it in the trash for me to take out with the used dental floss. What was wrong with him?

I trudged down the path to the creek, kicking at rocks. I'd walked that path probably a thousand times; it was my main destination whenever I went outdoors. My mother didn't like me in the creek because most of it was hidden from the house, etched into a steep crease in the valley floor well past our property line. She preferred I climb the opposite shore and go into the trees where she could see me again, though if I went all the way to the top, where a rocky spine marked the ridgeline, she got nervous because she thought I'd fall from there and tumble all the way back down the hill, like Jack and Jill or something. And if I went over the ridge I was hidden again, and she wasn't too fond of that, either. It was difficult to have any fun at all under such circumstances.

During the spring the waters of the creek were dark and cold, a sharp contrast from the milky pool water from which I'd been saving sevies all morning. From bank to bank the stream was more than thirty feet. In the summer, though, with the runoff down to a trickle, the creek bed was mainly dry, littered with rocks and mud and tree branches. The creek itself shrank back until it was only six feet wide, hugging the far bank and deep enough to swim in. That's where the fish liked to lurk, up under the tree root overhang. From the base of our hill the creek had only another couple hundred yards of independence before it joined the river, adding strength to the flow to town.

I started casting along the banks of the opposing shore, and it wasn't long before I'd hooked and pulled in a nice little brook trout. I put it in the creel, thinking that a couple more just like it and we'd skip the hamburgers that evening.

A few minutes later I had another one, and then another. Man, they were really biting! I left the creel lying on the bank and moved downstream a bit.

The fourth trout was the best of all, fat and glistening, bending my rod with authority while I wrestled it ashore. I was carefully pulling the hook from its mouth when I got the sense of being watched.

I turned and studied the opposite bank. The slight breeze gave the woods an empty sound, but I knew there was someone there, and I felt the hair on my arms stand up as my skin goose-bumped in alarm.

I gave a start when I looked higher up the hill. A pair of amber eyes met mine, unblinking.

It was a cougar, watching me from a jumble of rocks.

When he saw I'd spotted him, he leaped with nimble ability down the slope, closing the gap between us. With a soaring jump that was almost absurdly graceful, he cleared the part of the creek that was deep water and bounded to a sudden halt in the shallows, making scarcely a spray.

It all happened so quickly I never even had time to gasp. He stopped, staring at me, evaluating the situation. No more than fifteen feet of rocky creek bed lay between us.

There was no retreat possible. Behind me the bank was sandy, capable of supporting some sparse grass but no trees — as if climbing a tree would save me from a cat. If I tried to scramble up the bank the cougar could easily take me from behind. The deep water was too far away and there wasn't enough of it anyway. There were no good options.

The mountain lion was not running away. His rear end was lowered, his gaze intent. I was reminded of what my dad had said: *Ever see a cat jump on a string?* That's what the cougar looked like to me now, a cat getting ready to pounce.

There were no sticks nearby. My rod was

handy but so thin I doubted it would be intimidating. What was it Dad said? *A bite-sized boy like you could make a tasty meal.*

My fear was so strong and real I was sick with it. *Stand up big and tall,* my father had instructed. *What you want is for that cougar to see you as a meal that's going to cost him, put up a real fight.*

I took in a shuddering breath, raising my trembling hands over my head.

The cougar moved again, holding his body low, slinking toward me. There was absolutely no question of his intentions. He stopped, crouching. I stood my ground, quivering.

"Go away," I said in a whisper.

The cougar stood motionless. His muscles bunched; he sank lower; his lips drew back.

I found my voice. "Grrrr!" I roared at him. There was no reaction at all.

"Grrrr!"

I watched in terrified fascination as the tension built in the big cat's shoulders. His eyes were locked on mine. *This was it.* I braced myself for the attack. I would put up a good fight. I would make him decide that, as meals go, I was too much trouble to bother with.

I swallowed. I would put up a good fight, or I would die.

He was coiling to spring and then he froze, raising his head sharply, his eyes widening. I actually saw the irises turn dark with alarm. The cougar stood still for only a second and then turned and rocketed away, scampering up the bank and disappearing into the brush.

My legs were still weak and trembling. I wasn't sure what had happened. How had I gone from bite-sized to intimidating in mid-pounce? I stared after the big cat, terrified he might return, but after ten seconds, then twenty, there was no sign of him.

I was safe.

Then I was enveloped in a moist odor, dank and strong. I turned and found myself face-to-face with the reason why the cougar had broken off his attack and fled.

Standing on two legs, a dozen feet behind me, was an enormous grizzly bear.

CHAPTER THREE

I think now that the shock of seeing the bear and knowing my life was in peril for the second time in less than a minute simply overwhelmed my ability to process emotions. The flash of fear was like a slap: my whole body quaked with it. But then, just like a slap, the sensation receded quickly, leaving me numb. An odd calm overtook me.

The bear and I regarded each other. He was massive, close to six hundred pounds, taller on two legs than my father and immensely muscled in the shoulders. His front legs hung straight down from those shoulders and I took note of the light-colored claws at the tips of his forepaws, four-inch claws that might be the last thing I ever saw.

No wonder the mountain lion fled. There was simply no land animal as fierce as this one, nothing more intimidating or terrible to look upon. I stared at him, quaking, wondering what he was going to do and when he was going to do it.

The bear's expression was as serene as that of a man regarding a sandwich. I spotted a little drool in the corner of his mouth and assumed this meant he could already imagine what I would taste like on his tongue.

I raised my hands, feeling foolish even as I did so. How could I possibly persuade a bear like this that, as a meal, I would not be worth the bother?

"Grrr!" I growled. It sounded unconvincing, even to me. The bear watched me with a blank expression.

"Grrr!" I roared, showing my teeth, curling my fingers, tensing my muscles.

With a yawn, the bear dropped to all fours and turned away from me and went over to my creel, sniffing at it. As he walked I saw the shimmer of the distinctive silver-tipped fur that confirmed he was a grizzly.

The bear nudged the creel with his nose. I took a step backward. I could see events as they would unfold: the bear would rip apart the creel and devour my trout. While he was thus distracted, I would silently back away until I was out of sight and then run home.

That's not what happened. Instead, the bear turned and looked at me. His gaze

45

wasn't threatening or predatory; it was almost expectant. Pleading, even.

We stared at each other, the bear and I. I can't explain why I didn't continue to back away. I don't know why the bear's expression led me to take a step *forward,* violating everything my father had told me. I hadn't yet gotten around to concluding that the bear had saved my life; that would come later, when I was lying in bed recounting the day's adventure to myself. I just responded to what I saw as some sort of supplication, actually reaching *right past the bear's jaws* to pick up the creel.

I popped open the cover and let the fish flop out on the rocks. With almost comical delicacy, the bear pinned the largest one with his paw and bit into it, stripping the flesh away until, bones and all, the fish was gone.

The bear turned and regarded me with those warm brown eyes.

"Well, go on; it's okay," I said. With that, as if he had understood every word, the remaining fish were quickly devoured. When he was done, the bear lumbered over to the creek and put his snout down and took a long drink.

It was still a perfectly cloudless August day. The sun on the creek looked like diamonds flung across a black cloth. A euphoria spread through me, the joy of survival, as if every cell in my body was singing a song of life.

My fantasy now was that I would continue to fish, the bear sitting by my side like a loyal dog. I would turn my catch over to him and he would gratefully eat it out of my hand, and we would be friends forever.

When I was little there had been a show on TV called *Gentle Ben.* I couldn't remember much about it, except that it concerned a boy who had a pet bear.

I could be that boy. I could have a pet bear!

Obviously the grizzly bear had never watched the show, because after taking one last drink of water he waded through the creek to the other side and climbed the opposite bank without so much as a backward glance. I was surprised and even a little hurt.

"Hey!" I yelled without thinking.

The bear stopped and turned toward me, fixing me with that imposing stare.

I gulped. "I could bring you something else to eat, maybe tomorrow," I said.

I don't know what I expected in response, but what I got was nothing at all. The bear simply turned away and walked off into the woods.

Once he was gone it was hard to believe he had ever been there in the first place. Had I really just hand-fed lunch to a grizzly bear?

I gathered up my rod and creel and headed for home. I was still in an ebullient mode, excited to tell my father about my encounter in the woods. He wasn't home, so I put away my fishing equipment and went out to toss tennis balls at the pole barn door. My limbs were full of a kinetic, restless energy, and I threw those balls so hard and straight that they smacked loudly against the aluminum door and came bounding back as if served up by Billie Jean King.

The clink and rattle of gravel behind me drew my attention to the road. I turned around, the tennis ball in my hand.

My neighbor Danny Alderton and three boys I knew from school had already walked past my driveway and were headed down the hill, their hands in their pockets. They must have seen me, but none of them had called out, not even to shout a friendly insult.

"Hey, Danny!" I yelled. I dropped the tennis ball and it bounced around apologetically at my feet.

The boys came to a faltering halt. The way they met each other's eyes as I approached communicated something I couldn't interpret.

Gregg was a ninth grader, unpopular with his peers, which probably explained why he was hanging out with eighth graders — Danny, Mitch, and Jerry were in my grade. They were all, of course, bigger than I was.

Living up here on Hidden Creek Road tended to be isolating and Danny, like me, didn't have a lot of friends. He and I usually did things together, though this summer had been different for reasons never pondered or pronounced. It's just how it had been.

Gregg was one of those kids who were always in trouble at school. I'd seen him smoking in the woods. I didn't know anything about Mitch, who had just moved to Selkirk River, and Jerry was a friendly enough guy, though he wasn't very bright.

"Danny," I said, singling out my friend, though obviously I wanted everyone else to hear. "I was fishing in the creek today, and you wouldn't believe what I saw."

"It's 'Dan,' " he said coldly.

My narrative lost its excited momentum. I looked at him.

"Nobody calls me Danny. It's 'Dan.' Char- *lie*."

His expression was overtly hostile. The

49

three boys with him regarded me coolly.

And I . . . well, I was absolutely flab-bergasted. I had no idea what was going on, why Danny/Dan was acting so strangely toward me.

It was, of course, junior high. Seventh graders arrived at school like sailors washing ashore on a pirate island: they didn't know the rules; they only knew that after having been the cool sixth-grade kids in a building full of children they were now low-class sevies in a place where the oldest students were technically *freshmen in high school.* Ninth-grade boys carried themselves like men and the girls had breasts to gawk at. We all wanted to be like them in every way. Some of the boys even grew hair from their faces, a glorious thing. The jostling for position and social survival was agonizing.

That first semester of junior high I lived in a cocoon of polite pity. Everyone, of course, knew that my mother had died the previous April. Teachers were solicitous. Popular girls said hi to me. The guys mostly ignored me, embarrassed because they didn't know what to say to me. And I drifted from class to class, constantly astounded at how normal everything seemed, how people could behave as if nothing had happened, as if the world had not been knocked off its axis and sent spinning off into the dark.

Over Christmas break it was as if a vote was taken and I was stripped of the social status my grieving period had afforded me. Though it had been only eight months since the funeral, I was now expected to be like everybody else. I was a sevie, a nobody. The popular girls couldn't even *see* me. The guys went from ignoring me to ignoring me with malice.

I'd been aware of Danny . . . of Dan, Dan Alderton, suffering a different yet similarly rough passage, but it wasn't as if we ever discussed it when we got together. Guys don't talk about that kind of stuff. We just hoped to ride out the storm.

Everyone was still staring at me. I dropped my eyes. "Sorry. Dan."

"We saw you throwing your tennis ball at your garage." Gregg sneered. "What were you doing?"

Well, that was a stupid question. What I was doing was throwing my tennis ball at my garage. "Nothing," I said sullenly.

The boys all snickered a little at this, as if I'd said something funny.

"Wussy," Gregg hissed. He turned on his heel and the other boys fell in line behind him. I expected Dan to maybe glance back at me, give me some sort of signal with his eyes, but he was as bluntly uncaring as he walked away as he'd been during the entire exchange. I bit back my hurt.

The odd thing was, watching them go, I longed to be with them. I wanted to swing my arms and walk with the almost simian gate they'd adopted; I wanted to look tough and kick rocks. I pictured myself with them, one of the guys, and my heart unexpectedly ached.

By the time my father got home that afternoon, I'd had time to reconsider what I would tell him about the cougar and the bear. The cougar had probably been, as my father suggested during our game, a young one, newly turned out from the den and not good at hunting. He stalked me because we chanced upon each other, but the likelihood of another encounter was slight. A cougar's territory can encompass hundreds of square miles. Nonetheless, I didn't want my father to forbid me from leaving the property the rest of the summer, which was probably what he'd say if I told him about it.

And the grizzly . . . would my father even believe me? What would he say to the whole incredible story of me feeding brook trout to an animal infamous for its deadly temper? The whole thing sounded ludicrously fantastic even to me, and I'd been there to see it.

What I know now is that when grizzly bears are spotted that close to human habitat they are usually euthanized on the theory that they've become unafraid of man and therefore more likely to attack people. Reeducating them is also possible: using firecrackers, dogs, and even rubber bullets to teach the animals the lesson that hanging around houses was a bad idea. The problem is that bears are pretty smart and humans aren't: we'll move into a remote area and leave a bag of dog food on our front porch and then panic when we see a grizzly bear helping himself to a meal. The bears often conclude that they like the dog food people and don't like the rubber bullet people and work to evade the very individuals trying to save their lives.

Back in 1974, intervention was a seldom-used option. A bear that would approach people was considered a problem bear and immediately, one might even say gleefully, hunted down. I didn't know that, either.

All I knew then was that if I told my father I'd fed a grizzly bear in the wild, he would most certainly not believe me. I pictured the expression on his face when I told my tale. The skepticism.

And if he didn't believe me, the rejection would break my heart. I was loathe to meet his unloving eyes, to read the doubt, the lack of trust, in them. Just as I'd once told myself over and over that my mother was sure to survive her disease, I now told myself that my father loved me. If I revealed what had happened at the creek, he would treat me like a liar, and he despised liars.

So I said nothing, which was easy to do in our house. We ate dinner without a word to each other. Dad's mood was worse than usual, his gaze inward.

I woke up the next morning eager to grab something out of one of the freezers to feed the bear.

The person who sold us the house had been involved in dressing and processing elk, deer, and other wild game. The pole barn had sinks and hoses and big drains and two enormous freezers that my father bargained into the home purchase. I think my father saw those game freezers and pictured himself hunting and freezing a whole winter's worth of meat every year, but once my mom got sick he lost his taste for killing anything.

Now the freezers were full of foil-wrapped packages. When news of my mother's disease leaked out, the people of Selkirk River showed up in a constant stream, leaving pies, roasts, hams, and an absolutely endless assortment of casseroles in their wake. Most of it was still there: my dad didn't really like casseroles.

I hit the breakfast table with a fast bowl of cereal and a mind that had already left the house, but my father came out of his room with the worst kind of news: time to do some chores.

At the word "chores" my limbs grew heavy and I felt all of my energy drain out through my legs. I collapsed onto the couch with a groan.

"First thing to do is sweep the driveway," he said.

"Sweep the driveway?" I demanded incredulously. "Why? You're just going to drive on it!"

"It's got gravel that washed off the road from the last rain."

"It will rain again!" I predicted.

"Then we'll sweep the driveway again," he said, as if this made any sense whatsoever.

After the driveway he decided I should rake up the bark around the woodpile while he washed the wooden chairs on our deck. Then we cleaned house. Then we reset the mailbox, which had been knocked a bit cockeyed by the snowplow that winter.

"Are we done?" I asked him after each task. Finally, after the mailbox, he said yes, we were done. I turned to sprint away.

"Go wash up. We're going to the Becks' for Sunday dinner."

I looked back at him, astounded. "What?"

"We've been invited to the Becks' house. Shower and put on something clean."

As I stood in the shower I pictured a hungry grizzly bear pacing the riverbanks, wondering where lunch was. Walking up the road to the Becks' house, I thought of the way the bear looked at me, now believing that in his implacable gaze I saw affection and friendship, a friendship I was abandoning by putting on a pressed shirt and striding next to my silent father to the home of our neighbor.

The Becks lived next door to the Aldertons. They had a son named Scotty who was eight years old, with whom I was expected to "play" while my dad sat with the adult Becks and drank beer. Scotty Beck amused himself with toy soldiers, for God's sake! He was still at that age when he ran everywhere, like a puppy.

But there was no preparing myself for the betrayal that awaited me inside the Becks' home that afternoon. Worse than abandoning the bear, worse than playing with stupid dolls with Scotty, worse even than wearing a starched long-sleeved shirt on a warm August evening, was the woman who rose off the couch to greet us when Mr. Beck ushered us into the house.

"Charlie, you remember Miss Mandeville," Mrs. Beck gushed at me.

The lady worked in the grocery store, ringing up purchases. I never knew her name. The only times I'd ever seen her, she wore a smudged white smock of some kind and her hair and smile were a little dull. Now, though, she had on a black skirt, her brown hair was up, her watery blue eyes dark with makeup, and her lips bloodred. "Hi, Charlie," she said, as if we were old friends. A strong lavender scent spilled off of her. Her eyes sparkled at my father.

"Hello, George," she said to my dad, her voice full of a throaty mirth.

"Hi, Yvonne." He sort of stood awkwardly, but the lady came forward and turned her head to my dad and then he shocked me by kissing her on the cheek.

My dad kissed *her on the cheek.*

CHAPTER FOUR

Scotty Beck's idea of fun was for him to take his G.I. Joe, wrap it in a toy parachute, and hurl it out of an upstairs window. My assignment was to chase the plastic soldier down, so I stood in the backyard, loitering by a snowmobile that sat marooned in the grass. Through the windows I had a clear view of the adults sitting in the living room, drinking cocktails. Mr. Beck laughed a lot, and there seemed to be a connection between how much he laughed and how many times he went to pour himself another drink. He had the biggest, whitest teeth I'd ever seen on anything not wearing a saddle.

"Here he comes!" Scotty yelled at me, waving to get my attention. I squinted up at him. The G.I. Joe came flying out, the chute all tangled, and fell to the ground like a shotgunned duck. "Cool!" Scotty called. I could hear him tearing through the house to join me. I walked over to where G.I. Joe lay stiffly on the ground, wrapped in his plastic shroud. It appeared that rigor mortis had already set in.

"You want to throw it this time?" Scotty panted at me.

"No," I snarled, a flash of rage coursing through me.

Scotty had such an innocent face, his white skin so perfectly unmarred, his features so baby soft, that I felt a little ashamed at the hurt I'd just caused. He blinked at me like a dog being scolded, not sure what he had done wrong.

I held out my hand for the doll. "Okay, I'll throw it."

I passed the living room on my way to launch G.I. Joe on another mission. Miss Mandeville — *Yvonne* — was sitting closer to my dad on the couch, and her hem had ridden up a little on her crossed legs. She was smoking a Virginia Slim, holding it at the end of a bent wrist. I felt my face flush.

Dinner was lasagna. Mrs. Beck pulled it out of the oven like she was delivering a baby, turning to us proudly. "I'll bet you two bachelors haven't had lasagna in a long time," she trilled. Mr. Beck laughed. Yvonne touched her hair and looked at my father.

It was on the tip of my tongue to tell Mrs. Beck that, in fact, we'd had lasagna two

My sharp tone quieted the grown-ups a little. "A bear?" Mrs. Beck repeated uncertainly.

"There are some black bears around here, but they usually don't come down this far," my father said.

Yvonne smiled at him as if he'd just said the smartest, most admirable thing she'd ever heard come out of a man's mouth. Abraham Lincoln could be delivering the Gettysburg Address at the other end of the table and Yvonne would be ignoring him and mooning at my father, reeking of lavender, dimpling, and touching her hair.

"Scotty, you know why bears are em-barr-assed?" Mr. Beck asked. I don't know how the man could even talk with all those teeth in his mouth.

"Why, Dad?" Scotty asked.

"Because they're *bear* naked," Mr. Beck hooted. Scotty laughed, a single "ha," while Mr. Beck the Comedian stood. "Anybody need a refresher?"

Mrs. Beck put a hand on his arm as if to slow him down, but Mr. Beck walked very deliberately to the liquor cabinet, placing his feet carefully, not at all acting drunk. "Larry." Mrs. Beck sighed. Yvonne touched her hair.

"He was way over there, climbing up

Mrs. Beck was on her feet and had a towel to my mouth before anyone else had even moved. "It's okay, Charlie; you just go ahead," she said softly. I closed my eyes at the sensation of her soft hand on my back. This was what mothers did; they held you and spoke kindly to you when you were sick. When you had a fever their hands were cool and soothing on your forehead.

Mrs. Beck drove us home. I sat in the front seat and ignored Yvonne as she unhappily waved at us from the front deck of the Becks' house.

"You should go lie down," my dad said, though it was still light outside. I didn't fight it; the light touch of Mrs. Beck made me want to bury my face in my pillow.

I thought of my mother helping me one day when I'd skinned my knees falling off a rope swing. I was maybe eight years old. Her tanned skin at that point was more than a year away from the blotchy yellow pallor I would come to associate with her face when the disease — chronic myelogenous leukemia — took over and killed her blood. Her name was Laura, Laura Hall — we were a family with a Charlie and a George and a Laura, normal names, nothing at all like *Yvonne*.

My mom sat me down in the bathtub that

day and carefully cleaned my burning wounds. That's what mothers did; they took care of you.

And then when they got sick it was your job to take care of them. But I hadn't done that, not when it mattered most, and that was what made my tears burn my face as I lay in bed — that was my awful secret. When it was my job to take care of my mom, I failed her, and the consequences were life altering.

When sleep finally came it released me from both my grief and my guilt.

I was ravenous the next morning and ate so many bowls of Cap'n Crunch that the inside of my mouth burned. A note from my dad told me to call him, so I did — I liked phoning him at the shop, but I knew it pulled him off the floor, so I only did it when it was important. My father's company made furniture parts out of wood, and I could hear banging and drilling and cutting going on while the woman who had answered went to go find him.

"Hello?"

"Dad, it's Charlie. You said I should call you when I woke up," I said in a rush, so he wouldn't get mad at me.

"How are you feeling?"

"Not bad. I'm okay. I'm fine. I feel good,"

I said, adjusting the story when it occurred to me that anything less than a glowing report of health might result in me being ordered to stay inside. "I'm all better."

"Probably just something you ate, then," my dad speculated.

"Yes, I guess. I mean, I like the food here at home." As far as I was concerned, we never needed to go anywhere for dinner again.

There was a silence on the line. Someone hammered something. A circular saw shrilly ripped into a board.

"Okay, well, you stay close to the house. Call me if you feel sick again," he said.

"Okay."

There was another silence, this one so deep it felt like it was pulling me like quicksand into the phone. Why couldn't my dad just *talk* to me sometimes? Ask me about something, tell me something, give me something besides instructions?

"Okay then," my dad said, hanging up.

I pulled a big aluminum pan out of the game freezer and lifted up the tinfoil to see what I'd found. It looked like one of many hamburger casseroles. I could see cheese and noodles and maybe some canned peppers. We would never eat it, and my dad would never miss it. I marched down the path into the canyon holding the casserole like a waiter headed for the table.

I sat by the creek all afternoon, occasionally poking at the casserole with a stick to check on the progress it was making toward a thaw. There was no sign of the bear.

The next day I brought down a cooked chicken that was badly freezer burned. The casserole pan from the day before had been crumpled and ripped, but as I examined it I couldn't be sure what kind of animal had eaten the contents. Some of the scrape marks looked too sharp and tiny for a bear and probably were the result of a fox having a meal, but whether the fox was cleaning up after a grizzly had had supper or had hogged the whole thing I just couldn't be sure.

The chicken vanished: not even bones were left the next morning. I reluctantly left another casserole. "Bear!" I yelled into the woods. A tinny echo bounced back at me and then the trees whistled with the warm breeze, but other than that, there was no reaction.

"I'm not coming tomorrow!" I shouted.

Nothing.

"I'll be back in a few days. You'd better come out if you want food!" I threatened.

It's easy for me as an adult to wonder what the heck I thought I was doing. This was a grizzly, not a stray cat. But I wasn't the first person in the world to want to provide food to a bear: it had only been a few years since the country's animal experts had closed the dumps in Yellowstone that had for decades served up free food to the grizzlies. The park service had even built bleachers so people could sit and watch the bears eat garbage!

I make these excuses to myself now because as a bear biologist I know just how wrongheaded my impulse was. But still, had I known where it would all lead would I have stopped trying to feed the bear? I simply can't answer that.

What I can say, though, is that as incredible as it sounds, the remarkable encounter with the bear actually faded in importance for me over the next several days, shoved out of the way by a casual reminder at our junior-lifesaving class.

"Don't forget next week, you don't have to come in your bathing suits," Kay told us. "We'll be doing artificial resuscitation." Her dark eyes blandly looked us over. "Mouth-to-mouth."

Don't forget? Like any of us had been thinking about anything else? The Soviet Army could be attacking our town and the only concern I would have was whether it

67

would mean canceling mouth-to-mouth class.

Where once I luxuriated in the languid pace of summer vacation, I now cursed it. Like every teenage boy, I had managed to turn lethargy into a defining form of personal expression, but now I was almost angrily impatient, glaring at the clock, outraged by its lack of progress. I went down to the creek a dozen times or so and saw nothing of the bear and that, too, made me restless and grumpy.

I don't think I slept much the Friday night before the big day. That morning I ate breakfast and then brushed my teeth eleven separate times. I swished nearly a pint of mouthwash, until you could use my breath to thin paint. When my father came home at lunchtime from the Shelburton ranch he found me on the front deck where I had been sitting for an hour and a half. I yanked open the door to the Jeep and bounded in.

Dan Alderton had apparently dropped Lifesaving. This was the second class he'd skipped — miss two and you're out, Kay had warned us. The sixth grader was also missing — the prospect of what we were about to do was probably just too much for him to bear. But all four seventh graders were there, nervously bumping into each other. Kay waved at us, leading us down a hall and unlocking a door to a conference room.

"Come on in, guys."

We walked as if glued together, a gaggle of gangly geeks looking ready to bolt for the doors. The room was small, carpeted, with yellow walls and a black rubber mat on the floor. A large vinyl bag lay by the mat.

Kay smiled at us as we fidgeted our way into the room and spread out on one wall as if preparing for a firing squad. She was wearing short red shorts and a simple T-shirt. Her jet-black hair brushed her shoulders and gleamed with a metallic sheen in the fluorescent lighting. Her lipstick matched her shorts, which I found to be an almost unimaginably beautiful combination, though both the shorts and her lips were plenty nice on their own.

"So, did everyone read the chapter?"

We gave nervous nods.

Kay knelt by the bag, unzipping it. "Carl, come help me with this," she said.

Carl was a tall, sandy-haired seventh grader, who leaped forward with absurd eagerness. Kay had him unfold a life-sized mannequin and lay it on the mat. The plastic lips on the thing were open, the eyes shut. Carl lingered until he realized he couldn't really justify kneeling next to Kay on the floor, and then he sprang back up to be with the rest of us on the wall.

"Okay, so, we can do this two ways. You can do it either on the dummy or on me. Who's first?"

Relief and disappointment were written on our faces. The tension went out of our bodies like a breath we hadn't realized we'd been holding.

Carl, eager to exploit the incredible intimacy he felt he'd developed with Kay during the whole lay-out-the-dummy incident, stepped forward. He knelt by the mannequin's head, unmistakably picking plastic lips over real ones.

There was absolutely nothing in Kay's expression to betray whether she was kidding or not about the idea of doing live lip-to-lip training. She lectured us about compressing the water out of the lungs and made sure Carl squeezed the nose shut. I listened numbly. The next boy in line picked the dummy, as did the next. I held back, asking myself what would happen if I told her I wanted to try it on her. Would she laugh at me? Tell me I was stupid for taking her offer seriously?

The safe thing would be to do like everyone else and blow into the dummy.

I stood there, locked in indecisiveness, until all the other boys had gone and it was my turn.

"Charlie?" Kay said. "You ready?"

I nodded. I stepped forward. I cleared my throat. "I'll, uh, do you."

The boys on the wall straightened as if they'd just been hit with a cattle prod. As for Kay, those dark eyes flickered just a little — amusement? Pity? I stood, awaiting my fate.

"Okay," she said simply. She pushed the dummy off the mat and lay down. "What's the first thing?"

"Check the airway," I muttered. My pulse was hammering in my head so hard I couldn't really hear myself. I lowered myself to my knees. What was I thinking? Was I really going to do this?

Her nose was soft and delicate. I pinched it shut. Her head was back. I shakily put my mouth on hers.

If I did everything as I was trained — watched for her chest to rise, simulated rolling her over to press the water out of her lungs, timed my breaths — I have no memory of any of it. But I will never for a moment forget the light, warm, amazing sensation of touching my mouth to Kay's. It wasn't a kiss, not really. But it was close enough.

"Good, Charlie," Kay said with her studied blandness. I could feel that the boys on the wall were ready to raise their hands and ask for another go at it, but Kay had me practice on the dummy a few times so she could watch, and then class was over.

When I saw my father's Jeep waiting for me in the parking lot, it held none of the usual dread for me. For once I didn't approach the passenger door knowing that I'd spend the whole car ride wrestling with the thick silence from my father, seeking desperately to draw him into conversation. I didn't want to talk to anyone; I just wanted to think about Kay.

My dad waited for me to put on my seat belt before he yanked the Jeep into gear. Safety was his biggest concern, since Mom died.

"How'd it go, Charlie?" he asked.

I shrugged. There was simply no answer to that question.

"Well then. You want to go see what I've been putting all my time and money into, lately?"

No, I didn't, but this was the most engaging thing my father had said to me since *We're going to the Becks' for Sunday dinner.* I gazed at him with eyes that I supposed were as unreadable as Kay's.

"Okay," I said.

CHAPTER FIVE

Being with my father spoiled my mood, a little — his presence interfered with my intentions to wallow in sweet enthrallment over Kay, the way someone's radio can rattle you with a competing tune when you're trying to sing a song of your own. I decided to put Kay away to savor later, like a dessert brought home after dinner in a restaurant.

When my dad turned off on the rutted two-track that led up to the handful of graying, sagging buildings that was Grassy Valley Ranch, my stomach lurched independently of the bouncing Jeep. It was a familiar sensation that upset my insides whenever a strong memory of Mom collided with the unreal reality of her death.

My dad grew up with horses — when we moved to Selkirk River, he made glowing promises about how healthy we'd all be, out in the clean air, riding horses everywhere. I pictured myself going to school on horseback. I thought maybe I'd be sent into town to buy groceries on my own horse, whom I planned to name Flash.

None of that happened. When I got around to noticing I didn't own a horse, I put a heartbroken tone in my voice and asked about it. (As was true of any good child, I knew precisely how deep to stab my mother and father in their guilty consciences.) And it worked, to a degree: we started taking family trips to Grassy Valley Ranch to rent horses.

Grassy Valley was where my dad met Rod Shelburton, who bought the ranch for the same reason my dad moved us to a thirty-acre property on top of a hill, only the Shelburtons were from Chicago and not Prairie Village. My dad and Mr. Shelburton liked to have what sounded like loud, heated arguments about Vietnam and the environment and Richard Nixon, only they agreed with each other on everything.

More than two years before, when my mom's chemotherapy ended, the two of us took a horseback ride up into the hills. It was a wonderful May day, wildflowers dancing in front of us as we left the barn.

Normally when we rode, Mr. Shelburton put me on Nanny, a gentle old horse who could not be spurred into a gallop regardless of how many clicks I made with my mouth or unsubtle hints I gave her with my boot heels.

Nanny was sick that day, though, so I was on Ginger, a younger horse my mom didn't trust. She kept Ginger attached to her horse with a lead, which I felt was insulting for a boy my age. We marched along with me launching a barrage of bitter complaints the whole time, until my mom's shoulders sagged with the weight of them.

Then I was angry because she didn't want to ride up to take a look at what boys my age called Dead Man's Falls (located in an area known to us as Dead Man's River and close to Dead Man's Rock), saying she was tired.

"You're *always* tired," I told her viciously.

I brought my contemptuous attitude with me to the dinner table, infuriating my father.

"Charlie, you are being rude to your mother!" he barked.

"It's okay," my mom murmured.

"It's not okay. Go to your room, Charlie. No TV tonight. Let's see if you can be more polite in the morning."

The lash of my dad's anger stung me, but I didn't let him see any pain in me as I slid off my chair and flounced down the hall as if I didn't care what they did to me.

I think I know now what that was all about. A restlessness was starting to afflict me, a sense of not being able to fit into my own skin. Manhood was a long way off, but already I was becoming impatient with being a boy. I wanted to ride a horse by myself, without an umbilical cord. And mostly I wanted to push my mother away from me, to gain independence from her, as all men must eventually do.

At the time, though, these irrational impulses came to me like temporary insanity, goading me into churlish behavior and then fading away to leave me stewing in guilt.

The house darkened; my parents murmured; my dad passed my doorway without a word. I heard my mother clink a few things in the kitchen, and then she was in the hallway, pausing at my door.

"Mom?"

She looked into my room. Her face was different, her cheekbones sharper and her eye sockets more pronounced, and of course her hair was nothing more than a wispy fuzz trying to make a comeback on her head, but the smile she gave me was the same. I'd treated her like dirt all day and here she was smiling at me with all the love in the world.

"Yes, Charlie."

I'd say I was sorry now. God, how I wish I could say I was sorry to my mom, sorry for every single thing I ever did to hurt her. But instead I said, "Aren't you going to kiss me good night?"

More than a year had passed since I'd asked for — no, demanded — a halt to the nightly ritual of a kiss. But on my mom's face there was no triumph, nor surprise, nor self-satisfaction. I saw only affection in her eyes as she came in and gently touched her lips to my forehead.

"Good night, Charlie. I love you."

"Good night, Mom." I didn't tell her I loved her back. I don't know why. If I had it to do over again, I would have said it, and it would have been as true as anything I'd ever uttered.

This memory hit me like a sucker punch when the Jeep stopped at the ranch, the dirt cloud that had been pursuing us engulfing the vehicle, then drifting away like a dog who chases cars and doesn't know what to do when one stops. I watched the dust but focused on my memories, pangs of something like hunger clawing at my insides.

"What do you think of that?" my dad asked proudly.

I looked where he was pointing. On the

other side of a wooden fence a dark herd of maybe twenty-five buffalo were standing around, their tails swishing. Some sort of wooden pathway led from this corral to pass beneath an odd platform above the fence, as if the buffalo were going to walk down the chute and have somebody leap on them from the perch.

"Buffalo," I said.

"American bison," my father said. It sounded like a correction, but when I looked at him curiously he nodded. "Buffalo, sure."

"For rides?"

My dad grinned at me. It was a full grin, unburdened by any death or sadness. "For eating. Mr. Shelburton and I are going to raise buffalo and sell them for meat."

"Cool," I replied, though I was hardly sure of the sanity of his statement.

"Beef's got cholesterol in it, and doctors are saying cholesterol is what gives people heart attacks. Buffalo has a lot lower cholesterol, though we're calling it American bison because we don't think people will eat it otherwise. What you're looking at is the start of a herd we're going to let get to about five hundred head."

A red pickup truck was parked out beyond the buffalo pen — I recognized it as Mr.

79

Shelburton's vehicle. Mr. Shelburton himself was on a horse.

"Hey, Charlie, you going to help us inoculate these critters today?" he called. Mr. Shelburton used words like a cowboy, but his accent was the same as the gangsters we saw in the movies.

I was excited to help until my job was explained to me.

"You can sit on the hood of the Jeep," my father said to me, his voice singsongy with false promise. I pretty much knew that if I were up on top of the Jeep I wouldn't be on a horse or anywhere near the "critters."

"I got a clipboard here, and every time we inoculate a bison, you call out the number and keep a written tally," my father continued.

I pictured it in my mind. I'd sit on the front of the Jeep, holding a clipboard, with absolutely nothing to do but watch the two of them maneuver a buffalo down the narrow wooden chute. One of them would lean over from the platform and inject the bison, and then they'd open the door and the buffalo would walk out. I'd make a mark and then call out the number. In other words, I'd be a bookkeeper. "Why can't I help inoculate?" I demanded.

"Charlie, these are wild creatures, these

buffalo. They're not like cows."

There it was — no matter what, I had to be kept safe. My dad had buried one family member and was never going to risk losing another.

"Sure 'preciate your help, pardner!" Mr. Shelburton called out to me.

I wonder how my dad's worry reflexes would react if I told him I'd been cavorting in the woods with an animal so fierce he could *eat* a buffalo. Among the three of us men, who was the real rancher wrangler? Why, it was Charlie Hall, master of the grizzlies, that's who.

I obviously wasn't going to give voice to these thoughts or tell my father anything about the bear. Living with my father was so emotionally dangerous I'd learned to parse truth and dole out only as much information as was absolutely necessary — to do otherwise would be to risk the disapproval that always came charged with the clear and devastating message that with my mom gone there wasn't a family anymore, nothing to anchor Dad to my life, no connection. Avoiding the conclusion that my father didn't love me was my main pastime, and I'd withhold any amount of truth from him to keep it from myself.

Of course, I didn't have the advantage of

months of painful psychotherapy then, so I didn't have any actual insight into why I'd become such an artful dodger of integrity. I just knew that it was always smarter to keep my mouth shut than to give my father any ammunition he could use against me.

I climbed up on the Jeep, clipboard in my lap, and watched as my dad and Mr. Shelburton tried to coax a buffalo out of the corral and into the wooden chute. Before me the Grassy Valley Ranch, more than a thousand acres in all, spread out like a wide green ocean shouldered on either side by rugged, thickly wooded hills.

"Come on there!" Mr. Shelburton yelled in frustration at the beast they were working.

The buffalo herd stood around like parked cars. Flies buzzed at their faces. They were immense creatures, the males taller at the hump than I would be on tiptoes. Apparently, if they didn't feel like moving, they didn't move.

Finally one gigantic bull grudgingly bumped his way down the chute. Mr. Shelburton triumphantly leaped off his horse and onto the platform. He had what looked like a sharp stick in his hand — a long-handled hypodermic, most likely. He and my father grinned at each other.

Mr. Shelton stabbed down smartly and then, as they say, all hell broke loose.

CHAPTER SIX

The second that long-handled syringe jabbed him, the bull let out a bellow and leaped straight in the air, kicking his rear legs. His mighty hooves slammed the wooden walls of the enclosure with a tremendous boom, rocking the platform and nearly spilling Mr. Shelburton to the ground.

The panic went through the rest of the herd like electricity. They surged forward and the stout wooden fence of the corral broke apart with a ripping, splintering sound. Mr. Shelburton leaped back onto his horse as the platform toppled and the buffalo stormed past him. Many of them smashed into the red truck and it was hard to tell if it was by accident or if they were just plain mad. They hit that vehicle with blow after blow from their butting heads. The headlights broke and the windshield spiderwebbed as the truck rocked back on its shocks.

And then all we could see was the herd's backsides as they took off at a dead run, their hooves winking black in the dust cloud.

The freight train–like rumble faded as the buffalo, still going flat out, crested a small hill and dipped below its horizon. The only sound was the truck's tires, two of which were giving up the ghost in a slow hiss. The side of the vehicle was ruined, dented up and down its length. One half of the corral gaped open, wood fragments from the fence lying trampled into the mud. Mr. Shelburton and my father just stared at the destruction, their mouths open, unable to speak.

I stood and cupped my hands over my mouth to shout, "That's one!"

I made a careful mark on the paper and looked at the men expectantly.

My dad gave me an unreadable stare and then, for the first time in more than a year, he threw back his head and laughed. Pretty soon he and Mr. Shelburton were standing on the ground in the ruins of the corral, their hands on their knees, laughing so hard they could scarcely breathe.

For the first time ever I began to hope Dad and I were going to allow ourselves to enjoy life after all, no matter how unfair it was that we were here and Mom was not.

I had a lot to ponder that night, with the Grassy Valley Ranch and the brief visit by a grizzly bear who seemed to have disappeared as abruptly as he had come, but mostly, as I lay in bed that night, I thought about Kay. My love for her felt like a buffalo stampede thundering through my blood, capable of smashing through any fence I tried to put around it. It made me feel powerful one minute and weak the next. My bones ached with it.

By the time I eased myself out of bed the next morning my dad was back on the ranch. He left me a note telling me that he and Mr. Shelburton had "a lot of work to do."

My dad has always had something of a gift for stating the obvious.

It was Sunday, a whole week away from the next junior-lifesaving lesson. A car pulled in the driveway around noon. I guiltily snapped off the television — my dad hated when I watched television on a sunny day — and went to see who it was.

Yvonne. She emerged from a Chevy Vega, bending over to pull an aluminum-covered pan from the passenger side floorboards. She nudged her door shut with a hip. She was wearing a knee-length skirt and a white blouse with a big floppy collar. She set the pan on the hood of her car and messed with her blouse in the reflection of her car window. *What do you think, Yvonne, that I can't see you unbuttoning your shirt from in here?*

I toyed with the idea of not answering her knock but figured that maneuver would have consequences for me. You could see into the dining area from the driveway — I imagined she'd probably spotted me spying on her. I opened the door and she blinked at me, smiling.

"Hello, Charlie."

"Hi, Miss Mandeville."

She suddenly remembered the circumstances of our last meeting. "Are you feeling any better?" Her expression was now one of concern.

"Yeah."

We stood looking at each other. I not only was not inviting her in, my arm was on the doorjamb to let her know she'd have to physically overpower me to get in the house.

"Is your dad home?" Her moist blue eyes flitted around the empty house.

"No, he's working today."

"On a Sunday?"

"He's working."

She nodded in defeat. "Okay." Her smile brightened. "Say, I brought this for you. It's warm, but not hot. Can you take it?" She held out the pan.

My vast experience with casseroles told me the specimen I was being given belonged to the tuna noodle variety.

I knew exactly what I was going to do with it.

I think I pretty much had given up ever seeing the grizzly again, so I was surprised when I got to the creek and saw him standing in the shallows. His head was darting quickly from side to side as he stared intently into the water, which at that place in the creek was barely half a foot deep. I crouched down by the banks, the casserole, which I had dumped into a paper bag, at my feet. The wind was flowing into my face, keeping my scent from the bear.

All at once the grizzly pounced, making huge splashes as he pursued a fish in my direction, lunging back and forth and bounding with jabbing forepaws again and again. I was startled by the astounding agility of the bear, the way he could stop that huge bulk in an instant and spring to one side, stabbing those claws into the water. The contrast with yesterday's buffalo couldn't have been more stark: both immensely powerful creatures, but with bison it was all about charging in a straight line.

This animal before me could just as easily move laterally, turning tightly, graceful as he was strong.

He thrust his snout below the surface, blowing bubbles, then raised his head and sneezed. This struck me as so comical I couldn't help but laugh a little, but when I did the bear lifted his head and looked straight at me, and then I stopped laughing.

"I brought you some food," I told him, my voice taking on an involuntary quaver.

When bears walk right at you their amazing muscles bunch under their fur in a way that completely belies their dexterity. If I'd not seen this huge creature leaping about just moments ago I might assume him to be clumsy and slow. I took an easy, careful breath, holding my ground. This close, he looked as big as Yvonne's Chevy Vega.

I nudged the grocery bag with my feet. "I hope you like it," I stuttered as the bear stuck his head in the bag, exactly the way he'd held his nose underwater just moments before. He inhaled and the sides of the bag collapsed.

What I now know about bears is that there was no worry he wouldn't like it. Bears are amazing omnivores. They eat seeds, berries, roots, carrion, and honey. But they also graze like cattle and will attack a moth

89

swarm or an anthill with determination and gusto.

The bear ate the casserole and also the paper bag it came in.

"So, okay then," I said.

The bear and I looked at each other. I expected the same expression I'd seen in the eyes of the buffalo: black and implacable, seeing me but not assigning me any particular importance in their wild world. But there was something about this bear's expression that seemed . . . friendly.

I was friends with a grizzly bear.

Many years later I was in my office when a man phoned from Montana wanting to speak to a "bear guy." I explained what a bear biologist was, and he seemed satisfied, though not impressed, with my credentials. He was calling with a question. "What," he asked, "do you feed a grizzly bear?"

I tightened my grip on the phone. "You don't," I replied honestly.

He was a former aerospace executive who had purchased a Montana ranch to play on and who had discovered a grizzly living on the edge of his property. The man's wife thought the bear looked hungry.

I'll bet.

"Mister, if you feed that bear even once, he'll start thinking of you as a food source and will follow you home," I warned. "A grizzly can kill a man with a single swipe of his paw — you've seen his teeth, his claws? The only safe thing to do is to stay as far away from that bear as you can."

But there was no one there to give eighth-grade Charlie Hall that sort of advice.

That day I made four trips up to the pole barn, returning each time laden with frozen dinners the bear crunched up as soon as I pried them out of their pans. Each time I came back the bear was wading around in the water, jumping fruitlessly on fish I couldn't even see.

"You probably ought to give up on trying to catch a fish. It doesn't look like it's working out for you," I told him.

The bear gave me a look that I swear contained a little bit of irritation. I decided to let him go about his business without the commentary.

After I handed over a cheese-and-noodle dish that rained macaroni like little dried-up worms when the bear bit into it, I told him that maybe that should do it for the day.

"I don't know that my dad won't notice if I keep giving you stuff at this rate," I explained apologetically.

I figured there must have been something in my tone that the bear understood, because we stood there regarding each other for a minute and then he lumbered off. When I yelled, "Bye!" at him he did not look back.

I was in a good mood when I walked in the house, totally unprepared for the expression on my father's face. He was standing in the kitchen by the sink.

"Hi, Dad," I said cheerfully, unaware. "Did you finish rebuilding the corral?"

"Charlie," my father said gravely. He held up the pan that had contained the lunch that Yvonne had made for the bear. A little of the slimy casserole still clung to the sides — I'd been planning to wash it when I got around to it.

"What's this?"

Uh-oh.

CHAPTER SEVEN

"Yvonne called a minute ago to tell me I should put this in the oven for half an hour and then it'd be ready." My dad set the pan in the sink and then crossed his arms, facing me. "You want to tell me what you did with our dinner?"

"I put it in a bag and threw it away," I said, which, though not the exact truth, was practically truth's identical twin. Or similar-looking cousin, anyway.

"Why did you do that?"

"Dad, it was *tuna noodle*." What more defense did a man need?

My dad regarded me gravely. I fidgeted under his gaze. He drew in a deep breath and let it out as a whistle through his nose.

"Sit down, Son," he said to me. We settled in at the kitchen table and he stared at me, searching for words. The fact that he was wrestling with what to say caused me to feel a rising dread. This was going to be about more than just kidnapping a casserole. Suddenly I flashed on what life would be like if Yvonne were sleeping down the hall from me in Mom and Dad's room, if Yvonne cooked dinner at Mom's stove, if Yvonne stopped in to try to give me a kiss every night.

If that happens, I decided to myself, *I will run away.* I would run away with Kay, who had a driver's license. We would drive to some place in Canada, where it would probably be legal for us to get married — it was Canada where they let people do whatever they wanted because it was too cold to bother stopping them.

"Charlie, when a man . . ." He reconsidered and started over, correcting himself. "Charlie, there are things a man needs. . . ."

I stared at him in alarm. We weren't seriously going to talk about *this,* were we?

"Everyone thinks of me as being this lonely man who needs to have a woman around. They respect your mother, but they feel that time enough has passed and that I should have someone like Yvonne in my life, someone I can . . ." He sighed again. "So I'm really sort of helpless, here. I don't really *like* Yvonne. She's fine; don't get me wrong. But I don't like her in the girlfriend sense of the word." He shook his head in wonder. "I've had four people ask me over to their house this month and they all include Yvonne, like the town took a vote."

My dad agitatedly got to his feet. "There's nothing wrong with the woman. I don't want to hurt her feelings." He stared moodily out the window. "But it's as if the lack of any other alternatives makes her the default. Do you know what I mean by that?"

"So if you don't have a girlfriend, then you wind up with the person who is just there," I said to my father.

I briefly wondered if Kay had a boyfriend. If not, couldn't I be the default? She didn't act like she was going steady with anyone.

"Exactly." My father nodded.

I was the oldest student in Junior Lifesaving, now that Dan Alderton had dropped out. I was "just there." Who else could possibly be the default?

I looked at my dad, who was running a hand through his reddish brown hair. This was the deepest and most intimate conversation we'd had in a long time. What I should do, I realized, was tell him about Kay. It would be an equal trade of information, two men swapping *women, you can't live with them, you can't live without them* stories.

I opened my mouth, wondering where to

start. Talking to my dad had just gotten to be so *hard.*

"But Charlie. Throwing away her dinner, that was just rude. She was trying to do us a kindness. I was lucky I saw the pan in the sink and figured out what she was talking about, but when she first asked me I was without a clue."

I hung my head, unhappy with the shift in mood.

"I raised you better than that."

"You and *Mom* raised me," I retorted with a sharpness that startled both of us. I didn't know why I snapped at him. It wasn't something I did very often, that was for sure. When the surprise and anger seeped out of his eyes they turned cold and grave and unloving. I knew that look.

The upshot of it all was that I was grounded until the first day of school, not allowed to leave the house unless it was to do chores. August, dry and clear, was just getting glorious and I would spend the last half of it sitting inside. Then I thought of something *really* important.

"But can I go to Junior Lifesaving?" I cried.

Yes, I could do that — those lessons were paid for.

Most maddening was the fact that I was

pretty much my own warden. He was at work; how would he know if I snuck out during the day? Hadn't I already proven untrustworthy? How then did it make any sense that I was to police myself? It was the sort of crazy parenting my father employed all the time. He made me give my word and shake his hand and that was supposed to be good enough. If he had been as suspicious as a normal dad I might have succumbed to the temptation to head down to the creek to see if the bear was still around, but because of my father's faith in me I was completely stuck!

I saw Kay two Saturdays in a row, and though I gave her intense stares whenever she glanced my way she remained cool and professional with me. I couldn't decide if she was acting like we didn't have something special between us because she didn't want the other students in class to feel slighted or she was acting like we didn't have something special between us because we didn't have something special between us.

The second Saturday was the last lesson. We all practiced everything we'd learned, except, I'm sorry to say, mouth-to-mouth resuscitation. Kay told us we'd receive our certificates in the mail, and that was it. I lingered after class broke up to see if I could catch her eye, but she went directly into the ladies' locker room.

Would I ever even *see* her again?

I about went crazy during my incarceration, so bored that I sometimes did chores just to have something to do. The world was still reeling from President Nixon's resignation, but I didn't care about anything beyond my own miserable imprisonment. I was just on the brink of greatness, a boy who talked to real bears and put his lips on real women, only to be snatched back and tossed into solitary confinement. I was itchy with unexpressed energy, so stuck in the world of nothing to do that I didn't want to do anything. I had long and entirely impossible conversations with Kay in my mind.

Me: Kay, I'm not just a junior lifesaver. I often go into the woods and feed a grizzly bear tuna casseroles.

Kay: I love you! Let's kiss.

I was so bored that even though I had nothing to talk to him about I called Dan Alderton over Labor Day weekend, though he wasn't home.

"He's not here; he went into town. Are you going to the movies tonight?" Mrs. Alderton asked me.

"Sorry?"

"I guess all of your friends from school

are going to see a movie. *Sugarland Express?* With that woman from *Laugh-In,* Goldie Hawn? I know she's been in other things, but I still think of her as being on *Laugh-In;* do you miss that show? I used to love that show. You should go. How come you don't come over to play with Danny anymore? You tell your dad we're thinking of him. Is he seeing that woman, Yvette Mandeville? I mean Yvonne. She's so sweet. Are you okay, hon? How have you been?"

Mrs. Alderton, I decided, was one of those people who asked questions without ever really desiring any kind of answer.

I told her politely that it was a pleasure to speak to her and that no, I wasn't going to the movie. I didn't tell her I was grounded, nor did I say that with my dad there were no exceptions, no appeals. You took your punishment.

Fifteen cords of wood had arrived by truck a few days before and naturally it was my job to stack it all. I was digging around in the woodpile, not so much stacking as just heaving split logs around and thinking about Kay, when I heard the Jeep turn off onto Hidden Creek Road and head up to our house. By the time I went inside, Dad was in the shower, which was pretty un-usual. When he came out of the bedroom a while later, he was wearing pressed slacks.

"You okay on your own for dinner to-night?" he asked me. He was buttoning a shirt and it seemed to be giving his roughened fingers some trouble. His new tie, fancy and wide, was flopped over the back of a chair like a deflated snake.

"Where are you going?"

He wouldn't meet my eyes, so I knew.

"Just out with some friends. Out to dinner. Dinner with . . . Yvonne, she'll be there, too. Actually we're meeting friends for a drink and then after that dinner it'll be just me and Yvonne, Miss Mandeville, at dinner. It's a dinner date. I'm going on a date, Charlie."

For nearly a year my father had been silent as a broken clock, and now, with the advent of this Yvonne woman, he was unleashing a torrent of words and I didn't like any of them.

"When will you be home?" I asked him in a low voice.

"Don't wait up for me," he replied, turning his back on me.

That's how I wound up going to see a movie that night. I watched my father's Jeep pull out of the driveway and I cursed him out loud. I found myself going to the gun cabinet, but no, violating that rule wasn't enough; I had so much rebellion inside of me banging around like a buffalo head-butting a pickup truck that I needed to do something really *bad*. It wasn't ten minutes later that I was trotting down the road, drinking in the evening air, an escaped prisoner.

I was headed, as it turned out, for a hefty helping of heartbreak.

Chapter Eight

It took more than a little bit of walking to get to town, but I was used to it. Selkirk River didn't really know how to decorate itself for Labor Day beyond a back-to-school sale at the dime store, so it just left up the stuff from the Independence Day celebrations — the streetlights wore boas of red, white, and blue. The air was warm and I decided I'd be better off with an ice cream than without, so I headed toward Baskin-Robbins as the first order of business.

There were little white tables scattered around next to the big picture window at the ice-cream parlor, and my heart fluttered when I saw the short black hair shimmering on a girl sitting at one of them. It was my Kay, licking an ice-cream cone and laughing.

I went from glorious exaltation to crushing despair in just seconds. Kay was not alone.

Her companion at the table was a man I'd never seen before. He had the short haircut of a soldier, and he was handsome and muscular and taller than Charlie Hall by a lot. Compared to him I was just an eighth-grade kid from Junior Lifesaving.

I'd lost her.

I'm sure I'm probably not the only heart-sick boy in the world to self-inflict more damage by hanging around and watching the love of his life lavish affection on another male. Kay's lips eventually met his when they finished eating and stood outside the ice-cream shop. They kissed like they'd put in a lot of practice at it, entwined in each other's arms, and then broke apart with smiles on their faces.

Kay left in one direction and the boyfriend in another. I lingered for a minute and then set off in the direction of the movie theater.

I'd lost my taste for ice cream.

Naturally, because I hadn't yet suffered enough, Kay was out in front of the movie theater, meeting some girlfriends. She was wearing hot pants, her tan, slim legs adding desire to the nauseating stew of emotions bubbling up inside me. I hung back until she went inside, then purchased my ticket and slunk in after her.

The movie theater had big velvet curtains

and magnificent chandeliers hanging from the ceiling. Opulent faux box seats were built into the intricately tiled walls down by the polished wooden stage. It was a magical place for me, even if close examination revealed significant wear in the cushions and a carpet that was thin and ragged. The place was crowded, but as soon as I walked in I spotted a contingent of boys who were in my grade. Feeling better, I started down the ramp toward them, but a hand on my wrist stopped me.

"Hi, Charlie," said a female voice. It was, of course, Kay, sitting in the aisle seat.

It was my impulse to sullenly shrug her off as punishment for her betrayal, but I couldn't help it: a grin immediately lit up my face. "Hi!" I said. My whole arm was singing with the sensation of her hand touching me, even when she let go.

I stood there with my goofy smile, probably looking totally enraptured. If the thousands of volts of pure love I was sending her way registered with her at all, she gave no sign, though a small grin did twitch at the corner of her mouth.

Say something, you idiot! I cursed myself.

The lights dropped and the curtain began chugging its way to the ceiling, wrinkling up from the bottom. The noise level began receding.

"Well, enjoy the movie," I said to Kay. She smiled at me.

Just three rows down were my friends. Dan Alderton was sitting in the aisle seat. There were plenty of open places among them. "Hey," I whispered, starting to slide into the row to join them.

"Where you think you're going?" Dan demanded loudly — so loudly that it seemed like everyone in the theater stopped to listen. His leg was pressed against the back of the seat in front of him, like a railroad-crossing gate.

I was dumbfounded. "I just . . ." I pointed to an empty seat.

"Nuh-uh. Pick someplace else."

Sitting next to Dan were the same boys from the road that day, Mitch and Jerry and the ninth grader, Gregg. They were jeering at me with open hostility.

"Go sit down," Gregg said.

I didn't understand any of this, but the previews were starting and I could feel the people behind me getting restless. I glanced up and saw Kay gazing at me and there was something in her dark eyes I couldn't read — I loathed the idea it might be pity.

I found a seat down in front, where the floor sort of leveled out and anyone viewing the movie would get a crick in his neck by the end of it. I wasn't watching, though; I was still sorting through my confusion. I had done nothing to offend Dan that I could recall, but the contempt on everyone's faces was unmistakable.

I'd been focused on Dan and those next to him, but what about the other guys, several from my grade, all of whom had been watching as Dan blocked my passage? It felt as if a vote of excommunication had been taken. Or was it just that they were all so thankful that it wasn't happening to them that they kept their heads down?

Either way, I was an outcast. I swallowed back the hurt.

I was still wallowing in self-pity and perplexity when something light popped me on the back of the head. I thought I heard a snigger as well, and when something else struck me it fell into my lap: a kernel of popcorn.

So now my misery was complete. My dad was off on a hot date and would probably wind up getting married to the grocery gal, the love of my life was dating some *man,* and the boys from my grade hated me so much they were throwing food at my head.

If I left the theater my retreat would be noted and I would lose whatever slight standing I had among my fellows. If I stayed I'd be showered with popcorn and everyone in the theater would be witness to my humiliation. There were no good options.

A piece of hard candy shot past my ear, bouncing on the floor in front of the seats. The boys had escalated their ammunition. Now the projectiles would not only debase and disgrace me; they would *hurt.*

I was so saturated with wretched unhappiness I didn't even notice the person standing next to my seat in the aisle until I heard her whisper to me.

"Charlie. Move over."

It was Kay. I blinked at her in stunned amazement. She gestured that I should take the empty seat next to me, so I did, and then she took the seat I'd just vacated, but not before standing in the flickering light, giving all the boys behind her a long, full look — *this girl was no eighth grader!* — and fixing Dan with her unreadable eyes.

She didn't say anything, just sat and watched the movie while I gazed at her lovely profile in sheer dumb wonder. When she caught me staring she gave me a small smile and then, astoundingly, *laid her head on my shoulder.*

My only complaint about the movie *Sugarland Express* was that it wasn't near long enough, not by far. I didn't really follow the plot, I was just conscious of Kay, and I carefully refrained from moving the slightest bit even when her head on my shoulder gradually cut off the blood supply to my arm.

When the movie ended and people began filtering out, Kay put her hand on my arm, keeping me in my seat. We sat quietly until the place had mostly emptied, and then she stood. "Let's go this way," she said, leading me to the glowing exit sign in the front of the theater. We fumbled in the dark to a door that squeaked when we opened it, and then we were in the alley, facing each other awkwardly.

"That was a really good movie," I said reverentially.

"It was," she agreed.

"This is fun," I told her, cleverly thinking that by keeping my comment in the present tense she'd agree with me that the night was far from over.

"I have to go meet my friends," Kay replied.

Okay, not clever enough. I looked into her eyes. She was so nice and kind, so generous and caring, that there was no hint in her gaze that she knew she'd rescued me from social humiliation.

I nodded at her, struggling to come up

with something to say. *Thank you? I love you?* She smiled at me. "Bye, Charlie."

"Okay. Yes," I responded with admirable idiocy.

I watched her walk out of the alley and vanish from view.

The stars were out as I strolled home, a blaze of them against a black sky that was on occasion scored by the straight white line of a meteor making its mark. Because of an astronomy report I'd given in fifth grade, I could look up and identify Ursa Major, the Great Bear, watching over me. It didn't look very ursine to me, though.

Naturally, given what was to become my life's interest in bears, I've spent a lot of time thinking about Ursa Major. Why did so many cultures look up into the night sky and see a bear? The Romans, the Navajo, the Iroquois, and the Algonquins. Ancient texts in Greek, Hebrew, and Arabic speak of the great bear of the heavens. Homer, Shakespeare, Spenser, and Tennyson wrote about Ursa Major, and van Gogh painted it. Is there something comforting about having a bear up there? Is there some significance beyond needing to name the constellation something that they picked a bear even though it has a tail more like a lion?

Did I care about any of this that particular

night? Of course not. If it didn't have anything to do with Kay, it didn't have anything to do with me.

I figured that at that point my life had pretty much peaked. I was happier than I could ever remember being, certainly happier than I'd been since the day my mom and dad told me about the sickness. My ebullient mood lasted all the way home, right up until I turned down my driveway and saw, to my dismay, my father sitting in the living room, waiting for me.

CHAPTER NINE

As it turns out, the penalty for going off to a movie while grounded was to be confined to quarters *for the first month of school*. I didn't even get credit for time served, though I'd practically finished out my sentence for premeditated disposal of Yvonne's tuna noodle.

It was, I reflected as my dad scolded me, what happened when you didn't have a mother around to soften a father's harsh judgment. The first month of school, when friendships and alliances are formed, and I was grounded? My mother would have reasoned that what I had done was bad but not ruin-my-life bad. I mean, it wasn't like I went next door and murdered the neighbors. But to my father the whole issue was that he was the man in charge and I disobeyed orders. To drive home the point that my life was in his hands, he took it away from me.

I normally view the first day of school the way I'd view the bottom step of the gallows, but that year I was pretty much ready to burst out of the house and would have gladly joined a chain gang to get out of there.

Funny how it didn't occur to me until the school bus squealed and quaked to a halt at the top of my driveway that things were going to be different on the ride in. Dan and I had always sat together in one of the front seats on the bus, a habit we'd gotten into in grade school, but that wasn't likely to be true anymore, was it?

I stepped up the metal stairs to the bus interior that first day, nodded at the driver, and took an uneasy survey of the sparsely situated passengers. Dan's house was ahead of mine on the route, as was his buddy Jerry's. The two of them were sitting next to each other in one of the very back seats — that's where the older kids, the ninth graders, always took up residence. I started to head back their way, faltered, and wound up dodging into a seat just a few rows from the front. I didn't know where to sit. I didn't know who my friends were.

I was the freak with the dead mom. Maybe I didn't *have* friends.

I did notice that when the bus admitted a

group of ninth graders they made Jerry and Dan move up a few rows, but it didn't give me any particular satisfaction. When the bus got crowded and there were no more open seats a newly minted seventh grader, quaking with low self-esteem, slid in next to me and eyed me nervously, as if he had been assigned to be my prison cellmate because I'd killed the last one. I gave him a tough look to intimidate him and it worked: he blanched and turned away from me, perched on the lip of the seat so that he was practically falling into the aisle.

I sort of regretted doing that. It would have been nice to have someone to talk to.

It felt good to get off the bus, but as it turned out, that first day of school was nothing but one long, agonizing disappointment.

I'd been betrayed by my body again, which just hadn't been in the mood to grow taller or more muscular over the summer — I was the same size as most of the despised seventh graders and a bit shorter than a lot of them. That morning as I slipped into what I called my clean jeans — basically just the pair of pants I never wore to the creek — I had felt gratified at the familiar feel of the soft, faded denim. Many of the other boys, I knew from experience, would be wearing creaky new jeans, so darkly indigo they were almost black. Now, though, I realized my clothing announced my complete lack of growth as loudly as a broadcast over the school intercom system: *There's Charlie Hall, wearing the same clothes from last year!*

The girls all wore miniskirts because it was the first day of school. Somehow, girls just knew what to wear. I had on a striped T-shirt I'd first worn in sixth grade and believed people knew this. I looked like a kid from grade school who had gotten on the wrong bus, except that I had a pimple flaring on my chin — my body couldn't produce growth hormones, but it could crank out a new zit!

When the bell rang the hallways vibrated with happy energy, kids greeting each other and grinning. Not me, though. I belonged to a sad subspecies, scurrying from room to room with eyes down, part of no clique, member of no gang. Just hours into eighth grade and it felt as if I'd failed the year. I'd spend my days isolated and alone.

Dan was in my science class, sitting a few seats behind my desk. I noticed him as I slunk into the room but kept my gaze averted, not wanting to meet his eyes. As the teacher tried to figure out everyone's names, Dan leaned over and hissed at me, "Hey, Squirrel!"

I had never been called Squirrel before. It didn't sound as if it were intended as an endearment. I twisted around and looked at Dan with a question on my face.

"Why didn't you go out for football?" he asked. His freckles stood out against his skin more vividly than the year before — I don't know why, but this is what I focused on as I mulled over his question.

I wasn't able to come up with an answer. Football was, last time I checked, a sport that depended on size, strength, and speed. I had struck out on all three.

After science class was lunch. During seventh grade I'd sat at a table with a gang of boys that included Dan, a bunch of us, all low status, finding comfort in our numbers. Even though they were now eighth graders, the same boys sat at the same place. I didn't dare carry my tray over there — I'd no doubt that I'd wind up being treated exactly the same way as I'd been treated in the movie theater.

I felt like that guy everyone was talking about, Philippe Petit, who a week or so before school had walked across a tightrope strung between the World Trade Center towers, 1,350 feet above the streets of New

115

York. One wrong move and he would have been dead, and then when he did make it he was arrested.

I found an end spot at one table that was sparsely inhabited by a couple of nervous new kids and a seventh grader who never looked at anything but his lunch tray. I hurriedly bolted down my food, tasting nothing. I don't remember what I ate, but it was probably meat loaf, which was what they almost always served. Sometimes they put spicy gravy on it and called it Salisbury steak, sometimes they put it on a bun and called it hamburger, sometimes they served it in a hard tortilla and called it a taco, and sometimes they decided just to be honest and call it meat loaf. I'm sure we must have had other things for lunch, but when I remember junior high school all I remember eating is the same gray serving of ground beef over and over.

A couple of times during lunch I raised my eyes and spotted the searching glances of other rootless boys, but I didn't hold anyone's gaze for fear of being lumped in with a bunch of losers.

After lunch I made my way to the boys' room and sat in one of the stalls, my pants puddled at my ankles, letting my nervous stomach play out its undesirable symptoms.

I was oddly at peace in there, so naturally some loud boys marched in.

When I was in seventh grade and needed to go number two, some ninth-grade boys would stand on the toilets on either side of the stall, looking over the walls and jeering and laughing at me. I had no idea what was so funny; I was just a sevie hoping for some privacy while I pooped.

I had calculated that with those guys off to high school and me promoted to eighth grader I would at last be afforded some dignity, but alas, this was not to be so. The boys, ninth graders for only a day, banged into the surrounding stalls and their heads popped up on either side and they laughed and pointed at me. My misery was complete.

How did the new ninth graders even know to do this? Was there some sort of secret ceremony, an initiation into the society of boys who stood on the toilets to hoot laughter at some poor guy who was just trying to evacuate his bowels? Or did eighth graders witness the hazing and think to themselves, *I can't wait until next year when I get to do that?*

The last class of the school day took years to arrive. We were all itchy from being cooped up after a summer of freedom and

117

the students reacted to the bell as one giant reflex, leaping to our feet and rushing out of the classrooms even as teachers called final instructions to us, usually having something to do with the idea that we weren't allowed to leave until we were properly dismissed.

Dan, Gregg, Jerry, and a couple other boys were waiting at my locker for me. I didn't see them until it was too late to turn away.

"Charlie. You and me are gonna fight," Dan told me, his lips twisted in an ugly grimace. He stood close to me, crowding my space.

He really wasn't much bigger than I was, and I couldn't help but feel that this new-found hostility was somehow fake. We were *friends.* This didn't make any sense to me.

I looked into Dan's eyes and saw something unexpected there: fear. The skin had gone pale under his freckles. I don't think Dan was afraid of fighting; I think he was afraid of everything else, of trying to learn his place in this strange place, this in-between consignment where we were neither ninth nor seventh graders, where many of the boys — twelve- and thirteen-year-olds — had gotten it into their heads that it was time to tough their way into manhood.

"How?" I asked.

This call to the logical part of his brain unbalanced Dan a little. "What do you mean, how?" he responded, forgetting in his bafflement to sneer.

"How are we supposed to fight? We'd be suspended."

"Only if you fight on school property," Gregg objected.

"Or if someone tells on us," I continued. "And then how do we get home? Is your mom going to pick us up? Because my dad can't; he's at work."

The concept of beating me up and then getting in the car with his mother — *How was school today, boys? Why is Charlie profusely bleeding?* — froze Dan in place.

I slammed my locker shut and turned away. "It's not a good idea. It doesn't make any sense."

This response was so entirely unexpected that I was able to walk a good five yards before they reacted, and then it was with a chorus of jeering laughs rather than a pursuit and a hallway mugging. I made it safely to the bus and pretended my interest was entirely absorbed by the open English textbook in my lap when I sensed Dan swaggering down the aisle.

"Hey, Hall. Hall!" he called to me.

I couldn't hear him, so fascinated was I

with the description of adverbs and their uses.

"Squirrel," he taunted over his shoulder as he took his seat.

Please, oh Lord, don't let that become my official nickname.

CHAPTER
TEN

As soon as my feet touched down at the bus stop I was running. Maybe everyone on the bus thought I was running from Dan and maybe in some ways that was exactly what I was doing, but I always ran full speed up Hidden Creek Road and I hoped the kids on the bus knew that.

Hidden Creek Road was originally cut into the hill to give loggers access to the trees at the top of the rise and they didn't waste money on reducing the slope more than they strictly had to, so it was a pretty hard climb. On a couple of the turns the road had to be literally blasted out of the side of the mountain and the rocks were scored with thin half-pipes where the crews had hammered in the dynamite — the striations looked as if a massive animal had clawed the granite.

I walked in the front door panting and starving. I ate a bag of Hostess sugar donuts

121

and two glasses of milk, which made me think of another hungry animal. There was nothing, I thought glumly, I could do about it.

As I remember it now, I spent most of my incarceration that September standing in the big picture window at the back of the house, looking for signs of that grizzly bear. I took a page out of Scotty Beck's book and held binoculars to my eyes, spotting deer and elk and skunk and fox and all manner of squirrels and birds, but no bear. Some of the creek was visible from that window, but most of it was obscured by the landscape, including the shallows where I'd committed the crime that got me grounded to begin with.

Where was the bear? Had he wandered off to find some other boy to spend his time with? Was he hungry? If he was trying to survive on his fishing skills he was probably starving. I was anxious and concerned for my ursine friend but was honor bound to stay inside the house, going crazy with the conflict.

What he was probably doing, I now know, was eating berries and grubs. Back then I assumed grizzlies were savage carnivores who held the same opinion about vegetables as I did — a burger beats a carrot any day.

But grizzlies not only find berries and roots more abundant than meat; they actually seem to prefer them. I've seen a captive bear turn up his nose at hamburger in order to get to a pile of avocados. I also know that the younger the grizzly, the more likely he is to be frustrated in his search for food — and this was a young bear. He probably was not starving, exactly, but he also was most likely struggling to get enough to eat.

When the school bus came I went from one prison to another. Nobody was talking to me — I was alone and a loner. I evaded Dan Alderton as best I could, devising routes through the hallway that kept me from accidental contact and mastering the art of ignoring him in science class. I ate lunch with my eyes downcast. I hated every minute of it.

My father severely tested my loyalty during those four weeks by seeing Yvonne socially twice. That's how he put it: "I'm seeing Yvonne socially on Saturday." The whole lament about him not liking her was apparently a big fat lie. My father said no more about the matter, though he seemed to hesitate a little when he told me he was going off for his social seeing, like he was waiting for me to challenge him. I didn't give him the satisfaction. I just gazed at him with a blank expression on my face, hoping my lack of reaction was driving him insane.

If it was, he gave no indication. He was better at the expressionless look than I was.

Being stuck inside for the thirty days hath September gave me more than ample opportunity to wallow in the sadness that swamped me whenever I thought about Kay. She was the perfect woman for me in every way except her boyfriend.

Maybe her date with the military guy, whom I referred to in my thoughts as Sergeant Lunkhead, was all just for show, designed to make me jealous or something.

"Why did you put your head on my shoulder, Kay?" I asked the empty house.

Because Charlie, Kay's voice answered, *I love you. I've loved you ever since you gave me mouth-to-mouth resuscitation.*

My urges weren't sexual — for me those storms, while building on the horizon, were still a little ways off. I wasn't picturing Kay naked, though it had not escaped my attention during Lifesaving that she did know how to fill out a bathing suit better than the girls my age. I was thinking about her in a much more pure and frankly unrealistic fashion, as a woman who would be devoted to me forever, who would never leave me, ever. That's all I wanted.

Talking too much to yourself can lead you in unexpected directions. "Mom," I said out loud one afternoon, but I didn't finish my sentence. I'd tried a couple of times since her death to converse with her, to feel her presence and speak to it, but even in the cemetery it didn't work. She was gone. She couldn't hear me. My heart was aching and I needed to talk to my mother about it, but she was dead.

I felt a flare of anger, a twisted bitterness, at her for dying and leaving me motherless, trapped in a house with a man who often acted as if he were the one who died. It wasn't fair! I hated her for getting that wretched disease and taking so long to die that when it finally happened, yes, I felt relief. Who wouldn't?

This internal rant was immediately followed by shame and remorse. My throat tightened, my eyes squeezed shut, and tears tracked down my face. I was so, so sorry — sorry I had gotten angry at her, sorry for what I had done and could never undo. I didn't hate her. She was my mom. I missed her so much it felt like my insides were torn.

One Saturday I received my junior-lifesaving certificate — I was now officially qualified to pull seventh graders out of the pool. There was no mention on the diploma of the fact that I was the only student brave enough to put his lips on the instructor.

She had signed it: *Kay Logan.* I put my finger on the signature, a bit disappointed that it didn't give off an electric current.

Kay Logan. There was only one Logan family listed in the Selkirk River phone book.

"Hi, Kay; it's me, Charlie," I said by way of practice, the phone still safe in the cradle. "Really? Well, I missed you, too. . . . Now? . . . Well, I'm grounded, but you could come over *here.*"

Despite how well that went, I didn't immediately pick up the phone. My heart was pounding. Of course I could call her. We'd been to the movies together. I'd blown air into her lungs. We had a relationship.

I was a boy who fearlessly walked with a grizzly bear.

That's what finally gave me the nerve: how many other kids could claim something like that?

A woman answered the phone, but it wasn't Kay.

"Hi, can I talk to Kay?" I asked a little breathlessly.

"Is this Glenn?" the woman wanted to know.

"Who?"

Who was Glenn? Was that Sergeant Lunk-head's name?

"I'm sorry; I thought you were someone else. Kay's not here right now."

"Oh."

"Would you like to leave a message?"

Yes; when you see your daughter, would you tell her I love her?

"Hello?"

"Yes!" I blurted. "Tell her please that Charlie Hall called and that I got my certificate for Junior Lifesaving."

"Okay. Charlie Hall. I will tell her."

"Good."

"Thank you for calling, Charlie. Good-bye."

"Good-bye and thank you, good-bye," I said formally. Then I hung up and reviewed the conversation in my head, wincing.

Finally October 1st arrived and my house arrest came to an end. That afternoon I blew out of those school bus doors and dashed up the hill and into my house, spreading my arms as if to embrace the glory of it all. At last!

Then I watched television like I always did.

After an hour or so, though, I realized I was wasting time and thought of something

127

I could now do that I'd been grounded from doing.

The bear was not at the creek, and I carried my offering — a fruitcake — back to the freezer. I wasn't going to leave the food just sitting there, even though it was a fruitcake and therefore of no use to anybody. I wanted the bear to know this gift was coming from me.

That Friday after school I headed off into the woods, drinking in the strong pine scent as it wafted on October breezes. I didn't have any food with me — I wasn't really convinced I was ever going to see the bear again. I did call out, "Hey, bear!" when I got to the creek, but nothing answered but my echo and I kept wandering.

I did not have a destination in mind, but after a time I found myself working my way up to what I thought of as the Old Cabin. At the rocky outcropping that was the spine of the ridge visible from our house the terrain dipped back down and then flattened for a while before plunging down all the way to the river. In the center of the flat area was an abandoned hut, the windows broken out and the interior sagging from several winters of exposure. I suppose at some time it was a place where hunters took up residence for a few days at a time, but that was before Jules McHenry bought up so much of the land to use as his personal playground.

McHenry was estimated by the kids at school to be worth a bazillion dollars. He was a rich oil guy from somewhere south, like Texas, I guess, and showed up a few times a year to hunt on the acres and acres of land he'd purchased all over the county. It's what people did when they had so much money they didn't know what to spend it on.

I liked to go inside the cabin and smell the dank, musty air, though it was somewhat creepy. One time a gust of wind blew the front door shut on me and I nearly screamed. The door tended to stick a bit and the thought of getting trapped in there panicked me a little, though there was a big square window in the back, glass long broken out, that I could escape through if I needed.

The Old Cabin had a long driveway that led up to the paved road, Road 655. There was a junked car on the property where someone had gone flying into the trees after losing an argument about centrifugal force with one of Road 655's many curves. The driver wound up deciding the vehicle he'd ridden into the woods wasn't worth the cost to tow it out of there. Mice lived in the car, and boys had pounded the sheet metal with rocks. My loose plan was to go check out the car after messing around at the Old Cabin, but I never got there.

Years later, when I wrote my book, *The Bear from Selkirk River,* I sat down with what felt like half the people from town, asking them to tell me their thoughts and recollections about the events that occurred in the fall of 1974. From that I was able to piece together a narrative that included conversations that took place outside of my hearing and to understand the thinking of some of those involved.

People always answered my questions happily enough; they were cooperative and friendly. And then they had a question for me, and it was nearly always worded exactly the same.

Did it really happen?

CHAPTER
ELEVEN

I had taken just two steps inside the Old Cabin, fumbling my way, unable to adjust to the murky darkness, when the smell hit me. A dank, wild odor, both strong and familiar.

The bear had been in here.

Was he in here now? I froze, the bright square of light from the doorway cast on the floor in front of me like a piece of carpet. Gradually the interior images of the cabin worked to resolve themselves: there was the rusty sink, the door-less icebox, the pile of decaying tin cans. I held my hand up to block the light from the big broken-out window in the rear and saw more, including the torn and dirty mattress some unknown person had dragged in a year or two ago and placed against the left wall.

No bear. I let my breath out slowly. I strode over to the mattress, feeling the boards sag under my feet, the wood gone

131

even more soft than it had been on my last visit. The ceiling, too, looked worse, collapsing in the middle. The elements were working on this place and would soon pull it down.

I couldn't imagine a human being lying on the mattress, though it looked like a dog had left some fur on it. Mice had been busy burrowing in from the sides.

A shadow filled the doorway then. I whipped my head around and it was the bear, on all fours, watching me. I took a deep gulp of air, feeling cornered. I glanced at the big window, set a little high off the floor, but if I was motivated I knew I could dive through it.

"I didn't bring you anything. Are you hungry, boy?" I asked unsteadily. I held out my hands to show him they were empty, and they were shaking a little from my heartbeat.

The bear took a step forward. In the small confines of that place he was enormous, his bulk blotting out the light from the doorway.

Run! Though I had fed him and he seemed tame, some primordial sense within me was reacting to being this close to such a grand, awe-inspiring beast, urging me to try to bolt for the door.

"Okay. We're okay," I murmured.

I bit my lip as the bear pushed his head forward, virtually nose-to-nose with me. I shrank involuntarily against the wall. I looked into those eyes; I smelled his breath. His massive head, brown and round, with ears that popped up on either side like cupcakes, no longer looked doglike or cute to me.

He was far too close for me to try to get away now. If I had made a mistake by trusting him not to hurt me, it would be the last mistake I'd ever have a chance to make.

With a small chuffing sound the bear turned and lumbered away, grunting as he forced his way back through the narrow doorway.

I heaved a deep sigh and followed him outside. He looked over his shoulder at me.

"You want me to see if there's anything to eat in my freezer?" I asked him. My voice came out normal and easy. That had been the acid test — if he wanted to eat me he would have done it. I would never be afraid of the bear again. With the simple and uncomplicated trust of an eighth-grade boy I approached him and put my hand on the coarse fur near his spine. "You startled me a little," I said, feeling I needed to apologize since I'd nearly peed my pants in there.

There was a sudden squeal from above,

up on Road 655, followed by a dull concussion that I felt as much as heard. "Whoa!" I shouted. "Car accident!" Though the bear had whipped his head up at the sound, he didn't seem particularly excited. I turned and ran up the wide leafy trail that had once been the driveway of the Old Cabin, glancing over my shoulder.

The bear was still looking at me, but he was making no move to follow.

When I got to Road 655 I saw a Buick Estate station wagon about twenty yards away, pulled over to the side of the road. The brake lights were on, but then they winked out and the car accelerated away. I doubted that the driver had seen me.

Twenty feet from where the car had stopped, off on the shoulder, was a thick-limbed mule deer, small, a female. I walked up and looked into her blank, black eyes, the life gone from them. Blood was pooled under her and her legs were twisted — the impact had killed her instantly.

"Hey, bear!" I shouted. A light breeze made the branches creak over my head, the sound serving to accentuate how otherwise silent the woods were. "Hey, bear, come here!"

I sighed in frustration. Did the bear even know I was calling him? And though I had a fresh deer carcass for him, why did I think he would come at my command? Was he my pet? No, but what else would you call our relationship? "Friends" didn't describe it very well, either.

While I was stewing over all this there was a thrashing sound and the bear appeared, carefully looking up and down the road, his nose up to sniff for intruders. I gestured to the dead animal on the ground. "Look here!" I called.

It was October 4th, and I now know that the bear was well into hyperphagia — the huge intake of calories to prepare him for the winter's hibernation. He'd been eating acorns and pine nuts and berries but probably not, based on what I'd seen, fish. As he strolled up the road toward me, his eyes were on the fresh carcass at my feet, though he did glance at me as if to give thanks before diving into his meal.

Anyone who doubts the grizzly's position as top predator in the food chain has never done what I did that afternoon: stand by and watch as a bear tore into and devoured an entire mule deer. It was somehow even worse that his bites were almost dainty, using his front teeth like a polite person at a chicken barbeque. It was both awe inspiring and somewhat sickening, and when his energetic claws wound up pulling the deer off the shoulder and down the hill a little bit I didn't follow. The savagery of nature is sometimes too much for those of us who sleep in a soft bed under a wooden roof.

When the whole story of that afternoon and everything that followed was made known, my dad asked me what I could have thought I was up to. I was feeding a grizzly bear? Talking to it? *Playing* with it? What was I thinking?

The truth was, I wasn't thinking anything. Did I stop for one second to question the sensibility of my behavior? Absolutely, especially when the bear had me cornered in the Old Cabin. But the world had already lost all sense to me. Things that I knew in my bones could not possibly be true were, nonetheless, inarguable facts. Though it was impossible to believe, my mother was dead and I would not be seeing her again. Once a person tried to live within that inexplicable construct, nothing seemed too outrageous.

Did it really happen?

Here's all I can say to that: after the bear finished the deer carcass, he clambered back up the hill toward me like a dog tracking back to its master. It seemed as natural as anything in the world to put my hand out and touch his thick fur, to pat the huge head, and to say, "Come on." As the bear obediently followed me, it felt completely reasonable that I would take the bear home with me, maybe feed him a meal directly out of the freezer. That my dad would let me keep a live grizzly.

Well, okay, that last one didn't slide so easily into place: I wasn't able to conjure up a conversation in my head where my father said, *Of course you can keep a full-grown grizzly, Charlie.*

I'd have to think of something.

Rather than climb back up to the rocky ridge and on to my house, the bear and I walked past the Old Cabin, heading toward the river. The cabin was up on a bluff, and below it was a steep bank of heavy sand that ran all the way down to the rushing waters. One of my favorite things to do was leap from the bluff, the soft soil absorbing the impact.

"Ready?" I said. I launched myself into the air with a hoot, showing off for the bear, who stood up on two legs to watch me slide and tumble down the embankment.

Then the bear followed suit. I laughed in disbelief as the bear sprang into space, landing on all fours and then rolling down the hill in an explosion of flying sand. He came to rest at the bottom of the hill, lying on his back as if he, too, were laughing.

The bear took a deep drink at the river. There was, I reflected, time enough for me to grab my rod and see if I could coax a few fish from the water. The bear kept wading deeper into the stream until he was up to his neck, his big head serene in the clear, rapid river. Or maybe we'd just stay here and swim.

I grinned at the thought of Kay coming upon us just then. *I'm just watching my friend swim, in case he needs junior lifesaving,* I'd tell her. She'd be amazed. She'd sit with me and hold my hand while the bear frolicked. It would be our secret, something Kay and I would never tell another soul.

The easiest way back home was to follow the river upstream until the creek joined it, then walk along the creek's banks to the trail up to our house.

The bear came out of the water and we strolled side by side as if there were nothing more natural than the two of us together. He got interested in overturning some rocks to take a look at what was underneath: grubs and worms, it turned out, which I thought was pretty disgusting, but the bear slurped them up as if they were made of chocolate.

The riverbank here was a wide stretch of

light, sandy soil, striated from when the waters rose high but otherwise as pristine as a chalkboard on the first day of school. The soil was not as firm as sandstone but was packed solidly enough that when I took a stick and swiped at it I could draw a permanent mark. I made a big letter *C*.

"My name is Charlie," I told the bear. I stuck my tongue out a little as I drew my name in the dirt. When I stepped back, it was pretty easy to read: *Charlie*.

"That's how you spell it," I told him. "See? Charlie."

The bear looked at the marks I'd made as if trying to read them. He lumbered up to the bank, taking a closer look. Then he moved off down the bank a ways, where I hadn't yet written anything.

I cocked my head, regarding my artwork. Should I write *loves Kay* after my name? Or turn it around: *Kay loves Charlie*. Maybe Sergeant Lunkhead would come across it, think he'd lost her, and abandon Selkirk River forever. Or maybe he'd get in a big fight with Kay, acting all jealous, and then I'd show up to save her. I'd have the bear with me, which would sort of stack the odds in my favor, even if Lunkhead had military training.

I looked down at my feet and saw a small

painted turtle crawling glumly among the rocks. I almost shouted, *turtle!* at the bear but then bit my lip. The bear would probably just eat the thing, and I didn't want to have that on my conscience.

I glanced up, but the bear wasn't paying attention to me. He was digging at the soft soil of the bank with a single paw, a small trickle of dirt pyramiding at his feet. I frowned. What was he doing?

With a huff, the bear backed away from the bank, and now I could clearly see that he'd made his own marks in the smooth soil.

He'd written his own word, plain as day, easy to read.

EMORY.

"Oh boy," I said.

CHAPTER
TWELVE

The first psychiatrist I was sent to, the one I never liked, spent very little time getting to know me before he asked, "At what time did you become convinced the bear was trying to communicate with you?"

That one didn't take much thought. "When he wrote his name in the sand," I said simply.

The psychiatrist gave me a long, frozen, unamused look before speaking. "And then you took the bear to your house."

"To the pole barn, yes. Not inside the house or anything."

"And what were you thinking at that moment?"

That question again. Why did everyone expect me to be doing so much thinking all the time? How much thinking did *they* do at thirteen?

To this day, I can't really explain what I felt as I looked at the word "Emory" carved in the riverbank, nor why my only reaction was to say, "Hi, Emory." You don't shake hands with an animal with four-inch claws, so we sort of looked at each other for a minute, and then I said, "I've got some more food in the freezer."

Probably I just thought it was cool that someone had trained him to write his name. I'd heard of a horse who could do simple arithmetic, so why not this? I say "probably" because I can't look back at my first thoughts without filtering them through all of the events that transpired later. Asking me to isolate one single memory at the start of it all is just asking too much.

"What would *you* think?" I challenged the psychiatrist the second or third time he asked me about that day. He didn't respond, of course, because he didn't believe any of it happened.

That day in the woods it seemed as if the birds and all other creatures went quiet at the sight of a thirteen-year-old boy walking alongside a grizzly bear. The breeze died down, even, as if stilled in awe. I couldn't keep the grin off my face at the sheer mass of him moving next to me. Emory the bear.

I raised the big roll-up door to the pole barn and Emory watched it go up as if trying to figure out how it worked. "See, we have this big sink in here for water," I said, showing the place off like a Realtor. In the back was a big couch, too big for the living room, still wrapped in plastic from the move. I attacked the plastic, pulling it off as eagerly as a child going after a Christmas present. "And if you ever got sleepy you could take a nap right here. And there's food in the freezer."

Emory watched all of this with his inscrutable expression. I wondered if this meant he didn't understand I was hoping he'd live in our barn.

Because the air was so still I easily heard an unfamiliar car turn off onto Hidden Creek Road and start the climb toward our house.

"Hey! Uh, I have to close the front door, okay?" Anyone driving past our house would be able to see right in the barn, where it would be pretty hard to miss a six-hundred-pound animal. I ran to the garage-like door and pulled it shut with a crash.

The sunlight seeped in from the various gaps along the top edges of the walls like stars all lined up in single file, and there was a big square splash of light from the window in the top half of the exit door on the side of the pole barn, but even still, Emory's dark shape seemed to disappear in the shadows for a minute. I listened for the car, thinking I'd feel a little better when it passed and I could open the door again.

But the car didn't pass. It pulled in our driveway, making a squeak as it stopped. I heard the driver's door open and light footsteps hurrying to our front door.

Yvonne? Probably. I wondered if she would come to the pole barn when no one answered the front door. *That* would be bad. I walked over to the side door and put my hand on the knob. "It's my dad's . . . it's a friend of my dad's," I said to Emory. "I'd better go out there and see what she wants."

"Char*lie!*" a woman called. It did not sound like Yvonne.

I opened the door, stepped outside, and firmly shut it behind me.

I've often wondered what would have happened, how things would have been different, if I hadn't shut that door.

A woman I had never seen before was standing on our front deck. She was maybe my dad's age, with black hair pulled back from her face and wrapped in a knot behind her head. She was peering through the window into our house, knocking on the door. She looked a little frantic.

"Charlie, are you in there?" she shouted again.

I wondered what kind of trouble I'd gotten into now. I approached the woman and she caught sight of me out of the corner of her eye. She jumped a little, putting a hand to her chest.

"Oh!" she exclaimed. She took a breath. "Are you Charlie?"

"Yeah."

"I'm Margaret Shelburton. Rod Shelburton's wife? Your dad's partner in bison?"

"Oh. Right."

"Charlie, there's . . ." She pursed her lips together, as if she didn't want to say what she'd come to say. She came off the front porch and down to the driveway, leaning over a little to look in my eyes. "Your father was in an accident."

"What?"

"Something happened at the ranch and he fell off the fence. He had to go to the hospital. I came to get you."

All I could do was stare in dumb wonder. It simply wasn't possible that my father was hurt; he *couldn't* be hurt. He was the only thing I had to hold on to in life.

"Why don't we go inside and get some things. You can stay with us for a few days. Okay?"

I shook my head. "No, I'm okay here."

"Charlie." Her eyes were soft and caring

— mother's eyes, the kind that can look right into a child and see what he needs. "It will be okay. Your father's going to be fine."

That's what they said about my mom at first. She was going to be "fine." "Is he in a coma?" I asked tremulously.

"Oh no, nothing like that. He might have to stay in the hospital for a few days, though, and if you come home with us we can take you to see him. Okay? Let's go pack."

I certainly couldn't tell her I had a quarter ton of live grizzly in our pole barn, so I wound up passively following her into my house and leading her to my bedroom. I was numb with denial. None of this could be happening. At her request I pulled out a suitcase and opened drawers, not objecting when she picked out clothing for me, not complaining when she touched my under-wear. She told me to grab my toothbrush and as I did so I looked in the mirror and my face was blank.

I hesitated getting in the car, looking back over my shoulder at the doors to the pole barn, firmly shut. But what could I say or do? I would have to figure out a way to get back up to the house later.

When she caught me examining her in the car she gave me a reassuring smile. I was, oddly enough, thinking what a perfect match she made for Mr. Shelburton. She wore more makeup than the ladies around Selkirk River, but she dressed like a rancher's wife, with a thick plaid shirt and cowboy boots. She didn't have a Chicago gangster accent like her husband, yet there was something decidedly citified about her manner, a real sense that she was a transplant from a different world. It showed up in her manicured nails and the way the rings on her fingers flashed as she steered the car a bit too fast down the paved road into town.

The hospital hit me with a wave of dread so powerful it was almost nauseating. I hadn't considered what it would be like to turn up the driveway and into the visitors' parking lot, didn't give it any thought at all until I was there. This was where Mom died, curled up and shrunken down to the size of a small child.

I don't think I made a sound, but somehow Mrs. Shelburton knew what I was feeling. When we got out of the car she pulled me to her and hugged me. The tenderness in her embrace made my throat ache; I had to concentrate really hard on not letting any tears flow.

"I'm so sorry. I know how hard this will be for you. But this time is different. Your father is going to be okay, Charlie."

We went inside. Same carpet, same smells, same background noises. A muddle of TV sounds was occasionally punctuated by what seemed to my ears to be someone calling for help or mercy. Sharp antiseptic chemicals mixed their odors with sour, unhealthy air.

I loathed everything about the place. Everyone always acting so busy, industriously walking back and forth, none of it helping. Each patient room was a study in self-absorption, all attention focused on their insulated personal tragedies, none of them aware that Laura Hall lay dying of C.M.L. I deliberately picked a chair as far away from where I usually sat as I possibly could, though they were all beige chairs, uniformly stiff and uncomfortable. Mrs. Shelburton sat next to me and held my hand.

Mr. Shelburton hurried in a few minutes later, and his wife and I both stood up. He was taking the cowboy thing pretty seriously, with dusty jeans, cowboy boots, a denim jacket, and even some kind of handkerchief tied around his neck, like the Boy Scouts.

"Beth and Craig are with Mrs. Landers." Mr. Shelburton looked pale and all the folksiness had gone out of his voice. I gathered that Beth and Craig were their children. He patted his pocket absently for cigarettes, then gave his wife an *oh yeah, I quit smoking* look.

"What happened?" I asked him.

"Your dad was up on a fence and a buffalo decided to ram it for no reason. I'm getting so I hate those things," Mr. Shelburton told me. "He tumbled off and hit his head pretty bad." Mrs. Shelburton gave him a stern look. "Oh, but he's okay!" he said hurriedly.

As it turned out, my dad had dislocated his shoulder and had a skull fracture. Neither would prove life threatening, but he'd been knocked unconscious and the doctors wanted him to hang around so they could make sure he was okay.

He looked so weak in that hospital bed, a snakelike tube clinging to his nose so that he'd get extra oxygen, that I almost fell down. The strength just left my knees and I got really wobbly, but Mr. Shelburton grabbed my arm and propped me up.

My dad said his head hurt and that he felt really woozy. Then we stood around, not sure what to say next.

With my mother, there was always something to talk about. We never had these dead moments of silence. Mom always made an effort to engage me in conversation and to try to make me feel better, even though she was the one with C.M.L. Left up to our own devices, my dad and I would probably have just stood there and gazed at her, like I was doing right then with him.

Eventually the Shelburtons and I wound up feeling bored and then we felt guilty because we were supposed to be keeping my dad company. When he finally suggested to the Shelburtons that they should take me and head on out you could practically hear our relief. I shook hands with my dad and followed Mrs. Shelbuton out to her car.

The Shelburtons' house was sort of the opposite of ours. We lived high on a hill with a commanding view of the valley and could see distant mountains on the horizon. The Shelburtons lived right along the river, lushly surrounded by trees, the hills crowding around them. Their driveway had its own bridge over the stream, even. Where our house was two stories and felt even taller because of the way it was built into the slope, their home sprawled out just one story high, its shape following the bend in the stream in the backyard.

There was a boat on a trailer next to their garage for weekend trips to Priest Lake. We didn't have a boat. It had sort of gone the way of my horse. Another promise broken when my mom got sick.

Mr. Shelburton said he'd go get the kids and drove off. The air in the home was filled with a warm, sweet cinnamon fragrance that turned out to be homemade snickerdoodles. Even though it was before dinner I was allowed to eat several on account of what had happened to my dad. Then Mrs. Shelburton showed me a bedroom, one of what looked like four or five, and had me put my stuff in there. She set out towels and a washcloth, as if she thought I might be anxious to wash my face.

While she was doing all this, I felt a rising sense of alarm. How long did they think I was going to be staying here? I had to get back to Emory; I couldn't just leave him in the pole barn. What do you say, though, to a woman who is being so kind, so motherly? *No thank you, I have a bear to take care of?*

I heard car doors slamming and the sound of running feet heading my way. "Mom!" A boy of maybe eight barreled into the room and stopped, staring at me. This, I figured, was probably Craig.

Mrs. Shelburton introduced us. "I've got a new mitt. We could play ball," Craig said. I nodded — it would beat throwing G.I.

Joes at each other.

"And this is Beth," Mrs. Shelburton said.

My mouth dropped open in shock.

CHAPTER
THIRTEEN

A dark-haired girl was standing silently in the doorway, watching me with clear green eyes. Her features were petite: everything about her was small, her lips, her nose, her ears, even. She stood half a head shorter than I.

What stunned me was how perfectly beautiful she was. I hadn't really ever seen a girl with such an astoundingly pretty face.

I put her in fifth grade, which made me, an eighth grader, something like an adult in comparison. It gave me the confidence to say "hi" to her without stuttering — if she'd been my age, my brain would have been flooded with distress signals and I probably wouldn't have been able to squeak out a word.

"Hello, Charlie," she said. "What sort of music do you listen to?"

I opened my mouth at the unexpected question, then closed it. Music hadn't been much of a feature at my house the past couple of years. I couldn't think of a single artist who was currently popular.

"We were going to play ball," Craig objected.

I could see right away that my relationship to Craig would consist mostly of ignoring him. Beth raised her eyebrows, waiting for my answer.

"Beatles," I finally said, mentally pulling an album cover out of my dad's collection.

Beth's green eyes flared brightly. *"Yes,"* she said. "I can't stand Wings, though. Come on."

She vanished. Craig pouted at me as I hastened to follow.

Beth led me down the hall to a room with a fireplace and a couple of couches. She went to a shelf and began pulling out records. "White Album or *Abbey Road?*"

"Abbey Road," I replied, ready to say, *No, I meant White Album!* if she frowned.

Instead she smiled at me. Her teeth were absolutely perfect, white and straight in her mouth. *"Yes.* Also I love *Sergeant Pepper's.* You do, too, if you love *Abbey Road."*

She put the album on, carefully lowering the needle and then sitting on a couch. She indicated with her hand that I should sit on the same couch, so I did.

I was doing a mental calculation. Let's say she was ten years old. The age gap was less for us than for Kay and me, which had been my most serious romantic relationship to date. In three years Beth would be the age I was now and I'd have a driver's license and would therefore completely overwhelm any competition from boys in her grade.

"You never say hi to me. Didn't you know our dads were partners?"

"I'm . . . now what?"

She brought her feet up underneath her. Her pants were the plaid kind that were newly popular, wide up and down the length of her thin legs. "You didn't know I was Rod Shelburton's daughter?"

"No."

"Okay. I suppose I forgive you, then, though you completely ignore me even when I'm looking right at you. Is your dad going to be okay?"

"I guess he has a concussion. But when do I ignore . . . ?"

"In the hall."

"The hall," I said stupidly.

Beth gave me a considering look. "You really don't remember seeing me before, do you."

"So you go to Benny H.?" I responded, stupefied. Our junior high was formally

Benjamin Harrison Junior High School, named after the President who signed the law giving Idaho its statehood. Everyone called it Benny H. and felt cool doing so. It seemed impossible, though, that this little girl was a student there.

"Do you *think* I go to Benny H.?" Her eyes were laughing at me. "How old do you think I am?"

I supposed that this was what it was like to be drowning with nobody there from Junior Lifesaving to pull me out of the pool. I had no idea how I was supposed to answer this question and felt ridiculous and mocked.

She decided to let me off the hook. "I'm a sevie." She gave me another look at her pretty smile. "It's horrible. It's *ludicrous*. I feel like a little kid. The ninth graders are huge. You're going to say hi to me in the hallway from now on though, right?"

I nodded.

"See, that's how I'll survive. I'll feel like everyone hates me and then I'll say, 'Why, there's that Charlie Hall and he's saying hi to me, a big eighth grader.' " She slid off the couch. "Come on, Charlie; it's such a beautiful night out there and we're sitting inside. We can *always* listen to music."

Was that true? *Always?* I could always just

show up at the Shelburtons' house and sit in a room with Beth and listen to Beatle albums?

Beth led me to the river, energetically chatting about gymnastics, and I followed passively.

I think I managed to hold up my end of the conversation, though in retrospect most of what I had to say was communicated in one-word sentences. I said "yeah" a lot; I remember that. "Do you like gymnastics?" "Yeah." "Does your dad have a CB radio?" "Yeah." "Do you like living in Selkirk River?" "Yeah."

Especially now.

When my mom was in the hospital it seemed like I never thought about anything else. I had trouble paying attention in class and usually only snapped back to reality when I realized everyone in the room was waiting for me to answer a question I hadn't heard. Now, though, my dad was the furthest thing from my mind. I wasn't even thinking about Emory, trapped in our barn back home. My entire focus was on the girl walking next to me.

Beth was dainty and childlike on the outside and womanly and self-assured on the inside. She reminded me a little of Kay, whom I had been madly in love with when

157

the day started but who now seemed to be fading a little in priority.

At dinner I tried not to stare at Beth and when I failed I caught Mrs. Shelburton grinning at Mr. Shelburton and Mr. Shelburton looking cluelessly back at her, trying to figure out what she was communicating. Craig prattled on about one of the *Planet of the Apes* movies, which I gathered he felt represented the most significant accomplishment in cinematic history, and I completely ignored him. Beth shot me an occasional look of amusement over something and I did my best to look clever in return. For dessert Mrs. Shelburton produced a raspberry pie, still warm from the oven. I took my first bite and couldn't help moaning a little — my dad's pies were rung up whole at the cash register by Yvonne and then kept frozen until he stuck them in the oven. They always smelled great but were usually dark on the outside and mushy on the inside. Mrs. Shelburton's pie, on the other hand, felt as if it were handmade by the gods. The Shelburton family laughed at my reaction.

After dinner I helped Beth with the dishes. Several times I accidentally bumped into her. She came away from these soft impacts with a small grin on her face. I grinned back so broadly my cheek muscles quivered with fatigue. Mrs. Shelburton took Mr. Shelburton aside and whispered something to him and as she did his eyes narrowed at me, making me feel guilty.

It was Friday, so we stayed up and watched TV. It became evident why Craig was so excited about monkey-based entertainment — a new show called *Planet of the Apes* was on, though from the quality of the program it looked like the apes were not only the stars but also the writers. Mr. Shelburton sat in his chair with a newspaper that he snapped loudly in case we forgot he was there. The couch Beth and I sat on sort of sagged, pulling us down into the cushions with an irresistible gravity, and every time I readjusted myself I found I had moved closer to Beth and Mr. Shelburton would give his newspaper a workout. I couldn't help it; everything seemed to be revolving around Beth and my orbit was rapidly decaying.

My plan the next day was to get away to let Emory out of the pole barn, but the Shelburtons never gave me a chance.

First Beth went with me to visit my dad in the hospital. She had amazing power over the evil déjà vu that had ambushed me the first time — instead of feeling despair I was actually a little proud that I knew my way around the place so well. The doctors said he could go home Monday morning but no going in to work for a few days.

"Be hard to work with my arm so sore," my dad muttered. He seemed depressed. He greeted Beth with easy familiarity — apparently they knew each other. My dad had known Beth and never bothered to tell me about her?

We had a basket full of snickerdoodles for my dad from Mrs. Shelburton and I managed to leave one or two of them for him when we left.

Okay, now I *had* to get away, get home, and let the bear out. Except I wasn't allowed. First Mr. Shelburton took us out to his ranch to help with the horses and then we met Mrs. Shelburton for lunch and then she asked us to tag along while she ran errands in town. I appreciated being with Beth, but a dreadful anxiety was rising in me, like my conscience was screaming at me.

"What is it, are you worried about your father? He's going to be okay, Charlie," Beth said to me at one point, those clear green eyes seeing right into me.

"Yeah," I said.

When Mr. Shelburton came home I made sure I found a moment to be alone with him. I finally got my opportunity when he stepped out the back door to take out the garbage.

"Mr. Shelburton?"

"Yes, pardner?"

"How long do you figure a bear could go without any water?"

CHAPTER FOURTEEN

When I heard the family stirring that Sunday morning, my eyes snapped open and I took a shower and then surveyed the clothing Mrs. Shelburton had helped me select by doing it all herself. I was pretty much outfitted to stay a month, so I put on the nicest sweatshirt in my collection, intending to eat breakfast and then go. No matter what, I had to get back home and take care of Emory *now*.

I slid out of the guest room as if I had something to feel guilty about and stood on the threshold of the dining room until Mrs. Shelburton invited me in with a smile. This was a family that put all the food into big dishes instead of plating up individual portions at the stove. Sausage and juice and French toast were stacked up, feast-style.

I dealt with the awkwardness of being with a different family by keeping my eyes low. Mr. and Mrs. Shelburton spoke to me in the same concerned fashion that people had always used when my mother was failing; the tone of it left me cold. Craig, of course, was clueless as always and wanted to talk about football, submarines, werewolves, personal jet packs, the upcoming Ali-versus-Foreman bout, and James Bond, somehow making these sound like they were all part of the same subject. Beth was not there and no one mentioned her, which was distressing. As far as I was concerned, Beth was the only reason there was a Shelburton family.

I studied Mrs. Shelburton the way I would one day study bears, observing the behavior of a wonderful and mysterious species. She was a mom and did the type of mom things I had forgotten about. She poured Mr. Shelburton his coffee and whisked eggs with an efficiency that somehow communicated affection through sheer uncluttered economy of motion. When Craig ate his French toast into the shape of a pistol and pointed it at me, she told him in a gentle tone to stop playing with his food.

There was sunlight streaming in through the window by the sink and when Mrs. Shelburton stood in it her hair lit up like a halo.

"Charlie, why did you ask me about bears?" Mr. Shelburton asked abruptly, yanking me out of my thrall.

I blinked at him. "What?"

"Last night. You seemed pretty intent."

"Bears?" Mrs. Shelburton repeated innocently.

"Oh." I shrugged casually, but my heart was pounding. "I guess because it just seemed like you'd know the answer."

"A couple of days, at the most," he'd speculated.

Today was Sunday. It had *been* a couple of days. I had to get Emory food and water right away. It was urgent. I would have to come up with some pretext to get away.

Mr. Shelburton seemed satisfied with my reason for asking him the bear question. Craig abruptly bolted from the table, only to be halted by his mother: "Craig, clear your plate."

He trudged back as if sentenced to ten years hard labor. Mr. Shelburton stood. "Guess I'll swing by the ranch for a bit," he said. "Charlie, I'll check on your dad."

"Please let us know how he's doing and when I can bring Charlie in for a visit," Mrs. Shelburton requested.

"Hi," Beth said.

She walked into the kitchen amid the admiring silence she deserved. She wore jeans and a T-shirt and her hair was brushed

164

back, but even I could tell that despite the casual look, she had put considerable effort into her appearance before coming to the table that morning. I caught Mr. Shelburton and his wife exchanging a look: Mrs. Shelburton was smiling and Mr. Shelburton wasn't. Beth gave me a shy glance, and I tried not to appear to be an idiot.

"Hi good morning to you hello," I said, running my greetings together like Craig telling a story about werewolves and jet packs.

Beth had some of her mother's French toast and then she and I did the breakfast dishes. I'd never before much appreciated doing dishes, but now it felt like the high point of my social life, more fun than any party I'd ever been to. There was a magnetic field around her that made my insides flutter like iron filings whenever she passed close by.

"Today let's go into town, Charlie. We'll walk along the river and get some lunch. My treat," Beth said.

"Okay."

"We could go to the music store," she suggested.

"Okay." My mind was elsewhere — should I try to take Beth with me to my house? I needed to get up there but didn't want to spend a moment away from her.

"Are you always this easy to get along with, Charlie?" she asked me in a teasing fashion. "What if I said we should climb the hill and throw rocks at patrol cars? Would you say 'okay' to that?"

"You're probably not going to see very many patrol cars go by," I replied, an answer worthy of my father.

She laughed at that. "Craig threw a rock at a sheriff's car last year; that's why I ask. He said he didn't know why he did it. I'm worried it might run in the family and that I'll get the compulsion, too. If you're not going to stop me, who will?"

It was such a strange question it made my brain sort of seize up. I was so *drawn* to this girl, not just to her beauty but to the way she talked, the way she churned me all up inside with her rapid change of topics. We grabbed some of her mom's homemade chocolate-chip cookies. (My father's cookies oozed out of a tube, like toothpaste, and tasted like burnt toast.) While Beth chatted I followed her out the door and down the road toward town, feeling as dumb as a calf on a rope.

The Shelburtons lived much closer to town than we did out on Hidden Creek Road. A gravel path along the river was a less direct but prettier way to find our way to the shopping district, and as we walked I had the sense that if I had the nerve I could hold her hand and we'd be like the older couples, the kids in high school, who took the path along the river with their fingers interlaced or their arms linked.

"Isn't this river beautiful? Don't you love it?"

"Yeah."

"Yes." She drew in a deep breath, appreciating the clean smells. I was appreciating the cookies, which I'd started to munch on the second we were out the door. The chips were milk chocolate and still warm; each bite made me close my eyes in absolute ecstasy.

Before long Beth was talking about the dance that was coming up at Benny H., a dance I had never before thought of attending because I'd never been to a dance and now it seemed like it was too late — if I went, everyone would know how to behave but me and I'd do something stupid. The point of her conversation had something to do with how easy boys had it because we could just show up, but girls had to wear a new outfit. "It's a *burden*," she informed me. "Nobody wants to wear exactly what someone else is wearing, but nobody wants to dress different than everybody else. What is it?"

I'd come to a halt, and she was now searching my face with her eyes.

"I have to ask you something."

"Oh!" she exclaimed. I saw a small flush invade her cheeks and knew instantly that she assumed I was about to ask her to go to the dance with me. This flustered me into an anxious silence. I was utterly without clue as to how to address her expectations. I couldn't imagine ever having the confidence to ask a girl to a dance. And never *this* girl — Beth already had me so rattled I could barely converse.

If she saw the battle raging inside me, she didn't say anything; she just stood there, her green eyes resting lightly on mine. I pushed past it, reaching almost desperately for my original topic. "I need you to . . ." I groped for the words. "I need you to cover for me."

It was the first time I'd seen Beth Shelburton unsure of herself. "What do you mean?"

"I have to do something today. Back at my house. But I can't; I don't want anyone to know that I was up there. Okay? So can you go to town and do like you said, and if anyone asks you say I was with you?"

"Why?"

Well, that one was certainly unanswerable. "I just have to do something. Please, Beth."

She peered at me. "You," she finally said, "have some sort of mysterious secret."

I nodded.

"Are you going to tell me what it is?"

I hesitated, then shook my head no.

"Well, okay. I'll do it."

"Okay."

We smiled at each other. I looked around. "When I'm done I'll come back here, okay? I'll meet you right here at this bend in the river at around five o'clock."

"I'll see you right here, Charlie. Now go do what you need to do."

The parting was so unnatural and weird that I found myself holding out my hand like an insurance salesman. Beth laughed with delight and shook it. "Right here," she repeated.

As soon as I was away from her I ran, my feet light on the pavement. When I turned off onto the steep climb that was Hidden Creek Road the fatigue set in and each step landed with a thudding impact. Though I had sprinted from the bottom of this road to the top of its many switchbacks almost every day after school, I had never done it after first running what felt like a marathon, and my lungs were starved for air by the time I made it to my driveway.

On the other side of the big garage door of the pole barn was a grizzly bear who'd been trapped inside since Friday, two nights ago, trapped without water or food. The animal would probably be crazed, but I didn't hesitate to roll up the big door. I didn't even raise it all the way, just enough for me to enter.

What I saw inside the pole barn took what little breath I had left away from me. I put my hands on my knees, sick and dizzy, while the door behind me rattled back down and slammed shut, plunging everything back into shadow.

The light from the side door window and the spangles of sun leaking in where the walls met the roof made one thing obvious: there was no bear. What there was, however, was bloodred liquid splattered liberally on the floor.

I squinted at it, shocked and uncomprehending. In the gloom, my eyes still trying to adjust, it now looked black, but the brief flash of full daylight when the door was open had given me sickening confirmation of its real color. Cautiously I stepped forward. Emory's paw prints were all over, big as both my hands put together. Rivulets of the dark liquid ran among the prints.

The side window was broken out, and when I went to investigate I found two large smudges on the window frame, and these were easily identifiable in the stronger light as being the same bright red. I pulled the side door open.

"Emory?" I shouted, cocking my head to hear any response.

I spotted red tracks in the dirt, heading away from the house. I followed them at a run, but they petered out on me. Frantic, I ran down the path to the creek, stumbling a couple of times, heedless of the pain that flashed through me when I barked my knees against a fallen tree trunk. I burst out of the brush and leaped over the loamy embankment and fell more than ran into the rocky creek bed. My shoes splashed in the pockets of muddy water that were lying there in the rocks, waiting for the rains to liberate them.

"Emory!" I shouted, anguished. Tears were flowing down my face, gritty tears that burned on their way out. *"Emory!"*

The wind gave me a lonely, empty reply.

I sank to my knees, then, afraid and ashamed and guilty. It was not an unfamiliar mix of emotions. But the difference was that with my mother I knew what I had done — here my crimes were not clear enough for self-indictment. I'd left Emory alone, but what in God's name had happened back at the pole barn?

What could he have done to cause all that blood? Did he slice open an artery on the broken window? How could he have bled so much in the pole barn and then not tracked it more than a few feet down the trail to the creek?

After a time I managed to gather myself and numbly head back toward home. I had to hope that the bear's wounds weren't too bad, that he wouldn't get infected, that maybe he'd come out of the woods and I could put iodine on them. But the sheer volume of red blood I'd spotted belied this hope: something had happened to wound Emory, something deep and awful.

What if someone had come and killed him?

Back up in the driveway I opened the big pole barn door all the way and let the light flood in, sucking in air as I did so. The wreckage was even worse than I'd first thought: the tomato cages were scattered, more than one of them bent and twisted. Tools were strewn about; paint cans were lying here and there on their sides.

Paint cans.

I took a closer look at the blood on the

floor. It was indeed red, bright red, impossibly bright red. The dribbles and spatters gleamed as if wet, but they were dry to the touch.

Against one wall was a stack of paint cans that had followed us all the way from Kansas. The paint had been attacked by the bear, for reasons I could not fathom. A one-gallon can of fire-engine red paint had been opened — a grizzly bear has claws that certainly rival any man-made can opener. The paint from this can was undoubtedly what I was seeing all over the place.

I examined the side window. The glass was entirely on the outside, leaving little doubt that it had been smashed from within. The smudges on the window frame were paint, not blood, and careful examination revealed that the bear had meticulously busted out the glass, not leaving so much as a single sliver in the frame to cut him as he squeezed through to freedom. A tight fit, but obviously he made it.

I sighed in relief. As far as I knew, Emory was unharmed.

Crossing my arms, I looked around the garage at the mess he'd made. How would I explain any of this to my father?

Well, I *couldn't* explain it. I would have to clean it up. The paint wouldn't come off the floor, of course, but we had a couple of gallons of gray garage floor paint in our collection — the former owner had apparently found it easier to lay down a new coat of paint every so often than to try to scrub out the inevitable stains from his game-dressing business. As long as I didn't waste any time, I would have no problem meeting Beth back down at the river at the appointed hour.

The first thing I did was straighten the twisted tomato cages as best I could and lock them in a back cabinet — they were too precious to leave out, I thought, feeling a flash of resentment that my father hadn't put them someplace more protected.

I was gathering up a paint roller, a paint pan, and a stir stick when I glanced up at the wall of the pole barn opposite of the broken window. I'd been so fixated on the mess on the floor I hadn't looked over there until that moment.

The far-side wall was normally a pretty dull thing to behold. It was just an expanse of flat white, though sometimes in the oblique sunlight of late afternoon you could make out the ghostlike outlines of some shelves that had once stood against it.

The wall was no longer blank.

Big drippy letters were painted in red on the wall, drawn with a striking meticulousness. This is what they said.

I, Emory Bain, pvt. 3rd regt., inf. of GR Mich, May 1862 pursued rebels at Chickahominy, wounded, took fever, now returned. I have a message.

I sat down on the paint-splattered floor and read the words over and over again, my mouth open.

CHAPTER
FIFTEEN

The cryptic note was written in an odd
script, the capital letters twisting up in
ornate flourishes, the words painstakingly
inscribed in a stilted, schoolboyish cursive.
Some dribbles of red paint were all that
marred what was otherwise handwriting
better than mine.

When Emory wrote his name in the riverbank, his letters were all capitalized, drawn
from slashing swipes of his paw. These
words were as neatly painted as any brush
could make them. But how could a bear
hold a paintbrush? They had no thumbs.

The words made little sense to me. *I,
Emory Bain,* could be interpreted easily
enough if you were willing to accept the idea
that the bear had somehow managed to
write the words. He'd already told me his
first name, so why not his last? The next
several abbreviations, though, I didn't
understand, and when I did, I didn't under-

stand how they fit together. *Pursued rebels at Chickahominy.* Whatever Chickahominy was, I was pretty sure I was pronouncing it wrong. The final part was more clear: *wounded, took fever, now returned. I have a message.*

Thing was, I didn't care. The way I saw it, I had a big problem. The pole barn was a mess. My dad would be home within a day or two. I needed to put things back the way they had been.

A question a lot of people have asked me is why I did what I did next; what in the world could I have been thinking? (Yes, that question *again*.) All I can say is that I didn't want my father to be mad at me. I couldn't picture him being happy that there were bear tracks painted all over his floor and words scrawled on the wall. And I certainly wasn't about to tell him that I'd been consorting with one of the most dangerous species alive.

So it was not the content of the message on the wall but the fact that it was painted there in the first place that got all of my attention. *No,* I've responded patiently to so many people, *I did not stop to connect "1862" with "rebels" and I did not try to figure out what "inf." and "regt." meant.* I was a kid. I just didn't want to get in trouble. And anyway, my biggest concern had been for Emory, and he was evidently fine.

I had enough primer to coat the places on the floor where the bear had walked and drizzled a trail of red but not enough for the wall. To mark out his words, I used a roller and flat white wall paint, knowing as I did so that it would take more than one coat. Where the bear had left a smear crawling out the broken window I was forced to resort to sandpaper — I didn't have any stain that would match. In the yard, I scraped and dug at the red tracks with a hoe and a garden rake.

All of this I did in such a hurry my hands were shaking. The gray garage paint went on the floor so fast that little flecks of the stuff flew up in the air and got on my pants, but when I was done it looked really nice. The wall I repainted while it was still tacky from the first coat.

Despite my haste, several hours passed, and every time I checked my watch I was dismayed at how quickly the day was draining away. I was going to be late to my rendezvous with Beth.

I changed clothes because the outfit I'd had on was stippled with gray and white paint, but that cost me more time. It was already ten after five when I slammed the front door and raced down Hidden Creek Road.

A sharp wind had come up, cold air turning my sweat to ice and making the trees wave at me as if in warning. At 5:30 I was still running, now on the trail by the river, the uneven ground threatening to trip me up at every step.

I came to the rendezvous point at 5:34 by my watch. I slowed, panting.

She wasn't there.

So, okay. Though my skin was flushed red from the run, I could feel how cold it had gotten. She had probably waited here, freezing, for as long as she could.

I wasn't disappointed; it was worse than that: I felt as if I had let her down, failed her.

"Charlie."

I turned and there she was, hugging herself. "I went downstream a little," she told me. "I thought maybe I had the place wrong."

"No! It was my fault. I was late."

"Did you change your clothes?"

"Yeah. I'm sorry; if I had a jacket, you could wear it." This sounded pretty lame to my ears, but once you've said something stupid to a pretty girl there's no taking it back. It's a lesson I'd learn many times in my life.

"It's okay."

Mr. Shelburton was a little less forgiving than his daughter, clearly annoyed we'd been gone all day. "I need to get Charlie down to see his father," he told Beth.

"Well, you didn't say what time we had to be home," Beth responded reasonably.

"You had to know that I'd be waiting," he insisted.

"No, because you didn't say anything, Dad. If you'd told me to be home at a specific time, we would have been home when you said."

He gave her an exasperated look. "Okay," he finally said. "You stay and help your mother with dinner."

I watched this whole exchange in amazement. Beth didn't back down from her father's anger. I tried to picture talking to my own father in this manner — it was easier to conjure up an image of a grizzly bear holding a paintbrush.

We grabbed a basket of lemon bars from Mrs. Shelburton and headed out the door. Somehow she had managed to make the sour lemon and the sweet, crunchy crust work together in a silky delicious harmony. I ate four in the car and Mr. Shelburton had two and then he and I decided to split another one and not tell anyone. I wondered if my dad would be puzzled why we'd bothered with such a fancy basket when there were only three lemon bars left in it.

My father was sitting up in bed, glumly watching television, when we got to the hospital. He wore exactly the same type of hospital gown my mother had worn. Just seeing it made me a little sick. A too-fancy basket of flowers on the bedside table seemed out of place in such a grim room. I put the lemon bars down right next to them and gave Dad a look full of encouragement to offer me one.

"They say I can go home tomorrow, but they want me here another night for observation," my dad said to Mr. Shelburton. "I don't like to be observed."

I don't think my dad meant this as a joke, but Mr. Shelburton laughed. They chatted about a few things while I just stood there silently like the Invisible Man. Finally Mr. Shelburton seemed to notice my dad and I hadn't spoken to each other. "Well," he said, clearing his throat, "I'll go on down the hall for a minute, give you fellas a chance to chew the fat."

My dad nodded without irony, though naturally when Mr. Shelburton left he had nothing to say to me. We sort of stared at each other for a minute.

"The Shelburtons treating you okay?" he finally asked.

"Yes."

"That's good."

He looked around the room and I saw his eyes drifting uncomfortably past the flowers — plain as day you could read the card: *I love you, Yvonne.* I wondered if Dad told her if he loved her back. God, I hated being in this place.

"The window in the pole barn got broken out," I told him almost spitefully.

"Really? What happened?"

I was going to have to be very careful here, wasn't I? "Well, it was obviously an animal. Inside, the floor was all red, and some was on the wall, too." There, all completely true, as opposed to him telling me he didn't even like Yvonne.

"Ah, probably a duck. Didn't understand it was flying through the glass until it was too late, and then panicked inside. You didn't find a dead duck?"

"No, sir."

"How high up on the wall?"

I reached my hand up a little more than head high.

"Had to be a duck," my dad grunted.

"I cleaned it up."

"Good, Charlie."

"I couldn't get the red up, so I painted over it."

That surprised him. "You painted the wall?"

"Yes, sir. And the floor."

"You painted the floor of the pole barn?"

"Yes, sir, is that okay?"

"Why, sure, Charlie, I'm just . . . that's fine."

"Good. I wasn't able to do anything about the window, though."

"That's okay; I'll fix it."

"Okay."

Mr. Shelburton poked his head in the room. "If it's okeydoke with you, George, I'm going to take this fine young man home for some supper."

I figured "okeydoke" was an expression Mr. Shelburton had gotten from a book titled *How Those Hicks Talk in Idaho.*

"Sure, Rod," my father said. We both relaxed a little, now that the burden of being alone together had been removed from our shoulders.

As I was headed out the door my dad called out, "Charlie!" and I turned back with a questioning look.

"I'm proud of how you handled the duck.

You took responsibility. It was a good thing to do."

It was the most tender thing I could remember him saying to me in a long time. I nodded at him, my throat inexplicably tight, my eyes even a little bleary with unwanted, unshed tears that I wiped away when no one was looking.

On the drive home I realized I was far more worried about Emory the bear than my father the hospital patient, which was plain silly — why worry how a grizzly bear was getting along in the *woods*? It would be like worrying that your pet fish might drown. As for the words on the wall, well, that seemed like something to think about when there was less going on.

Dinner at the Shelburtons' was the most pleasant meal I could remember ever having. Beth and I sat across from each other at one end of the table, ignoring Craig, carrying on a conversation in quiet tones that the adults only occasionally audited.

"What did you say about sports?" Mr. Shelburton asked.

I cleared my throat. "I said I haven't gone out for anything yet," I explained, my face red.

The adults exchanged pitying glances and

I felt a flash of resentment course through me.

"Well . . . you'll hit a growth spurt soon," Mrs. Shelburton said soothingly. It was just about the worst comment she could have made, and I looked down at my plate for a full minute before I had recovered enough to meet Beth's eyes. Her expression was, as usual, confoundingly self-possessed and calm, and if she saw my embarrassment she made no mention of it.

The air was clear and dry the next morning as Beth and I walked to school together. I thought about what a delicious life she had, able to sleep in for an extra forty-five minutes because she didn't have a long bus ride to contend with.

"What lunch hour do you have?" she asked.

"First period," I said.

"I have first lunch, too. Imagine that, Charlie. You've gone an entire month of school and never noticed Beth Shelburton across the room having lunch."

I hated the idea Beth might have witnessed my daily anguish over trying to find a table where I'd fit in. "You never noticed *me*," I finally countered.

"Why do you say that?" she asked.

I had no evidence to submit and kicked at

some rocks, feeling stupid. How a mere girl could make me feel both wonderful and witless at the same time was completely beyond me.

"But you'll notice me now, won't you?"

"Yeah."

"And what," she asked gravely, "will you do then?"

I swallowed. It was a good question.

What *would* I do then?

CHAPTER
SIXTEEN

My first class was gym — the school's way of making sure that I would spend the rest of the day sweating unattractively in front of all the girls. The shower room could have doubled as a Turkish bath and the locker room a sauna; I was perspiring even as I changed into my gym clothes.

The outfits we wore were designed to make us look scrawny and weak. White shorts, T-shirts, socks, and shoes lent us an escaped-from-the-asylum appearance, especially on a boy like Charlie Hall, who wore a size Small in everything.

The two best athletes in our grade were in my gym class so that I'd never feel like I could excel at anything. Tim Humphrey and Mike Kappas both had men's bodies, with actual muscles under their cotton shirts. The resemblance between them ended there: Tim was blond and blue-eyed and Mike had a dark complexion and hair and eyes to match. They respected each other in a breezy, friendly way and were always opposing captains for any game we played.

I was always just about the last one picked.

Our gym teacher was Coach Briggs, a big hairy guy with a whistle around his neck. We filtered into the gym, bumping and pushing each other without discipline until the coach blew his whistle.

"Line up!" he commanded.

We organized ourselves into a line, looking like a row of little white lambs. He pointed to the chalkboard, where a crude map had been drawn.

"The new cross-country course starts here, goes to this yellow flag here, then down here, across the stream at the yellow flag here, up to here, then here. Everyone got that?"

Basically we'd be running the entire perimeter of the school, which felt like it had to be a thousand miles. We all looked at each other.

"A little more'n two miles," the coach said.

"Two *miles,*" someone repeated in horror.

I don't know about the rest of the country, but at that point in history the idea of folks running recreationally hadn't really taken hold in northern Idaho. We had some people in town we called joggers, but for the most part the local populace couldn't see any reason to run unless it was being chased by something. I shared the perplexed trepidation of most of the boys in that gym class as we stood around at the starting point, the first yellow flag so far away we could barely see it. Two *miles?*

"Line up outside!" the coach barked, like we were already in trouble for something. We shuffled out the door like a chain gang.

The coach blew the whistle and we all jumped and then settled into a bumpy, unpleasant pace. Tim and Mike, naturally, moved to the front and then accelerated like a pair of motorcycles, while everyone else around me put an expression of pain on their faces in anticipation of what was to come.

I've never been particularly fast or noticeably slow — just average, I guess. But I had no sense of the science of pacing myself and was lured to the front of the crowd by Tim's and Mike's sprint. It felt like we should be following our leaders.

Oddly, the boys who had always been the best at school sports were the first to drop back, their mouths open. Boys like me, gawky, all elbows and knees, kept running at the same determined speed.

Once my muscles warmed up and shook

out their reluctance, I let the steady beat of my shoes lure me into a hypnotic state, and, as had been true of every contemplative moment of the previous twenty-four hours, I thought about Beth and Emory the bear in roughly equal measure.

Emory Bain. Really? A bear who had a first and last name and could write them down? *Beth Shelburton.* Seriously? A stunningly beautiful girl who wanted me to say hi to her in the hall and sit with her at lunch?

At the first turn, a long, steady hill greeted us and more boys fell away. For a time a skinny boy named Kenny hung by my side, blinking at me through thick glasses, and then about halfway up the hill his expression changed and he seemed to lose ambition.

The next person in front of me was Ned, a knobby, muscle-less kid whose storklike legs hinged and unhinged in graceless, uneven rhythm. He never even looked at me as I passed him — his gaze was turned inward on his own agonies.

I had a knot in my side. Up ahead, Tim and Mike had stopped talking to each other and were now just determinedly slogging it out on the hill.

I was gaining on them.

They both turned in surprise when I was

about ten feet away. At that very moment we crested the hill and they put on a quick burst, zooming ahead again.

At the bottom of the hill was a tiny stream to vault over and then we were on flat ground. I kept my pace the same, listening for the sound of runners behind me. When I didn't hear any, I turned and looked and was startled to see I was fifty yards ahead of a staggering string of stumblers, none of them looking like they were enjoying their morning.

I had a solid cramp in my rib cage now, but there was something about the pain that felt liberating, like it was a wall I was punching through.

As I caught up with them again Mike and Tim didn't turn, even when the sound of my foot strikes merged with theirs. They did split, though, opening a gap that I moved up into.

"Hi," I gasped, which felt like it was going to be the last word I'd ever be able to utter. Neither of them responded. Tim nodded at me, though.

Now we were facing the hill from the back side of it, climbing up at an angle that felt almost as steep as the road to my house. I kept pounding my feet. When I glanced back at the top of the hill, Mike and Tim were twenty yards behind.

They beat me by finding some amazing strength at the end of the race and pouring on the speed. I didn't have anything left. I was, I now understood, a plodder, a person who put my feet down at the same rate whether I was going uphill or down. When they stormed past me, I didn't increase my pace by a step, pulling in third in the race.

Mike put his hands on his knees, wheezing, while Tim walked in circles, his face in a taut grimace. I turned and looked back at the rest of the class, who were one by one popping up at the top of the hill holding their sides as if they'd been pierced by spears.

I felt a slap on my back. Tim was nodding at me, grinning, still not capable of speech.

"Good job, Hall," Mike panted.

I couldn't have been happier if they'd picked me up and carried me around on their shoulders.

Coach Briggs was pretty impatient with our performance. He called us girls and asked us if we'd taken a nap somewhere along the line. He said he'd called the police and put in a missing persons report. He said we were supposed to run the course, not play hopscotch the whole way. He asked if we were worried that we'd get mud on our party dresses if we ran too hard or if we'd stopped to put on lipstick somewhere in the whole process.

Through this whole tirade, the boys in gym class winced and moaned with the pain like they were having dental surgery. "Kappas. Humphrey. You guys can hit the showers. Everyone else, drop and give me twenty."

The boys all groaned. I moved over to find a place to do my push-ups.

"Not you, Hall," the coach said. "You hit the showers, too."

I couldn't keep the grin off my face as I headed toward the locker room. Coach Briggs's eyes had regarded me without warmth and his expression was as severe as it always was, but I basked in it.

It felt like love.

The class before lunch was science, the only one I shared with Dan Alderton that semester. As I listened to the teacher explain photosynthesis I could feel Dan's eyes on me and wished he could have been in gym. I had the probably foolish thought that if he had seen me cross the finish line just a few steps behind Mike and Tim it would somehow put an end to the odd dispute between us.

I would be seeing Beth at lunch. I'm sure

that there was something in the lecture that I paid attention to, but for the most part my focus was on the clock, which doled out each minute in such a miserly fashion I wanted to yell at it.

I think Dan tried to say something to me as the class ended, but I was in a hurry. I dumped my books in my locker, then ducked into the boys' room to make sure my hair was still combed. There was nothing lodged in my teeth and my face hadn't grown any zits since breakfast.

I loaded up my lunch tray and wandered out into the lunchroom. I spotted Beth across the room and my heart sank; she wasn't alone. Sitting with her were several girls — if I went over there I'd be sitting with a whole group of seventh-grade females. I'd be the only boy and the only eighth grader. Everyone would be watching. It would be awful.

"Hey, Charlie!" Tim Humphrey called. He nodded toward a seat next to him.

Tim sat at the table occupied by the popular eighth graders. The prettiest girls, including Joy Ebert, would often be sitting there, though at that moment it was just a bunch of guys. It seemed utterly impossible that he was suggesting I sit with him. Was he talking to someone else?

I approached hesitantly, setting my tray down.

"You going to try out for cross-country this year?" Tim wanted to know.

"No," I said automatically.

"Why not?" he asked, puzzled.

I lowered my eyes. The truth of it was that joining in team sports or doing anything fun like that felt like it would somehow be a betrayal of Mom. Bit by bit I was letting go of this attitude, but it was still by and large my ethic. "I don't know." I shrugged. "Maybe I will. I never thought about it."

"You should," Tim said. "I was wiped out today in gym, but you looked like you could keep running."

All the way across the room, I could feel Beth looking at me. I knew if I turned our eyes would meet.

"Um . . . ," I said. Tim looked at me questioningly. "I sort of said I'd sit with a friend of mine. Some friends," I told him.

He shrugged. "Sure."

I've come to conclude that for every person like me — people who found junior high to be a nuanced, torturous negotiation, with inviolate rules and devastating punishments — there were students like Tim, who went through it all as if it were just normal school, with no rigid hierarchy and no social regulations. At the time, though, I believed we all subscribed to the same code and that surely Tim understood the significance of me leaving his table when I'd just been granted a free pass. Had I played it right, I might have eaten lunch there the next day, and then the next, and I'd be popular and happy.

But Tim gave no sign and I was drawn by a power far greater than anything I'd ever encountered. I carried my tray across the room, sure that everyone was whispering behind their hands about me.

The space across from Beth was unoccupied, and I sat down. The rest of the girls at the table instantly went quiet. "Hi," I said.

"For a minute there, I thought you forgot," Beth said.

"Oh, well, Tim just wanted to know if I was trying out for cross-country. You know. Tim *Humphrey*."

"I know who he is," she replied, ignoring my whole point, which was that I hung out with popular kids.

I was introduced to Beth's friends. I miserably mumbled my way through a greeting to each one. They were all perfect examples of why seventh graders didn't belong in junior high — gaunt, sticklike girls for whom puberty was only a concept in biology class. I lost track of their names because they all looked the same, though their expressions and quick head movements reminded me of birds. They cut their eyes back and forth at each other, grinned, and then sat back as if expecting me to entertain them. *What,* I wondered, *am I doing here?*

Beth turned to her friends. "Charlie," she told them, "is a man with a mysterious secret."

"What is it?" one of them immediately chirped.

"Well, it's a secret," Beth responded. "If we all knew it, we'd have to call it something else. Like 'common knowledge.'"

The girls all cackled and clucked and pecked at their food. I focused on my lunch as if I'd never in my life seen anything more fascinating.

"One time Charlie and his parents came out to our ranch to ride horses and I spied on him from the hayloft. Whenever he looked up, I'd drop down behind the window. But he knew I was there. It was the first time we ever saw each other."

I was astounded. "That was you?" I blurted before I had a chance to think. But that meant that I had seen Beth when I was in fourth grade. I remembered a little girl's face popping up and down like a monkey when we were mounting our horses.

The girl who'd asked about my secret had something else to say: "I'm really sorry about your mom."

When people said this to me they usually wore exaggeratedly sad expressions, like this girl now, or they looked a little afraid. At first I was convinced that the people with the sad faces were attempting to tear off a piece of my grief for themselves, to become uninvited participants. Now I figured they *were* sad, probably. The fear, though, I was still trying to figure out. Were they afraid of my reaction, that I would burst into tears and embarrass them? Or maybe they were worried it could happen to them, that they, too, could lose someone who should never, never be lost.

I looked up at Beth's eyes and saw warm sympathy, just the right amount, and no fear at all. It made my stomach drop inside me as if I were on the Tilt-A-Whirl at the Boundary County Fair. Kay had never made me feel like this. There was just something about this girl.

Beth was waiting for me after school and we walked to her house together. It was as if she were my girlfriend, or wanted to be.

If I thought about Emory or my father's

injury or anything else but the green-eyed girl from seventh grade that day, I simply don't remember it. When we entered the Shelburtons' house, Beth's mother told me my dad had been released from the hospital. She had me pack my things and she drove me home, but it wasn't like I skipped out of there full of joy. The only thing that made the ride bearable was that Beth sat in the front and talked to me over her seat the whole way.

I almost lacked the willpower to unbuckle my seat belt in the driveway. "Bye, Charlie," Beth said simply. I grunted in response, like a weight lifter doing a clean and jerk.

"Wait here; we'll be right back, Beth," Mrs. Shelburton said.

My dad came out of the house and stood and talked to Mrs. Shelburton as I hovered nearby with my suitcase, miserable because Beth was still in the car and I could have stayed with her but instead had elected to get out and now it would look stupid if I got back in. As Mrs. Shelburton backed away, she waved at my dad and I waved at Beth.

"Charlie."

I turned to look at my dad. He looked a little frail, somehow, and I flashed back to how he'd appeared in the hospital bed. I was glad I didn't need to see him like that anymore.

"You did a good job on the pole barn. I can't even tell where there was blood," he told me.

I nodded. We stood there, a slight breeze whistling in the pines, until it seemed to occur to both of us at the same time that the pause in conversation had lasted too long.

I put my stuff away in my room. "I think I'll go down to the creek," I said to my father.

"Charlie?"

I looked at him.

"What is my Polaroid camera doing out?"

CHAPTER
SEVENTEEN

My mom had given him the camera. The first time I was allowed to use it myself was to take an instant picture of her the night before her first session of chemotherapy. She put on a nice dress and did her hair all up and wanted a photograph of her with, as she put it, "all my hair intact." So I knew how to use it, but it was my dad's and I wasn't supposed to touch it without permission.

"Oh. I had been planning to take pictures of the pole barn before I laid on a new coat of paint."

He nodded. "Well, put it back then."

I did as he said and then went down to the creek. There was no sign of the bear anywhere. I yelled, "Emory!" a few times but didn't want to shout it too loud for fear my dad would hear me and wonder what I was up to.

When I climbed the hill back to our house

there was that stupid Chevy Vega in the driveway. I went inside and Yvonne was sitting in our living room holding a drink in one hand and an unlit Virginia Slim in the other.

"Charlie!" She carefully set her drink down and stood up.

I didn't know what she expected me to do: run over and hug her? I shied away, standing close to the opposite wall. "Hello, Miss Mandeville," I said stiffly.

My dad came out of the bathroom. He looked startled, maybe even guilty, when he saw me there talking to the grocery lady. "Hi, Charlie," he said.

The three of us stood for a minute. Finally my dad pulled a lighter from his pocket to set flame to the tip of her cigarette.

Why did he have a lighter all of a sudden?

"I came over to see how your dad is feeling. You had us scared half to death, George," Yvonne said.

I wasn't scared, I thought to myself.

Dad and Yvonne settled into some chairs and I went back to my bedroom and closed the door. My chest was tight, as if I'd just run cross-country. My dad had lied to me. He said he didn't like her, and now here she was. She sent him loving flowers in the hospital and probably visited him more than I did.

I love you, the card had said. That was a lot more serious than *Love, Yvonne.*

I decided that if she stayed for dinner I'd pretend to be sick again. Maybe my father would conclude I was allergic to her and tell her she couldn't come over anymore.

A few minutes later, though, I heard her get into her car and drive off. I went out to help my dad with dinner. He seemed to want to say something to me, but of course he didn't.

When I went to bed that night I reached into my sock drawer and pulled out a small cigar box I'd had for a long time. I kept stuff in it that I imagine no one would ever find of any value but me, stuff I'd found, mostly, like an arrowhead and the perfectly preserved skull of a small snake. I had a new item in there as well.

I hadn't lied to my father. I'd gotten the Polaroid camera out because I'd been planning to take a picture of the pole barn before I'd painted over it; that much was true. In matter of fact, I *did* take a picture of the pole barn before I painted over it. I turned the Polaroid over in my hands now, reading the mysterious words.

I, Emory Bain, pvt. 3rd regt., inf. of GR Mich, May 1862 pursued rebels at Chickahominy, wounded, took fever, now returned. I have a message.

Gazing at those words, I had, for the first time, the sense that my life was undergoing a profound change and that as a result, when I told the story of Charlie Hall people would no longer look at me with solemn eyes and say, *I'm sorry.*

On the bus the next morning I sat close to the front, as usual, marooned by my first day's choice in the middle of a field of seventh graders. From where I sat I could monitor what was going on behind me by looking into the huge mirror hanging over the driver's head, which was how I noticed Dan's friend Jerry stealthily making his way forward, moving from seat to seat even though you weren't supposed to get up when the vehicle was moving. At the next stop, just as the bus was lumbering to a halt, he darted forward, sliding into the seat next to me.

He didn't look me in the eye; he was watching straight ahead, as if he were a spy or something. I regarded him curiously.

"Dan wants to fight you after school

today," he said out of the corner of his mouth.

I thought Dan and I had pretty much settled this particular matter on the first day of school and was more than a little unhappy to hear it brought up again. What would be the point of a fight? We both knew that I'd lose.

It was on my lips to ask why, but I squelched the impulse. I *knew* why. I'd seen adolescent bighorn sheep banging their heads into each other when they were too young to do any mating — it was just a way of proving something to themselves and maybe to the other sheep who were watching. This was the same thing; we were all jockeying and jostling our way into manhood. Boys fought all the time, either because some spark of anger set them off or because of something like this, a formal, almost ritualized appointment, as if we were dueling with pistols.

Why couldn't I just forfeit?

"We'll go down to the city park, off school property so you won't get in trouble. You can take the late bus home," Jerry told me, anticipating my legal argument.

So, well, there it was. I shrugged. "Yeah, okay," I said. My heart was pounding as if I'd just asked a girl out on a date.

At the next stop Jerry slipped back to give Dan the good news that I'd agreed he could pound me into a pulp after school that day.

I bolted from the bus as soon as the doors flapped open. I didn't want to so much as make eye contact with my partner in pugilism. I was oddly embarrassed, as if Dan and I shared an intimacy now.

Word of the fight spread through the school fairly rapidly, and I found myself the subject of a few speculative glances in the hallways. I'd like to say there was admiration in those looks, but it was actually more as if they were picturing me lying in a chalk outline.

Why was I cursed with such a small body? Why wasn't I big and strong and tough like so many other eighth graders?

I'd have to wait until my twenties before anyone could answer these questions. I had finished defending my dissertation and was officially a Ph.D., but instead of luxuriating in the accomplishment I found I was restless at the sudden cessation of stress, plagued with an intractable insomnia. When my medical doctor's drugs didn't work I started seeing a therapist. Dr. Sat Siri was an American Sikh, an elegant, pale woman in white flowing clothes and a turban. Unlike some of the other professional listeners

I was sent to in the name of psychotherapy, she seemed to believe that the purpose of our sessions was to make their continuation unnecessary.

Sat Siri was the only person to tell me about studies done on the effect of grief and other stresses on prepubescent children. "It's no wonder your physical growth went dormant on you, Charlie," she told me. "You'd lost your mother; that's a great emotional shock."

Sat Siri also gently asked me if I didn't see something "worth looking at," as she put it, in the fact that when my yearning for some kind of communication with my father was at its most acute I found myself talking to a wild bear. I didn't have an answer for that one, because she, it seemed, like every other person in her profession, discounted my story about the words on the pole barn wall, choosing to believe they were the product of some rational, prosaic event, like a couple of kids committing vandalism or maybe a cry for help from a growth-stunted eighth grader.

At any rate, I was years away from that conversation, and whatever the cause, I was small and weak and, I knew, terrified. Several times that day I went into the boys' room, stared into the mirror, and admonished myself over and over, *Don't* cry.

This was all that I was afraid of. I didn't mind if Dan's fist broke my nose; I wasn't worried about losing the fight or feeling the pain. I was just terrified that I'd become so upset that I'd cry like a baby in front of the other boys and then I'd forever be rejected from the company of men. Just standing in front of the mirror I could feel my emotions fluttering inside my chest, reacting to the upsetting news that Dan Alderton, Danny my friend, wanted to hit me and hurt me.

I sat with Beth and her flock at lunch and it was easier, this second day. Compared to my upcoming humiliation on the battlefield, what did it matter if everyone saw me lunching with a bunch of seventh graders? Besides, Beth was *beautiful.* It never did any male reputational damage to be seen with a pretty girl. I felt lucky that some other boy hadn't swooped in already.

Beth apparently knew nothing about the title bout that was scheduled for that afternoon and I decided it would be best not to mention it.

I was at my locker when Dan suddenly appeared, flanked by Gregg the ninth grader and fellow eighth grader Mitch.

"Are you going to show?" Dan demanded hotly.

The funny thing is that once you've had a grizzly bear in your face, a skinny thirteen-year-old just isn't that intimidating. I mostly observed that he was flushed and had worked himself into a state of aggression that didn't come naturally to the Dan Alderton I knew. His freckles were scarlet and pulsing on his pale cheeks.

"Yeah," I said. "I'll be there."

"You'd better," he replied.

It was on my mind to remind him that I'd just said I would, but I bit back the smart remark. "I will," I finally said when the silence of Dan and his pals became awkward.

"You'd better," he warned again. I guess that's all he could come up with.

I turned my back on him then and I suppose there was some deliberation in my movements, a direct expression of contempt. I pulled my history book out of my locker and slammed the door shut, moving past Gregg, who had to step out of my way. As he did so, someone — I'm assuming Dan, but it could have been any one of them — hit me in the back of my head with his knuckles. It wasn't a hard blow, just one designed to insult, and it did the trick: my eyes were stinging.

Don't cry.

At the closing bell I trudged down the street to the city park, which was just a place with grass and some benches — probably the whole thing was constructed so that junior high students would have some place to fight. A few boys had already gathered and were milling around in excitement, but Dan and his entourage hadn't arrived by the time I got there, which put me in the ridiculous position of having to wait to be punched out. I noted glumly that Tim Humphrey and Mike Kappas both had shown up — I doubted they'd have much respect for my physical prowess once Dan had knocked me unconscious.

There was, as they say, a fairly good crowd. No one talked to me — they maintained a respectful distance. I pretended to do some stretching, as if I needed to get my body limbered up before I folded it into the fetal position.

When you were ready to surrender in a fight, you said, *I give.* It was, however, considered poor sportsmanship to say this before the other guy had even shown up.

Eventually Dan, Gregg, Jerry, and Mitch arrived. Dan's friends were grinning broadly, but Dan seemed pretty grim. His eyes didn't meet mine as he took off the light jacket he was wearing and handed it to

Gregg. If Dan's freckles got any hotter they'd probably burst into flames.

He knows this is ridiculous, I thought to myself. *He knows we have no reason to be doing this.*

Dan and I approached each other warily. Was this it? Were we supposed to just start fighting?

"Glad you could make it. Wussy." Dan sneered at me.

I could see that he needed to work himself into a froth before he could justify swinging at me, so I just waited for him to get there. Since I didn't want to do this in the first place, I didn't sling any insults back.

"Wussy," Dan said again.

Fine. Great. I'm a wussy. I'd like to see you hand-feed a grizzly bear. You'd probably mess your pants.

This actually made me grin, which seemed to disorient Dan a little. I was supposed to be reeling from his insults, and instead I was smiling at some internal thought. I guess he thought that if he called me a couple names I'd become enraged and fling myself at him and he'd drop me with a shot to the face.

"Come on," someone said in the crowd. They were getting restless. Fights aren't supposed to be boring; it was a rule.

"You're just . . . ," Dan floundered.

A wussy, yes, we've established that.

His lips twisted bitterly. "Your mother was a whore," he said.

The crowd went completely silent. Dan was staring at me, and he looked shocked at his own words. And I . . .

I . . .

I simply couldn't fathom how anyone could say such a thing. The idea that anyone in Selkirk River could so much as think a single ugly thought about Laura Hall, much less utter it in public, struck me literally dumb.

I had nothing to say. I let my fists, which had been up in a halfhearted mimic of Dan's stance, drop to my sides.

"That's it," I said, or think I said. I remember that as I pushed my way through the circle of boys who had gathered for the fight my face was frozen in a tight grimace. That the boys parted for me without a word. That Mike Kappas said, "*Jesus*, Alderton," with such contempt it instantly defined for everyone there how they and eventually the entire school would react to what had just happened.

I waited at the bus pickup without looking at or talking to anyone.

The late bus ran a spontaneously designed

212

route depending on who got on board. This meant you had to sit there while the bus driver took you on a meandering exploration of what felt like the entire county.

No one sat near me. They didn't mean any harm by their ostracism; they just didn't know what to say.

And Dan, of course, wasn't on the bus.

We had ground our way methodically up a long series of switchbacks in order to deposit one lone ninth grader at an intersection that looked like the crossroads where Nowhere meets Nothing. Why was he getting off here? If there was a house around those parts it was a secret to me.

What there was up there was a hunting lodge that belonged to the rich oil guy, McHenry. That was his last name and all most people ever called him, McHenry, though his first name was Jules.

He built a log cabin that people said had five bathrooms in it, a fact everyone repeated to each other as an exclamation: "Five bathrooms!" The bus swung around and I got a good look at both the five-bathroom cabin and then McHenry himself, who was unlocking a padlock at some iron gates to let his truck onto his property. He was certainly a character — that's another thing people would repeat to each other:

"That McHenry is certainly a character." The expression made no sense to me; weren't we all "characters"? What would the opposite be? Would you say someone was "not a character"?

McHenry's face was deeply suntanned, a stark contrast to the white hair he wore pulled into an eight-inch ponytail at the back of his head. The pickup's door was open and even from inside the bus I could feel its custom speakers vibrating the air with Led Zeppelin music. The truck bed had dog cages in it, with hounds who were pacing back and forth in their enclosures, eager to be let out. There were four dogs in all, rust-colored animals. Hunting dogs.

Bear-hunting dogs.

CHAPTER EIGHTEEN

At that point it wasn't strictly illegal to hunt a grizzly bear in the lower forty-eight. Grizzlies wouldn't make it onto the endangered species list for another year. It was, however, largely pointless to try to find one — as my dad had said, they were considered pretty much wiped out in Idaho. McHenry wasn't bringing out the dogs to track grizzlies; he was after black bears, which were more plentiful.

Bear hunting wasn't much of a sport — the bear would run from the dogs until, terrified, it climbed a tree, and then the hunter would come along and shoot the bear out of the tree. But then McHenry was rumored to not be much of a sportsman. People said he pretty much shot whatever he wanted, in season or not, figuring that if he got caught he'd just pay the fine.

The reason people all knew about his poaching but did nothing about it was that when McHenry came to town it injected a nice shot of dollars into the local economy. He could be counted upon to spend big at the restaurants and bars, to lease horses from Mr. Shelburton, and to add weight to the collection plate at Sunday services. McHenry was always buying snowmobiles and powerboats. If he shot a bear or an elk when he wasn't supposed to, nobody was going to complain.

I had no doubt what would happen if he and his dogs came across Emory in the woods.

When the bus dropped me at the foot of Hidden Creek Road I took off at a run, faster than usual, pushing myself. I dumped my schoolbooks on the front deck without even going inside.

"Emory!" I yelled. I sprinted down the path to the creek. There was no sign of him. What if I couldn't warn him in time? What if he didn't trust me, since I had shut him in the barn without food or water?

"Emory!" I shouted. I climbed the big hill on the opposite side of the creek, the vast expanse of forest that was visible from our back windows. At the very crest of this hill there was a ridge of rocks from which you could see for miles and miles, and it was toward this ridge I ran, an uphill climb that tore the oxygen out of my lungs until I was gasping so hard I could barely manage a croak.

It didn't matter that I couldn't shout; I was making enough noise as I crashed upward through the trees that the bear heard me coming. He was standing toward the top of the ridge, up on two legs as if he, too, wanted to see everything around him. He was massive, regal, beautiful. The sun was low in the sky, hiding behind some clouds, so that a soft light danced around the bear like an aura.

"Emory," I gasped. "There's a hunter. With dogs and . . . and guns. You have to come with me."

I'm not sure whether I thought he'd understand me or I just said the words out loud because other than gesturing with my arms I had no other way to communicate. But Emory gracefully dropped his forepaws to the ground and followed me passively as I made my way more slowly back down the hill. Apparently I was forgiven for having locked him up.

When I opened the pole barn door, I glanced up at Emory, thinking maybe his reaction would reveal something to me. Would he somehow indicate surprise that the words were no longer on the wall? Be angry? Notice I'd cleaned up his footprints?

He was maddeningly inscrutable, completely expressionless until I flipped on the light. Then he started in surprise, glancing around wildly until he saw the naked bulbs overhead. When he did he stood on two legs, sniffing, examining the source of illumination.

"They're called lightbulbs. They're like candles, only electric." I hesitated. Shoot, did he even know about electricity?

For the first time since I read the writing on the wall, the date of May 1862 assumed significance. Was Emory from the year 1862? Was he here by time travel? Was it a parallel universe, like in Craig's *Planet of the Apes* show? Reincarnation? Open the door on one element of the fantastic and the thirteen-year-old mind will let them all in at the same time.

I was at a point in my life where I thought it perfectly plausible that a radioactive spider could bite you and then you'd be Spider-Man. I believed the Starship *Enterprise* could travel at warp speed and that soon we would all have flying cars. I knew Superman was a fantasy but thought Batman and James Bond were reasonable constructs, all in all. I guess the people who are disappointed that I didn't faint dead away with all the spiritual implications of the words on the wall were more sophisticated when they were in the eighth grade.

Emory didn't seem to care about the new paint job anyway. He strolled over to one of the big freezers, sniffed its edge, and then faced me with what can only be described as an expectant expression.

I undid the latch, opened the freezer, and dragged out a tub of beef stew and took it to the sink and ran water over it until it dropped out of the tub, landing like a block of cement. "Here," I said to Emory. The thing skittered across the floor like a hockey puck. Emory stopped it with his foot, giving it a long sniff and then an experimental lick.

Satisfied that it was, indeed, food, the bear sprawled on the floor, holding the stew between his paws, and started chewing at it like a dog with a bone.

"I'll leave the side door open, but I need to close the big one," I told him. He didn't look up from where he was steadily crunching his frozen meal.

As I was reaching for the loop of rope to pull the garage door shut, I caught movement out of the corner of my eye. I glanced up and inhaled in sharp surprise.

Dan Alderton was standing out on the road. His eyes were wide in disbelief as he took in the sight of the bear lying on the floor of the pole barn, fully illuminated by the lights overhead.

Without saying a word or acknowledging him in any way, I shut the door. My heart was pounding, though — I knew that to keep the bear safe I had to guard Emory's presence, his *existence,* from the world. I couldn't think of a worse person to have spotted the grizzly bear in our pole barn.

But I had a more immediate problem: within half an hour of my chance encounter with Dan, I heard my father's Jeep turn off the paved road and start chewing up the gravel on its way to our driveway.

Emory raised his head curiously at the noise of my father's brakes squealing as the Jeep came to a halt outside the pole barn. I faced the bear, my hands open and spread in supplication. "Please," I said. "That's my dad. Please stay here until I talk to him, okay?"

As usual, the bear's eyes were unreadable.

I waited until dinner to talk to my dad. My delay wasn't strategic; I just couldn't think of how to introduce the subject or what I should tell him. And though I had irrefutable evidence in the form of a six-hundred-pound beast in our pole barn, I knew that my dad probably wouldn't believe me. The prospect of his cold rejection filled me first with dread and then with a grief so profound my throat went tight with it, choking me.

The silence probably just felt routine to my dad, who seemed more distracted than usual. He fried up fish on the stove, his back to me. I watched him move around the kitchen and he seemed tired and old. Life hadn't turned out the way he'd wanted and there was often a sense coming off him that he was sick of the whole darn thing.

"Dad," I said as we came to the end of another silent dinner. His eyes drifted down the table to where my mom always sat before they turned and looked at me.

I took a deep breath but couldn't seem to come out with it.

"What is it, Charlie?"

"Dad, it's bear-hunting season. I saw McHenry with his dogs. He's going to go after bear."

My dad considered this, no doubt puzzled that my words were shaking with so much emotion. His brown eyes watched me with almost the same lack of response as Emory's.

"There's a grizzly bear. If he finds him, I'm afraid McHenry will shoot him. We can't let that happen!" I blurted frantically.

221

My dad frowned in bafflement and I felt my frustration building. This wasn't going right.

"His name is Emory. He's not a normal bear."

"A grizzly?" my dad said. "Charlie . . ."

"We have to protect him, Dad! McHenry hunts whatever he feels like and people just let him do it. We can't let him shoot Emory!"

My father was staring at me with a perplexity that under any other circumstance might have been humorous.

"Dad, when you were in the hospital, I put him in the pole barn. And while he was in there, he got into the paint. It wasn't a duck like you thought. The red was paint, not blood," I told him in a rush. I *hated* having to tell him this — I might have explained to myself that I hadn't technically lied, but I knew my father wouldn't see it like that.

"You put a bear in the pole barn?" he sputtered, putting his finger on what was, for him, the most critical point. "A *bear?*"

"He's in there now," I said quietly. My dad's eyes bulged. "Dad, but look! Look what he drew on the wall!"

I handed over the Polaroid photograph. Another half falsehood exposed, but I thought I was probably beyond getting into trouble for using the camera.

My father accepted the picture as if it were fragile, barely holding it. His face was twisted into a grimace of absolute bewilderment. He read the words that Emory had written on the wall, then raised his eyes. "I don't know what to say, Charlie."

I didn't, either. I was almost holding my breath. It was so desperately important to me that my father believed me.

"How does a bear . . . ," he started to say, shaking his head. I knew the question: *How does a bear manage to hold a paintbrush?* But was that really the most important issue? How about the fact that the bear could write words?

And then my father translated the first sentence, which had been, to me, mostly gibberish. " 'I, Emory Bain, private, Third Regiment of infantry, of Grand Rapids, Michigan, May 1862, pursued Rebels at,' uh, 'Chickahominy, wounded, took fever.' " He paused a moment, then continued with the rest of it. " 'Now returned. I have a message.' " He peered at me. "This is what was written on the wall of the pole barn?"

"Yessir." I tried to keep the excitement out of my voice. Infantry! Emory had been a soldier; that's what he meant!

"And you painted it out."

I hung my head.

"And the bear is there now. Inside."

I didn't say anything.

"Charlie."

I lifted my eyes.

"There's a grizzly bear locked inside our pole barn right now."

"Yessir, there is. Well, not locked; I left the side door open." Now that it didn't matter, I was meticulously sticking to the truth.

His eyes were almost feverish with contemplation, and I suddenly had a sense of what was going on inside him. If he believed me on this, he'd be throwing in with me on something that was completely impossible. It would be my dad and me on one side and the rational world on the other.

But the alternative would tear me in two. If he abandoned me now it would be the final step in the long path toward complete separation that had started the day we put my mother in the ground. I wasn't without blame in the estrangement; I guarded an awful secret, locking myself behind its walls, but my father had not tried to scale those walls, not once. He'd never even noticed that we weren't communicating, so wrapped up in his own grieving he didn't bother to consider what had happened to me.

Resentment churned up in me then, an anger so tightly wound it felt as if I could strike him then, punch him in his doubting eyes. I swallowed it all back, trembling, waiting for him to say something.

"Okay then," he said quietly. "Let's go take a look."

I nodded quickly, turning away from him so he wouldn't see the tears that inexplicably sprang to my eyes. I hastily wiped them away when he walked toward the door, and then he stopped.

"Just a minute," he said to me. He reversed course and strode down the hallway to his room, shutting the door behind him.

I didn't try to puzzle through this odd behavior. I was caught up in a wave of cautious optimism then, a sense that things might actually turn out all right. My father was going to help me, help Emory, Emory the soldier.

Of course, not everyone would turn out to be as easily accepting of the whole thing as I was.

When Dad left his bedroom he wordlessly crossed the floor, a key in his hand, and unlocked his gun cabinet.

"Dad," I said, anguished.

He carefully loaded the .30-06, the safety engaging with an audible click. "Just in case,

Charlie," he said gently.

We went out to the pole barn. A square of light spilled out from the open side door, but we went around to the front. I reached for the handle to raise the door, but my dad stopped me with a hand on my arm. He cocked his head, listening, then finally gave me a firm nod.

What would I do, I wondered, if Emory had left?

I lifted the door with a rattle.

Emory was lying on the couch I'd pulled out for him, sprawled out like a drunk man. It was fully dark outside in the driveway, but I knew my father and I would be illuminated in the doorway by the spill of light from the overhead bulbs.

The bear saw my dad's rifle and came to his feet.

"Emory," I said tremulously, "this is my dad."

I felt my father tighten his grip on his gun when Emory stalked forward, moving slowly but with massive power. It must have taken all of Dad's willpower, but the gun stayed pointed at the floor even as the distance between us and the great bear shortened.

I took a step forward, deliberately putting myself between the bear and the rifle.

"Charlie," my father warned tensely.

"It's okay," I said, speaking to both of them. "Nobody wants to get hurt."

My dad drew in a breath between his teeth when I reached out my hand. Emory took another step forward and nuzzled my fingers with his nose.

"My God," my father breathed.

CHAPTER NINETEEN

I had the feeling, as I boarded the school bus the next morning, that there were just too many things to contain, that I was trying to manage a crisis in every significant area of my existence. I was filled with the sense of rampant momentum, of cascading events.

One of my biggest concerns was my father, in whom I had so little faith it was as if he'd become a stranger to me. His shock at seeing Emory, combined with the naked disbelief in my father's eyes when he spent what seemed like an hour reading and rereading the words captured by the Polaroid, led me to conclude he was the shakiest sort of ally, maybe even an enemy to me and my bear. He'd offered no encouragement or support, that was for sure — in fact, he said nothing at all, handling this new development in our lives the way he handled everything else between us.

As I slid into my customary bus seat up in seventh-grade territory, I noticed that Dan was well forward of his usual slot and nobody was sitting with him. By comparison, though, Dan was such a minor concern I dismissed him from any thought at all.

What I didn't know was that not long after I got on that bus my father would be literally face-to-face with our nemesis, McHenry.

My dad was always too impatient to be much of a storyteller, always skipping details, but in this instance he related everything to me word-by-word and blow-by-blow. He had been on his way to work and was rumbling over a wooden bridge when he saw Jules McHenry and his eager, baying hounds racing along the riverbank, clearly on the trail of something. My dad watched the hunter vanish around the bend, making a geometric connection between what he'd just seen and our house a few miles away. It seemed likely that my fears were playing out right there: McHenry was on his way to bagging himself a grizzly.

My dad turned his Jeep around and kept his foot into it as he headed home in the light drizzle.

He called his job and told them he needed some more time due to the head injury,

wondering what he could have been thinking to set off for the shop as if this were a
normal day. He poured himself a cup of coffee and watched in complete bemusement
as the bear came out of the pole barn
through the side door, went out into the
yard, and relieved himself of both bladder
and bowel, just like a dog except with a lot
more productivity. Then the bear yawned
and wandered over to my mother's ne-
glected garden, where a tangle of blackberry
and raspberry bushes drooped with unhar-
vested fruit. The berries were a little small
for human consumption, though to be
truthful I think the reason my father didn't
ever pick them was related to the reason
why I didn't want to put away the tomato
cages — my mother had spent hours out
there trying to manage her berry bushes,
painstakingly separating them the way she
had once carefully pruned some gum out of
my hair.

But then Emory stopped looking at the
berries. He turned his head toward the state
forest behind our property, cocking his head
as if listening. My dad set down his coffee
cup, seeing that some sort of change was
coming over the bear. Emory stood up,
lifted his nose to the wind, and sniffed.

And then he dropped to all fours and

moved with amazing alacrity into the pole barn. "Hard to believe an animal that big could move that fast," my dad said.

My father was just going for another cup of coffee, trying to figure out what had spooked Emory so badly, when he heard a noise floating on the wind, the cadence familiar and unmistakable.

Dogs.

My father found his binoculars and focused them on the hill on the other side of the creek. It didn't take long before a pack of hounds emerged from the woods, baying, their noses seeking the rich scent of live bear.

My dad put on his bright orange and yellow hunting vest and went out to the pole barn. Emory was pacing, nervously making a chuffing noise.

"Don't worry," my dad said, feeling a bit silly to be talking to a bear. He closed the side door and went to the edge of the yard and waited in the misting rain with his arms crossed.

Before long the four dogs poured up the hill, surrounding and ignoring my stationary father. They thronged the yard and waxed ecstatic over the sizable pile Emory had left in the grass, but eventually it was the crack under the door that attracted them the most.

Eventually McHenry came huffing up the path, his ponytail bobbing at the back of his head. "Name's McHenry," he said, pulling off a glove so he could offer my dad a hand.

"We've met, Jules," my dad said civilly but coolly. "I'm George Hall."

McHenry acted like of course he remembered my father. He was distracted by the commotion his dogs were making, so as he tendered his social platitudes he had one eye on what was happening over my dad's shoulder.

"I've got 'No Hunting' signs pretty clearly posted all along my property's edge," my father stated evenly. There was, in fact, exactly such a sign not far from where they stood, providing a convenient visual aid to his point. McHenry reluctantly nodded, but his eyes were getting suspicious. His dogs were still going crazy at the door. One of them had started jumping up as if to catch a glimpse of Emory through the window.

"We're tracking bear," McHenry said by way of explanation.

"No hunting," my father replied pleasantly.

McHenry flushed a little at this. Probably most of the people in Selkirk River would watch him shoot their chickens and pets and children and just say, *Why, there's Mr. Jules McHenry, pouring money into the local economy.*

"Call your dogs," my dad requested.

"I think maybe a bear must have just crossed through here. Maybe you have some dog food in your barn? Bears love that. He could've sniffed around looking for a way in and that's what's got my dogs so riled up. If I could cross through, I can maybe get them back on track."

As my dad related it to me, McHenry's voice was very reasonable, but his eyes belied his words. His theory made no sense if you knew anything about tracking dogs — they were acting as if the trail ended at the barn.

"I'd like you to return the way you came, please. There's no hunting on my property."

Though I wasn't standing there to hear him say it, I can hear the tone of my father's voice in my head. This was a man who watched a mysterious blood cancer eat away his wife from within, a man who cried out all the emotions a person has until he was nothing but a cold, mechanical dead zone of a human being. Arguing with my father when he spoke from this place was like arguing with a stop sign — all you got back was a flat, implacable notice that you were

233

not going to get to do what you wanted to do.

McHenry whistled at his dogs and they stared at him in disbelief.

My dad allowed him to pass to grab his dogs, which was a big mistake because it gave McHenry a view of the backyard. There was no misidentifying the spoor in the grass — his dogs couldn't have made that big of a pile, even if it were a group effort. McHenry turned eyes astonished and accusing on my father, who merely nodded at him.

"Call your dogs," my dad said again.

The canines were astounded they were being asked to give up the hunt and left the yard with great reluctance. McHenry's eyes were hot when he gave my father a parting stare. He didn't understand what was going on, but he knew he'd been made a fool of and he didn't like it. With a sense of misgiving my father watched him and the dogs descend the trail.

Emory and I had lunch about the same time that day. For Emory, it consisted of my father wrestling a big metal container filled with birdseed out into the yard once he was satisfied that McHenry wasn't coming back. The birdseed was an extravagance purchased when my mother first fell ill and no

234

gift or concession seemed profligate. She wanted to feed the birds, so my father put up two giant bird feeders, bird condominiums my mother called them, and dumped fifty-pound sacks of seed into a new trash container until the thing was brimming. I loved to plunge my hands into the seeds, most of which were hard and yellow. It felt the way I imagined beach sand might feel at the ocean. I was given a scoop and it was my job to facilitate my mother's project by keeping the feeders full.

Ironically, our neighbor Mrs. Beck told my mother she'd read that bird feeders often attract hungry bears, which dampened my mother's enthusiasm for the whole thing. And then my mother got sicker still, and the bird-feeding project went the way of her tomato plants.

After my dad lugged the big can of seed from the garage out into the backyard, he flung open the side door of the pole barn. He also ran the hose into a three-gallon bucket and let it trickle so Emory would have a steady water supply. My dad was back in the house when Emory came out and stuck his snout in the birdseed.

For me, lunch was whatever they called the meat loaf that day.

It was with a far higher degree of confidence that I approached Beth's table. She was still surrounded by her avian flunkies, but I'd learned to ignore them and just concentrate on the clear green eyes across the table from me. The soaring joy I felt when I saw her watching me approach was scarcely containable, and some of it broke out into a face-splitting grin.

"Hi!" I greeted her with burbling enthusiasm.

Beth's friends all glanced at her, waiting for her response to trigger their own. Her return expression was pretty much cold glare with a hint of anger mixed in, and I felt my grin fall off my face and plummet as if a hole had opened in the floor and swallowed it. She wasn't glad to see me — somehow, in the space of just a single day, I'd managed to lose her.

Naturally I took the coward's way out and pretended not to notice her attitude. "How's lunch?" I asked inanely. "Bring any of your mom's cookies?" Beth's friends all glanced at each other, exchanging huge volumes of information with their flitting eyes. Beth was still watching me.

"You were in a *fight* yesterday?" she demanded in her always-direct fashion.

"Uh, well . . ." I tried to decide which would put me in a better light. Should I claim to be a tough guy, a regular brawler for whom a battle of fists was just part of my life? Or should I climb on the peace train, explain that it had really been less a boxing match than some sort of misunderstanding?

Beth, I decided, would want to be with a real man. I sighed. "Yeah, Dan Alderton." I shrugged. Should I claim to have won? I didn't lose, but that didn't feel like the same thing.

"I can't believe it," Beth said. "Is that what you *do?*"

Maybe I should have gone for the peace train thing. "What do you mean?"

"You're like, the guys who meet at the park after school for fistfights?"

The unfairness of this question froze my reply in my throat.

"When were you going to tell me?" she demanded.

I didn't know what I was supposed to tell her or when I was supposed to tell it. I didn't understand why she was angry and just wanted to go back to yesterday when it was apparent we were going to get married someday.

A signal went through the girls and they all stood up at the same time, like a gaggle of geese hearing a noise and raising their heads simultaneously. Beth's eyes were flashing at me, but there was something else going on, some sort of uncertainty in those normally self-assured eyes. Even as the girls took flight, I had the sense that something about the drama we'd just played out had struck her wrong, like a badly played note in a song.

Regardless, it was junior high and so the girls were compelled by the rules of society to go stomping off with their noses in the air as if I'd just leveled some huge insult to all of femininity. Beth gave me a glance over her shoulder and I wanted to shout, *What? What's going on?* to her because honestly, I just didn't get it.

This wasn't like losing Kay — this *hurt.*

I was thoroughly miserable as I headed to the boys' room, and as soon as I entered I knew I had made a mistake. Several of the ninth graders who enjoyed laughing at me over the stall wall were hanging out by the sinks, carrying on a loose, sarcastic conversation. I involuntarily paused when I saw them, clearly telegraphing my cowardice.

I could, I decided, live with a little biological urgency for a couple of hours. I just didn't have it in me to put up with the humiliation, that day. I started to back up.

Then a boy separated himself from the

238

pack. It was Tim Humphrey. "It's okay, Charlie; come on in. We're not doing anything."

It would have killed me to suppose that Tim knew about the ninth graders laughing at me, but his comment seemed to suggest he thought my hesitation was because I thought they were smoking or something and didn't want to get caught up in a dragnet. I hurried past them and into the stall, blissfully left alone to do my business while the boys' room grew quieter with each departing student.

Finally, it sounded like I was completely alone. I flushed and exited and started a bit in surprise: Tim Humphrey was standing against the sinks, his arms crossed, looking like he'd been waiting for me.

"Hi, Charlie," he said, as if he hadn't known I was in there.

"Hi, Tim."

I washed my hands. Tim watched me. I dried my hands. Tim watched me. I was starting to get a little nervous.

"Hey. About Dan Alderton."

I froze, wary.

"You know." Tim's face became a little flushed. "Yesterday. What he said."

"Yeah," I answered.

"Don't worry about him." Tim leaned

239

forward, lowering his voice: "He's a Kotex."

I blinked at this. When we were all in grade school, "Kotex" was pretty much the worse insult one boy could hurl at another, mainly because we weren't quite sure what a Kotex even *was.* Tim was grinning at me, and I grinned back. For him to employ such an anachronistic expression now was somehow comforting, even reassuring. *Hey,* he seemed to be saying, *we've all been friends for years, remember? Remember when we were all the same size? When there wasn't all this pressure; when you hung out with your classmates and ate lunch at an assigned table and nobody staged fights after school?*

"Yeah, he is," I said. "A real Kotex."

When I got home after school it had stopped raining. My dad told me about McHenry's dogs, and, I'm sorry to say, the story upset me so much I missed the underlying implication, which was that, when it really mattered, my dad had stood up for Emory and me. "I don't know what's going to happen now, Charlie. But to have a man like McHenry as an enemy — we don't want that," he concluded.

"Where's Emory?" I asked impatiently. When my dad nodded in the direction of the creek I took off at a run but halted when he called me. "Charlie!"

240

I looked back at him.

His mouth worked as he struggled to come up with something to say to me to express what he was feeling, but that particular ability had long ago atrophied from disuse. Eventually all he could come up with was, "Stay close to home."

I found Emory at one end of the flat floodplain that lay upstream from our house, a wide section of sandy soil that was inundated whenever melting snow and spring rains combined. Junk tended to wash up there, and Emory was investigating an old burn barrel that was lying on its side when I approached.

"Nothing to eat in there," I said.

The bear looked at me as if I'd insulted him, then turned his back on me and strolled to the edge of the field.

"We should stick around in case of the dogs!" I called to him.

The bear dug his paw in among some bushes, trying to get at something, and when it rolled out I saw what it was: a basketball, dark with mud and a little deflated.

Basketball. Was there a sport less suited for me? I was one of the shortest boys in my grade. My hands were small, so small that the surface of the ball felt almost flat against my palm. When I sank a basket it was pretty much a random event, and any feeble attempt at a layup usually wound up with me driving my nose into somebody's armpit.

"That's nothing. Come on; let's go," I said.

Emory raised his paw and gave the ball a smack and it skittered past me, rolling to rest about twenty yards ahead. I started to walk toward it and flinched when I heard the bear coming fast. He ran to the ball and stopped, turning to look at me.

"What?" I said.

He hit the ball again and it bounced right up to my feet. I looked at it, then looked at him. He tensed, his shoulders tightening.

I kicked the basketball toward the far end of the field and Emory took off after it in a gallop. I ran, but he ran faster and got to it first and batted at it with one paw and then another. I sort of stuck my leg out, but he easily evaded me. As he rolled the ball back toward the rusty mouth of the barrel I gave chase, laughing out loud when he slapped the basketball inside like a hockey player scoring a goal.

"Okay, okay," I said. I dug the ball out, Emory watching expectantly. "Well, you have to back up," I told him, gesturing.

Emory swung around and trotted about twenty yards away, then turned to watch.

"Here we go," I said.

I tried to keep the ball close like a soccer player, but Emory snagged it easily from me and we both dashed back to the barrel for him to score another goal. "That's two," I told him. I also told him it was three, and four, and five, but by the time I got to ten Emory was panting like a dog and I thought he was slowing down on me. I poured on the speed and he only halfheartedly gave chase and I didn't think he was letting me; I really was tiring him out.

I was outrunning a grizzly bear!

I kicked the ball into the dead bushes at the far end of the field. "One for me!" I hooted.

I backed up and Emory put his paw on the ball. He was obviously resting.

"Well, come on. Are you worried you'll get mud on your party dress if you run too hard?" I asked him.

Emory lowered his head and slapped the ball. I got to it before he did and turned it with my foot and when I did he crashed into me and it was like being hit by a train. I went down, hard, my air gone. I clutched my stomach in pain, trying to suck in some wind.

Emory's enormous face filled my vision. I opened my mouth, but I couldn't say anything. I felt his paw lightly touch my shoulder. I looked into his eyes and could swear they were filled with concern.

"I'm okay," I finally managed to wheeze. I got on my hands and knees, doing an inventory of my bones. Nothing felt broken.

And then, in a moment I will remember for the rest of my life, Emory pulled me to him, hugging me gently for just a moment before releasing me.

Emory was in the pole barn later that evening, snoozing off the effects of our impromptu soccer match and the frozen hamburger pie I'd given him, when my father and I looked up at the sound of a truck coming down our driveway. I stood from the table and looked out the window and turned to my dad with panic in my eyes.

Written on the truck were the words "Idaho Fish and Game."

CHAPTER
TWENTY

The man who got out of the Fish and Game truck was Herman Hessler. He wore a gray uniform with green patches on it and had a hat that he seemed to always be carrying instead of wearing on his head. His blond hair was thin and wispy, tucked behind his ears. It was Mr. Hessler's job to make sure McHenry didn't shoot things out of season, an official function that, as I've said, mostly consisted of Mr. Hessler looking the other way.

"Hey there, George. Hi, Charlie."

I raised my hand a bit uncertainly, since I had never before directly met the man and therefore didn't know exactly how I should address him. My heart was pounding, though, and I was eyeing the side door of the pole barn, silently begging Emory to stay in there.

They stood and talked about various things: How many fish there were in the river, how many deer there were in the woods. What kind of winter we were in for. It was so pointless it made me itch.

Finally Mr. Hessler made of show of taking a long pause, and I knew he was ready to get to it.

"The thing is, George, we had an awful strange call from Katie Alderton up the road there."

My dad waited. Mr. Hessler cleared his throat. "Her boy. You know Danny. He said you all have a tame bear living in your pole barn, there." Mr. Hessler nodded at the pole barn. "Or maybe a cub; I thought it could be, you know, separated from its mother. They're mighty cute fellas when they're little. Docile."

"They are that," my father agreed.

"I thought . . . tell you the truth, I don't know what I thought, but then I heard from Jules McHenry. He owns the ranch up there on Road Six-fifty-five."

"I know him."

"I know you do; he said his dogs tracked a bear onto your property."

"There's no hunting on my property," my dad replied calmly.

"Yeah, well, he said you said that, too." Mr. Hessler increased the spin of the hat he

246

was tossing and I stared at it as if hypnotized.

"He did say his dogs were pretty interested in your pole barn."

"I've got some food in there," my dad offered.

"Well, his dogs . . . Look, George, I have to ask. Have you got yourself either a bear cub or a full-grown black bear in your pole barn right now?"

I sucked in my breath. Ever the truth splitter, ever in charge of parsing words, I saw a clear way out. We had neither a cub nor a full-grown blackie in our pole barn, and that was a fact. My dad could stay clean with the law.

But he surprised me. He scratched at his chin. "I guess I don't feel like answering that question, Herman."

I'm not sure that any one of the three of us expected him to say that, so we all sort of stood there a minute, pondering what it could mean.

Even back in the 1970s, northern Idaho had become something of a refuge for people who felt oppressed by the government and wanted to get to a place where nobody official and nothing bureaucratic ever had opportunity to bother them. So we probably weren't the first people to be obstinate in the face of an official Fish and Game inquiry, but still Mr. Hessler seemed disappointed. Probably what he was thinking was that if my dad had just said that he didn't have a bear Mr. Hesslcr could go back to his office and file a report and be done with it, but with this particular answer there was no real obvious course of action.

For what seemed like a full minute, nobody spoke. Then Mr. Hessler seemed to come to a decision. He stopped twirling his hat and placed it on his head.

"Why don't I just have a look, then," he said.

There was a long silence. Mr. Hessler didn't move to go to the barn and didn't take his eyes off my father. I had the sense that Mr. Hessler needed to put in his report that he'd asked to look into the barn, but that he already knew what my father was going to say.

"Rather you didn't."

He nodded, tossing his hat. "Well, that's that, then."

We all stood around for a minute or so. Finally Mr. Hessler cleared his throat. "Well, I was sent out to see if there was any evidence you had a bear in your barn, and I don't see any evidence and I didn't hear any, neither, so I guess that's what I'll report. No evidence." He put his hat on his head. "I'll ring up Katie and let her know that her son was probably just making it up."

"Good to see you, Herman," my father said evenly.

The Fish and Game agent opened his driver's door but didn't immediately get inside. He looked over at the two of us. "If you did have a bear in there, George, that could make a real mess for both of us."

We watched him back out of our driveway and head down the road. I waved and he waved back.

As far as I was concerned, things had turned out just fine. Dan had ratted us out to the Fish and Game, but nothing came of it. Now Emory was protected from Jules McHenry and I was no longer hiding his existence from my father. From my naïve perspective, it seemed that we had not only avoided getting in trouble but that the three of us — me, my father, and Emory — would be starting a new life together.

My dad's gaze, as his eyes met mine, was far more troubled. I turned away, a little irritated. The bear was fine. Dad needed to just let things *be*.

The next morning Coach Briggs thought it would be a wonderful day to run cross-country again. I guess he never bothered to check out what had happened during the recent rains to the stream at the far end of the track, but it had swollen from a spry little trickle we could bound across to a five-foot-wide mass of muddy water with slick, treacherous banks. Barreling down the slope, the three of us in the lead — Tim and Mike and I — fell in the stream, a tangled trio, and everyone who tried to stop on the slippery bank did the same thing.

Tim started laughing and the rest of us quickly joined in, having a great time hurling muck at each other.

The last boy to make it to the slope was a lumbering lad named Tank, who played offensive line in football and was pretty good at getting in the way of the pass rush but who had no accelerator and no brakes. He came crashing into us like a bowling ball taking out pins. Most of us went back into the water with him, and then we all brawled, throwing mud and laughing hysterically.

All of a sudden we heard a whistle, stabbing out shrilly from back up at the school.

"Uh-oh," Mike muttered.

Coach Briggs stood up there by the tennis courts, his hands on his hips, his whistle in his mouth like a baby's pacifier. He didn't look happy.

The coach marched us to the side of the building and told us to stand there in a row and shut up. When he picked up the hose, a murmur of concern rose from us. "Quiet!" he thundered.

The hose had a gunlike nozzle, and when Coach Briggs aimed the stream at skinny Ned the poor guy folded as if hit by bullets. One at a time the coach's hose sought us out, and I don't know which was worse: getting hit with it or anticipating how awful it was going to be. As the cleaner water flooded our clothing it rinsed out the dirt and our skinny bodies grew visible under the filmy white cotton: it was like being naked out there, our buttocks plain for all the world to see. Naturally, the girls' gym class picked that moment to go trotting past, so we were treated to the further humiliation of having them see us in such a state.

Inside, I couldn't feel my fingers as I peeled off my T-shirt, which was like pulling the skin off a raw chicken.

Nothing has ever felt so good as the warm embrace of that shower. I was vibrating with life.

I was still ebullient by lunch, so charged up that when I saw Tim Humphrey settling in across from Joy Ebert I went to their table as if I had an invitation.

"Hey, Tim," I sang out, setting my tray down. I launched myself onto the bench seat and even gave Joy a grin. "Hi, Joy."

"Hi, Charlie," she said, and it sounded exactly like all she was doing was saying hi and not, *What in the world is someone like you doing at this table? Don't you know I'm the most beautiful girl in the entire eighth grade?*

I saw Dan Alderton across the room but didn't acknowledge him. Nor, it appeared, did anybody else. His words had turned him into a person to be shunned, an outcast. A Kotex.

Tim related the story of what happened in gym class, making it sound like he and Mike and I were the star athletes of the school. I laughed along with Joy at Tim's descriptions of the facial expressions of the runners as they slid down the hill and into the water. I could see myself going to parties with Tim and Joy and hanging out with them all through high school.

I was shocked and even embarrassed when I felt a vibration and turned and saw Beth sitting on the bench next to me. Tim had finished his story and most of the people at the table were involved in more private conversations, but I was conscious of Joy giving the two of us a coolly speculative assessment. Beth was a seventh grader and as such really had no business being there, but wasn't that just like her? I didn't know if she was brave or confident or just stupid.

No, I knew she wasn't stupid.

"Charlie," she said. She was giving me an odd look, like there was something she couldn't figure out.

"Hi, Beth," I replied weakly. I'd gone from swaggering self-confidence to insecurity in a matter of mere moments.

"Can we talk? Maybe we could go out into the courtyard; it's nice outside."

I nodded numbly, dropping off my tray before following her out to the small treed courtyard in the center of the school. She was right: if you weren't soaking wet and being sliced to ribbons by a garden hose, it was nice outside.

Beth hopped up to sit on a low brick wall. It was funny how much that charmed me; it was just a little jump, her knees together as she scooted her fanny back a bit, but it made me grin with pleasure.

"What is it?" she asked. "Why are you smiling?"

"I don't know." *Because you're you*, I thought I would say, if I had the nerve to talk like that. *You're just so* you.

"You're not on drugs, are you?" she asked abruptly. The question was so unexpected it sort of slapped me into a state of guilt, as if I *were* on drugs.

"No," I protested.

"You don't take drugs, do you?"

"No."

"Good. I don't like that. It's stupid. Also smoking. Smoking's almost worse."

"No smoking," I agreed contractually.

Her green eyes probed my face. How someone could have eyes so clear and clean I had no idea, but I just wanted to sit and stare at them. "I heard what Dan said," she finally told me. "About your mom, I mean."

"Oh."

Sympathy softly warmed her gaze. "I guess I understand why you felt you had to fight him. When I heard about it, I wanted to hit him myself."

"Yeah, well . . . we didn't actually fight, you know."

She frowned. "Really? I heard there was a fight. That he said . . . what he said, and then the two of you fought."

I felt like I was in the position of having to explain something really inane, how boys were making appointments to punch each other with the same odd formality that we'd use to ask a girl out on a date. Worse, what

Dan said actually was tangential to the physical fight, which in truth had been neither a fight nor physical. So I took refuge in the universal body language of teenage boys and just gave her a silent shrug.

She pursed her lips. "I wish you'd explained this before. I feel like I was unfair to you. Why didn't you say anything?"

I stuck with the shrugging; it seemed to be working for me.

"Charlie." She sighed. "You're so hard to understand, sometimes."

I liked the sound of it: *Charlie Hall. Hard to understand. Mysterious. Sexy.*

Okay, *sexy* was probably going a little overboard. But I was willing to bet I was the only boy she'd ever met who had made friends with a grizzly bear.

"Why do you look so proud of yourself all of a sudden?" she asked. "Oh, I get it. Charlie Hall, man of mystery."

I could not believe how easily she read my mind.

"So what does that make me, in this equation?"

I had no answer to that. I was back to feeling like an idiot.

The bell spoke up then, shrilly announcing an end to lunch, and from back inside there was immediately the sound of students rushing the dishwasher station with their plastic trays and scuffing their way out of the lunchroom.

Beth put her hands on either side of her knees to help herself off the wall and I, drawing inspiration from some movie I'd seen sometime, put my arms out and sort of awkwardly placed my hands in her armpits to assist her. It was probably one of the dumbest things I've ever done, but when Beth dropped lightly to her feet I was standing there holding her as if about to pull her into a kiss. Her eyes sparkled at me.

"Oh *my,*" she said, laughing.

I carried that laughter with me the rest of the day; it rang in my ears like the tinkle of a small bell.

That night at dinner my father stopped his fork on its way to his mouth and blinked at me.

"What is it, Charlie?" he asked me.

"What?"

"Why are you grinning like that?"

I hadn't realized I was grinning, but I knew why. I was still hearing Beth's voice in my head.

Oh *my.*

My dad was pretty fidgety during the meal. "Charlie . . . ," he said at one point.

"Yeah?"

He looked out the window toward the pole barn. "We need to talk soon."

And though I'd spent the past year craving conversation with my father, what I felt at that moment was only a sense of relief that he'd grown so unaccustomed to talking to me he could only feint at it. I didn't *want* to talk. Emory was safe and Beth had forgiven me. My world was coming together perfectly, without analysis or commentary, and I didn't want to jinx it.

The rain started up again. I was doing dishes when I saw a large black shadow lumber across the yard: Emory was coming in out of the storm. Across the creek, garlands of white steamlike fog rose in stark contrast to the dark evergreen trees — it looked like we were witnessing the birth of clouds. Emory seemed to regard the phenomenon with real appreciation for a few minutes before he turned and walked through the side door of the pole barn.

I felt truly happy.

Later that evening I fed Emory a nice frozen pot roast, just like a normal boy giving his dog a dinner, except that nobody had a dog that big. I didn't imagine my father would be thrilled to see the pot roast go, either, but what was important was that Emory liked it and seemed to want to live with us in our pole barn now.

I crawled into bed when my dad told me to, but I wouldn't have bet on my ability to sleep — my brain was just buzzing with everything that was happening. But almost as soon as I turned off the lights I winked out. The fatigue that had settled into my bones from the day's physical toils had a marvelous, narcotic feeling to it.

A sharp crack of thunder broke me out of my sleep an hour or so later. The wind had kicked up and the rain was hitting the windows so loud it could have been popcorn popping in a metal pan. I drowsily lay in bed and watched the white light flare on my ceiling, not bothering to count the seconds for the thunder, though I could tell it was getting closer.

Then one of the strobes of white light caused me to sit upright in bed. Lightning flickered or burst, but it did not, not ever, trace a quick path across my ceiling in a tight white ball like a searchlight probing for enemy aircraft. Something entirely different had just happened.

I sat there holding my breath, waiting for the dancing ball of light to appear on my ceiling a second time, but there was no repeat. I slid out of bed and silently padded down the hallway and into the living room.

I felt more than saw my way across the floor and peered out the back window. There was nothing to see. I turned and went to the kitchen and looked out the side window over the sink, and that's when I saw three beams of light, man high, bobbing along as a trio of flashlights ran across the yard to the pole barn.

McHenry.

CHAPTER
TWENTY-ONE

I shivered then, but I wasn't cold. I knew I should do something but wasn't sure what. I leaned forward and peered through the wet glass, watching as the flashlights converged on the side door of the pole barn. Their beams bounced off the wet metal sides of the barn and reflected back on the people wielding them, and I saw I was wrong. It wasn't McHenry.

Dan Alderton, and his buddies Jerry and Gregg.

A flash of lightning illuminated them and I could see by their huddled postures that they were cold and terrified. They were four feet from the door and creeping toward it at what appeared to be about an inch an hour. Dan had his palm out to twist the knob, but at the rate he was going he wasn't going to have it in his hand until sunrise.

Still unsure what I should do, I just watched. The flashlights were all aimed at the square of new glass in the upper half of the door, and from where I stood I could see that the combined beams were illuminating the other side of the pole barn, a blank, newly painted white wall. If they wanted to see Emory, they'd have to open that door, and it didn't look to me as if they had the nerve.

I found myself smirking a little. I had never seen three such petrified people in my whole life. The thunderstorm, the rain, the wind in the trees, and their flashlights all combined to give them the spooks — and it couldn't help that they were convinced that on the other side of the door was a creature who could catch and eat all three of them.

Finally Dan straightened, overcoming his fear. He took a bold step forward, and the other boys joined him. Okay, he could reach the knob now, if he wanted. They kept their flashlights aimed at the window.

Bang! A flash of lightning came with a loud crack of thunder and as it did Emory suddenly appeared in the window, his huge face filling the space, his lips pulled back in a terrible snarl.

Dan dropped his flashlight, Gregg fell down, and even with all the rain I could hear the boys yelling as they backed away from that door as fast as humanly possible.

Their torches swinging in the night, they took off in a dead run, scampering past where I stood with looks of abject terror on their faces.

After a minute or so my dad came into the kitchen to ask me why I was standing at the sink and laughing. I told him and he smiled at my description, but then he stood behind me and stared at Dan's flashlight lying on the ground, its rays vanishing into the night, drops of rain flaring briefly as they fell through the beam.

"This could be big trouble, Charlie," he told me.

I didn't really see how, though, and fell asleep still smiling over how Dan and his buddies collapsed in dead terror in the rain. What could we have to fear from *them?*

We'd been back to school for more than a month now, and I guess the teachers found the whole experience so demoralizing they needed a day to themselves, so we had "in-service." I didn't care what it meant; for me it just meant "Sleep In Friday." So I was surprised when I felt my father's hand shaking my foot.

"I don't have school today," I mumbled at him, fighting desperately to stay asleep.

"I know. I took the day off work."

I pulled the covers off my eyes and peered

blearily at him. He was already dressed. My senses came alive one by one and I could hear rain falling on the roof and bacon sizzling in the kitchen. He gazed at me to make sure I was not going to wink back out on him and then turned and left the room.

After breakfast he told me we needed to go into town. We dashed out in the rain and jumped into the Jeep. I buckled in and gave him a questioning look.

"We need to get some food for your bear. I figure dog food'll work if we get the kind that has some real meat in it."

"Okay." I liked the sound of it. *Your bear.*

"Charlie." My dad scratched his chin. I waited for him, the wipers squeaking a little as they rattled back and forth.

"I don't know what this is, Charlie. I can't explain about the bear. I guess he could be tame. Raised by, I don't know. A circus?" He glanced at me, then stared back out at the road. "But that doesn't account for what was written on the wall. It said he was a private in the Civil War. That he got shot, or wounded somehow, and then, and then he *died*." My father's eyes were fierce when they flickered at me again. "And now he's back. From the dead."

Cool. That's what I thought and that's almost what I said, but my father's expres-

263

sion was so grim I strangled the word in my mouth.

"With a message," I reminded him.

He sighed and was silent for more than a minute. "Yes. Someone is trying to get us to believe that a bear wrote those words, that he is a Civil War soldier who has been reincarnated as a grizzly bear and has a message for us, or you, or somebody. A message from . . ." He frowned, not liking where his thoughts were taking him.

We pulled into the grocery store parking lot and stopped. Dad twisted in the seat and looked at me. "But Charlie, someone else had to have painted those words on the wall."

"How?" It seemed ridiculous; who would do such a thing?

"We've never locked the pole barn. Anyone could just waltz right in if they felt like it."

"His footprints were all over in the paint, Dad."

He cocked his head at me. "You're saying that if someone went into the pole barn, he did so while the bear was inside. A full-grown grizzly bear."

Contrary to my dread expectations, I loved that we were having this conversation, I suddenly realized. I loved that I had Dad's

264

full attention and that we were working the problem out *together.* To be truthful, I'd actually just meant that the presence of bear tracks on the cement floor implied, to me, that Emory had been there when the paint can was opened, but I immediately saw Dad's point. You'd have to be more than a little crazy to go into a pole barn with a live, trapped grizzly bear waiting for you inside.

"But, Charlie, a bear can't hold a paint-brush. Those letters weren't painted with paws; they're too neat."

"Okay."

"What we're probably dealing with here, the only thing that makes sense, is that the bear is owned by someone, his trainer, and his trainer wrote the words. His trainer wouldn't be afraid to go inside the pole barn." My dad was looking inward, nodding slightly, testing the theory and finding that it worked for him. "That's it. There just isn't any other explanation. It's a hoax, and not a funny one. I catch the guy I'm going to have him prosecuted for trespassing and vandalism."

There was still a little doubt in his mind, though; I could see it in his eyes. "We haven't seen anybody around," I objected. I didn't like the idea that Emory belonged to some bear trainer; I wanted him to belong

265

to *me.*

The difference between my dad and me was that to him, the writing on the wall was the most important and perplexing of all of the developments, whereas to me, the point was that I had the coolest pet ever. I even was beginning to regret I'd ever shown my dad the Polaroid — those words on the wall felt like they were going to be nothing but trouble. I decided it was critical I never mention what I had witnessed in person, which was Emory etching his name into the riverbank with his paw, something else his "trainer" could have taught him to do, I supposed. "If he did have a trainer, it's like he's abandoned his bear, right? He couldn't turn up and claim him now."

My dad picked up on my tone and gave me a direct look. "There's something else. Whether Emory's tame or not, he's foraging like any grizzly would this time of year. It won't be long before he needs to return to the mountains to hibernate."

"No," I protested.

"Yes, Charlie. That's what they do."

"Why can't he hibernate in the pole barn?"

"That's not what he needs. He needs a burrow and he'll be leaving soon to find one. All we can do is fatten him up."

I turned away from my dad and faced the grocery store. I did not like this conversation anymore.

"I'm just telling you the truth, so you'll be ready. You need to hear this."

The anger that flowed through me then was cold and ugly. *I needed to hear it. I needed to be ready.* But when my mom was sick, neither one of them told me the truth. Neither one of them said she was dying, that she would one day slip into a coma and die with my father pressing his face into her blankets and making sounds as if he was breaking apart. No, they lied to me; they hid it from me; they said she was going to be okay. They let me live in denial until my father's howls of anguish rang down the hospital corridor and I rushed in from the room where some well-meaning adults had kept me playing inane card games, shielding me from the truth even with the final seconds ticking off the clock. The shock of it all, the betrayal, the deceit, blindsided me when I saw her skeletal body motionless under those thin blankets and witnessed my father's explosive, *selfish* grief. Never a thought for what was happening to me; that I had lost my mom. As he grieved, he grieved alone, shutting me out.

I jumped out of the Jeep and slammed the

door in fury and ran to the grocery store, my feet making wet slapping noises on the pavement. The doors slid open and admitted me with a calm, oiled ease, not at all intimidated by my anger.

Naturally my father misinterpreted my expression and thought I was just petulant because I couldn't keep the bear. He grabbed a cart and followed me down to the dog food aisle and did what he always did when the emotions ran high between us: he removed himself from the equation, turning away, making himself busy by carefully reading the ingredients on the dog food bag.

"Meat by-products," he muttered. Eventually he heaved several twenty-five-pound bags of the most expensive brand into the cart and then added stuff we needed, like milk and eggs.

When my mother grocery-shopped she kept me by her side and we snaked up and down the aisles together and I would be bored out of my mind. My dad, though, sent me on missions. "Bacon," he'd say, and I'd fly off like a missile for bacon.

What I would give, though, for one more shopping trip with my mom. One more earnest discussion about how I needed to eat something besides sugar pops with sugar

268

on them. One more argument about why it was fair that she buy a square of dark, bitter chocolate for herself for when she "needed it" but that I didn't "need" a bag of Mars bars.

The grocery store looked exactly the same as when my mom was alive. Sometimes I resented that things could remain untouched by her death, hated that the walls didn't crumble and fall in the outside world to match what was happening to me inside. And sometimes I was grateful for the gift of being able to stand and gaze at something so unchanged it was easy to believe my mother was just around the corner, that if I just stood there she would walk up to me, smiling.

When we got to the checkout line, Yvonne was manning the cash register. She touched her hair when she saw us approach and gave my father a big grin. "There you are, stranger," she said. "I haven't heard from you in a while."

Good, I thought to myself.

My dad sort of shrugged and looked uncomfortable. Yvonne started ringing up our purchases, giving my dad smiling glances. Then her eyes suddenly widened and she gave my father a surprised look. "Did you get a dog?"

CHAPTER TWENTY-TWO

My dad and I were exchanging horrified expressions, Yvonne's question dangling in the air between us. We couldn't have looked more guilty if we'd been caught sticking up a bank.

"Thought I would someday," my father stammered, which sounded insane even to my ears.

Yvonne cocked her head at him. "So you're buying the dog food . . . ," she said.

"Yeah," my dad replied, nodding. Didn't everyone run out and buy a hundred pounds of dog food when they were *thinking* about buying a dog?

"It's for a friend," I said, master of the truthful untruth. My father gave me a grateful look.

"Right. A friend named Emory," my dad responded.

Yvonne shrugged. Then it seemed to occur to her that she should be showing me some fake affection so my dad would want to marry her. She beamed at me. "Charlie, what is your favorite dinner?"

I thought about it. "Steak," I answered, keeping my answer short in case there was some sort of trick lying in wait behind the question.

"And how about you, George?"

My dad blinked. I could tell that he, too, suspected there was some reason for this interrogation.

"I guess steak is as good an answer as any I could come up with," he agreed carefully.

"You're not buying any steak today, though," Yvonne pointed out. *That's right, Yvonne; you caught us! You are so smart!*

"Yeah, well . . ." My dad shrugged.

"Well, I have an idea," Yvonne said. I felt intimations of doom. I did not want Yvonne having *ideas.* "How about I get us a couple of steaks and bring them over tonight.

"I'll make a salad and my famous baked beans," she continued.

I couldn't imagine how dumb you had to be to believe you somehow had attained celebrity status for opening a can of beans. As far as I knew, Yvonne was famous for one thing, and that was ringing up the purchases at the grocery store.

"Well," my dad said.

Yvonne was smiling at him and I knew we were sunk.

"Okay, that would be great," he said.

"I'll bring beer," Yvonne said. "The whole meal's on me."

"No, you should let me pay for something," my dad protested. But Yvonne was insistent. This way, I knew, we'd be in her debt forever. My dad would have to buy her an engagement ring because he owed her for the beer.

Yvonne was as good as her threat, showing up with a couple of bags of groceries and wearing a medium-length skirt with a big belt buckle. If Yvonne fell in the water with that thing on, the buckle would drag her to the bottom and I would not employ a single one of my junior-lifesaving skills to save her, not even if Kay were there watching.

Earlier, when we first got home, Emory had, to my father's astonishment, eaten nearly half a bag of dog food in one meal. Then he lumbered off into the woods, which made me happy, since as far as I was concerned the novelty of cleaning up bear pies in the yard was long over. I made a mental note, though, to keep the back door open and listen for dogs.

Yvonne hummed around in the kitchen,

opening cupboards, not asking me anything. I was in charge of peeling potatoes to mash. I watched her and hated her for the silent judgment I saw in the way she explored my mother's system, feeling her think that oh no, she'd never put the spatulas *here,* and why in the world would the cheese grater be over *there?* In the end, though, she surveyed the room, the whole house, with a satisfied contentment, as if the place already belonged to her.

When she made her celebrity beans, she opened the cans, poured them into a baking dish, and put brown sugar and some ketchup on top before sliding them into the oven. There, I knew how she did it; so I guess I was famous now, too.

Her presence made me sullenly angry at my dad, so I wasn't talking to him, and I didn't want to talk to Yvonne, so I concentrated on my potato peeling as if I found the whole exercise to be more challenging than I could manage. If Yvonne had been a real cook, I reflected, she'd have made potato salad like my mom. That was famous. Everyone in town knew about Laura Hall's delicious potato salad, which was chockfull of mysterious secret ingredients and not ketchup.

Yvonne was stooped down, looking on a

lower shelf for something or maybe just snooping, when I looked through the window over the sink and saw, to my horror, Emory come plodding into the yard. The smoke from my father's efforts was wafting around and Emory had his nose up, tantalized. My father couldn't see the bear because the grill was on the back deck.

Yvonne stood up.

"Miss Mandeville!" I blurted, so sharply she whirled, blinking, emitting a quick, "Oh!"

"You, uh . . . this is so nice of you to cook dinner," I babbled.

She stared at me as if unsure she had heard me correctly. Then she smiled. The darn bear was still completely visible in the yard and if she turned back around our secret would be out. "Why, thank you, Charlie."

"Would you like to see my room?" I asked desperately.

Her grin was even wider. "Sure, that would be nice."

I shocked both of us by reaching out for her hand. I just couldn't take the chance that she would turn back to the sink, not even for a moment.

I walked her into my room and acted like I was doing a museum tour, showing her my model airplanes, my junior-lifesaving certificate, and everything else I could think of. I was running out of ideas and was practically ready to show her my underwear drawer when my father suddenly appeared in the doorway. He looked a little frantic.

"Hi!" he said loudly.

Yvonne smiled at him and touched her hair. "Charlie was just showing me his room," she told him.

"So you've been back here what, several minutes?"

"Yes, probably four or five minutes," I said.

Yvonne looked back and forth between us, a little puzzled by the conversation.

"So, okay, then," my dad said.

"We were just in the kitchen and I was looking out the window over the sink," I told my father, "and then I asked Miss Mandeville if she wanted to see my room."

"Ah." My dad nodded. "Steaks are done. I put them in the kitchen."

"I'd better get the beans out of the oven," Yvonne said. "Everything else is ready."

I gave my dad an intent look, which he interpreted correctly. "I put everything away in the pole barn that needed to go in there," he said to me.

The whole thing rattled me so much that

275

when I set the table I didn't think to put out a place for Yvonne. At least, that's what I assume my father thought. Yvonne didn't remark on it, even though it was pretty rude. What she did, instead, was grab her own plate and silverware and settle down into Mom's seat at the table. When I saw this I gave my dad a stare that was full of hot accusation, and he pursed his lips uncomfortably.

"Yvonne," my dad said, then stopped because he wasn't sure what he wanted to say.

Yvonne blinked at him, smiling, and then the smile faltered when she saw the expression on his face. Suddenly her eyes widened. "Oh!" she said.

She moved her place over and some of the tension went out of us.

After the steaks I did the dishes in silence while Yvonne and my dad watched television. Yvonne laughed out loud at *Sanford and Son,* which offended me for some reason. My mom never laughed at the television; she would just smile when something struck her as clever. It seemed a lot more classy than the guffaws Yvonne was blowing out like gusts of cigarette smoke. When something struck her as particularly hilarious she dropped her head on my dad's shoulder as if she were having some sort of sudden neck dysfunction.

I wanted to go see Emory after I did the dishes, but instead I sat at the table to do my homework. I didn't want to leave the two of them in the living room together.

Yvonne and my father watched *The Rockford Files* and then *Police Woman* and then sat and talked. My dad caught me yawning and rubbing my eyes.

"Off to bed, Charlie," he said.

"Good night, Charlie," Yvonne said before my dad barely had the words out. She gave me her big grin because we were buddies now. I gave them a surly look but didn't try to argue with my dad.

I went to bed determined to stay awake, vigilantly monitoring the hallway for traffic. If Yvonne went back to my mom's bedroom with my father I knew I would run away and never come back. I would live in the mountains with Emory while he hibernated, and there would be a legend about a boy who ran wild with a grizzly bear.

Of course, I'd sneak back into town to see Beth from time to time.

I drifted off to sleep and then awoke around one in the morning, angry at myself for dozing off. I slid out of bed and crept into the living room, where there were still some lights on.

My father was sprawled in the big reclining chair, and Yvonne was in the chair with him, sitting in his lap, her head on his chest. They were both fast asleep. I stood with my arms crossed, pondering what action to take. I wanted something dramatic, like maybe banging pots together or firing off a shotgun. Or even bringing Emory inside to snarl in Yvonne's face, to scare her so bad she never came back.

In the end, though, I did nothing at all.

Yvonne was gone when I woke up the next morning. I went about the business of my breakfast without a word, punishing my father with silence, but it was so much like every other day I wasn't sure he got the message. And Emory was gone, too — he'd eaten the dog food but, as I would figure out years later, needed a more varied diet than what he could get in the pole barn. As it would turn out, he spent the weekend foraging and only returned to the couch at night.

The phone didn't ring much in the house, so when it did and I went to answer it my father followed and stood looking at me with a questioning look on his face.

I said hello and for a second there was no response, and then I heard Beth's voice.

278

"Charlie?"

I waved at my dad that the call was for me. He cocked his head, not leaving, curious who it was. I turned my back on him, the cord wrapping around my torso.

"I'm glad your phone got fixed," Beth was saying.

"What?"

"Your phone. I'm glad they fixed it. That is why you haven't called me, because your telephone has been out of order, right?"

I found myself grinning. "Was I supposed to call you?"

"I don't know, Charlie, were you supposed to call me?"

"Um . . ."

"So anyway, I was just checking to see if your phone was working. Bye, Charlie."

She disconnected. I stared at the phone in disbelief.

"Who was that?" my dad asked.

"Beth Shelburton."

"Oh-h-h," he replied, drawing the word out so I'd know he was jumping to all kinds of conclusions. I felt my face flushing.

"It's not what you think," I told him icily.

He nodded. "Okay."

"She was just checking to see if our phone was working."

That one puzzled him, too. "Okay," he

said again, sounding less sure of himself.

That was Beth; she had the ability to confound even men as old as my dad.

I walked out of the kitchen as if the entire incident were behind me. I went out to the pole barn, but Emory was gone, probably out eating fifty acres of huckleberries. I scuffed my feet on the driveway a little and then went back into the house and asked my dad for the Shelburtons' phone number.

Her brother answered and then, with a taunt in his voice, called out to Beth, telling her it was a "boy" on the phone and making all sorts of irritating love noises in the background while she picked up the receiver. There was a short scuffling that ended in a muffled gasp — it sounded as if she had hit him in the head with something heavy.

"Hello?"

"Hi, Beth."

"Hi. Who's calling, please?"

"It's me. Charlie."

"Why, *Charlie,* what a nice surprise!"

She just had a talent for making me grin like an idiot.

That Monday at school I determined that after English class if I sprinted I could make it to her history class and walk with her to her math class and then race back for *my* history class. We'd have three whole minutes of conversation together. It was clearly worth the effort.

The novelty of having a boy call quickly went away for her little brother, since I had rung Beth six or seven times that weekend. We talked about a lot of things, but we didn't talk about Emory, or about my mother, or about Dad and Yvonne. I wanted to, though. I was ready to confide in Beth, but the truth is that she kept me so off balance I never felt like the conversation was mine to control.

I was on the phone with her when my dad came home Monday evening. He hadn't said anything about my sudden fondness for telephonic communication, but he couldn't help but notice all the activity, since the only place I could talk from was the kitchen. I planned to ask for a telephone in my room for Christmas.

I heard a car pull in our driveway, but Beth was telling me something about gymnastics, so I left it up to my dad to investigate. He went to the front window, then turned and looked at me.

"You'd better get off the phone."

I said a reluctant good-bye to Beth and hung up, joining my dad at the window.

What I saw made my heart freeze in my chest.

Herman Hessler, the Fish and Game agent, was back, and he had two more agents with him. There was also a sheriff patrol car.

The Fish and Game agents had rifles.

CHAPTER
TWENTY-THREE

The expression on my father's face and the stiff set to his spine as he opened the door to confront the Fish and Game agents was very familiar to me. I'd seen it more than once as my father had headed in to see Mom's doctors. He was ready for the worst, steeled against it.

We stepped outside together. "Herman," my father greeted softly.

Mr. Hessler started tossing his hat. "Hey there, George."

"So," my dad said.

Mr. Hessler nodded. "The Alderton boy won't let it go. He contacted the, the . . ." He turned to one of the men holding a rifle. "What is it?"

"Idaho Guild of Animal Rights," the man said. "IGAR."

"Yeah, the Idaho guild for the rights of animals, and they filed a, uh, an action." Mr. Hessler nodded at the sheriff's deputy, a big guy with doughy skin, who stepped forward and stiffly held out a piece of paper for my dad to take.

"You're George Hall?" the deputy asked, which was silly because everyone in Selkirk River knew my dad. My dad nodded and took the paper.

"So we've got that warrant to search the premises and determine if you're harboring a wild animal against the law," Mr. Hessler said.

"What are the rifles for?" my dad asked.

Mr. Hessler looked uncomfortable. "Well, you know, just in case."

My dad shook his head. Mr. Hessler shrugged. "I'm sorry about this, George. I'd just as soon not be here, but I have to do my job."

I left my father's side and headed over to the pole barn. "Charlie!" my dad called, but I didn't look back.

Emory was pacing back and forth. Clearly, he'd heard the men on the other side of the door — did he understand what was happening? "I'm not going to let anything happen to you, Emory," I whispered. I walked over to him, close enough to feel the heat coming off his body, and turned and faced the front.

When the door ratcheted up I was between

the men with the guns and the bear, my arms folded. The startled tension that went through them was almost comical, but there was nothing funny in the way they all reflexively jacked shells into their rifle chambers.

"Charlie. Come away from that animal," Mr. Hessler ordered. One of the men raised his rifle and sighted at Emory behind me and my father moved in a blur, shoving the rifle up in the air.

"Do not point a gun at my son!" he barked.

The deputy sheriff put his hand on his pistol and everyone looked scared and angry. Mr. Hessler set his hat on his head so he could have both hands free to raise up in front of him. "Hold it, everybody. Let's not escalate this thing. Hold on."

Everyone relaxed a little but still looked wary. The man who had pointed the gun seemed a little embarrassed when Mr. Hessler glared at him. Then the Fish and Game agent turned to my dad. "George, that's a full-grown grizzly bear."

"Yes, it is. And you've determined that it's here, so your work is done," my dad responded coolly.

Mr. Hessler thought about this, dourly regarding his fellow Fish and Game agents, who both appeared to be in bad moods. "I can't just walk away, now that I've seen him, George. It's against the law to harbor a wild animal; you know that."

"Herman, does that look like a wild animal to you?"

As if to help illustrate the point, Emory stretched his neck and sort of set his giant head on my shoulder. The weight of the thing almost made me collapse, but I shifted and kept my balance.

"Not legal to keep a tame one, either," Mr. Hessler observed. He pulled his hat off his head and started flipping it in his hands again. He probably wore out three hats a year with all the abuse he gave them.

"We're not keeping him. We leave the door open. He comes and goes. We didn't raise him and I never chose to have him show up. He chose us, or chose Charlie, anyway."

Emory yawned, lifting his head off my shoulder as he did so.

Mr. Hessler nodded. He turned to his men. "I guess we'd better bump this one up the chain of command."

The men looked a little disappointed that they wouldn't get to shoot anything, but they carefully disarmed their weapons and got back in their vehicles. Mr. Hessler didn't say anything else, but he raised his hand at my dad as he backed out of the driveway.

My dad turned to me. "Did you not hear me call you when you ran for the pole barn?"

I dropped my eyes. "Yessir. But Dad, they were going to shoot Emory!"

My dad sternly put his hand on the same shoulder where Emory had placed his head. It felt just as heavy. "Charlie, look at me."

I managed to raise my eyes to his.

"The only way we're going to make it through this thing is together, understand? No more running off to do things on your own."

I swallowed and nodded.

My dad regarded Emory, who was just standing there listening. Did the bear understand what had just happened? Could the bear comprehend our conversations? My dad opened his mouth as if to speak to Emory directly, then closed it again, unwilling to let go and plunge headfirst into the fantastic.

All I cared about was keeping everything about Emory secret. If it hadn't been for McHenry and his dogs and maybe the chance viewing by Dan, I'd still be hanging out with my grizzly bear at the creek and no one would be the wiser. That's what I believed, anyway.

After the confrontation with the law, it took a while for us to get back to feeling normal. To work off excess energy, my dad decided to tackle cleaning the house, something I preferred to regard as a spectator sport but which my father saw as very much a team effort.

By the time I was released from the housework squad it was too late to telephone Beth, and I went to bed feeling like a kid who had missed Christmas.

The next evening Mr. Hessler was back, as was the big, fleshy deputy. It was just the two of them, and they came to our front door and the deputy handed my dad another piece of paper after first asking him if he was George Hall, which was even more stupid than last time because now we all knew he knew.

"The people from IGAR, the Idaho animal guild or whatever they call it, they're keeping the heat on," he told us. "That's a subpoena for you to appear tomorrow in front of a judge for a hearing about your bear."

Despite what had to be years of practice at flipping his hat, Mr. Hessler dropped it, so that he had to bend over to pick it up. As he stood, he met my dad's eyes with obvious reluctance. "You might want to call a lawyer."

"I can't really afford a lawyer, Herman."

"Well, shoot, George. They might levy a fine on you. There's even . . . I mean, you could wind up going to jail."

I gasped.

My dad firmly shook his head. "No, I don't think so. The bear comes and goes; I told you that. Wouldn't be right to put a man in jail for an animal coming out of the woods to hang around on his property. I had a herd of deer standing in my driveway this spring when I came out to get the newspaper; you going to arrest me for that? Probably get me on multiple counts; there had to be thirty of them."

Mr. Hessler sighed. "Come on, George."

I realized then that my dad was angry. He kept such a tight leash on his feelings it was sort of hard to tell, but his eyes were cold and his conversation unfriendly. He looked down at me. "Charlie, go open the pole barn door."

Mr. Hessler stopped flipping his hat. The deputy looked a little pale, his hand drifting toward the gun in his holster as I dashed off the porch and ran over to the pole barn. I lifted the door and it rattled up loudly, stopping with a crash.

Emory was gone. He'd been out all day.

I walked back over to where Mr. Hessler was regarding my father with wary eyes. The deputy's big shoulders had slumped and some color was coming back into his face.

"See? The bear comes and goes," my dad said evenly.

"It's not up to me; it's the judge and these people from the guild of the Idaho animals."

"IGAR," the deputy corrected.

"Whatever it's called," Mr. Hessler snapped.

"I'll see you in court then," my dad said. He didn't seem angry anymore, just resigned.

"All right then," Mr. Hessler said.

As the cars drove off, Mrs. Alderton came up Hidden Creek Road, her son Dan in the passenger seat, looking out. His eyes swept over mine, then were riveted on the barn, still gaping open and empty. Then he looked back at me, and our gaze locked until the car bounced on up the road and out of sight.

I will fight you, Dan, I said to myself. My fists clenched themselves.

Emory didn't come back until after my bedtime, which I found so frustrating. Didn't he want to be with me?

Obviously I wasn't going to school the next day. Instead, my father woke me before dawn and instructed me to put on my suit, which I had worn exactly once before — when we buried my mother. There was still a copy of the service handout in the jacket pocket, all rolled up and stressed from where I had twisted and squeezed it. I threw it away because I had several of them in pristine shape and wanted to get rid of things that I had touched on that day. I would have tossed the suit itself in the trash, even, though instead I just stared at myself in the mirror and tried not to think too hard about the last time my reflection had been dressed like that.

We had a long drive to get to the hearing, a drive through some of the most beautiful country in the world, in my admittedly not-well-traveled opinion. The town of Selkirk River is in a basin that was blasted out of the mountains by an astounding series of prehistoric floods that violently re-formed the terrain when gigantic ice dams gave way during the Ice Age. The wave was said to have been eighty feet tall, containing two and a half trillion tons of water and carrying the strength of all the rivers of the world combined. Boys in my school liked to brag about this event as if it were proof of how tough a people we were, as if our ancestors survived the deluge by clinging to trees or something.

Selkirk River was unique among the towns in Boundary County because it was on the west side of the Selkirk mountain range, the only town in the county that was thus situated. It was mainly a logging town, with a single highway in and out of it that thundered with trucks barreling along with massive logs on their rigs.

Boundary County is so-named because it is on the boundary of every place that isn't Idaho — Canada, Washington, and Montana. That makes it sound bigger than it is, up in the Idaho Panhandle, but it really feels huge when you drive from Selkirk River to the courthouse in Bonners Ferry because the only way to get from one to the other is to drive all the way south to Sandpoint and then go east and north back up to get around the Selkirk Mountains, sort of like a boat going around the tip of Florida.

This meant my dad and I had a lot of time to ourselves as the Jeep's knobby tires growled along on the highway. "I don't know what's going to happen, Charlie," my dad said in response to my anxious questioning. "All we can do is tell the truth. The judge will decide what is right."

This sounded an awful lot like *the doctors will know what to do* and in the end I'd wound up wearing this suit and watching them lower a shiny box into a hole. I took a deep, shuddering breath.

"Will we have to witness?" I asked.

"Testify, you mean? I think probably yes," my dad responded.

"Even me?"

"Well, I don't know. You're a minor, so maybe not."

"What happens if I testify?"

"Well, they'll swear you in, and then I imagine they'll ask you questions and you'll answer them the best you can."

"Swear me in?"

"You have to tell the truth, the whole truth, and nothing but the truth."

I chewed on that a bit. I had gotten pretty good at telling something far short of the whole truth. Though I really didn't have anything to hide.

The whole truth. What would that be like, to allow the ice dam to fail inside me and let all two and a half trillion tons of guilt flow out? Just say it, tell everything, let my father know what I'd done.

I guess something was written on my face, because my father was giving me a curious look. "What is it?"

"Nothing." I looked out the window.

My dad assessed my expression and decided we should pull over onto the shoulder.

He put the Jeep in neutral and set the parking brake, twisting so he was facing me square, his features grim. "Charlie? What are you hiding from me?"

It wasn't as if he looked welcoming, or forgiving, or kind. His eyes had that steely coldness in them that I knew so well. I felt my anger rising in response.

"Nothing!" I shouted. Then I gasped at how much raw pain had come out with that one word. My emotions were betraying me. My dad watched the conflict working on my face, his eyes growing sympathetic. He put a tender hand on my shoulder and it broke me.

"Dad." I started weeping, then. I pressed my palms to my face.

"Charlie? What is it? You can tell me."

He waited solemnly and patiently while I fought for control. It took me a full minute before I could trust myself to speak without crying. "Dad, the day that Mom went to the hospital for the last time. You went to get some medicine and you told me to watch her."

"I remember."

Of course he remembered; no one would forget that day.

I couldn't bear to look at him. "I got bored. So I was looking around, and I found the little box stuck to the underside of your nightstand. I found the key to the gun cabinet. And I went out into the living room and I took your guns out."

"My guns?" Dad repeated. He seemed both mystified and angry at me, but it wasn't his anger that worried me, not about this, anyway.

"I like to take them apart and put them back together," I said.

"Charlie," my dad said, ready to pronounce sentence of some kind.

I put up my hand to stop him. "Dad, don't you understand? It was while I was in the living room that Mom went into her coma! You told me to watch her and I didn't!"

The sobs broke from me, painful, chest-cracking gasps of bottomless grief and guilt. I wasn't conscious of my father anymore; I knew nothing but my own horrible misery. My awful secret was out, my horrible, terrible secret.

I was a little surprised when my father gathered me in his arms, but I didn't fight him. I put my face into his chest and bawled like a baby. He held me and rocked me.

"Charlie, Charlie," he said. He held me so that I had to look into his eyes, and they were gentle and pitying. "Charlie, it's all right. It wasn't your fault, not at all. There was nothing you could have done to prevent it. She was dying, Son. We all knew it was just days away. It wouldn't have stopped anything if you had been there."

"No!" I shook my head wildly. "Don't you get it, Dad? Don't you get what I did?"

He plainly didn't get it, and I was forced to speak the words, my anguish pouring out.

"When she slipped into a coma, I wasn't there to be with her. She was alone, Dad! Her last moments of being aware and I left her alone!"

My dad's eyes were brimming with tears. "God, is that what you think? She was asleep, Son; she was at peace. She wasn't aware of anything. Her coma was just like a deeper kind of sleep, that's all. No one can say when she went from one state to the other. She didn't know you were even there. You didn't abandon her."

He bit his lip. "And I should never have left you alone with your mom. It was my fault. I let *you* down, Charlie. But I'll never do that again. Understand? I'm your father and I'm sticking with you and I will never let you down."

His grip on my shoulders was so tight it was almost painful, but through it flowed all of his strength, and all of the steel he'd built up as protection against a harsh, betraying world was now enveloping me instead of shutting me out.

I felt at that moment that the wound that had been inflicted on our family when my mom got sick had finally started to heal. We hadn't managed to forge a bond over the common loss of Laura Hall, but the odd quirk of fate that had brought Emory the bear into our lives was somehow bringing my dad and me together — together, as it would turn out, against most of the rest of the world, or at least as much of the rest of the world as was able to penetrate Boundary County, Idaho.

CHAPTER
TWENTY-FOUR

In 1974, the county seat of Boundary County — Bonners Ferry — was subject to so much flooding that a lot of the buildings in the lower areas of town were up on stilts. Over in Montana they were working on an enormous dam designed to end the periodic inundations, which was finished a year later.

The courthouse, though, wasn't up on stilts. It was a massive structure built of white stone in 1940 by the WPA. (I'd managed to write a report about it in the sixth grade without ever actually learning what the WPA was.) Carved into the rock by the people struggling with the Great Depression were three massive reliefs respectively showing loggers, miners, and farmers, each faceless and gray, appearing crushed under the burden of their labors. It was oppressive and grim, giving no hope to us as we mounted the steps and passed beneath their impassive countenances.

298

But what I found most intimidating was the courtroom itself, the sheer, vast emptiness of it. *You are small,* the giant space told me, *and we are large and powerful.* It was so isolating to sit at the table up front with my dad while Herman Hessler and four men I didn't know clustered at another table on the other side. No one was talking, so every time my dad nervously cleared his throat the sound echoed off the walls.

A deputy was up front. He had a gun on his hip, but mostly what he seemed concerned with was filing. He kept rearranging folders, ignoring us.

A woman dressed in a severe brown suit sat quietly at a small table — the court stenographer. The deputy ignored her, too. He was apparently really good at filing papers.

Then the judge entered and the deputy said, "All rise," but I was already on my feet, hoping to score some points by being first.

I had expected a really crusty ancient guy with hair like Thomas Jefferson, but the judge was a woman, and she wasn't as old as I expected, either, with youthful cheekbones. She put on glasses that had brown frames matching her hair and read through her files, then looked at us.

"All right," she said. "Everyone may be

seated. This is a hearing, and I want to keep it informal." Her eyes found me and softened. "My name is Judge Reimers."

One of the men at the table next to us stood up and said he had a motion. He was there to represent the Idaho Guild of Animal Rights, and he just kept talking and talking while the judge looked at him with increasing exasperation until finally she interrupted.

"No, I'm not going to entertain motions at this time. As I was saying, I want to keep this informal. Will that be all right with you, Counselor?"

The man dropped his eyes and sort of mumbled that he thought it was a swell idea. The court stenographer silently recorded everything, her face so completely expressionless she could have replaced one of the WPA workers carved in stone out front.

The judge told her bailiff to have my dad swear to tell the truth and the whole truth. "Well, let's get right to it," she then said. "Do you have a bear living inside a building on your property, Mr. Hall?"

No. I wanted to shout. *He comes and goes.*

"Yes, Your Honor."

Judge Reimers regarded my father for a long minute.

300

"Your Honor, if I may," the attorney from IGAR said, standing up. The judge shot him a *no, you may not* look and he sat back down.

"You do know that harboring a bear . . . it's a grizzly bear, Mr. Hall?"

"Yes, ma'am."

"Harboring a grizzly bear is not only against the law, but it's dangerous as well. You have a child."

"Yes, ma'am."

I gave my dad an incredulous look. Wasn't he going to say anything else?

"What happened? Did you find it as a cub?"

"No, Your Honor," my father said, shaking his head. "He just sort of came up on my boy one day in the woods and followed him home, more or less."

"I see."

The judge held her glasses as if not sure she wanted to wear them, looking through the lenses at the papers on her desk. The court stenographer sat motionless. "I guess the Fish and Game Department has already considered relocating the animal. . . ."

The man from IGAR stood up and this time was determined to talk. "If I may, Your Honor, relocating the animal is contraindicated because he is too socialized. The odds of an attack, or a return to the site of his

301

dependency, are too great."

Judge Reimers frowned at the man. "Are you under the impression I did not read your brief?"

"Well, of course not, Your Honor."

"So why are you telling me something I already know?"

He didn't have an answer for that one. I felt my heart soar with hope: she obviously didn't like the IGAR man one bit.

The judge returned her gaze to us. "As I was about to say before I was interrupted," she said meaningfully, "Fish and Game has already looked into relocation and doesn't believe it would be successful. We can't just take it to the Canadian border and let the creature go."

Mr. Hessler was nodding. His hat was on the table in front of him and he was touching it a little, probably aching to pick it up and start tossing it.

"We also, I understand, have looked into the idea of a zoo —"

A *zoo!* I must have gasped out loud, because the judge stopped and gazed at me. Her expression was sympathetic as she continued.

"Though I guess we can't find a suitable location and the matter, or so I've been led to believe, is urgent."

The IGAR man shifted in his seat but froze when the judge impaled him with a sharp glance.

"Mr. Hall. You've got some people pretty worked up. They'd like to file charges against you. You do understand that, don't you?"

My dad nodded, swallowing. The stenographer raised her eyes to the judge.

"Please answer out loud, Mr. Hall."

"Yes, Your Honor. I understand."

"But my primary concern here is for the safety of the community. I also, if there's room, must consider what is best for the animal. You do understand, a bear who feels free to wander around people's homes — that bear poses a very real threat. What would happen if a family came home and surprised a full-grown grizzly foraging in their garage? That's a tragedy I can't allow to happen."

This was such a mischaracterization of Emory that I wanted to jump out of my seat.

"I can't explain why this animal has decided to become friends with you, but unfortunately, there's a long, sad history of interaction with bears in this part of the country, and the people always come out on the losing end."

"But he's not just a bear!" I cried, anguished.

My words seemed to echo around that empty courtroom for a full ten seconds, ringing in my ears while the judge regarded me with stern yet gentle eyes. "What's your name, son?" the judge finally asked in quiet tones.

"Charlie Hall."

"Well, Charlie, you're not old enough to participate in these hearings. This is something for grown-ups to decide, okay? I'm sorry, but I have to ask you to sit still."

Sit still while she decided that Emory had to be killed, she meant. I gave my father a long, beseeching look. He said he would never let me down, but if we didn't do something, these people would decide to send men with guns to shoot my bear. My father regarded the pain in my eyes, biting his lip. He glanced over at the man from IGAR, who was sitting stone-faced, and at Mr. Hessler, who was watching back with sad eyes.

"The law is clear when it comes to situations like these," the judge said.

Like these? *Like these?* Since when had there ever been situations like these?

Dad cleared his throat, standing back up. "Charlie's right, Your Honor."

"I'm sorry, Mr. Hall. Right about what?"

"It's not just a bear. In fact, it might not be a bear at all."

You could have heard a fly walking on the ceiling, it was so quiet in that place. My father had a look on his face that I recognized — he didn't enjoy what he was doing, but he was determined to go through with it.

"Did you not tell me earlier you had a bear on your property?" the judge finally asked.

"Yes, Your Honor."

"I'm not clear on what you are trying to say. Do you mean not just a bear because, as a pet, it is a member of your family?"

"No, that's not it. I'm trying to say that it's a bear on the outside, but not . . . it's not a bear on the inside, Your Honor. It's something else entirely."

"And what would that be?"

Dad closed his eyes as if he were jumping off the high dive at the pool. "It's a Civil War soldier named Emory Bain. He was apparently killed in battle, wounded and killed, and now he's come back as a grizzly bear."

Mr. Hessler's mouth was open. The judge was giving my father a penetrating stare, as if trying to figure out if he was crazy, or joking, or what. Even the stenographer reacted,

305

a flicker passing through her eyes as she silently made note of what my father had just said.

It was more than the man from IGAR could take. "Your Honor . . ."

The judge held up a hand like a crossing guard and he shut up. "Why do you believe this, Mr. Hall?"

"Because the bear wrote the words on the wall of my barn in red paint, Your Honor."

"He wrote . . . what, exactly?"

My dad's eyes raised up to the ceiling and he recited it all. " 'I, Emory Bain, was a private in the Third Regiment of infantry from Grand Rapids. In May of 1862 pursued Rebels at Chicka . . . Chickahominy, was wounded and took fever, and now I'm back with a message.' "

The judge blinked at him. "Civil War."

"Yes, Your Honor."

More silence.

"You saw the bear write these words in paint in your barn?" the judge finally asked.

"No, ma'am."

"Did your son see it happen?"

"No, Your Honor. He came home and the words were there."

The judge held out her hand, demonstrating what it would be like to have a stiff paw. "How would a bear paint words on a wall?"

306

"Believe me, Your Honor, I've thought that through and I have no idea."

"But you nonetheless believe the statement was written by the bear."

"Yes, Your Honor."

"Why, Mr. Hall, would you believe such a thing?"

My dad put his hand on my shoulder. "Because my son told me and he wouldn't lie to me, Your Honor."

I felt my throat tighten at this declaration of trust. I found I couldn't look at his face for fear of starting to sob right there in the courtroom. I focused all of my attention on Judge Reimers.

"Well." The judge looked down at her desk for a few seconds, mulling things over. Then she raised up her eyes and looked at the bailiff. "I'm going to take fifteen minutes or so in chambers."

"All rise," the bailiff intoned smoothly.

"Thank you, Mr. Hall. Everyone. I'll be out in a few minutes," the judge said. She left the room and the deputy immediately went back to his filing.

My dad and I exchanged glances. I was frightened and hopeful. Mr. Hessler stood, grabbed his hat off the table, and came over to see us, tossing it lightly in his hands like he always did.

"Hey there, George."

"Herman."

"You didn't say anything about this soldier boy idea before."

"I guess I thought it would sound crazy," my dad responded.

Mr. Hessler nodded, a small smile twitching in the corners of his mouth. "Sort of does, George."

My dad shrugged.

"No doubt in my mind he's a special kind of bear, though. The way he is with your son, I never imagined such a thing before."

Mr. Hessler regarded us both for a moment with eyes that were not at all unfriendly. Then he deliberately looked away from us, first up at the courtroom deputy, then over his shoulder where all his allies were sitting at the other table. The IGAR attorney was speaking vehemently with the other men in suits and they all kept staring at us. Mr. Hessler leaned in, lowering his voice.

"You know, if it was me, I'd take Charlie and leave."

This obviously surprised my father. "Why? We're not finished here."

Mr. Hessler's expression was patient and kind. "Yes, we are, George. You know the judge isn't going to come back through that door with anything other than an order to euthanize that grizzly, and then we'll be out there to take care of it straightaway. You understand? If you leave now, though, you'd have a head start."

My dad was letting the words sink in. I had never heard the term "euthanize" before but got the general idea and it froze my blood in my veins.

"I imagine that if we show up at your place and the bear's not there, there's someone who will want to go hunting for him," Mr. Hessler continued.

McHenry.

"But I'm not personally motivated to chase the bear down, understand? For reasons I don't understand, the only house he's been at is yours. We get complaints he's raiding bird feeders, we're going to have to trap him, but if nobody calls, I got better things to do than try to track a grizzly up into the mountains with winter around the corner. Unless I get orders to the contrary, I mean. Gotta follow orders." He glanced over at the IGAR man as he said this.

"Thanks, Herman," my dad said softly.

"Don't mention it," Mr. Hessler said. He winked at me and returned to his table, still flipping his hat in his hands.

We sat still for a moment or two, and then

my dad turned to me, holding his head as stiffly as if he were wearing a neck brace, and carefully said, "Let's get up very slowly and leave. Just like we're taking a break, going to the men's room or something."

"Okay, Dad."

I followed my dad out of the courtroom at a slow dawdle, but when we got to the front doors we sprinted down the steps and dove into the Jeep. My heart was racing as we tore out of there. Nobody followed us, no one opened fire, but I still felt like I was a fugitive from justice.

My dad waited until the courthouse was long gone in the rearview mirror before he spoke, as if he was making sure we were out of range of listening devices. When he glanced at me, his eyes were a little wild, and I gained an instant appreciation for just how much he had joined my side against the world, back in that courtroom.

"Do you think Emory understands you? When you talk to him, I mean."

"I don't know," I replied honestly. "He doesn't really react one way or another."

Sort of like you, Dad, a voice continued unbidden in my head.

My dad drove in silence for a few miles. "Well, when we get home, you're going to have to somehow convince him to run away.

He gets up into the mountains far enough, no one's going to bother him."

I took a deep breath. My dad's brown eyes found mine for a second before he went back to concentrating on the road. "There isn't any other way, Charlie. They're going to come out and shoot him."

"I know, Dad. I know."

"He gets up in the mountains, he'll be fine," my father repeated. I nodded, feeling hopeful. Emory was going to be okay. He just needed to go hide.

Evening was falling when we pulled into the driveway. I hit the ground running and threw open the door to the pole barn. Emory was inside, lazily sitting on the old couch like me when I didn't want to do chores.

"Emory," I called. My father approached more slowly, halting just outside the barn to watch.

"You have to run away," I told him. "It's worse than last time. A judge said the police can come out and shoot you. You have to go far, far away, up into the mountains. Okay?" I wiped a tear away from my eye. It was so *unfair*. Seeing Emory's blank expression made me want to fall to my knees and wail. Why did things like this keep happening to me? I made a shooing motion with my arms.

"Emory. *Go.*"

Instead of leaving, Emory went over and sniffed at the big metal can that now held his dog food. I had to laugh at the absurdity of it. Here I was terrified for his life and Emory's main concern was that he wanted to eat.

The thing was, he could have knocked that trash can over and popped that lid off any time he wanted, but he waited for me to use a scoop to fill the big pan. It was like me being in charge of my own grounding — we could *trust* Emory; didn't that prove something?

"We have time. He should probably eat," my father told me.

So I poured the food into the pan and as Emory bent his head to feed I ran my hands up and down the thick, coarse fur on his shoulders. It was, I realized, the last time I would ever see my friend the bear. I kept sniffing back the tears — it helped that Emory didn't seem too upset, just mainly hungry, as always.

When he was done and he'd lapped up enough water to put out a small fire, Emory lumbered out into the yard. I shut both doors to the pole barn with a bang, illustrating my point.

"Now go, Emory. Go away."

With one final, impenetrable look, Emory went. As he descended the trail to the creek where the shadows had gathered to wait for nightfall, he never once looked over his shoulder at me. Didn't I mean enough to him for a farewell glance of any kind? I stood at the edge of the yard and watched his retreating back until the gloom swallowed him up.

We were having dinner when the Fish and Game cars showed up. As my dad was raising a bite of food to his mouth his face lit up with red, pulsing flashes from the cherry lights. Mr. Hessler had his two buddies back, and they had their rifles at the ready, plus there were two sheriff's deputies with heavy shotguns.

"Stay here," my dad ordered me.

I stood in the front window to watch. I saw my dad have a brief conversation with Mr. Hessler and then walk over to the pole barn, the men with the guns on high alert. When my dad raised the door the men all flinched. The inside was well lit with headlights and clearly there was no sign of Emory, but Mr. Hessler still made a show of looking around, his team following him in silly, creeping steps, as if they expected the bear to jump out of one of the freezers.

My dad waited until the cars pulled out of

the driveway before returning to finish his meal.

"He said his boss might make him come back in a day or two, but I told him the bear ran off to the mountains, and he seemed pretty satisfied with that."

"Thanks, Dad," I said, meaning "thanks for everything."

"It's okay," my dad told me, smiling.

I was happy Emory was safe, but it was like giving away a dog — he was my friend. I crawled into bed worrying about him, hoping he was already miles away and looking for a den to hibernate way up where nobody would find him, but aching at the idea of him being all alone with no friends to comfort him.

And me, I felt alone, too. I pressed my face into the pillow until it was wet with tears, a familiar sensation.

I awoke with a start just before dawn. The light was gray-blue through my window, with a red flush building up strength in the east. Something had awakened me, some sound that shouldn't have been there.

I strained to hear it, willing the noise to repeat, and when it did it was slightly louder. A high, shrill baying sound. I knew instantly what it was.

McHenry's hounds.

CHAPTER TWENTY-FIVE

I knew that the hounds meant Emory was close by. He hadn't run far enough away. McHenry was on his trail. McHenry, who probably had someone on the payroll who called him the second the judge handed down her decision. McHenry, who didn't care that grizzlies were essentially extinct in Idaho. I had never despised anyone the way I despised McHenry.

I got out of bed and into my clothes as quickly as I could and ran down the hall. I pushed open my dad's door and fumbled quietly for the key to the gun cabinet.

It was gone. Though it had been less than twenty-four hours since my confession, my dad had already relocated the key, *as if,* I thought furiously, *his guns had been the point of the story!*

There was no time to try to find the key. My father slumbered under his covers, oblivious to the buglelike barking and baying from the woods. I went into the living room, wrapped a towel around my fist, and punched the glass in the gun cabinet. It shattered with a racket that sounded all the louder because of the morning quiet.

"Charlie?" my dad called as I pulled out the .30-06 and slipped a box of shells in my pocket. I felt the vibration through the floor as he jumped out of bed, but I was already at the back door. "Charlie!" he shouted, but I was running.

The gathering dawn lent a surreal glow to the path beneath me as I ran. I knew with absolute certainty where Emory was, where the dogs would find him. The old, abandoned hut.

The forest still clutched the night to itself, each tree trunk barely visible in the gloom. The climb was far steeper than the cross-country course, and I faltered, slowing, hating my body for failing me.

The rocky crest made for slow going, but once I was at the top I was out in the sunlight, actually above the Old Cabin, with a full view of the river and of McHenry and his hounds. I deliberately didn't look behind me, for fear I'd see my father on the balcony of our deck, ordering me with hand signals to get home. The Old Cabin was visible, too, its mossy roof covered with a light frost.

Down in the river valley the dogs were thirty yards ahead of McHenry and pulling away fast, hitting the river with separate splashes. A man could pick his way across all the deadfalls and not get wet, but the canines scrabbled without plan, the current adding drift to their progress, their nails unable to find purchase on the slippery tree trunks, which they gripped with their forelimbs, dangling, before dropping back into the water. Under any other circumstance it would have been comical.

I didn't see Emory at first. The door to the Old Cabin was open, and I measured the distance from the top of the sandy riverbank to that door, considering. It was at least thirty yards. I swung my gun up. Could I pick off four dogs as they crossed that gap? They'd be slow and probably exhausted from fighting their way up that steep bank.

I peered through the telescopic sight. The dogs were digging their way up the riverbank now, weighed down by the heavy sand, struggling but tantalized by bear scent.

Of course, if Emory wanted to get away from the hounds, he could find himself a tree. That was the point, anyway — bear hunters didn't want their dogs tussling with a bear, just terrorizing their prey until it

317

treed itself. The real threat came from McHenry, who had gained a few yards on his dogs while they thrashed around in the river; he held a large hunting rifle under his arm as he jumped from log to log, nearly across the rushing waters.

Could I shoot McHenry?

I was pondering this when I saw Emory move. He'd been standing in the trees, absolutely motionless, invisible in the weak morning light. He was watching the dogs approach, but now that they were most of the way up the steep bank he turned and headed for the Old Cabin, not running, calm as you please. Didn't he understand what was happening?

I stood up and began making my way down. Emory disappeared inside the hut's front door. A second later, the dogs surged up over the lip of the bank. They were so tired they barely managed to bay, but that didn't stop them from charging after the bear.

I watched in utter dismay as they streaked across the flat grass toward the cabin. I would never have been able to hit a single one; it was worthless to raise my rifle now. All I could do was watch as they launched themselves over the threshold into the Old Cabin.

The second the last one had leaped through the open door, Emory came whipping around the corner of the hut, moving faster than any animal I'd ever seen. He must have climbed out the big back window and run around to the front of the building. He lunged for the front door and banged it shut. The dogs were now locked inside.

Immediately the tenor of the dogs' barking changed; it became muffled and more distant sounding even as their distress pitched their tones higher. Emory eased himself back around the corner of the hut until he was once more hidden from view.

I kept walking, but more slowly, fascinated by what I had just seen. The rear window of the cabin was far too high for the dogs to leap through. They were trapped inside until McHenry arrived to let them out. Emory hadn't yet done any running and could put a huge distance between himself and his pursuer while McHenry tried to figure out what had happened and got that sticky door reopened.

The man himself was just clearing the sandy bank and looked much the worse for wear, his ribs cranking like bellows and his face red, his mouth slack. He raised his rifle, though, visibly turning off the safety, his instincts telling him there was something wrong with this picture.

I squatted down in the brush so a chance glance wouldn't find me. *Go, Emory. Go,* I thought to myself. I hoped he was already a hundred yards away.

McHenry cautiously approached the Old Cabin. "Hello?" he called out. Though it was clear that no one lived in the place, it wasn't clear there couldn't be someone hiding inside holding McHenry's dogs hostage. He looked baffled, but he was taking no chances, his rifle held like a soldier, off his shoulder but at the ready.

He looked to his left and there was a blur to his right and he spun and Emory was *right there.* McHenry fired a single wild shot and then the bear was upon him, knocking him to the ground. He fell on his back and started to kick himself away, but Emory put his paws on McHenry's shoulders and he was forced to lie still.

All of this happened in an instant. I abandoned my crouch and ran down the hill, now, slipping and stumbling in my haste, my own rifle held away from my body so if I fell it would land clear.

Emory laid bare his teeth and let loose with a thunderous roar so loud and fierce that the dogs inside the cabin momentarily fell silent. His fangs were just inches from

McHenry's face.

The man looked up, facing his own death, the terror draining all the color from his skin. I stepped out of the trees as the dogs started howling again, and that's when I saw that Emory was bleeding.

The bear's shoulder fur was sodden with blood and a trickle of it went down his foreleg in a steady pulse. McHenry had shot him; he had shot Emory. Emory gave vent to another roar, loud as a jet plane, and now I could hear the pain in it, the pain and the rage. And I, too, became enraged, and it overcame me like a fever. I fumbled for the box of shells in my pocket, still walking forward. When I jacked a shell into the chamber, Emory looked up.

Could I shoot McHenry? Yes, yes, I could. A black hate was flooding through me, an unrestrained fury at everything that had happened in my life, the injustice of losing my mom, the unfairness of the courts, my lonely, awful life, and now seeing Emory get shot. I could shoot McHenry.

"You shot my bear, McHenry," I hissed, my voice actually quivering with wrath. I stepped forward so that he could see me. McHenry's eyes were filled with a wild light, his face a milky pale, his chin trembling. We locked stares and his look was beseeching, hopeful. I knew my expression was as pitiless as my heart. "You shot my bear, and now I'm going to shoot you, McHenry. I'm going to shoot you dead."

I was thrilled to say it. I wanted to rampage; I wanted to kill him and beat his body. I've never felt such a berserk anger, such an out-of-control bloodlust. I pointed the gun at his face and lowered the barrel until it was just inches from his nose.

Emory stopped me. He lifted his paw and pushed the gun away. "No," I cried, attempting to aim, and this time the bear released McHenry and knocked the rifle out of my hands.

Hot tears gushed from me as the fever passed. I felt giddy and sick now, and without thinking I plunged my face into Emory's coarse fur, hugging him and, after a moment, feeling him hug me back.

I recovered with a flash of fear when it occurred to me that McHenry was now free to grab his own rifle, which was lying just a few feet away. I broke from Emory's embrace and looked to the hunter, but I needn't have worried. He was still lying there in the same paralyzed position, his eyes wide with shock, beyond terror, beyond comprehension. I bent over and picked up his gun, my hands shaking from the aftereffects of what I'd almost done.

"I'll keep this for you, but I'm not stealing it. I'm no thief," I spat. "Don't let your dogs out until we're long gone. Understand what I'm saying?"

He nodded, his face still a sickly white.

"Come on, Emory," I said. As we turned away and headed back toward home, I tried to act as if I weren't fighting a rising panic.

Emory had been shot. I had no idea what we were going to do now.

CHAPTER
TWENTY-SIX

When Emory and I reached the top of the rocky ridge, I glanced back at McHenry, and he was still lying there, looking like he might never recover from having a grizzly bear's teeth just inches from his throat.

Good.

If Emory was limping at all, I couldn't tell, but he was still bleeding from his shoulder. He followed me docilely, and again the unfairness of it all embittered me. Why couldn't people just leave things alone? We hadn't been hurting anybody.

My dad was waiting for me on the back deck. His face looked tired.

"Emory's been shot!" I shouted at him. I went straight to the pole barn, as if physically avoiding my dad's wrath would be possible. Emory strode over to the couch and eased himself down on it. My dad came up from behind me.

"Give me my rifle, Son," he said quietly.

I snapped the bolt back and released the shell, then handed him the weapon butt first, barrel down. He nodded at the other one.

"Where did you get that?"

I told him what had happened with McHenry and the dogs at the Old Cabin. My father listened without expression at first, but he grew contemplative when I explained that Emory had pushed the rifle away when I pointed it at the man lying on the ground. I didn't tell my father about the nearly demonic rage that had infused my blood with a lust for murder, but I think he concluded something like that must have happened.

"What you did was just about the most stupid thing possible. You could have been killed. You could have shot a man. You broke into my gun cabinet when you expressly knew I had locked you out of it, locked you out for what turns out to be a very good reason. You must never disobey me again like that, understand? We said we were in this together, but Charlie, you violated that pact, Son."

All of this was true and all of this could have been said with a hot anger, a cold fury, or even physical blows, and it would have been justified. But there was something almost gentle in the way my father pronounced his words that made me feel that there was a different meaning to it all.

Later, as I was thinking it over, it occurred to me that there was an unstated possibility at work in this whole injustice. If the words on the barn wall had, in fact, been written by Emory and if he was, in fact, a Civil War soldier somehow returned in the form of a living grizzly bear, then what McHenry had been up to was nothing less onerous than hunting a man down with a pack of dogs and then shooting him out of a tree, murdering him in cold blood. Not a bear, a man.

And though he was not by any means helpless, Emory couldn't hold a rifle, couldn't fight back. I had done wrong, but it had been in the name of defending something we might not understand but which had the potential of being innocent human life. So Dad needed to work it all out in his mind, and he wasn't there yet. It was wrong to disobey, but was it really wrong to disobey when it meant saving a man's life?

As I said, all of this came to me later. Right then I was fixated on the fact that Emory was bleeding. We couldn't really see the wound through the fur, though he allowed my father and me to lean in and peer at it. It would not heal without help.

My dad departed in the Jeep to go get the vet. He left me there to keep Emory company, though I suspect that he also didn't want me along to see what sort of tale he told the veterinarian to convince him to return with his large-animal surgical bag. Later, when I asked my dad about it, he flushed and said that he may have given the impression that the emergency concerned a horse, though he never said so directly.

"You'll be okay, Emory," I said, hoping it was true. Emory gazed back at me with oddly serene eyes. Maybe I was imagining it, but I suddenly had the impression that he knew more about what was going on than any of us.

Several hours passed while we waited for the vet. Outside, the clanking and rattling of the school bus on its way to Benny H. sounded like a long-distance call from another time zone, a faint reminder that far, far from here I had another life. During all that time, Emory just sat there, not crying or panting or anything despite his wound. I was the one who felt like crying, frankly — when I thought back to what happened at the Old Cabin, where I'd been ready to shoot McHenry, I felt like I was going to throw up. What if I had actually done it?

The vet was Tim Humphrey's father. His

name was Jim, and I believe that in the family there was also a sister named Kim and for all I knew a dog named Pim. Dr. Jim Humphrey had Tim's blond hair and blue eyes and muscular frame, and gave me a toothy grin as he was getting out of the Jeep.

The smile went away when he saw what was in our pole barn.

"My God!" he exclaimed. At first he stood stock-still, staring at Emory lying there on the couch, and then he retreated, stumbling over his own feet. He yanked open the passenger door of the Jeep and jumped in, slamming the door behind him as if the canvas roof of the vehicle couldn't be shredded by a grizzly bear.

"You said . . . you said . . . ," Dr. Humphrey stammered through the open car window.

"I know. I'm sorry," my father said sadly. "I had to get you out here, Jim."

My father gave the vet the short, easy version: this was a tame bear who had followed me home. We'd set the bear free, but a hunter had winged him with a bullet and we needed the shoulder patched up so the bear could recover.

It sounded reasonable to me, but Dr. Humphrey was hanging on to the door handle as if he were on a wild carnival ride.

He shook his head in terror when my dad got to the part about the town's veterinarian treating a grizzly bear for a gunshot wound.

"Isn't there something we can give him to knock him out?" my dad asked when Dr. Humphrey remained intransigent.

The prospect calmed the vet a little. He agreed that yes, he could tranquilize the animal, or rather, *we* could do so while he sat in the Jeep and clung to the door latch. He fussed in his bag and before long produced a large hypodermic, into which he drew some clear liquid from a glass bottle.

He handed the shot to my father. We left the animal doctor in the Jeep and went back to the pole barn together, but my father put out an arm to stop me. Emory was acting strangely. He was off the couch, and his eyes were big and round. He was drooling heavily.

I was both baffled and alarmed, but my father read him better than I did: "He's scared." My dad looked back over his shoulder at the vet, realization clicking. "Ah, okay. Wait here, Charlie."

Unhesitatingly my father stepped closer to a mad-looking, anxious, frightened grizzly bear. It was at that moment that I realized with wonder that my father really did believe me; he truly thought Emory was more than just a bear.

"It's different now, Emory," my father said. "We won't have to amputate. And we have medicine a hundred times more powerful than whiskey that will take the pain away."

During the Civil War, bullets were mushy, fragmenting metal balls and getting hit with one pretty much guaranteed amputation as the only way to prevent infection and death. If Emory had been a soldier in that war, he had no doubt heard the screams as his compatriots were held down and had their legs and arms literally sawed off, the lucky ones getting a few sips of alcohol before the surgeon operated.

"See how thin this needle is? I'm going to poke you with it, in your other shoulder. All right? This is the medicine that will make you sleepy."

Dr. Humphrey had heard all this and now watched in amazement as Emory calmed down and went back to the couch and sat there while my father injected him. Almost immediately Emory's eyes clouded and his head drooped, and he collapsed into a deep slumber.

The Jeep door creaked open cautiously. Dr. Humphrey entered the barn. "How did you . . . I'm not sure what just happened," he whispered.

My dad reached a decision. "Charlie, show Dr. Humphrey the Polaroid."

I handed over the picture to the veterinarian, who accepted it and stared at it numbly. My dad nodded at the newly repainted wall. "The bear wrote those words. We painted them out, but they were right there."

Dr. Humphrey handed the photograph back to my dad with an absolutely disbelieving expression on his face.

As it turned out, it wasn't as serious a wound as I'd thought. The bullet came closer to missing Emory than hitting him, furrowing a path that was, as Dr. Humphrey described it, "through and through." He sewed up the wound with quick efficiency, giving us some antibiotic tablets.

We'd shut the door to the pole barn, which is why we only heard but didn't see a vehicle crunch into our driveway. My dad indicated with his eyes that I should go see who it was.

McHenry stood in what was now noonday sun. He still looked worse for wear, haggard and drained, his face twitching with residual emotions from his encounter up at the Old Cabin. His ponytail trembled at the back of his head. He came around the front of his big gleaming pickup truck.

"Are you here for your rifle?" I asked him in even tones.

He regarded me with a puzzled expression.

"Your rifle?" I repeated pointedly.

"Oh. No, I just . . . I wanted to see."

What I knew he meant was that he wanted to *understand,* but I wasn't going to go easy on him and explain that none of us had gotten that far yet. What I said instead was, "Wait here and I'll fetch it."

When I came back out of the house with his rifle in one hand and the shells from it in another, he was standing just inside the pole barn, staring at the sleeping bear. His mouth was open in awe.

"Here's your gun, Mr. McHenry." I handed him the bullets, too, which he put in his pocket.

"Will he recover, Jim?" McHenry asked the vet.

Dr. Humphrey, like everybody in town, did business with McHenry. They shook hands now. "There's no reason he shouldn't make a full recovery. I can't tell without an X-ray, but I'm all but certain there are no bullet fragments in the wound. It's through and through. So you're, uh, part of all this, McHenry?" Dr. Humphrey asked.

"Part of it," McHenry repeated, as if unsure what that meant.

Dr. Humphrey didn't know what to say. He didn't want to offend someone like McHenry. So he just shrugged. "I've never seen anything like it," he finally allowed, a neutral statement that could mean that he believed the bear understood English or that he believed my father and I were lunatics.

"You know, Jim," my father said, clearing his throat, "I'd really appreciate it if you didn't tell anyone what you saw up here today."

"Of course," Dr. Humphrey replied, with just enough hesitation so that I knew he thought the request ludicrous. There was a bear with a bullet wound sleeping on a couch up on Hidden Creek Road; how could he *not* talk about it?

They stood awkwardly for a moment, as if not sure what to say next.

"I'll walk you to your car, Jules," my father finally announced firmly but politely. McHenry nodded, took a final long look at Emory, and then followed my father up the driveway to his truck.

"How would a bear do that, do you suppose, Charlie? Write those words?" Dr. Humphrey asked. It was a question I was tired of. I didn't know how a bear could

333

paint such clear script onto a wall. No one knew.

And there was a larger significance in the question, though I didn't recognize it at the time. By focusing on the mechanics of how a bear managed to hold a paintbrush, the veterinarian was shying away from the implications of the words themselves. It was as if Emory had drawn meaningless circles and squares, instead of informing us indirectly that we all needed to adjust our bedrock assumptions. Dr. Humphrey was looking at the words as objects and not part of a coherent sentence, so that the main mystery was how the bear had written them.

As Dr. Humphrey cleaned up I kept an eye on my dad and McHenry, who were having what looked like an urgent conversation up by McHenry's pickup truck. I quailed inside when I saw my father showing him the Polaroid — McHenry was the last person I would trust with anything about Emory!

It was decided that McHenry would swing through town on the way back to his lodge and deposit Dr. Humphrey at his clinic, saving my dad the drive. The last I saw of him, Dr. Humphrey had fully recovered his normal demeanor and was talking animatedly to McHenry, for whom recovery would doubtless take a while longer.

Meanwhile, my dad and I had a serious problem. Emory's wound meant he was going to be a sitting duck if the Fish and Game came back.

"What's going to happen now?" I asked anxiously.

"I don't know."

"Will Mr. Hessler still come after him? After all he's been through?"

"I doubt that makes much difference to the Fish and Game Department, Charlie."

"But Dad, he can't run away now, not with his shoulder like that."

"I know."

I sat on the cement floor of the pole barn and watched Emory snooze away the anesthetic. I'd never felt so helpless in my life.

CHAPTER
TWENTY-SEVEN

I don't remember sleeping at all that night. Mostly I just lay rigid, straining my ears for any one of a number of dangers. McHenry's hounds. The Fish and Game trucks. The faceless people from IGAR. I even worried Dan and his buddies would show up again, this time armed with weapons to shoot themselves a grizzly bear.

My dad let me stay home from school to take care of Emory — I guess he knew that to try to make me go would force a battle we'd both regret. All Emory did was sleep, though. I didn't know if it was from the antibiotics I faithfully gave him or the wound itself.

I was tired and grouchy all weekend, which describes Emory's mood pretty much to a T. He didn't eat much and wandered off the couch in the barn only to make the short trip to the yard to relieve himself. Whenever he was outside I stood nearby, watching anxiously for Fish and Game.

To make matters worse, Beth was occupied with some sort of gymnastics clinic that I guess she'd told me about but I'd not registered as meaning she'd be unavailable until she got home late Sunday night. "You'll see her at school Monday," Mrs. Shelburton told me. *Monday.*

I didn't know if I was just being acutely sensitive or if traffic was heavier than usual that weekend, people driving past slowly. They all looked at me out their car windows as I stood solemnly regarding them from the driveway. They didn't wave or react and I didn't, either, as if the glass made us each invisible to the other.

Astoundingly, my father expected that after all that had transpired, I should get up the next Monday morning and go to school, telling me he'd let me take care of the bear before, but now the danger was past.

School? I could not imagine anything less relevant to my life at that moment than junior high school. I got on the bus that morning with a sense of total unreality.

I hadn't been in the hall for more than five minutes when Tim Humphrey grabbed my arm. He pulled me over to the wall, out of traffic, his face flushed with excitement. I was quickly encircled by his jock friends, ironically the center of attention among the people with whom I had long craved association, though my plan for the day had been to keep my head down.

"God, my dad told me!" Tim said without preamble. "How long have you had it?"

"Well, like, I don't know, awhile," I responded slowly.

"How big is it?" someone asked. "Male or female?" someone else demanded. "Does it do tricks, like a circus bear?" a third asked. "Like ride a bicycle!" someone hooted, and people laughed.

"Never seen him do that," I answered cautiously. I was enjoying the attention. The group of people was getting larger, the ring deeper, and I was the one they wanted to talk to.

Mike Kappas sort of shoved his way forward because he was Mike Kappas. "So what's the deal with the bear?" he asked, which was such a broad and general question it rendered me mute. So many people were talking now, speculating and explaining to each other what was going on, that I wasn't really sure I was necessary to the exchange anymore.

I kept my eye out for Beth, but that conversation, I soon realized, would have to wait for lunch.

Right before lunch was science class, and though my newfound social prominence had put me in a good mood, I felt my stomach lurch at the prospect of seeing Dan Alderton. I'd managed, since the day of the non-fight, to not only keep my distance but to also avoid his eyes, skipping my glance past his part of the room whenever I needed to look anywhere close to where he sat.

I hated myself for it, but I was afraid of Dan Alderton. He made me feel awful inside, just thinking about him and his betrayal and his insults. That's what I was afraid of — how he made me feel. And now, of course, I had Fish and Game and IGAR in my life because Dan told his mom about Emory. It was all Dan's fault, all of it.

I entered science class and maneuvered to my desk, so practiced at averting my gaze I wasn't sure he was even there, at least not until the bell rang and we all settled down. And then it was as if I could feel him staring at the back of my head.

The teacher stood, pushed the glasses back up the steep slope of his nose, and began talking about something while I sat with my book open and stared at it. Slowly the room went away and I was back in the pole barn with my bear.

When would Mr. Hessler return with his

posse? Would Emory now, finally, head up into the hills? I couldn't believe, after all that had happened, that it would wind up with my bear getting *shot.* When would life decide it had been unfair enough to me and move on to some other kid?

The proximity of Dan Alderton brought it all home to me: this was going to end soon, and it was going to end badly.

Dan Alderton.

"Hey," he whispered at just that moment. I felt my face grow hot. I knew it was him, and I knew who he was talking to.

"Hey!" he called again. "Hey. Squirrel."

That's what broke me. I took a single, deep breath and then, my hands curling into tight fists, I stood up. The teacher stopped talking. I turned stiffly, facing Dan. He had a smirk on his face, his eyes taunting me.

"Charlie?" the teacher asked.

I took a step in Dan's direction, just one step, and that's what triggered the explosion. I suppose that deep down I might have understood how I had evolved to be the focus of all of his frustrations, but I was still surprised at the fury with which he boiled up out of his chair and came at me, his fist swinging.

His knuckles caught me right in the mouth and a stunning pain blurred my eyes, and then I was swinging, too. It was clumsy and brutally violent, with me taking several blows to the head and giving back very little, though when my fist hit him in the face I could actually feel the softness where his left eye lived and I knew it had to hurt him.

That turned out to be the last blow in the fight: I connected with him, and then the teacher and a couple other guys swarmed us, pulling us apart.

Dan and I were put in the detention room while our parents were called and the principal read us the riot act, telling us that fighting in school was serious, that we were in serious trouble, that we needed to take things seriously. The message, as I understood it, was that things were serious. Dan and I didn't look at each other during the harangue. I stayed silent, but Dan felt compelled to protest that I started it, which was as ridiculous as it was false, but as it was explained to us, it didn't matter who started the fight because of the serious nature of how serious it was.

I guess that no matter what age you are, after you've been through a certain amount of hardship and trauma in your life being lectured to by a junior high school principal just doesn't seem like that big of a deal.

What did he know about *anything?*

My dad, though: I wasn't looking forward to the conversation with him. When he came into the building, he and the principal went into an office and closed the door. Dan and I were left sitting not ten feet apart and if we'd wanted could have gone right back at it, but the mood had passed. A school secretary glared at us from behind her typewriter, as if she had any authority.

Eventually my father came out and, with a jerk of his head, indicated I should follow him out to the Jeep.

"You want to tell me what that was all about?" he asked as we drove home.

"Dan Alderton's the one who called the Fish and Game," I blurted, "and then when Mr. Hessler said he didn't care they called IGAR. He's the reason Emory got shot!"

My dad didn't comment on the shortcut in my logic. Instead he went straight to it: "So you attacked him. In class."

"Dad, I . . ."

"What?"

I knew how I could turn this whole thing around. All I had to do was tell my father what Dan had said about Mom. Then my dad would probably drive us up to the Aldertons' so the two of us could beat up the entire family.

Of course, I didn't tell him. I *couldn't* tell him. I just looked at the floor mats. "No excuse, Dad," I mumbled, which was what I'd been taught to say when I'd been caught red-handed doing something.

"First the gun cabinet, and now fighting in school. I don't understand what you think you're doing, but I want to see an attitude change starting now. We clear?"

"Yessir."

"I had to leave work early. Again. I can't keep doing that."

My eyes bulged. "You went to work?" I demanded incredulously.

"Of course."

"But Dad, what if the Fish and Game came while you were gone? What would happen?"

"I have to earn a living. I can't afford to lose my job. Not in this economy, with inflation the way it is."

This was the biggest non-answer I'd ever heard. "Dad," I protested, unable to articulate the anxious plea stuck in my throat. Emory was more important than any *job*.

My dad sighed. "I know how hard this is for you. But you have to understand, whether I'm there or not, the Fish and Game Department is going to do what it is going to do. I left the side door to the pole

343

barn open — all we can hope for is that when they show up, Emory is gone."

"His shoulder is shot!"

"I know. But there's simply nothing else I can think of to do. Understand? If I knew what do to, I would do it."

The look he gave me was a little wild and more than a little helpless, and I bit off whatever argument I had been planning to make. For the first time I considered just how out of control things were for my father, not just with Emory, but with me, with his entire life. He wasn't supposed to be a single parent — I was supposed to have a mom.

When we got home, Mr. Shelburton was parked in our driveway. He waved his hat at us as we got out of the Jeep. "Hey there, George, uh, my wife made some brownies for ya, and . . ." He shrugged and then grinned. "Could I see the bear?"

We opened the front pole barn door. Emory groggily got off the couch and went over to drink some water. I poured out some dog food for him.

My dad and Mr. Shelburton talked while I made short work of a half-dozen brownies. They had little kernels of caramel in them. Obviously the main attraction of the Shelburton family was Beth, but man could her mom *bake.*

I saw my dad showing Mr. Shelburton the Polaroid. Then Mr. Shelburton handed my dad something and drove off.

"What was that?" I asked.

My dad had a funny look. "He gave me twenty bucks for food for the bear. It's weird. McHenry tried to get me to take two hundred dollars from him the other night. At work, a couple of the guys wanted to pass the hat."

"Two hundred dollars!"

"I refused it."

"Why?"

"Jules McHenry isn't . . . he's not right in the head. I think the shock of it all, what happened that day, he's still trying to get a handle on it. So I said no, I wouldn't take his money. I think he'll be back, though. He asked a lot of questions." My dad's eyes focused on me. "We need to talk about school, Charlie."

It turns out that the punishment for fighting is to be suspended from school for a week. To me, that was like letting inmates out of prison for bad behavior, but I wasn't going to question it.

My father, probably sensing that the school hadn't exactly provided me with a deterrent, had additional considerations. I would have to keep up on my studies. I was grounded. I had to do my regular chores, plus some other jobs he thought of in a burst of creativity I could have lived without.

Yvonne showed up during the middle of my father's impromptu piling on of tasks, interrupting him just as he was hitting his stride — it was the first time I could recall being happy to see her.

"I came as soon as I heard," she said breathlessly. "My God, George, are you all right? Is Charlie all right?"

Charlie, of course, was standing right there and could have answered the question himself. And she obviously had not come right over; she'd stopped at her house to change out of her grocery store uniform and put on a sweater that even I could appreciate made her look very womanly.

Yvonne stared with obvious distress at Emory shuffling around in the yard, and Emory looked back grumpily. His shoulder seemed to be hurting him a lot more than it had the day before and all he wanted to do was sleep and, of course, eat.

"You want to come see the bear, Miss Mandeville?" I asked her a bit wickedly.

She gave me a startled expression, reaching up with a hand to close the open V of her sweater as if worried the bear might want to shove a paw down her cleavage. "Oh, oh no," she said.

Mrs. Beck from up the road was driving by and swung into our driveway when she saw Yvonne, blocking in Yvonne's Vega, which I sourly concluded meant that they would all be there for a while.

I went in to fix myself a hot dog for lunch. The glass around the gun cabinet had been swept up and all the guns now had trigger locks, which made me angry to see. I wasn't a *baby*.

By the time I went back outside, there were five cars parked on Hidden Creek Road and maybe a dozen people standing around, watching the dozing bear show. The local paper, it seemed, had cobbled together a hasty and mostly incorrect accounting of the doings up at our place.

After straining so hard to keep it all a secret for so long, this open exposure seemed nothing short of crazy. My father looked especially unhappy, particularly when some people started taking pictures. Dr. Humphrey showed up with the announced intention to "check on my patient," though when he arrived all he really did was tell the story of the surgery, omitting the part where he was too scared to come out of the Jeep. If he'd had a pen I swear he would've signed autographs.

I sat on the front porch and bemusedly watched the crowd gradually thicken. At one point Emory went out into the yard and left me a steaming present, which was the subject of about thirty photographs. People started wandering in to use our bathroom and I noticed with a curious lack of resentment that Yvonne served as the restroom attendant for these people, ushering them in and out of the house. The whole circus was growing increasingly bizarre.

I was pretty much unprepared to see Kay and her big ugly boyfriend separate from the crowd and come over to talk to me. I stood up, my mouth dry.

The funny thing was that even though my heart was kicking around in my chest, I understood that what I'd had with Kay was never the real deal. But she wore a crop top and high-waisted pants, and the slim band of tan flesh below the hem of her shirt, dimpled with her belly button, was enough to give a guy a seizure.

"It's really amazing, Charlie. I saw the picture. Oh! This is Glenn. Glenn, this is my friend Charlie."

She could have introduced me as anything from "my student Charlie" to "little boy Charlie" and it would have been accurate, so I was grateful for the status upgrade. I shook hands with Glenn. Up close he was unmistakably military, with his hair short and his stocky shoulders held square, his posture disciplined. His muscles were ridiculously large, so big that he probably couldn't brush his own teeth — his biceps would block the crook of his elbow like a doorstop.

Out of the corner of my eye, I saw someone else approaching the porch. It was, naturally, Beth, because I simply didn't have enough awkwardness in my life.

"We're here to help," Kay said simply.

Beth came over to me expectantly. As clumsily as is humanly possible, I introduced Kay and Beth and Glenn. Beth gave me a shrewd look as I fumbled my way through the whole thing, and I felt completely exposed as I stood there between the only two women I'd ever loved during my whole life. Well, as an eighth grader, anyway.

"I don't know what you mean, 'help,' " I said to Kay.

"Just . . ." She shrugged. "Whatever you need, okay? I've got more friends coming."

Later I was to wonder at this instinctive assumption of Kay's, her unsupported but ultimately prescient conclusion that my dad and I and Emory were in need of some sort of assistance. We certainly hadn't sent out an appeal. But at the time I was more struck by the sort of person Kay was — someone so motivated to help other people she would lay her head on a young boy's shoulder to erase his humiliation in front of his friends. That she was on my front porch to "help" now was entirely in keeping with her character.

I told Kay I was grateful for the offer and would let her know if I could think of anything. My uneasiness was growing with the size of the assembly of townspeople on our property, and I could tell by the way my father kept looking around him that he wasn't sure he was happy about things, either.

And, of course, I needed to deal with Beth.

"Who was that?" was her first question.

She meant Kay. A whole menu of choice responses presented itself to me. *The first girl I ever kissed,* I could say with at least 10 percent accuracy. *She used to be my girlfriend,* I could also claim, because as far as I was concerned, from about twelve minutes into a Goldie Hawn movie until the ending credits had completely rolled that's what Kay had been. I could also just say she was my Junior-Lifesaving instructor, but I knew that for Beth the issue was the way I'd behaved when I'd had the two of them together in front of me. So instead I gave her some risky, rare honesty. "I used to have a crush on her," I explained.

"Oh. Ah," Beth said. Kay was chatting with some people her age and Beth sized her up and down. "She's pretty."

"Yeah."

Beth turned to me. "So who do you have a crush on now?"

I didn't answer that one, but I knew my grin gave me away.

I wasn't smiling a minute or so later when Beth asked why I'd kept Emory a secret from her. I was learning an important lesson about women — if you start getting the cocky impression you're doing really well with them, they'll put you in your place pretty quickly. Since honesty had worked when it came to Kay, I came clean with everything, starting with the first time I'd seen the bear and leaving nothing out. Somehow Yvonne got mixed up in there, too, and I found myself talking about seeing my dad in the chair with Yvonne, how disturbing it had been for me.

"So now's the part where I say I'm mad at you for not telling me any of this," Beth said when I had finished. "And then you say you're sorry, and I make you promise never to keep secrets from me again."

"Okay," I said.

"I get it about Yvonne. My mom says she's trying way too hard."

"Really?" I blinked at this. I thought everyone in town saw Yvonne as the default.

"But you should have told me about the bear."

I hung my head. "I know."

"Anything else you want to tell me now? Owls in the attic? Alligators in the bathtub?"

"No. We don't even have an attic."

That made her grin a little. I felt like I'd just been given a pardon by the governor, but I did my best to keep the look of relief off my face.

By that time, it looked like another twenty people had shown up, and there were cars parked all the way up and down Hidden Creek Road. My dad shut the pole barn door, but if he thought that was going to change anything he was wrong. The buzz of conversation was constant; it was like the county fair out in our front yard. Some kids were chasing each other, and I saw a Frisbee soar elegantly over people's heads.

The people seemed happy enough, but some of them were starting to look restless and impatient. There was an air of expecta-

ething was going to happen.
ething did.

with the
cted to it
en, a long
nd of the
e distance.
ed.
was looking
sirens ap-
two Fish an
ng their
use they
nctio
dle c
?

Chapter
Twenty-Eight

I guess because I was more in tune
normal traffic noise on 206 I rea
first: the thin wail of a police sir
distance off. I went to the far
front porch and looked off into th
"What is it, Charlie?" Beth ask
Eventually the entire crowd
in the same direction as the
proached, two sheriff cars and
Game vehicles carefully maki
up the crowded street. Becau
the law, they had no compu
stopping right out in the mid
They got out of their cars
together in a knot of author
cers and four Fish and Gan
Mr. Hessler — and began
down our driveway in a gro
stiff as pallbearers.
Beth and I went over to
father in front of the pole

I tried to swallow down my dread, to be brave, but inside I felt sick with foreboding. My father put a grim palm on my shoulder, and then I felt Beth's fingers shyly reaching for mine. I gratefully held her hand.

They weren't really going to shoot Emory; they couldn't do that, could they?

Of course, everyone moved forward to hear what the law had to say, which slowed any forward progress they had hoped to make. Then the sheriff showed up — Sheriff Nunnick, a white-haired guy who was generally pretty well liked in town. His cowboy hat was soft and worn, as if it had spent a whole year being pummeled by Herman Hessler. The sheriff lit a Marlboro and stood by his car up at the top of the driveway so we could all get a look at his imposing presence — his job required a fair amount of electioneering and he had developed a sense for the dramatic. He made his way down to where his men were standing, raising his hands for quiet. I could see in his eyes that he was surprised there were so many rubberneckers.

It being a law-abiding town, the people started shushing each other, and gradually they fell silent.

"I want to thank everyone for coming out," the sheriff said, as if this had been a pep rally on his behalf. "We've got the situation under control, now, so we'll need everyone to just move on. There's no need to stick around for this."

"For what?" Rod Shelburton asked.

The sheriff didn't like the question. He drew on his cigarette, squinting. Everyone was so quiet and intent on his answer I could hear him blow the smoke out over his weathered lips. "We're here to execute a legal warrant," he stalled. The crowd started to murmur.

"Folks," Sheriff Nunnick said a little sternly. His deputies picked up on his tone and straightened. This was, I thought suddenly, how bad things happened. The sheriff's department was going to get angry, and then they wouldn't care what was right or wrong; they would execute my bear just to make a point.

"Dad," I whispered. He looked down at me, his eyes sad.

"Folks, it is time to disperse," Sheriff Nunnick told them in hard, commanding tones. The murmuring was growing louder. I caught Kay's eye — she looked distressed.

"Not right," said a man I recognized as the cook at the diner. The people standing next to him nodded in agreement. Yvonne stepped out of the house and stood pensively on the porch, hugging herself.

"We have to let the Fish and Game people euthanize the creature before anyone gets hurt!" Sheriff Nunnick said over the mounting buzz.

The Fish and Game guys looked unhappily at him. The sheriff had just made them the bad guys.

"Obviously a tame bear," someone said loudly.

"Not hurting anyone," another observed.

"A boy's pet," a third person lamented.

And because it was Idaho, more than one person was talking about "private property" and "leave folks to their own business."

"People, now," Sheriff Nunnick warned.

"Don't hurt the bear!" someone shouted, much more loudly than anyone else. That gave license to everyone to yell out their opinions as well, and before long someone started chanting, "Save the bear! Save the bear!" which caught on until there were dozens of voices, mine included, all raised together as one. "Save the bear!"

The funny thing was, Mr. Hessler was grinning and when he caught my eye he gave me a wink. He turned his face away from the sheriff, but I could read Mr. Hessler's lips, and he was chanting, too.

The sheriff tried a couple of times to get

everyone to shut up so he could say something else, but the crowd had been so bored that they seized with complete delight on this opportunity for recreation.

After about five minutes, Sheriff Nunnick gave up. When he signaled his men to turn back around, everyone cheered. People were laughing and hugging and jumping up and down and when Beth turned to me I embraced her and then, to my absolute astonishment, I kissed her right on the mouth.

She was smiling underneath my lips, and maybe I was, too.

Kissing Beth was nothing like kissing Kay, but I was glad to have had both experiences. Frankly, kissing Beth was a lot better, and not just because I had been holding Kay's nose and blowing air down her throat. Kissing Beth made me want to sing out loud. It felt as if my insides were jumping up and down in tandem with the crowd.

When I broke off my lip-lock I saw my dad regarding me with a shocked expression, but I didn't care, not at all.

The law was in full retreat. The people of Selkirk River had spoken. Emory the bear was safe.

Or so we all thought at the time.

Once the authorities left, there seemed to be a general consensus that the show was over, and people began heading home for dinner shortly thereafter. The ones who stayed were mostly people Kay's age, and they organized their spontaneous protest rally along the lines of what they'd seen in *Look* magazine. We'd sort of missed out on the riots and sit-ins during the sixties, up in Selkirk River, so this was the closest they'd come to having a chance to participate in something like that. Some sheets hanging from clotheslines made for makeshift tents, and one guy started playing a guitar until it became evident people wanted him to stop.

As night fell it looked more like a party than anything else, with a lot of laughter and beer drinking. At one point they all broke into a ragged rendition of "The Bear Went over the Mountain," the chorus collapsing under the weight of their giggles. I imagined how much fun it would be to sit out there with them in that circle, bathed in flickering light from the campfire, holding Beth's hand and kissing her a little. Or a lot; I'd probably kiss her a lot.

Yvonne had to work the late shift and my dad walked her to her Vega and I saw him shaking his head over the idea she should come back after the store closed. His kiss good-bye was pretty awkward, somewhere between the way I'd kissed Beth and the way I'd blown air into Kay's mouth.

Kay and her friends held a candlelight vigil through the night — when I looked out into the yard the next morning, there were half a dozen people in sleeping bags, ready to jump into action if the law tried something. It was a pretty sparse army, but it comforted me to see them there.

Emory came out of the barn, yawning, giving the campers a sleepy look. The ones who were awake, including Kay, jumped up excitedly, talking to each other, and then Emory wandered away in the direction of the creek. I hoped he had the good sense to stick close to home — we couldn't be sure the Fish and Game people wouldn't try to sneak up on us from behind.

I couldn't call Beth — she was at school, even if I wasn't — so the morning went by pretty slowly. Just before noon, though, a delivery truck edged its way up Hidden Creek Road and pulled into the driveway, inching past the curious people.

I was stunned when I saw what the driver hauled out: boxes of frozen salmon, bushels of apples, a huge basket of strawberries from California, and sacks of nuts and seeds. This cornucopia of bear delights was astounding enough, but it was the sender who really floored me: Jules McHenry.

It was testimony to Emory's amazing nose that by the time I'd poured nuts and strawberries into a pan he'd wandered up from the creek to see what smelled so good. As he put down what was for him a light lunch, the people in the driveway watched in awe, and laughed when, after eating, he strolled to the edge of the yard and deposited a big pile. Sure, I thought sourly, they could laugh — they didn't have to clean it up.

After my dad thawed the fish in the sink, Emory ate another meal. His shoulder seemed a little better. As I watched him eat with such gusto, it was on my lips to say something like *good boy* or even *good bear,* but the words faltered before I uttered a sound. Every time I went to treat Emory like a pet, I was reminded of the writing on the wall, and then I didn't know how to treat him at all.

More people were drifting in, most of them people I recognized from town but a couple I did not. I probably should have had a sense of foreboding over the latter group, but to be dead honest I was more interested in the subject of how much time would pass before I could get in some more kissing practice with Beth than anything else that was happening. Every single time I thought of her it felt as if my internal organs were shuffling themselves like a deck of cards.

Mrs. Shelburton and Beth arrived so soon after school I knew they had driven right over. My mouth went dry when I saw Beth, and my heart hammered at my rib cage. She was wearing a simple blue dress with a belt and long white socks, and her hair was tied in a ribbon. I just couldn't believe how pretty she was. I wondered briefly if I should tell her that, then dismissed the notion because I thought it would make me seem unmanly.

Mrs. Shelburton sat on the deck to talk to my dad while Beth and I went for a walk through the back property line. I guided her to where the path conveniently dipped down out of view of the house as it aimed for the creek. My scheme to get her alone and out of sight was working perfectly, but I was immensely nervous because this time my kissing would be premeditated, with no cheering crowds to provide inspiration. How, I wondered, does somebody go from having a conversation to having a kiss? I kept slowing down, thinking Beth would get the hint that I had more on my mind than a mere stroll, but she maintained her pace and then I'd have to jog to catch up.

She informed me that Benny H. Junior

High was absolutely abuzz with conversation about the bear and that despite the fact that everyone knew about the Polaroid, there was a substantial number of students who maintained that my father and I claimed the bear could actually *talk*. Everyone also knew that Dan Alderton and I had been ejected from school and were serving out a weeklong suspension, with the consensus being that the fight had erupted because of what Dan had said about my mother and that I had beaten the crap out of him. In truth, I'm not sure that's how a fight referee would score it, but it seemed my schoolmates didn't feel I had lost, which was the important thing.

All of this was interesting, but the reason I was watching Beth's mouth had less to do with the words coming out of it and more about my intent to home in on it with my own, moving target or not. In fact, I was so fixated on her lips I felt sure she'd notice and understand what I was intending, but if she did she gave no sign whatsoever.

At the creek she turned downstream and I followed, though I felt an instant stab of guilt when the creek joined the river and I pictured us coming to where Emory and I had etched our names in the riverbank. *Charlie loves Kay.* I knew I hadn't written those words, but I'd been contemplating doing so, and that made me flush with consternation even though it was ridiculous.

I needn't have worried. The recent rains had erased all signs of both "Charlie" and "Emory."

Beth was still talking and walking, oblivious to my inner turmoil, and I despaired that I would ever get her to shut up long enough to romance her any.

"Oh, and Mike Kappas says hi," she said breezily.

That one stopped me — it felt like ice landing in my stomach. *Mike Kappas?* If Mike Kappas was interested in Beth, she wouldn't be my girl for very long. Maybe I'd already lost her! Maybe she'd kissed *him.*

"Mike?" I repeated with forced casualness.

"I went over and talked to him at lunch."

"Why did you do that?"

She seemed surprised. "He's your friend, isn't he? I thought he'd want to hear about what was going on."

"So you went over to talk to Mike because he's my friend." I tried, but I couldn't quite keep the flat disbelief out of my voice.

"What do you mean? What's wrong?"

"He's not my friend. He's, like, one of the most popular kids in eighth grade."

"Right," she said slowly.

I found myself getting a little angry at her now, mainly because I'd promised myself all day that the second we saw each other we'd make out like fiends and instead we were talking about another boy. "How can you just walk up to a guy like Mike Kappas? You're a seventh grader."

"I know." She was searching my eyes with her own, trying to puzzle it out.

"It's just . . . it must be because you are so pretty."

"You think I'm pretty?" she responded softly. Had I been a little better at it I might have picked up on the vulnerability in her tone, but I was chasing a different thought entirely.

"I mean, God, it's so easy for you."

"What do you mean, easy? What's easy?"

"The whole thing. Benny H."

"No, what, you mean junior high?"

"Yeah, the way you just . . ." I trailed off.

"*Easy?* It's horrible. I hate it," she declared.

"But you just, I mean, you walk up to people and start talking. You're not scared or anything."

"How can you say that? I'm scared to *death*. I feel like if I do something wrong everyone will despise me."

This was so out of keeping with my image

of her that I stopped walking and stared. She stopped, too, which meant that I now had a shot at kissing her, except the mood felt all wrong.

"Really?" I asked. It was exactly the way I felt. I couldn't imagine her having the same issues.

"Sure. What do you think?"

"I just think you're the most confident person I've ever met."

Her eyes danced across mine, flattered and speculative. Now. I should kiss her *now*.

What I did instead was turn and start walking. I'd lost my nerve again. This whole kissing process was turning out to be far more complicated and stressful than I'd thought it would be.

"I just thought you would want me to tell Mike what was going on, Charlie."

Great, now we were back to talking about Mike Kappas.

"Hey, what's that?" Beth asked me, pulling on my arm.

I didn't see where she was pointing at first, but then gradually out of the carpet of pine needles and yellowing grasses a shape resolved itself that wasn't supposed to be there, something man-made. I stepped forward, peering at it.

"Oh!" I exclaimed when I figured it out.

It was a wire-framed, triangular structure that, when I stood it on its broad base, looked a little like an oil rig. This particular one had a thick wad at the top where a homemade flag had been wound and carefully taped in place, like shoving a cork on top of the point of the oil rig.

It was one of Mom's tomato cages. What was it doing here?

"It looks like a tomato cage," Beth said.

"Yeah, from our garden." On closer inspection, this one was different from the others that I had locked in the cabinet in the pole barn. At the end, where the taped-up flag made a tightly wound lump, it was covered in dried paint.

Red paint.

It all came together for me in a flash. I picked up the tomato cage and slid the big end over my arm. It came all the way to my shoulder and still stuck out several feet. At the tip, the rolled-up flag would make a pretty fair paintbrush. At its base the cage was as big around as a basketball.

Wide enough for a bear to stick his paw in, if he wanted.

A very *smart* bear.

I stared at her. Her expression was non-comprehending. We were standing close to each other, so close that she heard me clearly, even though my voice was a murmur. "That's how he did it, Beth," I said simply.

And it was with those words and with the stupid tomato cage still hanging off my shoulders like a giant robot arm that I pulled her to me and kissed her.

CHAPTER
TWENTY-NINE

Maybe Beth had known what I'd been planning all along, because she didn't scream or flinch, just sort of focused on my mouth as it was closing in for the kill. I got about 80 percent lip involvement, but I was a little high and to the right. Then I dropped the tomato cage and did it again, and this time, with this kiss, I was filled with a warm sensation that spread through my body, a wonderful feeling that combined the way Beth fit in my arms with the smell of her hair and, of course, with the soft touch of her lips against mine, a melting of our mouths that was a vast improvement over the last one. When we finally parted our faces remained close — I just wanted to stand there and hold her forever.

"You're the first boy I've ever done this with. I mean, kissed like *this*," she whispered.

I nodded. "Me, too," I confessed.

"I knew you would be. That day I saw you from the barn window," I thought to myself, 'That's Charlie Hall, and one day I'm going to let him kiss me for real, like lovers, so I'm going to save myself for that moment.' "

What could I say to that? Beth always left me speechless.

The air was chilly and Beth was trembling a bit, so I picked up the tomato cage and we headed back to the house, holding hands. We didn't talk much — I felt too good to put anything into words, and Beth was just smiling, her face turned up to an October sun that was losing potency as the afternoon waned.

My American Sikh therapist, Sat Siri, rather gently asked me in one of our sessions if I thought I should "take a look" at the fact that I had "come to believe" that the bear was communicating with me using an object that I revered as one of the last normal things my mother ever touched. I nodded as if I were pondering it, but what I was thinking, as Sat Siri waited patiently for me to respond, was that at the time I didn't really register what an epiphany I'd had over how the bear had written the words on the wall. I had just kissed Beth Shelburton; my whole body was singing with it. I didn't have room in my field of vision to be "looking at" anything else.

For an adult, a kiss is often part exploration and part negotiation. It's sort of like two people resting their hands on a Ouija board pointer and waiting to see if it will drift up to "no" or "yes." But for me, as an eighth-grade boy, kissing Beth was everything, the whole package, complete and joyfully romantic.

When we got back to the house I saw that the changing weather was having a dampening effect on the crowd. I imagined the novelty of hanging around waiting for something to happen was wearing off and my dad was keeping the pole barn shut to ensure Emory's privacy. I locked the tomato cage in the cabinet with the others, noting that Emory was sound asleep on the couch.

Mrs. Shelburton had been looking for Beth and briskly motioned that it was time to go. Beth turned her face up to me and I thought maybe it was an invitation for a good-bye kiss, but I just wasn't sure I could muster up any technique with that many people watching.

As Beth left with her mom Kay came up to me. "Is that your girlfriend?" she asked.

"Yes. I mean, we're not going together officially. No," I said.

Kay laughed at me. "Well, you better make

up your mind before someone else claims her. She's very pretty."

"Yeah." I could feel my face flushing.

Kay's dark eyes traced around my face, easily reading all my secrets, giving me a small, affectionate smile. "I have to leave, but there will still be some people here, and I think a friend of mine's coming back tonight. You'll be okay," Kay told me.

"Thanks," I said inadequately.

I was pretty surprised to see whom my father was sitting with at the kitchen table when I walked inside the house: Pastor Klausen, the minister, and his new youth minister, who always told us to call him Pastor Jamie, so I didn't know his last name.

Pastor Klausen was one of those guys who didn't have much hair, and what was left of it seemed to have taken up residence mostly in his ears. He smiled at me now, his spotted skin a waxy pale color, crisscrossed with wrinkles, like paper that's been read and folded many times.

The youth minister was fresh faced and attractive, with clear skin and brown eyes and lots of dark hair that touched his shoulders. As he nodded at me the gulf between the two holy men looked like a thousand years. The plan was for Call Me Pastor Jamie to take over running things when Pastor Klausen retired, which would be quite a change for the congregation to get used to, in my opinion. Pastor Jamie was pretty new out of minister school and knew a lot of stuff about the rules in the Bible, while Pastor Klausen had lived in Selkirk River for most of the century and knew a lot about his neighbors.

Pastor Klausen was saying that he just wanted to make sure things didn't get all stirred up.

"You've introduced a lot of troubling notions," Pastor Jamie interrupted.

My father raised a mild eyebrow, which I knew from lifelong experience meant he was getting irritated.

"*I've* introduced?"

"The idea that the bear is human," Jamie said scornfully.

"I never said that," my father replied.

"I think the issue, George, is this idea that he's somehow got the soul of a man in him," Pastor Klausen explained.

Jamie snorted, and Pastor Klausen cut a quick look in his direction before turning back to my father. "Do you believe this to be true?"

My father fished around inside himself for the most honest answer he had at that moment. "I don't know what I believe about that. I guess I do believe the bear believes it, though."

That made me grin.

"But think of what that *implies*," Pastor Klausen urged. "And how could a bear do such a thing, anyway?"

I knew, but I wasn't going to say anything until I'd figured out if it would be good or bad for Emory.

"I'm not sure why you're here," my father said after a long moment.

The older minister's face was kind but a little concerned, like maybe my father and I were getting ourselves into some kind of trouble and he wanted to help us out of it. "Because, George, people look to us for an explanation about all of this," he said.

"And there's nothing in Scripture about a talking bear," Pastor Jamie said. The tone in his voice was so close to being a sneer I was surprised his lips didn't curl. I looked at him, startled. He sounded so mean, but his face was so handsome and nice, I had trouble reconciling the two.

Pastor Klausen was still looking at my dad, but his eyes flickered a little in what I thought was amusement. "Well, Numbers Twenty-two," he said to the youth minister. Jamie looked away in disgust. "In Numbers," the older minister elaborated to my

374

father, "Balaam has a donkey who speaks to him."

"Not the same thing at all," Pastor Jamie said.

I had to agree with him on that one. I didn't know who Balaam was, but a donkey was not a bear.

Pastor Jamie leaned in toward my dad. "The point is that you've got half the town believing in this, this superstition, that a soldier has been reincarnated as a bear," he said.

My dad gave Jamie a very cold look but didn't say anything.

"George. It's our job to help people understand things by way of the Word of our Lord," Pastor Klausen said gently. "Even things that defy explanation, if we look hard enough, we see that God provides an answer." He gestured with a slight hand motion toward the Bible that I only now noticed that Pastor Jamie held. We all respectfully turned and looked at it, and a long, long moment passed before I spoke.

"Like my mom?" I asked quietly.

Pastor Klausen's watery blue eyes turned sad. "Charlie. I wish I could say I understood why things like that happen. Why our Lord chose the course for her He did — maybe it is something we'll never understand in this lifetime. Your mother was called home at a very young age, and we all miss her terribly. You, especially, I know you miss her."

I nodded, swallowing. Some part of me, I now realize, just wanted to hear this, to hear that someone knew how much I missed my mom. Yes, it happened to our family, to her, to my dad, and I was part of all that, but it separately happened to me, all alone with it, and I had long craved recognition of that sad fact.

"It must have been so, so hard for you," Pastor Klausen continued. "A terrible shock."

I nodded again.

"And if maybe it seemed like a good idea, when this tame bear showed up, to write some words on the wall in paint," Jamie interjected eagerly. "That would be perfectly understandable."

Pastor Klausen shut him up with a look.

My father cleared his throat. "Then let's get to it. Charlie, did you write those words on the wall?"

"No, sir."

"You see who did?"

"No."

"You think Emory did it? The bear?"

"Yes, I do."

"So do I. There's not much I understand, but I do believe that's exactly what happened. Gentlemen, thanks for stopping by; I do appreciate your concern," my father said, not sounding appreciative at all.

Pastor Klausen shook my hand with what looked like real regret in his eyes, like things hadn't gone as planned. Pastor Jamie shook hands, too, but his eyes were scornful and displeased, like I was the boy who hit a baseball through the church window but was standing by my story of innocence. If he ever decided to give up being a preacher, Pastor Jamie had a good future in him as a junior high school principal.

As the two men walked out the door, I turned to face my father. "Dad, there's something else."

I couldn't blame him for the wary look in his eyes — I'd been throwing a lot at him lately.

"I knew Emory's name before he wrote it in the pole barn. His first name, I mean."

My father regarded me patiently. I explained about the names Emory and I had etched in the riverbank, now washed away. I kept talking faster and faster, as if I could run right past the question I knew was coming.

"Why didn't you tell me this before?"

I bit my lip. Withholding facts from my father was such an inveterate habit that I often wasn't sure *why* I felt such a compulsion to control the flow of information.

"I don't know," I said miserably. I felt pretty guilty about it now.

And, of course, there was something else I hadn't told him, either. I opened my mouth to advise him about finding the tomato cage by the river, but before I could say anything we heard footsteps on the porch. There was a knock on the open door, and then McHenry was standing there.

"Come on in, Jules," my dad said, surprising me. Despite the food shipment, McHenry was, to me, the *enemy.*

McHenry came in carrying a briefcase. We didn't see many of them in Selkirk River. He set the briefcase on the table.

"What'd you find out?" my dad asked him.

"They're coming at midnight," McHenry said.

CHAPTER THIRTY

My dad looked grim faced at the news, while I'm sure I just appeared mystified. Dad peered past McHenry out the window at the campers, who were standing in a tight ring, listening to Pastor Klausen and Pastor Jamie, who were talking and shaking their heads. Drawn together like that, it didn't look like much of a defensive force against the Fish and Game, and even as I watched two of them deserted, heading up to where their cars were parked on Hidden Creek Road.

"Who is that in the truck?" my dad asked. I looked up on the road and could see a white pickup parked near McHenry's truck, a man sitting behind the wheel.

"His name's Ransburg. He's the one I told you about," McHenry said.

"He can come in, if he'd like. No need to wait out there," my dad said.

"He's supposed to remain neutral, he

says." McHenry shrugged.

I followed this exchange with my comprehension running on empty and my anxiety on full. I was liking it less and less that my dad was talking to McHenry as if they were buddies. The man shot Emory!

"How's the bear?" McHenry asked. Meaning "How's the bear I tried to kill in the woods?"

"He seems to be able to move around just fine, but all he's interested in is the food you sent. Odd thing is, he goes straight for the berries and only eats the apples and the salmon when they're all gone. I guess I thought that given the choice he'd gorge himself on fish."

McHenry smiled in delight. "I guess I'd better call in another order of berries."

"We do appreciate it," my father replied.

"Dad!" I said. I meant it to sound casual, planning on communicating my distress with my expression, but my call came out more like a hiss of alarm. The two adults turned to gaze at me. My dad read me instantly and met eyes with McHenry.

"You need to tell Charlie what you told me, Jules," my father said softly.

"Why don't we all sit down," McHenry suggested.

We arranged ourselves in the living room.

I took what was normally my dad's big soft chair, the one that swiveled, and turned it so I could see them both on the couch. My dad's expression was, as usual, frustratingly unrevealing. McHenry just appeared uncomfortable.

"Charlie," he said. He wrestled in his mind a minute and then nodded at me as if we'd both agreed on something. "Well, first, I'm really sorry I shot the bear, that I hunted him with dogs, all of it."

I gave him the cold stare my father gave me whenever I did something boneheaded and my first attempt at an apology was too halfhearted.

McHenry sighed. "This isn't easy to talk about because I'm not sure how to explain it. I mean, that bear's teeth were practically on my throat. I could feel his breath." McHenry agitatedly stood up. "I thought I was going to die; I *knew* I was going to die. But that bear, he not only didn't kill me, he looked me in the eye, and he . . . he *forgave* me." McHenry said these last words in a whisper. Now he was staring out the back window into the night as if we were no longer in the room with him.

"I'm not the best man, Charlie; I've done some things in my life . . . well, I don't need to go into that. I'm not, I mean, I have sinned. I believe . . . anyway, I, I just . . . despite everything, the bear, he . . . my God, it was . . ."

This was starting to sound like a conversation McHenry was having with himself.

"And then he pushed your rifle down, pushed it away from my face. He *saved* me." McHenry turned back to look at me. I was avoiding my father's glare, so I kept my gaze locked on McHenry's, and I saw an odd, intense light in his eyes. "I don't believe in reincarnation. I don't believe in God. But I do believe everything happens for a reason. I realized there had to be a reason I was spared. I'm meant to do something, and my fate is tied up with that bear. He saved me, and now I need to do whatever I can to save him. We *cannot* allow him to be killed. He's here for a reason, too."

McHenry seemed to sense that he was coming on a bit strong and sort of got control of himself. He relaxed his shoulders. "It was almost a religious experience for me," he said, sounding apologetic.

My father and I didn't say anything for a long moment, out of respect for McHenry or maybe just because we were worried he'd crank up again. Eventually he shook himself out of it and explained what he meant when he said they were coming at midnight.

Just as I'd always suspected, a man of means like McHenry was able to curry favor, and he'd managed to find out that the sheriff and the Fish and Game Department would be returning that very night.

So naturally, my father wanted me to go to bed.

I was outraged. In less than two hours we'd be under armed assault and my father wanted me to *sleep?* I thought I should be up with them, loading weapons to repel the invasion. But you don't disobey my father when he gives you a direct order. Fuming, I did as I was told, but I made sure I banged cupboard doors and brushed my teeth loudly in protest against his unfair directives.

"Good night, Charlie," McHenry said.

"Night, Charlie," my dad echoed.

I punished them by remaining brutally silent. I slid into bed and stared at the ceiling, still steaming. They were treating me like a child. Obviously there was a plan in place to resist the sheriff. My father and McHenry both carried themselves with a grave resolve, committed to some action from which there would be no turning back. And I, the person who found the bear in the first place, was being excluded from the operation.

As it would turn out, I was betrayed not only by my father but by my own body. My eyes were wedged open by an iron will-power, my brain a fully engaged sentry, wakeful, alert, tense. That I dozed off was unforgivable, and I was furious with myself when I opened my eyes and my room was dancing with reflected red lights.

They were here.

I dressed hurriedly. It had gotten much colder in the short time I'd been asleep, so that I shivered a little as I yanked on socks. I was bent over my shoes when I heard a squeal from a megaphone.

"Anyone interfering with police business will be arrested," Sheriff Nunnick's voice announced through a bullhorn.

I ran to the front window. The popular Save the Bear uprising had dwindled to four of Kay's friends, who were blinking in the strong glare from the headlights. Thoroughly cowed, they meekly began assembling their camping gear, hastily rolling up the sleeping bags. Nobody said anything as they trudged up the driveway, slipping into the deep pool of blackness beyond the vehicles.

My dad and McHenry were standing on the front porch. Sheriff Nunnick lowered his bullhorn, cocking his head in a *is that all you got?* sort of way. I saw the dome light in the white pickup truck come on up there on Hidden Creek Road as McHenry's mysterious friend opened his door. Ransburg, McHenry had called him. I'd completely forgotten he was there. Several flashlights from sheriff's deputies swiveled and found the man, who squinted at them.

"You should let that man through, Sheriff. He's involved in this," McHenry called. Two deputies cautiously moved toward the stranger, who raised his hands for them to see.

I slipped out the front door then. My father turned at the sound of my footfalls and nodded at me, thankfully not insisting that I return to bed. The three of us left the porch and walked up to the sheriff, our breaths all coming out as gusts of steam.

"Now, George," Sheriff Nunnick warned as we stopped in front of him. He handed his megaphone to a deputy without looking and pulled a pack of Marlboros from his pocket. "This thing has gotten out of hand and it's my duty to see to it that we get back on track with the law. I'm here to ensure that the Department of Fish and Game executes a valid court order unimpeded and I mean to do so even if I have to arrest you in front of your son." He pointed his cigarette pack like a weapon.

Mr. Hessler stepped forward from behind the sheriff, joining us. He looked a little sheepish.

"Hello there, George."

"Herman."

"McHenry," Mr. Hessler greeted.

"Herman."

It was like a Western, except we didn't have any six-guns.

"He's a cop!" someone called from the pack of people surrounding the guy named Ransburg. Sheriff Nunnick accepted this news with a tilt of his head, eyeing us.

"Let him through!" the sheriff called over his shoulder.

Ransburg trudged down to join us. He was tall and thin, with a scary scar drawn across his left cheek in a straight white line. He reached into his jacket pocket.

"Evening. I'm Marshal Richard Ransburg," he said dryly.

The sheriff and Mr. Hessler glanced at each other. "I'm Sheriff John Nunnick," the sheriff finally said, sticking his cigarette pack back into his pocket so he could offer a hand to shake. The marshal dropped an envelope into the sheriff's open palm.

"You've been served," the marshal said in the same inflectionless tone. He turned to Mr. Hessler.

"Are you Herman Hessler?"

Mr. Hessler nodded, swallowing.

"You've been served," the marshal said. He held out a piece of paper that Mr. Hessler accepted with great reluctance.

A third and fourth envelope came out. "These court orders were issued today by Judge Raymond McNichols and are directed to your respective departments. You accept service on their behalf?"

Sheriff Nunnick looked angry, but Mr. Hessler was reading his sheet of paper and appeared almost ready to cry. The sheriff nodded curtly and took another piece of paper from the marshal.

"Herman?" my dad said gently to get his attention. Mr. Hessler looked up, blinking.

"You accept service for the Idaho Department of Fish and Game?" the marshal asked.

"Um . . . yeah," Mr. Hessler finally said. He took the paper.

I had the sense that at this point we were winning the war, but I was absolutely in the dark as to how. Fortunately, Mr. Hessler was as confused as I was.

"What's this all about, George?" Mr. Hessler asked plaintively.

McHenry answered. "The court order is an injunction against any further action against the bear by your department or the Boundary County sheriff pending a hearing in court in five days' time — Monday. And then I am suing you and Sheriff Nunnick personally."

"For what?" Mr. Hessler protested.

McHenry shrugged. "Trespass. Endangering wildlife. Endangering a child. False testimony. Causing damage to property."

"It's a load of manure, Herman," the sheriff snorted contemptuously. "He can't sue us for doing our jobs."

"You'd better get a good attorney. I've got one," McHenry said simply.

Everyone stood looking at each other for a long, tense moment, and again, it felt just like a Western. Then Marshal Ransburg nodded. "Good evening, gentlemen." He turned and walked back up the driveway, got in his truck, and drove off, carrying a lot of the confrontational feeling with him.

Within fifteen minutes the entire posse was gone, Mr. Hessler shooting us one last betrayed look. We trooped victoriously into the house, where my dad built a fire in the fireplace and we sat and watched him do it, the two men drinking whiskey in celebration. I had warm milk, the only beverage made available to me by the house bartender.

The warmth from the milk and the familiar snap of the fire filled me with good feeling. Emory was saved by subpoena. The courts had given him a stay of execution. He could spend the winter in the barn, and in the spring we'd go fishing together.

"So basically, we've got five days," my dad said as he settled down with his drink.

That took the grin off my face.

"We might be able to file for a delay, but I doubt it. The sheriff's angry and he'll get government resources on his side. I won't be able to ambush him again," McHenry said heavily. "Monday morning my attorney is going to be taking a lot of heat and I don't think the judge is going to be too happy."

I sifted through these words carefully. "I thought we were suing," I finally objected.

McHenry gave me a steady look. I liked how he held me with his eyes, including me in the conversation. "The lawsuits against the sheriff and Hessler are junk. They'll get thrown out. And the injunction — do you know what an injunction is, Charlie? Okay, good. The injunction is based on a lot of allegations I wouldn't want to actually defend in court. My lawyers are creative, but they can't work miracles."

I was crushed and I guess my face showed it.

McHenry's smile was sad. "We couldn't really argue that the bear is a reincarnated man. No judge would ever rule in our favor on that; he'd be impeached. We've made the issue that Emory is a tame bear, but it's pretty clear from historical precedent that they won't let Emory stay."

"So in five days the whole thing will happen again," my dad concluded.

"Today's, well, it's technically Wednesday morning," McHenry said, looking at his watch. "But yes, five days until Monday." He looked at me. "We've got to get the bear to go up into the mountains. He's fat enough to make it through the winter, and it's getting cold. He should have left under his own volition by now."

"He's no ordinary bear," my dad reminded McHenry.

"No." McHenry pursed his lips. "But if he doesn't behave like one soon, we don't have a hope of saving him."

"He's eating like crazy," my dad said. "So in that way, he's acting like a normal bear."

"Right. That's what I'm thinking, that the rest of his instincts will kick in and he'll go find himself a den."

I watched the fire leaping up, gloomily reflecting on what I'd just heard. When my mother had been sick there had been so many days like this: good news, then bad news, then good news. She's getting better; she's not getting better; she's not as sick as we thought; she's not dying; she's dead.

With Emory, there was at least a chance he might get through this, but only if he left. My fantasy of him hibernating in the pole barn was childish and silly.

I fell asleep in front of the fireplace and awoke in my own bed well past my normal waking time. My dad had gone to work, but McHenry was in the kitchen, talking on the phone. I ate Puffa Puffa Rice with sugar on it and went outside. Emory was not in the barn.

It was too cold for anyone to hang out in the front yard, though a lot of traffic streamed by all day, the people of Selkirk River driving up to spend some time staring at our open pole barn. The folks I knew personally sometimes came down to talk to me and to verify with their own eyes what they could see for themselves, which was that there was no bear in there. A lot of them asked me if I believed the bear wrote words on the wall, and I said I did, and they asked how, and I said I didn't know. It was the truth; I didn't *for sure* know. I was splitting hairs again, my chief testimonial talent.

Sat Siri told me one time that keeping

secrets and hoarding even trivial bits of information was classic behavior of the children of alcoholics, who feel compelled to exert what control they can over their chaotic family lives.

"My dad was never a drinker," I responded.

She gave me a patient, serene look, like she always did when I pretended not to understand her point.

Roughly translated from Sanskrit, "Sat Siri" means "Great Truth."

I went off to find Emory and came across him right away — he was standing on two legs, leaning on the split-rail fence that bordered the edge of our property nearest the pole barn. He didn't hear me approach, and for a minute I stood there looking at him. The expression on his face, the way he was resting his head on his front paws, seemed wistful, pensive, even sad. Did he know what was coming? When I remember Emory, I often think of him the way I found him there that day, so humanlike in his posture and expression. He turned when I walked up to him.

"You need to leave, Emory," I told him intently. "You need to go up to the mountains and hibernate."

My voice caught in my throat, but Emory

didn't react at all. His eyes lifted to mine and there was that warmth in them, that human quality I'd noticed from the very first day I'd seen him, but I could not say for sure he knew what I was saying or understood how hard it was for me to say it.

"You could come back, though, next spring," I said softly, looking back at the house to make sure my father and McHenry were not within earshot.

Again, no reaction. My heart hurt so much I had to hug my arms across my chest.

We went back to the barn together, and Emory ate more of McHenry's food plus a freezer-burned casserole I had thawed for him for old times' sake.

At that point, I thought our biggest problem was looming five days away, when the judge would pass down another ruling. But I was mistaken; the threat was much closer to hand.

CHAPTER
THIRTY-ONE

When things started to go wrong, it happened so gradually and with such little fanfare I wasn't in any way alarmed. The next morning, Thursday, a car stopped on Hidden Creek Road and a man I'd never seen before got out and there was just something odd about him. He had long hair and a beard, which wasn't unusual, but it was wildly unkempt, and his face was deeply tanned and kind of dirty. He walked down our driveway and stopped in front of me.

"I'm here to see the bear," he told me. He looked at me with eyes that were tired and bloodshot.

I stuck out my hand like I'd been raised to do. "My name is Charlie Hall."

He shook my hand. "I drove all day and all night, Mr. Hall, from San Francisco, California. My car broke down in the town of Kennewick, state of Washington. I have come to join my brother."

The first part of what he said sounded so normal that I didn't initially catch the last part. "I'm sorry, sir?"

"I served in the Army of the Potomac alongside Emory Bain. He saved my life at the Battle of Gettysburg. We are brothers in arms, he and I. I have served under General John Pershing and General George S. Patton and I was most recently an enlisted man in the United States Army from 1964 through 1966, honorably discharged. Medically. Though I was well qualified, I did not see battle during my last enlistment."

"Okay," I responded.

"War is a terrible thing."

"Yessir."

"My actual driving time was twenty-one hours and eleven minutes."

"The bear's not home right now, sir," I told him.

He gazed with empty eyes at the hills around us, then looked at me. "I'll just lie down in my car, then," he told me.

I went in and told McHenry about the conversation I'd had with the guy now sleeping in his Oldsmobile. McHenry listened to me, his frown deepening. Frankly, I was willing to give the guy the benefit of the doubt because he sure seemed to have his facts down, but McHenry thanked me and picked up the phone with a grim expression on his face.

The soldier in the car was by far not the first out-of-towner to show up that day. My father came home from work at noon, looking stunned at the number of automobiles that were parked on both sides of Hidden Creek Road. The license plates were from California, Washington, Oregon, Montana, and Utah. Some of the people wore strange outfits and some of them sang songs. One man carried a sign saying: "You shall have no other gods before Me." Another man wore a Daniel Boone raccoon hat and seemed to be totally intoxicated, because he kept falling down and laughing at himself.

Two motorcycles blasted up the road as if announcing a battle, but the guys who got off the bikes were so fat and old they intimidated no one.

My father turned people away when they asked to use the bathroom and rather firmly instructed them to leave his property, which they pretty much ignored.

My dad went in and reluctantly called the sheriff's department. As he dialed, I heard a loud insistent honking, experience telling me that it was coming from where Hidden Creek Road turned off the paved county road and was getting closer.

As my dad later related it to me, the sheriff thought it was ironic to get the phone call. That was the word he used, "ironic," as in "It's ironic for you to call me, George, since not too long ago you were serving me with a court order to vacate the property."

My dad explained that the situation was rapidly deteriorating. This wasn't the county fair atmosphere we'd seen when the locals had turned out; this was carload after carload of strangers.

"And good luck," Sheriff Nunnick replied with a cackle that I could hear all the way across the kitchen.

My dad hung up and looked at McHenry. They both appeared worried.

"I called a security firm. I can get some Pinkertons up here, but it's going to take more than a day," McHenry said.

"Not sure what this place will look like in a day," my dad muttered.

The honking ceased as a big white van with a TV logo on the side wheeled into our driveway. My dad shook his head.

"Now what," he said.

The side door of the van slid open and a woman and a man got out, stretching their legs and arms. The man was short and muscular, with dark, oiled hair. He wore a brown suit with a light blue shirt and a tie with the same brown and blue in it, pretty much the fanciest clothes I'd ever seen on a man. What I noticed about the woman was that her hair was soft and blond and that she was trim and, when she turned to the house, pretty. She had on a vivid green dress with a big collar. The driver of the van got out and handed her a microphone on a cord and pulled a huge video camera out of the van, hoisting it up on his shoulder. The woman shook her head, tossing her hair, and began speaking to the camera, looking over her shoulder at the pole barn as she did so.

"We need to get them out of here," McHenry said.

I went outside with McHenry. People being the way they are, they were clustered around the camera, the ones behind the woman waving and grinning. The man with the black hair said something to the cameraman, and he dropped the camera off his shoulder and the woman let her arm fall to her side, still holding the microphone.

"Excuse me; can I help you?" McHenry asked coldly.

The woman smiled at him and held out her hand. "My name is Nichole J. Singleton, KHQ Channel Six, Spokane. I am so very pleased to meet you, Mr. Hall?"

"Name's McHenry," he said gruffly. "You people need to leave."

The woman's smile didn't falter. She seemed so friendly I just had to speak up. "My dad's inside," I told her. The last I'd seen of him, he'd been heading back to his bathroom, but I didn't think that was a topic for the evening news.

"You're Charlie!" she exclaimed. I found myself grinning with pleasure at her reaction, but my smile dropped when I caught sight of McHenry, who was still giving her a cold stare.

"This the kid?" the man with the black hair asked. He had very dark eyes and a good tan, and he was handsome in sort of a movie star way, with a strong jaw. He didn't look very friendly, though, sizing me up and down like I was a piece of furniture he was thinking of buying. He chewed gum, his jaw pulsing.

"This is private property," McHenry said.

"Yeah?" The guy stopped chewing and gave the growing assembly of trespassers an appraising look. When he turned his cold eyes back to McHenry, they were mocking.

"This is Tony Alecci, our producer," the woman said smoothly. Tony Alecci didn't offer to shake hands.

"And that's Wally Goetz, my cameraman."

Wally was a folksy guy in jeans.

"Call me Wally. I'm just the driver," Wally Goetz said from inside the van, where he was working on the equipment. "The driver, and everything else."

Nichole laughed even though I had the feeling she and Alecci had heard the joke a few times before.

You didn't have to know Jules McHenry very long to realize he was pretty much accustomed to people paying attention to what he said, so there was no surprise that the expression on his face was one of slow burn. He elected, though, to try logical persuasion. "Look," he said, stepping forward and lowering his voice. Most of the crowd had lost interest and had gone back to their activities, which from my point of view seemed to consist mainly of littering. The backings from several Polaroid pictures were curled up on the lawn, like fallen leaves from a black plastic tree. More than one beverage can had been tossed in our bushes, and, astoundingly, a group of four people had set up a camping stove on our property, not a hundred feet from our front door!

"Things here are already pretty much out of hand," he said, gesturing around. "If we have TV out here, people are going to come from all over. It'll be a zoo."

Alecci snorted. "Late for that," he said.

Nichole was still smiling, though she gave Alecci a quick, impatient look. "This is a really big story, Mr. McHenry. We drove a long, long way to get here."

Our front door opened and my dad came out. My eyes widened a little when I saw him.

He'd showered, shaved, and put on a nice shirt and clean pair of pants. He came across the driveway and straight up to us, looking only at Nichole J. Singleton from KHQ Channel 6, Spokane. He was smiling in a way I hadn't seen in a long, long time.

I watched him as he introduced himself, saw the way he stared into Nichole's blue eyes.

And though my understanding of adult relations was far from sophisticated, it did cross my mind at that instant that my father hadn't cleaned himself up just for the cameras.

"We have just a few questions," she said to him. I caught McHenry frowning at this — he apparently didn't much like the woman.

I heard the telephone ring and ran in to answer it, so I missed my dad's interview. I had planned to take a message and run right back out, but it was Beth and she was by far my number one priority.

"Charlie, have you seen all these people?" she asked without preamble. "The town is full of cars!"

I told her about the steadily building crowd of gawkers mingling out on Hidden Creek Road and hanging around on our property, littering and singing and establishing communes.

"How does the bear react to all those people?" she wanted to know.

I explained that Emory had left the pole barn that morning and hadn't been back since. As I did so, I wondered at how much had changed in so little time. A few months ago I'd been locked in the house of grief, virtually friendless, wasting hours messing with my father's rifles while the summer petered out, dreading the onset of school. I was a no-name student with no friends and no prospects. Now here I was at the center of a media beacon that was attracting crazy people like ants to a picnic. I had a girlfriend in all but name and a pet bear whom Beth and I were talking about as if it were the most casual, normal thing in the world to live with a grizzly in your pole barn.

"So when does your suspension end?" Beth asked.

"I'm back to school on Monday," I replied. *If I can get past the mob,* I thought to myself. I looked outside where people were jumping up and down behind my father while Nichole interviewed him.

"Monday, huh," she said.

I snapped to attention. There were stress fractures all over the way she pronounced the word, as if I had disappointed her. Monday. Why was that a bad thing?

"So you're probably suspended for the dance," she observed.

"Oh." I hadn't given it much thought, but hearing her tone made me want to try to fix things for her. "Actually, I think my suspension is through Friday. Tomorrow," I speculated. "I mean, what point would there be in having me suspended over a weekend, when there's no school?"

"Right," she agreed.

There was a long pause. Was I supposed to say something else? Ask her to the dance? I didn't know what to do! Why didn't they issue some kind of manual when you started junior high, operating instructions for this sort of situation?

"So," I said slowly. "I guess I'd better get back outside."

"Sure," she replied, her cheerfulness so phony that I wanted to shout, *Stop! No!* even as she was saying, "Good-bye, Charlie Hall."

403

I hung up the phone. Okay, that had gone just about as badly as it could have. I looked outside. The TV people had stopped filming my dad. He was standing and talking to Nichole in the front yard while Alecci and Wally wandered down the driveway toward the pole barn.

Right then, as abruptly as I had kissed Beth by the creek, I made the biggest decision of my life. I would, I decided, not only go to the dance, but when I got Beth alone I was going to tell her I was in love with her.

My heart immediately began to pound away at my chest wall. Beth wasn't a normal girl, not that the phrase "normal girl" had any application to my life thus far. She was pretty and smart and in control. I needed to be bold, and that meant doing more than dragging her off into the woods to sneak kisses. I'd just flubbed a perfect opportunity to ask her out on what I presumed would be a date, my very first unless I counted Kay putting her head on my shoulder out of pity. I wouldn't get very many more turns at bat.

But if I told Beth I loved her, that would fix everything. Girls at Benny H. often signed their notes: *Love,* but only the school's Official Couples said, "I love you," to each other.

Besides, it was true. I did love her. My bones ached; my stomach was upset; I felt like I was short of oxygen. What else could it be but love?

"I love you, Beth," I told the coffeepot.

I slipped out the back door and wandered out to where the two TV guys were talking to each other. They were facing away from me and didn't hear me approach as I treaded on the yellowed grass.

"We handle this right, this could be big for us," Alecci was saying. "We got the dad; we need to get an interview with the kid."

I halted, eavesdropping, amazed at what I'd just heard. I was going to be on television!

"You need to talk to Nichole," Alecci continued.

"Well, I don't know; you're the producer," Wally drawled. "You should be the one to talk to her, seems like." There was something a little mocking in the way he said it to the shorter man.

"Yeah, well, she's not happy with me because of that thing that happened."

"You're married, Tony."

"Jesus, not you, too," Alecci said. He ran his hand over his hair, smoothing it back.

"I'm just sayin', that's what's got her

upset. You get a couple drinks in you, doesn't change that you got a wife at home," Wally observed. "Didn't change it for Nichole, that's for sure."

"I was just kidding around."

Wally snorted. He stroked the sparse hair on his chin — he was as grizzled as Emory. "I'd like to get a shot of the bear."

Alecci nodded vigorously. "Hell yeah, the bear, we have to get the bear or there's no story. But you see all the people showing up for this thing? We're exclusive on this. By the time the networks wake up, our feed will be the only thing they've got. You can't even *get* here; it's the middle of the wilderness."

Wally caught sight of me and turned, surprised. Alecci gave a start, his dark eyes reflecting hostility for just a second before he put filters on and suddenly was all friendly. "Hey, kid, you want to be on television?"

I nodded, feeling shy. Alecci gave Wally a triumphant look.

"Still gotta get the dad to say okay," Wally told him.

Alecci nodded back up to where Nichole was chatting with my father. "She'll get that done," Alecci said confidently, apparently thinking a mere kid couldn't understand what they were saying. Obviously it would be Nichole's job to manipulate Dad into doing what they needed for the story — something she'd be pretty good at, I imagined. Even now, she was smiling a dazzling smile and reaching out to touch my dad's arm, and he was nodding and grinning back. Watching it, I had a little sickness in my stomach, a sad, sour feeling.

Courtesy of Beth Shelburton, I was newly wise in the ways of love, which was why I had the sure conviction that my father was going to wind up getting his heart broken by Miss Nichole J. Singleton.

CHAPTER
THIRTY-TWO

Eventually the TV crew left to go get a hotel room. It took them a long time to get back to the paved road; I could hear them honking at traffic the whole way down the hill.

Dad and McHenry came back into the house, and I asked my dad when his interview would be on television, deciding that for now I would withhold the fact that I might be interviewd by Nichole myself. He said he thought it would be on that night. He was animated, more excited and lively than he'd been in a long time, but McHenry seemed gloomy and dour.

"It will only attract attention," McHenry observed.

"Dad, do you think I'm suspended from school just until Friday, or does it last the weekend?" I asked.

The two men seemed a little surprised at the question, like maybe I was changing the subject, but for me I'd just put my finger on the paramount issue of the day.

My father said he didn't know and agreed to call the school first thing in the morning. "Hey, Charlie, Nichole wants to interview you, too," my dad told me, so he already knew. McHenry stiffened. Dad turned to him. "What is it, Jules?"

"On television? Charlie's going to tell the story of how he met the bear, and the words on the wall?"

"Yes," my dad responded slowly, trying to figure out the cause of McHenry's agitation.

"He can't do that," McHenry objected.

My dad just looked at him. I felt my shoulders slumping in disappointment — I wanted to be on television; no one else I'd ever met had been on television before! "It would be fun," I ventured.

McHenry sighed in frustration. "Think about it, George. You know how some people are. They hear that you're claiming that a human being is reincarnated as a bear, it's going to make them angry. They might . . . they might take it out on the bear. We need to protect the bear. Above everything else, we must protect the bear."

I didn't understand why it would upset anybody — either they believed what Emory said or they didn't. I looked to see what my dad had to say.

"Then what are you suggesting?" my father asked McHenry.

"I'm saying, okay, Charlie goes on television. But Charlie, when you do, you can't tell them about the writing on the wall. You can't say what's really happening here."

My father pursed his lips. "I'm not sure we even know what's really happening, Jules."

McHenry's eyes had that strange light in them again. "Can't you see? Emory. He's been *sent*."

My father mulled this over. "Charlie can't lie. I won't have him tell lies," he finally warned.

"It doesn't have to be a lie." McHenry turned to me. "Charlie, I know what you believe to be true, but you don't actually know, do you? I mean, we know, we *believe*, but you didn't see the bear write those words on the wall. You don't even know how it is possible."

I bit my lip because I *did* know.

"So if you have any doubts at all, it isn't a lie to say you don't know, is it?" McHenry reasoned.

Ah, Jules McHenry was a truth splitter, just like me.

"Okay," I said. My dad looked unhappy,

but he nodded, too. I wouldn't say that Emory wrote on the pole barn wall; I would instead say it was possible anyone could have snuck in and done it. I would agree that a bear couldn't hold a paintbrush in his paw.

A while later a roar went up from outside: Emory had returned. He stood on two legs at the edge of the property while his eager fans surged forward, the people literally so stupid as to rush up to a grizzly bear with their hands held out to touch him. Then he lowered his head and sprinted for the door, knocking aside one guy who was dumb enough to block his path. I knew what *that* felt like. The guy went down hard and lay there on the grass, stunned but ultimately unhurt.

Emory dashed into the pole barn through the side door.

"Stay here!" my father barked at me. He and McHenry ran outside, pushing their way through people, and slipped inside the pole barn and shut the side door.

Before long the side window was covered with a tarp from within, and I knew the front pole barn door was still locked in place because when some idiots tried to raise it, it wouldn't move.

The crowd milled around in agitation for

411

about an hour, but it was getting signifi-
cantly cold, below freezing, out there, and
most of them hadn't come equipped to
spend the night in the elements. There was
a lot of honking from the traffic jam as most
of the cars left.

That morning I made sure that the first
thing my father did was call the school and
find out what it meant to be suspended for
a week: a school week, ending that evening,
or a calendar week, meaning I was punished
through the weekend? The news was grim:
the principal claimed I was out until Monday, though I was willing to bet this rule
wasn't written down anywhere.

I couldn't call Beth until she got home
from school, but it was just as well because
I didn't know what I was going to tell her. I
hated the idea of her going to the dance
and meeting other guys there and dancing
with them. My hold on her heart felt so
tenuous. What if some ninth graders, kings
of the social order, noticed the delicate
beauty flowering two grades below them?
There was no way I could compete with a
ninth grader.

When I crossed from the house to the pole
barn people reacted like I was Elvis Presley.
Honestly, were their lives so empty that the
sight of a thirteen-year-old boy was *that*

412

exciting?

Emory ate what I fed him and then did something remarkable: he went to the far end of the pole barn, turned his back to me, and relieved himself right there. It was as if he understood just how delicate the situation was: the people in our yard all wanted something from him, and we had no guarantee it wouldn't all turn ugly if he were to go out there.

What it smelled like in that barn, though — *that* was far from delicate. I hosed down the cement, feeling like this was a pretty good indication as to how the day was going to go.

There were so many cars on Hidden Creek Road that it took the news van until almost noon to make it to our property. We had two people wearing robes and chanting who were a couple of real odd numbers, with bald heads and spangled jewelry. Mr. Von, the grave digger in town who everyone said was not right in the head, had made his way up and was wandering around with a bemused expression on his face, approaching people and standing and staring at them as if he thought they were street performers. More than one portable cassette player vied for dominance from different picnic areas that had been assembled on our property. One man held up a sign that I thought said: "PERSPECT," which didn't make any sense to me, and then he moved his hand and I saw that it said: "PERSPEC-TIVE," which still didn't make any sense to me. A woman had set up a table with a red velvet tablecloth that had a picture of a man's palm stitched into it, and she was dealing cards and telling people's fortunes. Under any other circumstances I might have headed over there to see what she had to say about me, but I sensed that interacting with any of these people would just legitimize their trespass.

I couldn't shake the feeling that all this was adding up to something bad.

The family Jeep was parked sideways at the top of the drive, but when my dad saw the TV van he pretty much skipped out the door to unblock their entrance. He was clean shaven and smelled nice again, I noticed.

Wally looked as good-humored as Alecci did sour. Nichole J. Singleton slid from the truck and held her hand up to her eyes to shield them from the sun and smiled at my father in a way that didn't seem at all phony. That was probably why she was a famous TV personality, because she had a genuine way of smiling at people when she was being phony.

For the third time in my life, I put on my suit. It was time for my interview. Man, did it feel good when Nichole painted my face with a makeup brush. I closed my eyes so that I could concentrate on the light, soft sensation. When she told me I was done we headed outside.

"Need to get something different in the background," Alecci was saying to Wally.

"Maybe the porch?" the cameraman said to Nichole.

"Would it be okay if we shot this on the porch?" Nichole asked my father. It was like watching an order make its way down the chain of command. My dad nodded at her and I half-expected her to say okay to Wally and for him to say okay to Alecci, but instead they all just trooped up the steps and moved the deck chairs around.

Nichole took out a mirror and checked her makeup. She smiled at my dad, who was hovering around her like an imprinted duck.

I sort of hated the idea of him getting a crush on someone like Nichole, though I didn't have the heart to advise him what I'd overheard Alecci say — that she was being so nice because it was her job. Nothing I could tell my dad would matter anyway; he was too far gone. (I knew this because I was in exactly the same position, love-wise.) Besides, there was a potential benefit: when Nichole left for Spokane, I doubted Yvonne would look like anything to my dad but just a lonely grocery gal.

I knew that my father needed to move on from Mom, that a man can't stay faithful to a dead woman forever. I expected that if it hadn't been for the fortuitous arrival of Nichole J. Singleton from Channel 6 News, my dad and Yvonne might have gotten pretty serious with each other. Now, though, his eyes were open to the possibility of other women and maybe he wouldn't settle for the default. If he took his time we'd both be a lot better off.

I had this worldly perspective because I'd kissed two women so far that year and it wasn't even November.

"Look at that," Alecci said. "Wally, get a shot of that."

A man in a really dumb bear costume was dancing around out in the driveway. It looked homemade out of brown carpet samples. My dad and I glanced at each other in disgust.

"Okay, Charlie, are you ready? This is taped, so you don't have to worry about making any mistakes," Nichole told me. Her smile was so warm and genuine it made me

grin right back. "Wally?"

"I'm ready," said Wally.

Alecci pulled out a piece of paper and read it to himself so we'd know he had a function of some kind, too.

I was pretty sure I would be nervous, but Nichole's eyes were so kind I just talked to them and forgot all about the camera. She asked me questions to lead the story up to the bear being locked in the barn.

"And then when you got home from school, what did you see?" Nichole asked me.

"Well, no, I wasn't in school that day," I corrected.

Alecci was a man so impatient that he could signal displeasure with no more than a subtle shift of some papers in his hands. Nichole gave him a sharp glance and then smoothly corrected herself: "When you got home, what did you see?"

I explained there was paint on the floor and words on the wall. As I did I looked around for McHenry, but he had gone home the night before and hadn't yet returned.

"Stay with me, Charlie," Nichole said softly. I snapped my eyes back to hers.

"So the bear wrote those words himself," Nichole said.

I closed my mouth.

"Charlie? Who wrote those words on the wall?"

"Well, we don't really know."

Nichole just stared at me with those warm eyes. Alecci slapped the papers against his left palm. "For chrissakes," he muttered.

Nichole turned to the camera. "Let's take a minute," she said.

"Cut!" Alecci barked. He was giving me an accusatory look. I glanced over at my dad, and he met my eyes and shrugged.

"Charlie, can we go somewhere and talk?" Nichole asked.

Her tone was exactly what the teachers use when they ask you politely to go somewhere with them so they can read you the riot act. I figured I was in for a real chewing out, since probably the whole reason why the TV crew was here in the first place was to cover the story of the bear who wrote on the wall. Otherwise, it was just a bear in Idaho — not exactly something for the evening news.

We went around to the back deck and sat on the wooden chairs. A ridge of dark clouds was coming up the valley like an advancing army and soon we'd have wind and rain to contend with.

Nichole took in a deep breath, looking

around. "This place is so pretty. I grew up in Los Angeles; we have mountains there, but they are nothing like this." She turned and smiled at me. I braced myself for the question: *Why did you just lie on camera?* Instead she said, "Tell me what she was like."

I must have looked as stupefied as I felt.

"Your mother. Laura Hall. Tell me about her."

When I finally found my tongue again, I told Nichole about my mom's upside-down tomato cages. I guess they had been on my mind a lot. I explained how I made these dumb cloth flags for them and how carefully she had taped each flag into a tightly wound spool of cloth at the top. "That was her last good day."

Nichole was looking away and wiping at the lower part of her eyes with a tissue. She didn't say anything for a few minutes, and then she turned back to me. "Charlie," she said, "you get to say whatever you want in that interview. Don't let Tony Alecci or anyone else tell you anything different."

"Okay," I said.

"Between you and me, though, what do you think it means that he has a message? A message for whom? About what?"

Funny how having her ask me that one

simple question made everything clear for me. I knew why Emory was still hanging around, why he ignored my urgings to get up to the mountains. *I have a message.* He was still here because he hadn't delivered his message!

Nichole was watching me speculatively. "What is it?"

"I know what we need to do," I said simply.

We went around to the front of the house. My father was lingering at the near edge of the front porch and sort of lit up when he saw Nichole and me rounding the corner.

There was a man talking to the camera on the porch. "Civil War expert," my dad told Nichole in a whisper. The guy was pretty much bald, but he had some hair growing above his ear that he'd oiled and plastered to the top of his head to fool everyone. He seemed pretty nervous and tugged at his tie a lot as he blinked at the lens Wally had focused on him.

"So what is your opinion, Professor?" Alecci asked.

"Well, the people behind this were clever, but they made some mistakes," the professor responded. "There was, indeed, a Michigan Third Regiment of infantry that mustered out of Grand Rapids in May of 1861, and ultimately did see some action in Virginia, where the Chickahominy River lies. But it was actually the Fourth Michigan Regiment, under the command of Colonel Dwight Woodbury, that fought the Rebel army at New Bridge."

I could see from Alecci's expression that he didn't understand this any better than I did.

"So you're saying . . . ," Alecci prompted. Nichole fidgeted by my side.

"The account is not historically accurate as far as we know," the professor stated.

"Were you able to find a soldier listed on the rosters for the Third Regiment of the Civil War?" Alecci asked.

The professor didn't like the way the question was phrased. "The Michigan Third Regiment of the Army of the Potomac," he said deliberately and slowly. "No, I was not able to locate a roster with the name Emory Bain listed on it."

"Okay then," Alecci said. He turned to Wally. "Cut."

"What are we doing?" Nichole demanded instantly. She sounded angry.

"We're keeping the story alive," Alecci responded smugly. "Adding controversy."

"And *you* conducted the interview?"

"I'm the producer," he replied.

"That's right, Tony. You are the producer. I'm the reporter." She turned to the professor, who was just standing there looking nervous. "Tell me, Professor, are the rosters from the armies of the Civil War so complete that you can say with certainty that no man named Emory Bain ever fought for the Michigan Third Regiment?"

"No, they are —"

"And isn't it possible that a soldier from the Third Regiment might have somehow been involved in the fighting on the Chickahominy?"

"The battle at New Bridge is fairly famous," the professor said cautiously. "We know it was the Fourth Regiment."

"Do we know that no soldiers from the Third Regiment were involved?"

"Of course, we can't say anything for sure about individual soldiers who might have moved between regiments. It was war. Anything can happen in war."

Nichole turned back to Alecci with a defiant expression on her face. He spread his hands. "We got writing on the wall and this guy says it may not all be kosher," he explained defensively. "He's the expert. Controversy sells. It gets us airtime."

"We're standing here on this man's front porch," Nichole responded, gesturing to my

422

father, "and you're saying he's a liar."

"No, the *kid* said the words could have been written by anyone! After that, do you think we even have a story? At least the professor here gives us something to talk about," Alecci exploded. "Look at this god-forsaken place! Look at these *people*. You want to have come out here for nothing?"

"It wasn't for nothing," I said quietly.

Everyone looked at me. Wally's gaze was as blank as his camera's lens — he recorded; that's all he did. Alecci's eyes were snake-like, Nichole's were encouraging and kind, and my father looked pensive. I sighed.

"It's what's the most important, and we forgot all about it," I explained. "He has a message."

CHAPTER
THIRTY-THREE

There are days when the weather comes
storming out of the north and lashes the
area so violently it's easy to believe Nature
has completely lost her temper over something, and moments after my big TV interview that's what happened. The Woodstock
festival out in our yard fled before the assault, pelted with icy rain and cutting winds.
The guy in the bear costume found out
what it was like to try to walk wearing wet
carpeting, and at the top of our driveway he
shed the whole assembly and ran down Hidden Creek Road clad only in his Skivvies.

Wally and Alecci raced to their van and
jumped inside and took off, but Nichole followed us into the house. She was a little bit
like Beth, in that way: she always seemed to
know what to do.

My dad made coffee and gave me hot
chocolate and built a nice fire. It was so cozy
I could feel myself being lulled into the

same strange delusion that my father was entertaining in his own mind — it seemed like Nichole was here to stay. She'd come over for meals and we'd sit and talk in front of the fire while a storm roared outside and slapped rain hard against the windows.

What snapped me out of it was a telephone call my dad answered. He turned and looked at Nichole. "No, no interviews," he said firmly. Nichole gave him an encouraging nod. *Another reason she's so nice,* I thought to myself. *Eliminates the competition.*

"So, Charlie, you said the bear has a message. What do you think it is?" Nichole asked me. I liked being asked questions by her. It was really comfortable having her attention, feeling those blue eyes focus all their warmth on me. I guess in some ways I knew she was using her charm on me for the same reason she was buttering up my dad, but I wasn't inclined to resist it, not at all.

"I don't know," I said truthfully. "But I know it's important."

"Whatever it is," my father said, "we need to hear it by Monday."

I nodded, but I couldn't help the sad feeling that seeped through me then. All the pieces had come together in my mind. I knew that I was the only person who had figured out how the bear had written his words on the wall and that if I just went out to the pole barn, opened a can of paint, unlocked the tomato cages, and slipped one over Emory's paw he'd be able to tell us his message. I hate to admit it because I know it is selfish, but I wasn't ready to say good-bye, so I didn't say or do anything.

Nichole was looking at me with a concerned expression. "What is it?"

She barely knew me and yet was more keyed into my moods than my father ever had been. I didn't want to tell them why I was so wistful, though, so instead I told her a different truth.

"I'm not going to be able to go to the dance tomorrow."

My father gave me an odd look. Though he had seen me kiss a girl with his own eyes, he just didn't seem to understand how my life had changed — I was no longer a little boy tossing G.I. Joe dolls out the second-story window; I was a man who could have gone on an actual date this weekend if I hadn't been suspended and also had had the nerve to ask her. I explained to Nichole about the suspension from Benny H.

"Fighting in school is very serious," she said slowly, processing the story.

"Yes, but I was only supposed to be suspended through Friday and now it's the weekend, too," I explained, essentially fabricating a technicality.

Nichole turned to my dad. "How do you feel about it?"

He shrugged. "It's a shame he can't go. It does seem arbitrary and unfair. I get the feeling that if I hadn't called his attention to it, the principal would have let Charlie in without giving it a thought."

I was astonished. My father hadn't indicated anything but complete indifference about the matter until now.

"Why don't I call him?" Nichole suggested pleasantly.

Her conversation with the principal was one of the most delicious I've ever heard, and I only was privy to the one side of it. After introducing herself and her news channel, Nichole asked him all sorts of questions for which the answer could only be, "I'm an important man."

"It must be difficult to run a school with children that age; how do you manage? . . . You seem awfully young to be in such an important position; why have you risen so quickly? . . . Education is so crucial; what called you to the profession?"

Ten minutes of this and he was as relaxed

as a nursing baby. "So, regarding Charlie Hall," she said smoothly. "He's been through so much, I'm sure you and your staff are doing everything you can to help him reclaim a normal life."

The principal probably said something like, "We're doing everything and I'm an important man."

"It's a shame, then, that he won't be allowed to go to the dance tomorrow, don't you think?" Nichole asked. "If there's anything that could help a boy forget all the furor surrounding a national news story, it would be going to a party with his peers. So tell me, if we were to go down to the school tomorrow night, could we interview you about the dance? . . . Wonderful! Perhaps we could shoot some tape of Charlie at the party? . . . That would be great!" Nichole winked at me. "Thank you very much; I so look forward to meeting you in person."

It took her about three minutes to extricate herself from the conversation because the principal was so in love with talking about himself he just couldn't give it up. When she finally set the phone down she gave me a big grin. "You're going to the dance, Charlie!"

The storm howled for most of the rest of the day, but just as the light was fading the precipitation let up and the wind backed off a little. Everything was scrubbed clean by the rain, the air so pure it almost hurt.

I gazed sourly at all the wet trash that had been tossed in our yard. It would be Charlie Hall, the house janitor, who had to clean it all up.

Emory lumbered past me without so much as a glance when I opened the pole barn to air it out. I imagined that being cooped up in there was making him pretty grumpy.

It was a real relief to stand there and look around and not see any strangers. The weather Saturday was supposed to be even more inhospitable, which I hoped would keep the crowd away.

My interview was aired on television that night and I came off looking like a real smooth operator, in my opinion. They'd cut my conversation down from five minutes to about ten seconds, but they were my best ten seconds. It came out that I believed Emory was somehow a Civil War soldier now living in a bear's body because he'd written words in our barn to that effect. Despite McHenry's misgivings, that's what I had wanted to say.

I was less happy with the way the reporter sitting at the news desk treated the whole thing. After cutting to the dancing bear man and then some woman who said she figured the whole thing was a publicity stunt, the look to the camera the anchorman gave seemed to imply that I was a liar and everyone who believed me was crazy.

My dad asked Nichole to stay for dinner and he thawed some fish and fried it up with potatoes and onions. She set the table and put herself next to my dad, not at the other end where Mom used to sit.

I remembered we had some candles and it just seemed right to light them and set them on the table. Dad opened a bottle of wine, which I hadn't seen him do in more than a year. Everything was relaxed and comfortable, but then my ears picked up the sound of a car coming up the road and I recognized the labored, tinny clanking of Yvonne's Chevy Vega. I slid out of my chair.

"Excuse me for a moment," I said. Dad and Nichole were talking about something in which I'd lost all interest, and she gave me a small smile but kept nodding at my dad, who didn't so much as glance up.

I went out the door and walked up the driveway, which still had the Jeep blocking it. Yvonne was just emerging from the darkness, carrying a cake box. She had escalated her outfit to a short skirt and precariously

430

high heels, with a long raincoat flaring open and framing her legs.

"Hi, Miss Mandeville!" I called to her.

She looked up from where she'd been concentrating on how to place her feet.

"Hello there, Charlie. My goodness, can you believe the fuss? All because of your bear, we have out-of-towners, and TV people, and everything."

While I didn't want her for a stepmother, I had no reason to hurt Yvonne Mandeville. Letting her barge in on Dad and Nichole would have been just cruel. Yet I wasn't really sure how I could stop it.

"None of this would have happened if not for you. You're famous!" she exclaimed.

"So, hi," I said as she got closer. "Hey, uh, listen."

She picked up something in my voice and stopped, regarding me warily. "Is your dad home?"

There was no way to half-truth my way out of that one. "Yes," I admitted reluctantly. "But he's busy."

"Oh." She gave me a puzzled look. No doubt my tension was communicating better than my words. "I brought a cake," she said, making to move on.

I sort of slid sideways, as if to block her, and that seemed to startle her. She frowned

431

at me, then raised her eyes and of course could see my father and Nichole sitting at the table, drinking wine by candlelight.

Nobody should have to watch the realization and hurt sink into another person like that, but I was as trapped in the situation as Yvonne was. It didn't take more than a few seconds of seeing my father fawn over his dinner guest to know just how smitten he had become.

When the shock had worn off, Yvonne's eyes narrowed down to hard points. She glared at me in the dim light. "Charlie," she hissed at me, "you are a hateful, hateful child."

Her shoes were so spiky her return ascent up the wet driveway was treacherous, so despite her obvious agitation she had to carefully pick her way, her head and arms making odd, jerky motions. At the car she had to contend with the cake, grappling with the box, but I didn't dare go help her with her door. Eventually she managed to get inside her Vega and drive off, her tires spitting gravel at me.

Neither Nichole nor my father had noticed the interaction.

It started to rain again.

I stopped in to see Emory, who was lying on the couch. He raised his head and looked at me, and I stood there, unsure. What I wanted to do was go over and pet him, but if there really was a man inside him, that seemed like the wrong thing to do. Eventually I waved at him, to which he provided no reaction, and turned and went back into the house.

At some point in the evening, my father began referring to my bedroom as "the guest room," so I went in and changed the sheets and put some blankets on the couch. Nichole slept in my bed and I slept in front of the fire, drowsily aware of the storm howling away outside.

Saturday the weather couldn't decide if it was ready to fully entertain winter or if we were still stuck in the fall. The temperature was in the thirties, with wind and sleet adding to the general misery. Yet despite the meteorological onslaught, more than a dozen people came to see the bear, or at least to see the pole barn, which was the only show they got that cold, sodden day. One man carried a sign saying: "There Is No Reincarnation" that disintegrated in the wet. I wondered if he'd had the opportunity to meet the fellow who said he'd fought in all the wars.

I called Beth and she wasn't home, so I told Mrs. Shelburton to tell Beth I would be at the dance. Mrs. Shelburton gushed that it was so nice to hear it, but I had the sense that passing the message through Beth's mom wasn't going to win me any points. But how does a person ask a girl for a date? What topic could I start with that would eventually lead to such a question? In my opinion, it was a lot less scary to arrange a fistfight.

I, like Emory, had a message. *I love you, Beth,* I would tell her. *I love you, too, Charlie,* she would reply. Kissing would ensue.

Nichole and my dad sat and talked while I concentrated on the serious question of what to wear to the party. Were you supposed to dress up, or would that look stupid? What if I wore jeans and everyone else was in nice slacks? What if I wore nice slacks and everyone else was in jeans?

Nichole was hanging up the phone as I came out of my bedroom carrying all of my pants.

"Tony's got a bear expert coming to 'evaluate' the situation. He wants to let the man examine Emory tomorrow; is that okay?"

"It's okay with me if it is okay with the bear," my dad said gaily. His mood was irrepressible with Nichole around.

I asked Nichole about my clothing situation and she said that as far as girls were concerned, wearing nice clothes was always the right choice. That one hadn't occurred to me.

Nichole was on the phone with Alecci when McHenry parked out on Hidden Creek Road and hurried down the driveway out of the rain. Another vehicle pulled up behind him, and then another one after that — big four-door AMC Matadors, painted black. I opened the door for McHenry, one ear trying to listen in on Nichole's argument with Alecci. "I think it would be interesting to hear what the principal has to say about all this," she was telling him.

McHenry greeted my father and me somberly — he'd seen the TV interview, and I knew he wasn't happy about it. But I also could tell by the way he deferred to my father that he didn't feel he had any vote in the matter.

"I've got two carloads of private security out there, but it doesn't look like we need them right now," McHenry announced.

"Weather's driven everyone away," my father agreed.

"Well . . ." McHenry glanced over at Nichole, who waved, the spiral telephone cord bobbing up and down.

"Your men want to come in?"

"Oh no. They've come prepared to secure the area around the pole barn. I should let them get to it."

"Now?" My dad looked out at the weather. "Seems like a waste. How about if they come back tomorrow?"

McHenry thought that would be okay. "We're using CB channel five," McHenry replied. "You need anything, you call out."

Nichole came over and shook hands with McHenry. "Tony's not going to go for talking to the principal," she told us. "He says the interview would be a waste of time. Wally would do it for me, but with Tony here, Wally's not able to make decisions."

"He's the driver, and everything else," I said.

Nichole smiled at me. "But I don't think you should worry. The principal told me you could go to the party. Tell him I'll call him Monday morning. And I will; I'll call him."

"You know what you could do," my dad said to McHenry. "Drive Charlie to the party. Drop him off at school. I'll come down after the party is over and pick him up."

So that's how I got what amounted to an armed escort to a junior high dance. McHenry drove his truck, and when we pulled up in front of Benny H. a man jumped out of the Matador in front and the Matador in the rear and came and opened the door for me like I was the President of the United States. A whole procession of cars was disgorging students at that time and they gawked at me as I went into the building, an irrepressible grin on my face, completely oblivious to the disaster that awaited me inside.

CHAPTER
THIRTY-FOUR

I had never been to a junior high dance before. My mother probably would have insisted I go, but living with just my father all I needed to say was I didn't feel like it and that was good enough for him. He didn't know that I was shy and needed prodding. But that night I would have sung a solo in front of the whole school if I thought it would allow me to secure my relationship with Beth Shelburton.

Man, I was nervous. I was wearing plaid bell-bottom trousers with a wide black belt and a cotton dress shirt with a very long, pointed collar. My shoes were brown suede with big thick chunky soles that would probably make dancing impossible. I smelled like my dad's Old Spice plus my dad's Brut plus my dad's Jade East.

The gym was lit up with red and blue lights and the band was already playing when I stuck my head in to look around. It was a pretty good band from a volume perspective, not so great on the quality. I noticed that I was better dressed than a lot of the guys and not as well dressed as most of the girls, which struck me as perfect.

A hard hand gripped my shoulder and I turned around and Mike Kappas was grinning at me. "Saw you on TV, boy!" he shouted over the music. He pumped my hand in congratulations.

"Yeah!" I shouted back.

We nodded and grinned at each other awhile, until that got tiresome. Then he slapped me on the shoulder and moved on.

I found that a lot of people wanted to tell me they saw me on television and nobody wanted to tell me what they thought of my performance. Did I do a good job or not? If I *had* sung a solo, these people would have come up to me afterward and said, *I heard you sing!*

Being a junior high school celebrity wasn't all I thought it would be, in that a lot of guys wanted to talk to me and then I'd break away and somebody else would grab me, so I was passed around like a plate of cookies. I just wanted to get it over with and head off by myself so I could get down to business with Beth, but it felt like an hour went by before I was able to maneuver like a lone wolf.

For an occasion that was supposed to be social, there sure were a lot of people who seemed to be doing their best to avoid any male/female interaction. Because it was the gym, at the far end, away from the band, there were boys actually playing a game of basketball. Sometimes the ball would get loose and they'd have to chase it down, going on the dance floor and retrieving it without once making eye contact with a girl.

Groups of guys stood against the wall and talked sideways to each other, cracking jokes, and then sometimes one of them would break away and go talk to a girl. Usually this happened when the girl went to get some punch. Otherwise, the girls formed dense, circular packs.

When I was researching Alaskan brown bears for my Ph.D., I witnessed the protective behavior of the oomingmak — the Alaskan musk ox. When a bear approaches the herd, the musk oxen form a tight circle and push their young into the center. Then they face outward, fierce and ready for anything. It would take a Sherman tank to penetrate the ring of oxen, and even a starving bear will move on rather than try to attack such a fortified defense.

That's just what was going on at the

dance, only the girls were all facing inward. I spotted Beth: she was wearing a short, light-colored dress with a square neckline and sleeves that were puffy down to the elbows and then were normal from there on out. She had on clunky black platform shoes that laced up, and her hair was all straight except two pieces on either side which were pulled back and were tied with a thin ribbon. She was standing with her birdlike friends and I had no idea how I was going to separate her from the flock for what I intended to be a life-changing conversation. I made a couple of passes at the group like an airplane buzzing a platoon of enemy soldiers, but she didn't break from the protective ring of seventh graders.

"Hey, Charlie, I saw you on TV!" a female voice called. I turned and Joy Ebert was grinning at me. She, too, had puffy sleeves and a square neckline, along with a choker necklace of velveteen ribbon with a little cameo in the center of it. I yanked my eyes away from that necklace because I didn't want her to think I was trying to look at her boobs.

It would be difficult to overstate the impact a girl like Joy could have on a boy like me when she focused her smile like she was doing. It was like being caught in a *Star*

Trek tractor beam — I was transfixed. I nervously agreed that I had been on television and fumbled my way through what had sort of become my stump speech for the evening, explaining how nice Nichole J. Singleton was in person.

The funny thing was, when the conversation hit the point where it had always petered out with everyone else Joy started asking me about other things, like my dad's American bison business. Several times she put her hand on my arm, sending a warm sensation all the way up to my shoulder.

More than once during this process — and later I did come to realize that it *was* a process — Joy would longingly glance out at the dancers crowding the floor, but even when she said, "I really like this song!" I didn't get the hint. Finally she grabbed my hand. "We should dance!" she called out.

Me, dance with Joy Ebert? I numbly followed her, feeling foolish, and then we were facing each other and dancing.

There were two types of people out there on the floor: (a) people who could dance and (b) boys. I fell into the latter category, but I gave it my best shot. Joy was so lovely when she moved it was hard for me to keep the grin off my face.

We danced through two songs and then,

when the band announced they were going to "slow it down," Joy sort of spread her arms and I found myself, contrary to all the rules of the universe, clutching the most popular girl in the eighth grade to me, drinking in her perfume, swaying to the music.

"You're so normal," Joy told me.

"What do you mean?" I pulled my head back so I could see her, and having her beautiful face up so close nearly sent me into a full swoon. I hastily bent back to my original position, my jaw resting on her shoulder.

"I mean with the bear and all. The whole town's talking about it. There's TV here. Yet you just come to the dance like everything's normal. That's so cool."

I thought about this. After my mom died it seemed like everyone expected me to act normal. So I changed my outward behavior, pretended I wasn't hurting inside, and I got pretty good affecting normalcy. What an odd talent to praise, out on the dance floor at a junior high party.

Several couples on the floor kissed as the song ended. That was strictly against Benny H. rules, but we were starting to figure out that if one or two students misbehaved, it was considered criminal, but if a bunch of us did it, it was considered political protest. I got the feeling that Joy would kiss me, if I wanted, but when I was making up my mind about it I caught sight of someone staring at me from across the gym.

It was, of course, Beth.

She turned and marched away from me and I felt hopeless with loss. What in the world did I think I was doing?

Joy didn't notice anything. She was smiling at someone over my shoulder, and then Tim Humphrey was there, smiling back. He gave an approving look at the two of us as a couple, which I now felt was ridiculous. He was the person who should be with Joy Ebert, not me. They would get married and produce model-quality children who would go on to become movie stars and NFL draft picks.

"You come over to ask me to dance?" Joy asked flirtatiously.

"Oh," Tim said uncomfortably. He looked at me, seriously contemplating that I, Charlie Hall, might have a claim on the most popular girl in eighth grade.

"You should!" I told him as the music cranked up. I practically threw the two of them together. I received a strange look from both of them, but then they got swept up in the band's semiclose approximation of "Crocodile Rock."

I went after Beth and she retreated into the impregnable fortress of the girls' room. I saw her as the door swung shut, and then one of her friends came out and stood sentry, her face frozen in disapproval.

I turned away from the gargoylelike glare. I figured I could wait this one out. I folded my arms and leaned up against a fire extinguisher mounted on the wall. Beth would have to come out eventually and then I would tell her . . .

Well, I didn't have it worked out exactly what I would say.

An electronic buzzer filled the air, followed by the sound of someone blowing into a microphone. "Charlie Hall, please report to the principal's office immediately," the principal boomed at the world.

Just great.

I trudged to the principal's office. Naturally, he wanted to know what had happened to all the media attention he'd been promised. I dutifully gave him Nichole's message, but he'd put on what I knew to be the best suit in his collection and looked more than a little unhappy with the way he'd been manipulated. I found myself talking about how great it was that he, the principal, would consider granting an interview, though inwardly I seethed with resentment that he had the authority to keep me in his office at his whim. I didn't have *time* for this man!

When I finally escaped I ran as fast as I could down the shiny floor, my rubber soles squeaking. The girl guarding the girls' room had abandoned her post, which could mean everything or nothing. "Beth?" I called to the door. No response. What if she was in the gym and I was stuck here at the bathrooms? When another seventh-grade girl drifted over I desperately seized her and asked her to go into the sanctum to see if Beth was still there.

Beth was gone.

I dashed into the dance area. The boys were still playing basketball at the far end, but the band had stopped and most of the students were leaking out the doors and into the night. I joined them, jumping up to scan the crowd for any sign of her, but I saw nothing. Beth had vanished.

My dad's Jeep was parked out in front, waiting for me. The stars had come out and when I looked into the night sky I could see all the way to forever, but nowhere in any of the astrology was written what was going to happen to me next, and I felt tired and unhappy when I opened the passenger door.

Nichole was sitting there, smiling as usual, and she leaned forward so I could clamber into the back.

"How was the party?" she asked.

"Fine," I said bitterly.

She twisted in her seat. "What's the matter?"

If my dad had asked me, I would have said, *Nothing,* and that would have been the end of it. Instead, I found myself telling her about Joy Ebert and the horrible mistake I'd made with Beth.

"Rod Shelburton's daughter?" my dad wanted to know, sounding a little surprised. How clueless was he? He'd seen me *kiss* her!

"You do understand why she's upset," Nichole said.

"Yeah."

"When will you see her again? Monday?"

"Yeah."

"Well, you'll have to apologize to her. Tell her you're sorry."

I looked out the window. That didn't sound like much of a plan to me. I felt completely miserable.

"Charlie." Nichole leaned the seat back so she could put a hand on my shoulder. Her eyes were gentle. "Trust me on this. If you say you are sorry and you really, really mean it, if you tell her it was a mistake and you don't know what you were thinking, she will forgive you. Girls like an apology; it's a way of saying to her that she matters to you."

I spent the night on the couch again. I figured Nichole had an exclusive on this story and wasn't going to let my dad out of her sight. At dawn, I heard car doors slamming and saw that McHenry was back and he had his men with him. They were wearing security guard outfits, complete with big hats like Sheriff Nunnick wore. They stood sipping coffee and talking as the light brightened, but they all froze in place when Emory strolled out of the pole barn and left me a steaming present in the backyard.

I walked outside and went over to the bear. "It looks like your bullet wound has healed up just fine," I observed.

As usual, the bear didn't react at all.

"Probably today's the day for your message, Emory," I told him. "I know how you did it, now, so we'll use the same method." We regarded each other. "And then you'll need to leave, because tomorrow is Monday and McHenry says the judge will order you to be shot."

All my life I've wondered why Emory never gave me any indication that he comprehended anything I ever said. I don't know what he could have done — nodded, maybe, or pawed the ground once for "yes" and twice for "no." At any rate, I had no idea, gazing into those chocolate eyes, if he understood that he was going to die the next day if he didn't run away.

Even though it was barely daybreak, I could hear some people tramping in the woods down below our property, calling to each other. Emory heard them, too, and he returned to the pole barn. I closed the door behind him, putting the tarp back up over the window.

When I walked out into the yard, McHenry was waiting for me.

"Just heard it on the CB," he told me grimly. "More people are coming. Cars and cars of them."

CHAPTER
THIRTY-FIVE

At first McHenry's men tried to prevent the flood of people from getting on our property, but there were only six of them, plus McHenry, and they were quickly outflanked. The guards drew back and formed a protective barrier at the doors of the pole barn, looking ominous and official.

The weather had gone from hostile to welcoming, and people took advantage of the sunshine to make absolute fools of themselves. I couldn't keep myself from staring at the situation as it deteriorated. There were people having picnics and prayer meetings; there were protestors from IGAR and from church; there were people smoking marijuana and people drinking beer. All kinds of trash littered the ground. McHenry put a man on our front porch to turn away bathroom seekers so most of the crowd went into the woods to do their business.

A lively discussion started between two men, rising above the hum of conversation. They were both normal-looking guys, in T-shirts and jeans, one with a thick mustache and one with a bushy beard.

"You don't know what you're talking about!" Mustache yelled.

"No sir, no sir!" shouted Beard.

"You'd better shut your hole!"

"Try it!"

With that, their friends from both sides grabbed them and separated them, though it hadn't looked to me like they wanted to fight each other — it was more like the way Dan Alderton was at the park, yelling because hearing himself shout made him feel angry.

Alecci and Wally arrived and stood in the driveway getting footage of the people carrying signs, many of which had biblical quotations and some of which proclaimed they were against animal cruelty. I didn't see any that were in *favor* of animal cruelty, though. One of the signs said: "It is Wrong to Keep Animals in Cages." I argued with that one in my head — it wasn't a cage; it was a pole barn big enough to park two tractor-trailer rigs inside. Another sign urged people to "Believe the Bear," and, it being Idaho, there was a sign demanding the government "Lower Our Taxes." The people with signs tended to want to move around, always careful not to step on the people sitting cross-legged on blankets.

A man in a blue suit had emerged from the news van and stood around nervously while the crowd put on a loud show for the cameras. I wondered who he was.

Alecci seemed really angry when the security guard stopped him from walking into our house like he owned the place. He and Wally and the man in the blue suit fidgeted while McHenry came over and poked his head in our door and asked my dad if it was okay for the TV people to come in. Nichole nodded at my dad and then the whole group was inside.

The man in the blue suit was introduced as Phillip T. Thorpe, there to help the TV audience understand the "unique situation we are all facing." Mr. Thorpe was a Bear Expert with Experience in These Matters. Nobody questioned how someone could have experience in a unique situation. He actually sort of looked like a bear, with a heavy, squat body and a dark shadow where his razor had lost the battle with his beard that morning. When he spoke, though, his voice was high and whiney.

"I will be able to quickly ascertain what

we have here," Mr. Thorpe said.

I could tell by the look in my dad's eyes that he didn't care much for Mr. Thorpe. "What we have here is a bear," my father said laconically.

McHenry turned to the side so Alecci wouldn't see his smile. I was just a kid, though, so I felt free to grin away.

"See, what we got here is the problem of the bear paw," Alecci lectured. "So what Mr. Thorpe is going to do is figure out how he wrote the words on the wall. That goes out tonight, keeps the story going, along with the footage we shot of the mob scene, there." He gestured and we all dutifully looked out the front window. Pastors Klausen and Jamie had arrived from church and were speaking to one group of people while the folks from IGAR were listening to someone else, like opposing football teams huddling up before the ball was hiked.

"Sunday's a slow news day. Tomorrow, Monday, the court reaches its decision. We'll be here to catch your reactions to that." Alecci nodded at my dad and me. "Monday's the biggest news day."

Nichole was staring at Alecci, who faltered. "What?" Alecci demanded.

"Their reaction? Charlie's *reaction?*" she repeated.

It took him a lot longer to get it than it took me. *So Charlie, they just condemned your bear to death; what is your reaction?* My dad looked disgusted. Probably if there were a button that ended the world, all Alecci would care about was getting a shot of the person pushing it.

"Okay, so," Alecci said uncomfortably, "we need to start with Thorpe getting to the bottom of how the bear drew on the wall."

It was, I knew, time to quit withholding information. "I already know how," I said.

Well, that sure got everyone's attention. I explained what I had concluded about the tomato cage.

"When did you figure this out, Charlie?" my dad wanted to know. I didn't like that question.

"Tuesday," I admitted reluctantly.

"Tuesday," my father repeated. I expected a chewing out then, but when I timidly raised my eyes to his he looked contemplative, as if instead of immediately reacting to what I'd done he was trying to figure out why I'd done it; why this son of his, Charlie Hall, kept holding things back, hoarding information, covertly guarding the truth from people and doling it out only when it suited him. I hadn't ever seen that expression on his face before. It was as if I no longer was merely this boy he needed to carve into a man the way he carved wood at his shop. I was also someone he needed to get to know, to discover.

"That's why he hasn't gone up into the mountains yet. He said he has a message, and I don't think he can leave until he delivers it," I concluded.

Everyone processed this in their own way. My dad looked thoughtful, Nichole admiring, McHenry awestruck. Alecci looked as self-important as he always did. Wally didn't seem to care; he was just there to drive and do everything else.

As far as I was concerned, the next order of business was to go out to the pole barn and give Emory a tomato cage paintbrush, but two things got in the way: first there was the fight, sort of a brawl, out in the yard. I couldn't tell if rival groups were going at it or it was just some rowdies who couldn't pass up the opportunity to skin their knuckles on each other, but there were at least ten people kicking and punching, a real riot. Some women screamed and a lot of folks looked expectantly at the security guards, but their job was to keep people away from the pole barn and they didn't budge.

Fighting makes for good television, so Wally and Alecci ran out to tape the thing. Eventually the combatants quit out of exhaustion, panting and giving manly stares at the camera. A few minutes later we could hear sirens making a very slow climb up Hidden Creek Road, so then Wally and Alecci went to the top of the driveway to film what turned out to be three sheriff's cars and two tow trucks. One of the sheriff's deputies got out of his car and began nailing "No Parking" signs to trees on both sides of the road.

Sheriff Nunnick unslung his bullhorn and aimed it at the crowd. "By order of the sheriff's department, there is no parking on Hidden Creek Road until midnight Tuesday. Same goes for two miles of Highway 206 on either side of the turnoff for Hidden Creek Road. Move your vehicle or it will be towed."

People grudgingly began heading up to their cars. A couple of them had pulled too far off the road and were stuck in the drainage ditch, so it was a good thing the tow trucks were there.

Alecci motioned for Nichole to come out and talk to the camera. She sighed, glancing at my father, and then joined the news team. Mr. Thorpe followed her out, as it

456

seemed he suddenly realized that if he didn't he'd be surrounded by unfriendly faces.

Sheriff Nunnick came down the driveway, nodding and smiling at his constituents and the out-of-towners as if he had just done them a big favor. He gave McHenry's man a cool glance and walked right past him with an *I outrank you* air and knocked on our door, opening it and sticking his head in. "Mind if I come in?"

My dad offered the sheriff some coffee. They went over and sat at the kitchen table. McHenry excused himself and went out to talk to his men.

"Quite a spectacle out there," the sheriff observed, blowing on his coffee.

"They don't leave," my dad replied. We all glanced outside, where some people still stood around in our yard. Most of the crowd, though, had gone to move their cars.

"I imagine when they park a couple of miles down 206 and make the hike up here, it'll dampen their enthusiasm a little. That's quite a climb up Hidden Creek Road," the sheriff said. "Soon as we get the cars out of here I'm going to send the deputies into the woods and start ticketing people for camping without a permit, and I've set up a roadblock down there so that only your neighbors can come up."

My dad nodded.

"I imagine you're wondering why the change of heart."

"You did pretty much imply I was on my own," my dad replied.

The sheriff leaned back in his chair. "The folks here are only about half the story. We got people coming into town from all over. The hotels are full. Some families are even renting out their guest rooms for top dollar, and you got to wait two hours to get a seat in a restaurant. It's a bit of a strain on my department to keep everyone in line, but nobody's complaining. You get my drift, here? This show has put some money in people's pockets."

Even then, I understood that when money was in people's pockets it was good for whoever was an incumbent, come election time.

"So you decided to come out and thin the crowd before it turned into a riot," my father speculated.

"Well, that and . . ." The sheriff glanced at me. There was a long pause.

"And you don't want a lot of witnesses when you execute the judge's order tomorrow," my father finished for him.

The sheriff rubbed his face and then nodded.

"But if the bear were to leave, head off into the mountains, say, this afternoon . . . ," my father said speculatively.

The sheriff shook his head. "Oh, we're not going to try to follow it, if that's what you're asking."

My dad met my eyes and nodded, and I understood. We needed to give Emory the means to deliver his message right now, while the mob was nearly gone.

The sheriff shook hands with Pastor Klausen and Pastor Jamie on the way out. In a decision that was probably the exact opposite of separation of church and state, Sheriff Nunnick allowed the two of them to keep their car parked on Hidden Creek Road. Jamie was earnestly addressing a small knot of nodding people, folks who probably had caught a ride to our place with someone else and didn't need to move cars.

My dad went out and explained the plan to McHenry, and the news team came over and heard enough to figure out what was going on. I noticed Nichole touched my dad's arm when she came up to stand next to him.

"So wait, you're going to put a special cage on his arm with a paintbrush and see if the bear writes some more words?" Alecci asked. It was close enough, so my dad nodded.

"Right now?"

"Seems like the best time to do it," my dad replied, looking out at the near-empty lawn.

"No," Alecci objected, "that's not what we want. This is not the best time. Tomorrow would be better. Monday morning, that's our biggest audience."

McHenry looked him over. "I'm sorry you got the impression we care what you think."

"Well . . ." Alecci glanced around for allies and found none, though Mr. Thorpe didn't seem hostile, so it gave him an inspiration. "Okay, so, we shoot the bear doing his writing and we have Phillip provide his expert opinion on the whole shebang."

Wally snorted. "I'm not going in there; there's a *bear* in there, Tony."

"Well, I know there's a bear in there, Wally; that's why we're here, isn't it?" Alecci snapped.

"He sees my camera, he's going to think it's a gun, man," Wally said.

"If you're going to shoot any video, we should leave the tarp over the window," McHenry observed. "Less threatening to the bear if we're not all out there peering in at him through the glass."

"I'm not going to go in there, either," Nichole said. "Are *you,* Tony?"

There was a long pause. "Well, no, I'm the producer," he said.

"I think it should be just Charlie and Emory," my dad said.

"George," Nichole said cautiously. I picked up on what she didn't ask: *You sure you want your son in there alone with a bear?* Like everyone, she wasn't sure what she believed.

"It will be okay, Nichole," my dad said. Seemed like he understood her pretty well, too.

"So just the boy and the bear," Wally said.

"Well, and Thorpe," Alecci said.

"What?" Mr. Thorpe squeaked.

Alecci glared. "You knew that was the deal, Phillip. You're here to examine the bear."

"But . . ."

McHenry snorted, shaking his head, his ponytail flapping as he did so.

It took some working out, but eventually it was decided that I would go into the barn and get things ready and then Mr. Thorpe would stand inside by the side door, which would be cracked open enough to allow

461

Wally to have a view.

I didn't know what good it was to have a bear expert who was afraid of bears, but no one asked me my opinion.

I opened the back door and stuck my head in. "Emory?" I said tentatively. "You okay?"

The bear just stared at me, implacable as always.

"You need to give your message," I told him. "We're out of time."

I went to the paint cans and selected a deep blue. I popped open the lid and stirred it up real well. I considered turning on the lights, but as my eyes adjusted to the gloom I decided to stick with the ambient illumination. I unlocked the back cabinet and pulled out a tomato cage.

"Are you ready, Emory?" I asked quietly.

CHAPTER
THIRTY-SIX

Emory was ready. He rose up on his rear legs. I stuck out the tomato cage, and he slipped his paw into it.

There it was: proof that he had written the words on the wall.

I went to the back door and opened it a little. A wedge of bright light leaped across the floor. "You ready, Mr. Thorpe?"

He gave a trembling nod. Behind him my dad smiled at me. He was standing close to Nichole and I could somehow tell that he wanted to hold her hand but lacked the nerve. Thorpe edged into the pole barn, standing as close as he could to the exit.

I picked up the paint can and set it down close to the blank expanse of white wall directly across from the door. Then I guided the wrapped, taped flag into the paint, and when I pulled it out it dribbled a little like a marshmallow on a stick when you pour chocolate syrup on it.

Emory had trouble with the thing — no wonder there'd been so much paint spatter the first time; it really was unwieldy. I helped him get the tip of the tomato cage up and pointed at the wall, then held my breath. Emory touched the wet end of his tomato cage paintbrush against the white surface and began to write his message.

I was pretty astonished at the words that flowed out from under his brush. It must have shown on my face, because Thorpe hissed at me, "I can't see; he's blocking my view!"

Emory turned and looked at our bear expert and I thought the man was going to faint dead away. He'd already been hanging half out the door and as he reflexively retreated the rest of the way he jerked sharply on the tarp over the window and it fell away, blasting the room with light.

Wally had his camera on his shoulder and he rushed forward even as Mr. Thorpe fell back, so that the two collided. I've seen the footage and it's pretty funny, with Mr. Thorpe's out-of-focus head swimming past, big as a blimp, and then the sky and the ground and the door all flashing into frame.

Finally Wally got focus. Emory had dropped to all fours and beaten a retreat to the corner when he saw Wally — maybe he did think it was a gun, or a weapon of some kind. The tomato cage was at my feet and I picked it up.

Wally's camera caught me standing there with my mouth open, the tomato cage in my hands, dripping blue, and the words on the wall next to me:

God Loves

"It's okay, Emory," I told him. For some reason, my heart was pounding. I went back over to the window and rehung the tarp. To help calm him down, I shut the door behind me when I walked outside. Everyone was standing in a tight knot in the backyard, still processing what they had seen.

"You get it, Wally?" Alecci asked.

"What I got was Thorpe here blocking the whole thing with his fat ass, then a few seconds of graffiti," Wally replied laconically. "No action, unless you count our bear expert falling over his own feet."

"I guess we should have expected something like this," Nichole was saying.

"So you believe . . . ," my father started to respond.

"Yes!" McHenry said.

"So you got nothing?" Alecci demanded incredulously.

"What did you want me to do: say something, get my voice on tape? You're the damn producer," Wally spat. "You were hiding behind me like a scared rabbit instead of doing your job."

"What, what do you believe?" Nichole asked McHenry.

"It's a message from God!" McHenry said exultantly. He raised his fists up into the air like he'd just scored a touchdown. I thought it was an odd statement from someone who said he didn't believe in God.

"Or maybe just a message from a reincarnated soldier who believes in God," my father speculated. "Or a bear who . . ." He trailed off, unsure.

"It's a direct message, clear as anything," McHenry insisted. It seemed pretty important to him that we agree.

"So we didn't get the bear writing anything. All we got is some words that are already on the wall," Alecci said angrily.

" 'God Loves,' " Nichole mused.

None of this really mattered to me — not at that moment, anyway. I was just feeling deflated. It was over. Emory had done the thing he'd come to do, and now he would be leaving.

"Great, just great," Alecci muttered, rubbing his hand through his hair.

"What's the problem?" Nichole asked him. "It's the message that's important."

"The message? This isn't the story people want," Alecci said scornfully.

"But we saw — ," she objected.

"What did we actually see?" Alecci turned to Mr. Thorpe. "What did *you* see, Phillip? Since you were standing directly in front of my camera."

We all gazed at our bear expert expectantly. The truth was, I'm not sure he could see anything, there was so much of him that had been poised for retreat. But he was, after all, the man with experience in unique situations like this. He gathered himself, straightening his tie.

"I need to reflect on this for a bit. Go back to the hotel. I'll have an announcement in the morning," he responded.

Alecci stared at him in disbelief. "What? We're not electing the Pope here, Phillip. We need to get you on camera now."

He shook his head stubbornly. I figured I knew why he was being intransigent. We'd all heard Alecci say Sunday was a slow news day.

"All right. Okay," Alecci said, as if some huge emergency were under way and only he could save us. "Those padres still here? Let's get their reaction. We need *something,* for crissakes."

It occurred to Nichole that our bear expert was stuck without a ride, so McHenry gave him a lift back to the hotel just to get rid of him. My dad allowed Nichole to use our house for the interview, and Pastor Jamie was delighted to be on camera, while Pastor Klausen refused, saying no one would be interested in what an old man like him had to say.

"He really wrote that, Charlie?" my dad asked me. I gave him a solemn nod. He looked over to where Nichole was applying makeup to Pastor Jamie's face. "I have to say, I thought it would be something about bears. Or war, maybe. Not to fight any more Vietnams."

We regarded each other, just like a normal father with his normal boy.

I wandered over to where Nichole was finishing up her makeup job on Pastor Jamie. Pastor Klausen stood with his arms folded. "I'm just observing that it is ironic that we of all people should cast doubt on a message of God's love simply because we don't like the messenger," Pastor Klausen was saying.

"We of all people," Jamie repeated. "Come on, Mark."

"What would be wrong with leaving the

468

door open for a little doubt, a little hope?"

"It's not Scripture," Pastor Jamie said stubbornly.

"All done," Nichole said.

Pastor Jamie pulled the paper bib off from around his neck and stood, turning to Pastor Klausen. "Mark," Pastor Jamie said in low tones, "tomorrow morning they're going to come up here and euthanize that bear. Can you imagine the uproar if people believe he's a messenger of God? And can you imagine what would happen to our faith if people start comparing that bear to our Savior? Another life sacrificed, they'll say. A bear. An animal. And then what? You're not seeing the big picture, Mark. This is a *crisis*."

It was hard for me to care about any of this. For me the only pressing issues were that I had to get Beth back and that Emory needed to be kept safe. Compared to that, what else mattered?

Nichole interviewed Pastor Jamie and he patiently explained why it was simply impossible that the bear was really a person or that he had really been reincarnated to bring a message about the Lord. "There's only one man who has risen from the dead in the history of the world," Pastor Jamie gravely reminded the camera.

Alecci and Wally left after the taping, and

McHenry followed shortly after. New security men came out to replace the ones who had been on duty all day. The number of gawkers was small enough that when they were told by the guards to get off the property they went, walking down the road with the slow gait of people who know they've got a big hike ahead of them.

Nichole cooked dinner, and it was chicken parts fried up in a lemon sauce with spaghetti noodles and spinach, which sounded dreadful but tasted absolutely wonderful. It was pretty comfortable, sitting there at the table, the three of us. The phone rang and it was for Nichole, who talked quietly and then turned to us with a troubled look on her face.

"Tony was right. Our news director doesn't want to run the story the way it is right now. He said we need to wait until we hear from Phillip and then we'll see."

"Really? It seems like a pretty big deal to me," my father observed. "Maybe the biggest deal, if you consider the implications."

Nichole shrugged. "Tony said they said it looked staged; I don't know. And, um, hokey."

"Hokey," my father repeated, turning the word over on his tongue.

After dinner I went out to check on

470

Emory. My throat tightened a little as I approached the side door of the pole barn — I knew he'd be leaving now, probably first thing in the morning. He'd delivered his message.

I opened the door. Emory eased off the couch and went out into the night.

"Hey," I said softly. "You coming back?"

He looked at me a moment, then turned and walked down toward the creek. If this was the last time I would ever see him, he'd done nothing to mark the occasion or give me any sense that I meant anything to him at all. I felt bitter and empty over the possibility.

I turned on the light in the barn to see if there was anything I needed to clean up. I stopped in my tracks when I saw that Emory had written more words on the wall.

CHAPTER
THIRTY-SEVEN

While we were eating dinner, Emory had apparently put the tomato cage back on his arm and finished the sentence. Now it read,

God Loves All

I have to confess that my initial reaction was that the additional word didn't change much. What was the difference between "God Loves" and "God Loves All"? But then a few days later, pondering it, I applied it to myself. If I just said, *Charlie Hall loves,* it meant that I was capable of loving and did love somebody, but if I said, *Charlie Hall loves all,* it said I loved everybody. So that was it; that was why Emory was here; that was his message. God loves everybody.

Again, to my thirteen-year-old mind it wasn't very controversial — but I was missing the big picture, wasn't I? Suppose for a moment you believed in God and, further, that you believed Emory when he said he was here with a message and the message was that God loves all. Did that mean God loved atheists? Buddhists? Muslims? Was this the Christian God I'd been raised to believe in? Or maybe some other God, a bear God, even.

And, as I said, I didn't really give it much thought at the time, because there were other words on the wall, written below and to the side of the central statement, almost like an afterthought.

Now this bear will be bear once more.

I ran to the house, bursting in the front door. "Dad!"

I stopped. Nichole looked very sad, my father sitting really close to her on the couch. They were obviously having an intent conversation that I had interrupted. Nichole abruptly stood and turned away from me, facing out the back window and wiping her eyes.

"What is it, Son?"

"Emory's written more stuff on the wall."

Nichole turned at that. Her eyes were red and I glanced away from her, a little embarrassed. My dad cocked his head at me in a way that left me cold — for just a second, I saw doubt there, like maybe I was lying. But then his vision cleared as he apparently reminded himself that he had already made his choice to believe me.

My dad and I went out to the pole barn, and Nichole arrived shortly after, her face glowing with fresh makeup. She gave me the same odd look as my father had as she contemplated the new words, a look I would become more and more accustomed to over the course of my life. No one but me and Phillip T. Thorpe had seen Emory write anything, and even the bear expert admitted he hadn't seen much. Now, after Emory had been unsupervised in the pole barn, there were more words on the wall.

Did it really happen?

Now this bear will be bear once more.

My dad, of course, was able to translate. "He's saying he's leaving. Emory's leaving, and the bear will go back to being a bear."

Dad went inside to call McHenry. Soon our core group — McHenry, Nichole, my dad, and me — stood in a huddle, looking at each other in the harsh light from the overhead bulbs in the pole barn. McHenry had no doubt in his eyes at all — if anything, he was ecstatic, ebullient. For some odd reason this immediate acceptance made me uneasy, as if having him so solidly on my side only served to cast further doubt on my story.

There was, however, reason to treasure McHenry as an ally. "I called my attorney and told him to request an emergency extension of the injunction, make up whatever reason he has to," he said.

"I thought you said that wasn't likely to happen," my father objected.

McHenry nodded. "I know that's what I said, and that's what I was told. But we have to do it, don't you think, George? We need more time. The bear's still here."

"Unless he's already left," my father suggested, gazing meaningfully out into the tenebrous forest where Emory had gone.

I gave my dad a wild look. Could that be true? Again I thought of Emory passing by me without so much as a second glance. I couldn't believe my last glimpse of him would be so bereft of any personal recognition.

Nichole gave me a comforting smile. "I don't think so, Charlie. I think he'll be back. You'll get a chance to say good-bye."

"We don't know that," my dad objected.

Then he sort of blinked when Nichole gave him a narrow look, and, after a second, he got it and looked at me. "But we don't know he won't come back, either, Charlie," he said reassuringly. "We just don't know."

The whole exchange reminded me of when my dad would say something harsh to me and then completely reverse himself after a single glance from my mom.

I felt pretty good about what McHenry said about his lawyer. When everything had been at their most bleak, he'd served the sheriff and Mr. Hessler some papers and they'd had to completely back off. It seemed pretty clear to me that Emory and I would have more time.

When Emory came plodding back up the path from the creek an hour or so later he headed toward the food I'd set out for him in a clear indication that he wasn't yet ready to go be a bear once more. He gave me a look as he passed inside. "I read it," I told him. I put my hands on my hips like a disappointed parent. "So you're going to become a bear again, a wild bear? Like, live in the woods?"

No reaction. It didn't really sound right when I said it out loud — Emory already *was* a bear.

That night I was conscious, as I slept on

the couch, of a lot of moving around and whispering, but I was too tired to open my eyes to see what was going on. I figured my father and Nichole were having trouble sleeping, with everything that was happening.

I guess it was a few years later when it occurred to me what they were really up to.

We were awake at dawn again. The news van showed up early, too. Everyone looked grumpy as we assembled in the chill morning air. It was bitterly cold. *Good hibernating weather,* I thought to myself.

No spectators had yet arrived, so it was just us. Nichole had been up for more than an hour and looked beautiful, ready to go on camera. While Wally and Alecci discussed what they wanted to shoot, she sat with me on the front porch.

"So you're off to school pretty soon?" she asked.

"Yeah. Bus will be here in about an hour." The conflict was making my stomach cramp — I needed to see Beth, but I wanted to be here, with Emory. I wasn't looking forward to seeing Beth, though, and if being here with Emory meant watching him leave, I wasn't much looking forward to that, either.

Nichole's eyes were sympathetic, as if she could read my inner turmoil. "Remember what I told you about when you see Beth. Girls like apologies; I promise."

"I was really stupid," I said.

"Tell her *that*," Nichole said with a smile. She started to stand up.

"Nichole?" My voice cracked a little, surprising me.

"Yes, Charlie."

I started to talk, but nothing came out. It must have appeared really peculiar, my stare intense and my mouth working soundlessly, but Nichole just put her hand on my arm and gave me a patient look.

"Take your time," she said quietly.

I took a deep breath. I had no idea why I wanted to confide in her, but the urge was as strong as it had been in the Jeep when I was headed to court with my dad. It was like the current in the river, pulling me along irresistibly. With no plan at all, I opened my mouth and said it: "When my mom slipped into her coma, I wasn't in the room. I was supposed to sit with her, but I got bored and went into the living room to mess around with my dad's guns. When she, I mean, in her final moments, she was all alone by herself." I stared up at Nichole, my eyes filling.

"Oh, Charlie," she whispered. She pulled me to her, my face against her soft shoulder.

"When you're loved by other people, you're never truly alone; you know that."

Probably I did know that, but when Nichole said it the tight grip of guilt loosened for me, just a little.

A few minutes later, Nichole was gazing into the camera, explaining the happenings of the day before. Phillip T. Thorpe wore a different suit — a black one — with a pale blue shirt and a wide maroon tie. He stood there fidgeting as Nichole explained that the mystery of what was happening in Selkirk River had electrified the nation, which was probably something of an exaggeration, since even her own channel had refused to run a segment on what Emory had written. When she mentioned that the bear had put up an additional word, that the message was now "God Loves All," Alecci looked angry. Then she explained that Phillip T. Thorpe was a bear expert who had witnessed the entire process, using the form of the word "witnessed" that meant "cowered behind a door and could barely see what was going on."

Thorpe looked nervously at the camera.

"Mr. Thorpe, what can you tell us, in your professional opinion, about yesterday's amazing events?"

He swallowed and then started talking

haltingly in his high, whiney voice. "I was present when the bear, affixed with a custom-made paintbrush, made markings on the wall."

Since Nichole had just said that, she smiled and nodded for him to get on with it.

"The bear did, indeed, appear to write what seemed to be letters."

Seemed to be? His handwriting was better than mine!

"However, the entire time, his handler, Charlie Hall, was standing nearby, giving signals to the bear. Also, Mr. Hall guided the paintbrush into the paint can, and I saw him assist the bear in writing the words. It is remarkable, really, that a grizzly would put up with it. To the uneducated eye, it's a miracle. But what we're actually looking at here is a trained bear. In my opinion, this animal is probably a circus beast, enlisted in a hoax far above its understanding."

It was so quiet I could hear branches creaking in the faint morning breeze.

"Cut," said Alecci. Wally shrugged the camera off his shoulder. Nichole wordlessly handed the cameraman her microphone, looking furious.

"You could have told me this back at the

hotel, saved us the trip out here," Alecci said.

"Charlie's not a *handler;* he's an eighth-grade boy," Nichole said contemptuously.

Thorpe was still focused on Alecci's words. "What do you mean, saved a trip?"

Alecci had his roll of paper and slapped his palm with it. "If the bear's a phony there's no story here. It's over. Wally, let's go. Nichole, you got a bag here? We'll stop for the one at the hotel on the way out."

"I'll get her suitcase," my father said stiffly. He turned and walked to the house, carrying his head oddly.

"But wait," Thorpe said, confused. "I don't understand."

"What?" Alecci snapped. "You don't understand what, Phillip?"

Thorpe looked bewildered. I figured he thought that the most dramatic thing he could say was that the whole thing was a sham. Then everyone would see him as this big expert who saved the world from some huge con job. To Alecci, though, the story of "boy invents tall tale" was not a story at all. Everything unraveled from there — if the bear was some sort of circus freak, if he had to be helped to write on the wall, then the content of the message was irrelevant. It might just as well say "Charlie loves Beth" for all anyone cared.

Nichole had been gazing after my father, biting her lip. Now she turned to Alecci. "There's more, more words," she said. "I think we ought to —"

"What?" Alecci interrupted scornfully. "You think we can keep going now? It's over, Nichole. Get in the van, Phillip."

Nichole had shock in her eyes. "But this morning the court meets to decide Emory's fate."

"Right. That's a story? The Fish and Game Department bags a tame bear? Or doesn't?" He swept his eyes across the littered landscape of our lawn. "At least before there were some people, added energy to the whole deal. Now, we got nothing."

My dad emerged from the house carrying Nichole's suitcase. His face looked grim and shaken, and when he met Nichole's eyes he gazed into them with an unreadable intensity.

"This is sudden," he said awkwardly.

Alecci grabbed the bag from my dad's hand and headed to the van. "Say your good-byes!" he called over his shoulder.

"George," Nichole whispered. She stepped closer to my dad.

Dad shook his head. "It's like you said. Your life is in Spokane, Nichole. I live here.

It would never work. It's okay. I understand." He gave her an uneven smile. She
touched his face with her open hand.

"Come on, Nichole!" Alecci shouted from
the open van door.

I heard the rumbling of the school bus up
the road, squeaking and banging its way
down the hill. I ran and grabbed my books
off the front porch, and when I returned,
my dad and Nichole were clenched in a
deep hug. My father's eyes were pressed
shut in pain. I hated to see it. My poor dad.

He broke from the embrace, sniffing, and
nodded, blinking. "Okay, Nichole. Good-
bye, then," he mumbled. He turned and
walked into the house.

Nichole turned to me and threw her arms
open and I gave her a big, unreserved hug.
"You be good, Charlie," she whispered to
me. Then she got in the van. Wally tossed a
grin and a wave at me and I waved back; I
liked Wally.

I knew it would be the last time I ever saw
Nichole, so I burned an image of her in my
memory as she sat in the van, her face staring at me out the side window. It looked to
me like she was crying. And then the bus
was there and I was on it and headed to
school, an air of unreality settling over me.

The week I'd missed felt more like a lifetime.

I had no use for any of my teachers or classes that morning. My insides were roiling, my brain buzzing with everything that had been going on. Then there was lunch, and what I would say to Beth to put my life back together. I had to do that; I couldn't imagine anything worse than losing her.

But between being dropped off by the bus and breaking for lunch I had science class, which meant Dan Alderton would be there, having served out his suspension for fighting as well.

I wanted to walk in like a man, fix Dan with a glare, and invite him with my eyes to another round if he had it in him, but in truth my nerve failed me and I sort of slunk in just before the bell rang. I was focused on my desk as if there were a treasure map affixed to it, but I clearly heard Dan's voice.

"Hey. Hey, Charlie."

I pretended not to hear, another cowardly move.

"Charlie!" He was more insistent this time.

Okay. This was it. I steeled myself, finding some strength that had probably been there the whole time had I looked for it. I took a deep breath and turned and faced him, ready for anything.

His smile was tentative. "Hey, Charlie. How you doing?"

"Hi, Dan," I said automatically.

We looked at each other for a second, both of us with weird smiles on our faces, and then the bell trilled and I turned to face the teacher.

Observing Dan the rest of the school year, I think I put together what happened. None of his strange hostility had been about me, really; it had been about the social pecking order, about trying to figure out where he fit in. Fighting me was supposed to earn him some currency — oddly, he probably picked me because we knew each other, so that it would seem less arbitrary. But then he made the remark about my mother that sent him into social ostracism, and then everything he tried after that just made it worse.

And as it got worse, he hated me more and more — until we fought, that is. Because once we traded blows in science class he could lay claim to what was probably the highest badge of tough-hood a boy could earn — he was *suspended from school for fighting.* I'd done him a real favor.

I wouldn't say we were friends, after that, but we weren't enemies, either. For a pair of junior high boys, that was almost the same as intimacy.

When the bell rang for lunch I lowered my head and ignored the people who called my name in the hallway. My appearance on television still ranked me pretty high up on the list of cool, but I had only one mission at that moment, and she was sitting at her usual table when I approached.

"Here comes the pest," squawked the girl who had stood guard outside the girls' room. They all glared at me with cold hostility — all except Beth, who was eating her lunch and not looking at me.

"Beth."

She raised her eyes and they were hard and accusing.

"You think we could talk, maybe? Out in the courtyard?" I implored.

She shook her head. "I'm eating lunch."

Fine. I settled in on the bench seat, the girls all leaning in to hear what I had to say, eager for it.

I took a deep breath. "I'm sorry."

No reaction.

"I was stupid."

Beth took a sip of milk.

"Beth . . ."

Her friends were exchanging glances of deep significance. I stayed focused on Beth.

"Look, I should have asked you to go to the dance with me. I was going to, but . . ." I shrugged helplessly. "I mean, the only reason I even went to the dance was to find you, to dance with you. Just you. But you were standing with your friends and I felt, I don't know, embarrassed." I was embarrassed now, actually, but there probably wasn't any point in bringing that up. "And then Joy Ebert came up to talk to me. Like you do, just walked up to talk, like it was easy. And then she was the one who said we should dance, and then they played slow music, and I didn't know what to do."

Beth regarded me with her clear green eyes. It was the first time she'd looked at me. I took it as encouragement.

"I know I should have said no, or something. I didn't think."

"Do you like her?"

I bit back my reflexive answer and gave her a more truthful one. "Everyone *likes* Joy Ebert, Beth. She's really nice."

Honesty wasn't gaining me any points. Beth's gaze was cooling. I remembered what Nichole had said.

"But I was stupid to dance with her. Really stupid, and I'm really sorry. I didn't think how it would look to you. I should have. It was wrong of me. Because when I said just now that I like her, I didn't mean that I *like* her like her. I don't love her."

The flock of girls froze, sensing what was coming.

"I love *you*, Beth."

CHAPTER
THIRTY-EIGHT

Like Emory, I had delivered my message. My face felt like it was on fire. Beth regarded me calmly and she didn't say she loved me, but she didn't say she didn't, either. Seconds ticked past — long, hard seconds filled with the sound of my heartbeat and the shocked expressions of the girls, who couldn't decide if they should start chirping or take wing. Then she said, "Let's go out into the court-yard."

I had to keep from skipping as I walked next to her. We settled in under a tree that had recently dropped the last of its leaves, and for the first time Beth smiled at me. That smile filled my whole chest cavity with warmth even as it made my stomach drop. Neat trick.

Now that I had said it, I wanted to say it again, and her expression was encouraging. I opened my mouth and at the same time heard an electronic buzz, followed by,

"Charlie Hall, please report to the principal's office."

Oh, no! I looked desperately at Beth, the intercom's summons still ringing in my ears. Had I done it? Had I fixed everything? Her green eyes wouldn't tell me.

"You'd better go, Charlie. Probably now President Ford needs to talk to you or something," she said lightly.

She was teasing me; that was good, wasn't it?

"I guess I'd better." I stared at her. I wanted to fall on my knees and beg.

"So go."

She said it a bit coldly. I felt my shoulders start to slump. "Okay," I muttered. I turned.

"Oh, say, Charlie?"

I whipped back around. I know my face was probably lit with desperate hope, but I didn't care.

"Your phone still working?"

"Yeah," I croaked.

"That's good," Beth said, and now, finally, she smiled.

Yes.

I felt pretty much on top of the world, nodding and waving at people who called my name in the hallway, the luckiest, happiest kid at Benny H. Some of the air went out of me, though, as I turned into the

490

principal's office and saw my dad standing there, waiting for me. He looked grim. The principal was there and he looked grim, too, but his face had been locked in that expression as long as I'd known the man.

"I need you to come home with me, Charlie," my dad told me. I gulped and nodded, following him out to the Jeep. He didn't speak until we were pulling out of the parking lot.

"I got a call from Herman Hessler. McHenry's lawyers didn't get the job done. The court threw out our injunction and reinstated the original order, like we knew it would eventually. Only now it's happening today." My dad glanced at me. "They say we have an hour, Charlie. After that, they'll be on our property with guns. We need you to try to get your bear to head up into the hills now. It's our last chance."

"Okay," I said solemnly. I felt ill. The day before I'd been in happy denial, willing to postpone saying good-bye to my bear day after day, but now I felt panicked and impatient. He'd delivered his message; why was he still here? *A bear once more.* Okay, why didn't he go be a bear once more? He was going to be *shot.*

My dad was silent and I studied him. His eyes were red and he looked exhausted.

"Dad?" I said quietly.

"Yes, Charlie."

"I'm sorry Nichole had to leave. She was nice."

My dad swallowed and gave a tight nod. We stopped at the last stoplight on the outskirts of town, and he looked at me.

"Charlie," he said. He bit his lip. "Charlie, I know I haven't been that good of a father."

"Dad," I gasped.

"No, listen. I think I was too wrapped up in losing your mom to pay any attention to you. That was wrong. It's going to change, though, Charlie. You and me, we're all we got now. There's nobody else."

"Okay, Dad."

We drove up Highway 206. The deputy parked across Hidden Creek Road gave us a wave as we turned off the pavement and started bouncing up the rutted dirt road to our house. I was staring off at the trees, thinking about Beth, when I heard my dad inhale sharply. I turned to see what he was looking at.

Nichole J. Singleton stood in the driveway, two suitcases at her feet. My dad braked, turned off the Jeep, and sat there a second with the engine ticking at us, his mouth open.

Nichole shook her head and she was crying and laughing at the same time. My dad jumped out of the Jeep.

"This is crazy," she said, and then they were running toward each other. I sat in the passenger seat and grinned at them through the dusty glass as they kissed. It was as good as anything I'd ever seen on television.

McHenry had been standing with his security men in the road. Now he crossed over and opened my door. He seemed to make a point of ignoring what my father was up to, concentrating on speaking just to me. "I heard," he said curtly. He looked at his watch. "Forty minutes."

"I think Emory will leave now," I said. I felt sure of it — everything was going to be better. Everything.

"He . . ." McHenry scratched his neck. "What if he doesn't? What if he has to stay?"

"What do you mean?"

"What if he wants it? What if he has to be, you know, put down? Like maybe that's part of it."

"Part of what, Mr. McHenry?"

He had that same passionate look in his eyes. "I don't know. Part of getting the message out, Charlie. Part of making a point. Like, his sacrifice."

It just seemed like a lot of the time McHenry would say really intense things

493

that didn't make any sense. "I'll go talk to Emory now," I said.

But I didn't, not right away. I felt the need to stall, to put off losing my bear for just a little while longer, so first I detoured to say hi to Nichole. She gave me another hug. "I'm glad you came back," I told her, though to be truthful I had a feeling I was going to get sick of sleeping on the couch.

Of course, that's not exactly the way it turned out.

I carried Nichole's luggage in for her and then went back out to where McHenry, my dad, and Nichole were standing in the driveway. They all looked grim, and I had a feeling it was because McHenry had shared his speculation that Emory maybe wanted to be killed, that he *had* to be killed. But that couldn't be what it meant to be a "bear once more," could it?

"I'll go let Emory out, see if he'll leave, now," I said reluctantly. Nichole's expression was full of sympathy. One way or another, this would be good-bye.

My dad nodded. "You go on, Charlie. We'll watch from here."

I swallowed and went to the side door and peered through the window.

What I saw inside shocked me. The couch had been torn to shreds — tufts of it lay everywhere; it looked like the wispy stuff they used for the fake Santa beards at Christmastime. Cans were scattered; boxes were destroyed; a whole shelf of tools had been ripped from the wall.

But what was most disturbing of all was Emory himself. He paced back and forth in the barn, drooling, chuffing, agitated and angry. His eyes caught mine and it was full of wild fury and he immediately charged across the floor, growling, pulling up short just inches from where I stood.

I fell down as if he had bowled into me. I crawled backward, then scrabbled to my feet and raced around the side of the barn, yelling for my dad.

"There's something wrong with Emory!" I shouted.

They all came at a run. My dad, reading the alarm on my face, motioned Nichole to stand back, then edged up to the door and peered in the window. I heard another roar, and he dropped down, dashing back over to us.

"What's happening?" McHenry asked.

"George?" Nichole said, looking frightened.

My dad was pale. We'd both just gotten a view of a very angry *Ursus arctos horribilis,* and it was terrifying. My dad and I exchanged stunned looks.

"It's happening," he said.

"What is, George? What's happening?" Nichole asked, her hand to her mouth.

"He's gone back to being a bear," I said.

McHenry's eyes went wide. He glanced up at the door but didn't approach it. "Oh," was all he said.

"We've got a wild grizzly bear trapped in our barn, and he's not happy," my father agreed, recovering from his shock.

We all went silent for a second. I don't know what the rest of them were thinking, but all I could do was process hurt feelings. I was *Charlie;* why would Emory act like that toward *me?*

McHenry and my dad decided that none of us were foolish enough to try to open the pole barn and then get out of the way of a charging, paranoid, claustrophobic grizzly. McHenry ordered his security men to get in their vehicles, and my dad shepherded Nichole and myself into the house. We all went to the window over the sink and watched as McHenry backed his truck up to the big door at the front of the pole barn. He got out and grabbed a towing chain from the bed of his truck, wrapping it around both the doorknob and the trailer hitch. He glanced at us once before running back and getting behind the wheel of his truck. I noticed that not only did he roll up his window; he also locked the door, as if the bear might be able to figure out how to open it to drag him out of there.

All four of McHenry's wheels bit the driveway as he accelerated. The chain snapped taut and then with a crash the door came flying off, flapping flat and dragging behind the truck in a shower of sparks. He drove up to the top of the driveway and then sat there, waiting.

I think we all held our breath. And then Emory appeared.

He held his nose up to the wind, getting his bearings. He looked at the house and just for a second it seemed as if his eyes met mine, but there was no recognition, no sign he even knew who I was. And then he turned and loped off down the path to the creek.

I couldn't stand it. Without even thinking, I broke away and burst out the back door in pursuit.

"Emory!" I called, my voice full of anguish.

"Charlie!" my father shouted. "No!"

The bear was moving fast, quickly pulling away from me, making a beeline for the creek. I kept running. "Charlie!" my dad yelled.

"Emory!" I screamed again.

The pain inside me felt exactly the same as when they told me my mother was gone for good. I'd never had a chance to tell her good-bye, tell her how much I would miss her. That's what hurt, even now, even today: I missed her so very much and I never got a chance to tell her. I could barely see through my tears, but I kept running.

The bear must have stopped to drink in the creek, because all of a sudden I jumped over the bank and there he was, twenty yards away. He took a look at me and bolted, heading up the hill. It was comical, really: I was a thirteen-year-old boy, small for my age, and he was an immense grizzly bear, all power and teeth and claws, fleeing me as if frightened for his life.

I pursued, tired but still going, drawing on my cross-country lungs. We reached the part of the hill that was visible from the house, and even from that distance I heard my father's thin wail: "Charlie! No!"

Later he told me what happened, how after I left he went to the gun cabinet and got out his .30-06, his hands shaking as he unlocked the trigger guard, nearly dropping the shells as he loaded it, slapping the bolt.

Nichole stared at him with wide eyes as he took up position on the deck, sighting through the scope, using the railing to steady his aim, hoping that the bear would keep retreating, praying that if he didn't, he wouldn't make a stand until he was up from the creek, in the sparse trees, where my dad could get a clean shot.

He had the scope on Emory when the bear finally grew weary of the chase and turned, pounding his forepaws on the ground, snarling at me in fury.

I kept running. The bear showed his fangs, snapping them at me, drooling, chuffing, banging his paws again. He felt cornered and threatened and he was getting ready to attack.

Up at the house, my father gave a helpless gasp, resting the crosshairs just below the shoulders, going for a heart/lung shot.

The bear glared at me, locking eyes with me, a final warning before he charged.

My father's senses cleared and he became aware of everything around him. He could feel that behind him Nichole stood tense and weeping, McHenry mute next to her.

My father thought briefly of what McHenry had said, that maybe the bear *had* to die. That this sacrifice was somehow a necessary part of the whole process.

And it didn't matter. Nothing mattered to my father right then but that his son was recklessly pursuing a wild grizzly bear. He could see me now in the scope, looking so small compared to Emory, as I heedlessly ran up the trail.

He had no choice. The bear was going to kill me.

He squeezed the trigger.

There was a dry, impotent click.

Cursing, he quickly moved the bolt, chambering a fresh round.

Back on the hill, I was close enough to Emory to see the wild fury in his eyes. I reached my arms out.

My dad pulled the trigger again and again, all with the same result.

When I was less than ten feet away from the bear he abruptly stood up on two legs. The tension went out of his body, and a warmth flooded his eyes. The transformation was immediate and complete: Emory was back.

I crashed into him at full speed, and he wrapped his front legs around me.

"Emory. I'm going to miss you, Emory," I said, my voice muffled by his thick, coarse fur.

Up at the house, my dad let the rifle sag in disbelief.

We'd figure it out eventually. What seemed like a lifetime ago but was actually only back in August I'd hastily reassembled the rifle when I heard his Jeep pull onto Hidden Creek Road, the small parts scattering on the hardwood floor. Inadvertently I'd stepped on the spring that made the gun fire, warping it just enough that the firing pin no longer hit true, disabling the weapon.

I cried, saying farewell to Emory, a harsh sobbing that hurt my throat, as if all that emotion was scraping me raw on the way out. And then it was time; I knew the sheriff would be pulling in our driveway any second. I gave my bear one last hug.

"Good-bye, Emory. Good-bye."

He dropped to all fours. He held my gaze with those wonderful brown eyes for a minute, and then he turned to leave. I watched him climb slowly and deliberately up the slope, higher and higher, and then when he got to the top of the rocky ridge he rose up on his rear legs and lifted his nose to smell me one last time. I raised a hand and he looked at me for a long, long moment, holding my gaze, and then he turned and disappeared.

EPILOGUE

Though a lot of people tried, no one could track Emory more than a few miles up into the mountains. He seemed to vanish like a wisp of smoke, which lent mystery to those who needed the whole affair to have mystery and frustration to those who needed to have explanation. It didn't help that winter showed up in an angry, punishing fury just as the really serious search parties were getting organized. And then, by the time the snow melted, no one could seem to remember what all the fuss had been about. It was just a tame bear, right?

A few weeks after the bear left, my dad bought me a puppy, a half-Lab, half-who-knows-what bundle of energy. Dad understood that losing Emory broke my heart in several different ways and that despite the literal writing on the wall, emotionally it still felt as if my prized pet had run off.

A lot of people expressed their unsolicited

opinion that the entire affair implied that my dad was not a good father and that something had to be done for my "welfare." I was sent to a smarmy psychiatrist with fat, wet lips — I guess you could say I didn't like him very much. He insisted we talk about the "delusions" I had and the "stunt" that I'd pulled. I eventually agreed that maybe it was possible I'd written the words in the pole barn myself, just to get him to back off.

When it came to my welfare, that puppy helped a lot more than the shrink, I'll tell you that much.

Years later, my American Sikh therapist, Sat Siri, was too polite and professional to pass judgment on the quality of the treatment I'd received from her colleague with the fat, wet lips when I was in eighth grade, but during one session she said something that gave me a little insight into what she thought about the psychiatrist pushing so hard for me to admit I'd made everything up. I was talking about Emory with her when I abruptly halted the monologue.

"What just happened? Why did you stop?" she asked me.

I sighed. "I forget, sometimes."

"Forget?"

"You don't believe me. About Emory."

"Why do you say that?"

"Well . . ." I was always a little irritated at her style of conversation. If she'd been pointing a gun at me and I'd said, *You're pointing a gun at me,* she would probably have said, *Why do you say that?*

"It's because for the past year you've been asking me to 'take a look at' everything," I explained. "The timing of Emory's appearance, a bear who rescued me from the loneliness of my life with my depressed father. The fact that he used the tomato cages, which you said I should 'take a look at' because they were the last things I could remember my mother touching, when it had been just my mom and me, out in the garden. That I wanted to believe that my mother wasn't really dead, that there was an afterlife, hence reincarnation. And that I desperately needed love and forgiveness, so 'God Loves All.' Your opinion couldn't be more clear."

"Did you ever hear me say I didn't believe you?"

"No."

She leaned forward in her chair. "Is it possible that because you think no one truly believes you, you read into my questions what you expected to hear?"

"What else would I think?"

"Charlie, it was never my intent to imply, directly or indirectly, that I doubted you. I would never be so arrogant to question an article of faith, to tell someone to believe or not to believe in the Resurrection, or reincarnation, or Communion. That's not my role here. The psychiatrist you saw when you were a child thought he was doing his job, but please understand, regardless of what else I believe in, I believe in *you*."

A month after that, Sat Siri fired me. My word, not hers. She just suggested I was finished with her — my insomnia had passed and, though I was still enjoying my sessions, I didn't need any more therapy. She told me I should call her if I ever needed to talk to her, and from time to time I do.

My father and Nichole J. Singleton were married the summer after Emory, making official an arrangement that pretty much settled into place the day the bear went back to being a bear. I continued to call her Nichole, and she became my second mother. She bought Selkirk River's newspaper and took over as its editor and, for the first few years, was its only staff. If she missed life in the big city of Spokane, she never said so.

I never heard from Tony Alecci again, though Wally Goetz came to Dad and Nichole's wedding. When I became a bear biologist I tried to track down Phillip T. Thorpe, Bear Expert Extraordinaire, and never located a single person who had ever heard of him. For someone who so clearly wanted to be famous, he remains the most anonymous person in the entire story.

Not long after Emory left, McHenry paid for some kind of expert to come out and shine oblique lights on the wall and carefully, stroke by stroke, re-create the original script that Emory wrote on the wall, the one I painted out. When the expert was finished we all stood and stared at it in wonder, but after a while it lost its novelty and I'll sometimes go months without reading those words. Then I'll catch myself ignoring them and feel a little guilty about it, like someone who thinks he should be going to church more often but never manages to do so.

People still come up to see the pole barn, especially in the summer. For some of them it's the place a miracle happened; for others, just confirmation that we don't know everything. I think many folks find the whole thing exciting, like Bigfoot, maybe, or a haunted house. They accept, or at least contemplate, the notion that Emory wrote those words because it's fun to do so, gives them a little shiver, a frisson. They don't look too hard at the profound conclusions one might draw from it all. Instead, they come to the pole barn for the entertainment value. I don't mind it at all; we each have our own walk.

A lot of the visitors leave little stuffed bears that they buy in town, placing them at the base of the wall as offerings. Every few months I ship a box of the critters off to a children's hospital. Folks like to stand and gaze at Emory's words, which are protected from vandalism by sheets of Plexiglas. There's a bucket we discreetly set out and people sometimes drop in a few coins or dollars. I send the money to a bear charity.

For every one of them, though, there are ten people who think I faked up the whole deal and a hundred people who have never even heard of Emory the bear. I've learned to accept their hostility and their indifference, to shrug off the people who are angry and to be patient with the ones with the dumb questions, like whether the bear could have been a robot.

A question I can't answer: Why does a photograph of me standing in my room, taken by my mother in 1972, clearly show two books on my bookshelf, one right next to the other? The first, *General McClellan and the Peninsular Campaign,* was written for young readers and, I'm sorry to say, has a chapter on how the Yankee forces routed the rebels at Williamsburg and then "pursued them across the Chickahominy," using those very words. Listed in the back of the book are the regiments that fought under McClellan, and yes, it's right there on the list, Emory's regiment, the Michigan Third Infantry. The other book, *Native American Stories for Boys,* has a chapter on the Ani'-Tsâ'gûhï — an ancient clan of Cherokee who were reincarnated as bears.

I admit, it looks pretty fishy that the two books are right there together, though I have to question the sanity of the magazine writer who first pointed it out. Didn't he have anything better to do than to scrutinize my bookshelf with a magnifying glass? At any rate, the picture pretty much satisfied conspiracy theorists that they could close the case on this one.

Yet, I don't even remember reading either one of these books, though I vaguely recall looking at some Civil War pictures that could, I suppose, have been in the McClellan one. I can neither spell nor pronounce Ani'-Tsâ'gûhï. People who want me to confess I either consciously or unconsciously cobbled together the entire story of

508

Emory out of these two books because of juxtaposition are just flat out of luck. It's my life to remember the way I remember and to live the way I want to live, though in the latter case I sometimes make an error or two.

I'd like to say that Beth and I remained together through college and then got married, but alas, the trauma of having me go off to high school while she stayed back in Benny H. was simply too much for us to endure. It was more my fault than hers — I was stupid again. I was jealous of the boys at Benny H. because they had Beth to themselves every school day and then I'd be angry with her, even though she hadn't done anything. I provoked fights because the negative thoughts with which I tormented myself needed an outlet. She put up with that nonsense for a few months and then showed me the door.

I changed a lot as a sophomore, finally getting my growth spurt, becoming a track star, gaining confidence. Senior year my time in the mile was only half a second behind that of the guy who took home the state trophy. Beth, on the other hand, remained petite, almost little girl–like, pretty as ever. I'd see her around town, often with one boy or another, and feel miserable inside.

Beth became a lawyer and moved to Minneapolis. The day I heard she got married I put on my hiking boots and tromped down the trail and stood where I'd kissed her and closed my eyes, remembering.

I stayed in Selkirk River. Jules McHenry made his ranch his permanent home and set up a foundation to study and protect grizzly bears and I went to work for him straight out of graduate school. Maybe it showed a lack of imagination, but whenever I was in an urban area all I could think about was when I could get out. Selkirk River was plenty big enough for Charlie Hall.

I dated a girl from Coeur d'Alene for a few years but didn't propose to her because it felt like everyone expected me to and I had an aversion to going with the default. After we broke up I prepared myself for someone else to show up, but no one did.

Kay Logan married her soldier and left with him and never came back. I was at her wedding and as the car pulled away with her in the backseat, waving and smiling, I felt pretty sure she was looking right at me for a long second, giving me one last gift.

Life flows past pretty quickly when you're

not moving very fast yourself. One July evening I realized I was thirty years and three months old, and went into town to find something to do to justify that fact. I was wandering the streets, trying to settle on a course of action, and I turned the corner and saw Beth, watching me with amusement in her eyes.

"And there's Charlie Hall," she greeted me.

"And there's Beth . . ." I paused. "I don't know your last name now," I admitted.

"It's back to being Shelburton. That happens sometimes," she replied. She slid up next to me so that we were walking in the same direction. "Where are we going?"

I told her about my meager ambitions for the evening. "I'm thinking either a drink or an ice cream," I replied.

"No reason we can't do both. Drink first, though," she said, self-assured as always.

We sat in a restaurant and made each other laugh until suddenly the lights went up and the manager was standing at our table telling us he was closed. The ice-cream shop was shut by then, too.

"Probably seems pretty tame, now that you've been in Minneapolis," I apologized.

"Actually, it seems kind of nice," she told me. She still had those clear green eyes. The childlike features I remembered so well from junior high — smooth skin, small nose, delicate hands — had combined to make Beth Shelburton a real beauty.

"Tomorrow, then. Ice cream tomorrow," I suggested.

She gave me a lingering, speculative look. "Okay, Charlie," she said. "Tomorrow."

I picked her up at the Grassy Valley Ranch, where the Shelburtons had built a house and now lived full-time. Mr. Shelburton had bought my dad out of the American bison business and was still selling buffalo meat, which had finally started to catch on with consumers a little bit. Beth and I decided that instead of eating ice cream we felt like walking the horse path that eventually led up to the trickle of water we still called Dead Man's Falls.

She told me the man she married was a nice enough guy but that he was a secret drug addict and had nearly bankrupted her and then he got another woman pregnant. So she had divorced him and was taking the summer off after winning a big case for her firm. She needed to "reset," she said.

I told her I was studying grizzly bears and how critical they were to the ecosystem. How every year we had to euthanize several who became unafraid of mankind. It was the part of my job that bothered me more than anything. Beth said she could understand that.

We sat on a log along the path and I told her she was my first love and that I would always cherish the memory of her. She smiled her wonderful smile and said she felt the same way. With no awkwardness at all I leaned forward and kissed her, and it was the same sensation as in eighth grade, the same soft lips, the same loud thumping of my heart.

I knew in that moment there was love to be found and redemption to be had in the arms of this girl from long ago.

Her trip to Selkirk River turned into an extended stay and then she decided to open a law office right there, across the street from the Baskin-Robbins where I finally managed to take her on our fifth or sixth date. McHenry shifted all the foundation's paperwork to her so she had a client on her first day, and her business grew slowly but steadily enough that she managed.

I decided I wasn't going to let her get away this time. We were married almost one year to the day after I ran into her on the streets of Selkirk River. We have three children: two boys and a girl. Beth was my first love, and now she's my forever love.

I call her the Beth of Both Worlds.

My dad died not long ago. It was a sudden shock, because he'd only been diagnosed with stomach cancer a few days before. That's how he would have wanted it, though: after seeing what the chemo did to Mom, after fighting that long, losing battle, he didn't have it in him to put any of us through it again. The doctors told him he only had a few weeks and they were way long in their estimates.

He knew I loved him, though, because I told him often, and he knew that when he died I would miss him because I told him that, too. I did not suffer the same awful lack of completeness, closure I think they call it, that I felt when Mom passed away.

Nichole let me bury him next to Mom and actually bought the plot on the other side of him. "When we all get to heaven we'll sort it out," she told me with a laugh. My dad had many more years with Nichole than he'd had with Laura Hall, which gave me a start when I first thought of it. Nichole moved to Pittsburgh because of an ill sister, but she calls and visits frequently.

It occurred to me that after my dad died there was no one left alive who remembered my mother. Oh, I do know that there were plenty of people in town who could muster up an image of Laura Hall in their minds if they were challenged to do so, but not people who really *knew* her. I'm the only one who knows what it was like to sit at the dinner table, just the three of us, before she got sick and her illness became the focus of our lives. I'm the only one who remembers her touch and her smell, her kind eyes, the way she loved me and loved my father. I can hear her voice in my head, a gift I can't share with anyone, not even Beth. She just has to take it on faith.

I still think about my mom every single day. She was the most wonderful mother a boy could have, and I will always, always miss her.

Did it really happen? That's what people ask me about Emory the bear, usually with cautious skepticism in their eyes, wanting to be drawn in, hoping to be convinced by me, but always with the reserved enthusiasm with which people will throw themselves into a magic act, knowing that in the end it's all just sleight of hand.

Sure, they all know there was a bear. They all know that for a few weeks in the autumn of 1974 the bear lived in my pole barn. They can drive up and look at the words painted on the wall, and I wrote a book about the events they can buy right there on the spot.

But I can't prove that Emory was anything other than a tame bear, any more than I can prove that my mother was a wonderful, loving person. You either believe me or you don't; you have faith or you don't.

Here's the question people should be asking: not *Did it really happen?* but *Why?*

Sometimes I will gaze up at Ursa Major in the night sky and reflect on what Nichole J. Singleton told me: no one who is loved is ever truly alone.

"God Loves All." Doesn't that mean that whatever is out there, we're not facing it on our own?

Could that be why Emory was sent with his message?

Most written accounts of the mild hysteria of that time suggest very convincingly that I wrote the words myself. That I, a little boy who had lost his mother, was so starved for attention, and so wanting to believe in life after death, fabricated a backstory for a lost circus bear who had turned to me for shelter. That I came up with the whole story, drawing inspiration from a couple of books I'd read as a kid, and that I cleverly positioned myself so that the words "God Loves All" were secretly written by me, while the sheer bulk of the grizzly bear hid my actions from the rest of the world.

Hey, could be. If we all accept the theory that I'm crazy, then clearly it's possible I've deluded myself into believing Emory wrote those words. That's possible, right? And what could be more insane than suggesting God exists and loves all of creation?

When I start asking these questions of people, Beth always gives me a warning look and I shut up. We've long ago decided there's no point getting involved in this type of conversation. I just sometimes can't help myself.

And as for Emory . . .

Sometimes I think I see him when I'm out among the bears. They are wondrous creatures, and to see them moving with ponderous grace along the rivers, doing their work, is something that takes my breath away. I'll catch the eye of a grizzly and for just a moment I'll believe I see Emory's warmth, that glint of intelligence.

In a way, I'm always searching for Emory. And I believe that someday, I don't know when, I will find him.

ACKNOWLEDGMENTS, EXPLANATIONS, AND EXCUSES

If you're a student of geography, or perhaps just well informed about Northern Idaho, you're possibly a bit perplexed over the location of the town of Selkirk River. It should be easy enough to find: just head up the highway on the west side of the mountains, going north out of Sandpoint, well east of Priest Lake, and there, stitched into a valley at the foot of the Selkirks, you'll find a charming town with a movie theater, a junior high school, and its own newspaper.

Actually, no you won't. Find it, I mean. I built it in my imagination, using spare parts from around the area. For example, there's a road heading out of the town of Wallace that tracks a river in just the way that the unnamed stream flows into the fictional town of Selkirk River. The high school in Kellogg offered me the view and the terrain that I imagined for Charlie's cross-country course. When Charlie went to the movies, it was the Panida Theater in Sandpoint that I pictured him attending — though I placed him in the theater prior to its magnificent restoration. In the end it was just easier to piece together the town in my mind until it exactly fit the story than to struggle to change Charlie's experiences so they could take place in an existing location.

And some things I didn't make up: the courthouse in Bonners Ferry looks, to me anyway, exactly as I described it. I didn't invent the Missoula Floods or the fact that logging trucks storm up and down the highways all day long.

Everything I know about how Northern Idaho smells and feels and tastes came from the time I spent at my cousins' houses in Coeur d'Alene and Priest Lake. Thank you, Cam and Sara, for your hospitality, and for your personal support all these years.

If you'd like to read those two books whose presence Charlie finds so disquieting — the ones written for young readers entitled *General McClellan and the Peninsular Campaign* and *Native American Stories for Boys* — I am sorry to report I fabricated their existence as well. If I made any mistakes about Civil War regiments or battles, I blame the inaccuracies on mistakes contained in the fabricated books.

The grizzly in this story is, of course, a very special bear, so his behavior was mine to invent. But I did, where possible, stick to what I learned about grizzly bears, depending on the work and generosity of others to assist me. It takes years to become a bear expert, however, so if I made any glaring errors I apologize. I heartily recommend *True Grizz,* by Douglas H. Chadwick (Sierra Club Books, September 2003), *The Grizzly Bear,* by Thomas McNamee (The Lyons Press, June 1997), and *The Grizzly Almanac,* by Robert Busch (The Lyons Press, May 2004) as excellent and entertaining resources for learning more about *Ursus arctos horribilis.*

I'm also deeply indebted to Chris Morgan, bear ecologist and conservationist and author of *Bears of the Last Frontier* (Stewart, Tabori & Chang, April 2011). Chris was kind enough to answer my questions about grizzlies, which I fear were numerous and grounded in ignorance.

Louis Dorfman gave me tremendous insight as to the behavior of grizzlies who, through no fault of their own, can no longer live in the wild. He is animal behaviorist at International Exotic Animal Sanctuary, Boyd, Texas, (www.bigcat.org) and can be found at www.louisdorfman.com. Louis is the author of *Dakar, A Wolf's Adventure* (AuthorHouse, May 2003), *Otters on the Loose* (Windsor House Publishing, February 1998), and *The Fairies' Quest* (1st Books Library, February 2003).

I never write anything about animals without reading and rereading Temple Grandin's books *Animals in Translation* (Scribner, December 2004) and *Animals Make Us Human* (Houghton Mifflin Harcourt, January 2009). Dr. Grandin is a national treasure.

Evie Michon turned to her personal archives and found photographs, magazines, articles, and other items from the early 1970s to help me see the look and understand the talk of the times. Before there was Google, there was Evie.

This novel was something of an artistic risk for me. Thank you to Scott Miller at Trident, and to Linda Quinton and Kristin Sevick at Forge, for encouraging me to think big.

Thank you, Cathryn Michon, for reading, editing, and advising on early drafts. I'd ask you to marry me, but hey, you just did.

So much of the life of one novel flows from what happened with the one that came before it. *Emory's Gift* was conceived when *A Dog's Purpose* was not yet even in galleys, but I imagine that if you are reading these words now it may very well be because my first novel led you to take a chance on picking up the second. In the Acknowledgments of *A Dog's Purpose* I did my best to identify everyone who helped me with that novel, but subsequent to publication there were others who I really need to, well, acknowledge.

Sheryl Johnston, when she's not terrorizing the streets of Chicago, is simply the best publicist and the best friend anyone could ever want.

Karen Lovell at Forge ran the publicity fort at that end, and I am delighted that you will be working on *Emory's Gift* as well.

Gavin Polone took *A Dog's Purpose* to DreamWorks. Thank you, Gavin, and thank you, Steve Fisher, David Boxerbaum, and Steve Younger, for helping to get the deal done.

Norma Vela put me in touch with Temple Grandin — I will always be grateful, Norma. Lisa Nash not only helped me with personal insights into life in Northern Idaho, but she introduced me to Dr. Marty Becker, who was such a strong supporter of *A Dog's Purpose.* Lisa, I so appreciate everything.

Bob Bridges has done so much for me in the past and, as I write this, has been in the hospital for months, struggling to recover from H1N1. You are in my prayers, Bob.

Thank you, Emma Coleman, for being production assistant on the book trailer we made for *A Dog's Purpose.*

Claire LaZebnik serves as a sort of one-person writers support group for me. She's prolific, talented, funny, and a great writer. She's at www.clairelazebnik.com.

Thanks to Hillary Carlip, for her artistic design of www.adogspurpose.com and wbrucecameron.com. And thanks, Max Lapiduss, for agreeing to marry me.

My own personal rescue squad: Marcia Wallace, Jennifer Altabef, and Julie Cameron. Just like the movie, *I Know What You Did Last Summer* . . . and I appreciate it so very much. I simply would not have made it without you.

A Dog's Purpose was on the *New York Times* Best-Sellers List from the first day it was eligible — that was due to a lot of people doing a lot of work to see that the novel got the attention they felt it deserved. Many of those individuals are the owners and managers of the independent booksellers scattered across the country. Visit them by name on the buy-the-book page of www.adogspurpose.com. Geoff Jennings of Rainy Day Books in Fairway, Kansas, in particular, has been my godfather in the world of books. Thank you, Geoff.

Finally, though I am not supposed to be in the "Facebook Generation," I'm a Baby Boomer, so we're taking it over like we did everything else. The fans on Facebook's *A Dog's Purpose* fan page are the best people in the world, posting pictures of their dogs, supporting each other through hard times, and celebrating the message of *A Dog's Purpose.* Come hang out with us at www.face book.com/adogspurpose.

W. Bruce Cameron
February 2011

ABOUT THE AUTHOR

W. Bruce Cameron is the *New York Times* bestselling author of *A Dog's Purpose* and *8 Simple Rules for Dating My Teenage Daughter*, which was turned into the hit ABC series. He has twice received the National Society of Newspaper Columnist's award for Best Humor Columnist and his weekly nationally syndicated column is published in more than fifty newspapers. He lives in California.

The employees of Thorndike Press hope you have enjoyed this Large Print book. All our Thorndike, Wheeler, and Kennebec Large Print titles are designed for easy reading, and all our books are made to last. Other Thorndike Press Large Print books are available at your library, through selected bookstores, or directly from us.

For information about titles, please call:

(800) 223-1244

or visit our Web site at:

http://gale.cengage.com/thorndike

To share your comments, please write:

Publisher
Thorndike Press
10 Water St., Suite 310
Waterville, ME 04901